Sacrifices

Maggie Voysey Paun

For Leonard
with love from Maggie
x

Cover design by Rich Voysey at Forge Branding Ltd.

ISBN: 978-1-326-42124-3

PublishNation, London
www.publishnation.co.uk

Acknowledgements

Thanks to the staff of the British Library and the archivists at the library of the School of Oriental and African Studies for their help in tracking down some little used texts. Also to staff at the University of Birmingham special collections and the Church Missionary Society.

Many thanks to Father Hans Boerakker, keeper of the archives of the Mill Hill Fathers for enlightening conversations about missionary work in Uganda. Also to my husband Rashmi who lived in Uganda in the 1950s and who is always ready to read and discuss my writing; to Jignesh Lakhani for his memories of Iganga and to Kamlesh and Sheila Madhwani for their hospitality in Kakira. I am very grateful to Dora Mindham for giving me a home in Chichester and much encouragement in the early days of writing the book.

I am also very grateful to my tutors, especially Stephanie Norgate, at the University of Chichester, where I began this book as part of the MA in Creative Writing; to my workshop colleagues, in particular Gabrielle Kimm and Joanna Howard, who read the first draft of the manuscript; to Helen Clark, then MP for Peterborough, and Adrian Weston for twice reading and commenting on later drafts, and to Todd Kingsley-Jones and other members of my current writing group who helped me finish it.

The book is dedicated to my dear friend and ex-teacher, Marion England, miraculously rediscovered after several decades, who was not only a most supportive reader and critic but who inspired me to try to understand lives guided by religious belief. As her gravestone says, she is surely now *'singing with angels'*.

1

The tide is on the turn. Rose loves this moment. It makes her pulses quicken, her heart lighter. The incoming wave sinks slowly into the sand, leaves its outline along the beach in a fine line of sparkling foam and strands a few lengths of seaweed. A small breeze picks up somewhere out to sea and the next wave, though still very shallow, swishes in with confidence, teases the weed into its own shape and erases all trace of its predecessor.

She lays her knitting in her lap, breathes in deeply and looks about her. The gulls that have gathered, one to each post of the breakwater, know it is time. They are shifting their feet, paying beady attention, poised for action. The oyster catchers that have been running back and forth feeding at the water's edge all afternoon have become nervous, each watching its own back, as if afraid of getting its feet wet.

I must move, she tells herself. Another five minutes at most. Make the most of it. She lies back in the deckchair and half closes her eyes. The sun, though declining, is still strong; her body is saturated with its warmth. It has been such a lovely day. Now, as forecast, small clouds have begun to drift in: there may be a storm tonight. Only one or two yachts and a red-sailed windsurfer out to sea. There is never much on this stretch of coast. A sudden flurry of black and white to her right attracts her attention.

'*Namunye*!' The word surprises her.

The bird is quite close. It has landed on the wet sand and is looking at her, as if it has something to tell her, has brought a message. She feels a faint stirring of hope.

'We will ask the namunye.' Heads nodding wisely.

'Little *katikkiro*, God's own Prime Minister.'

The ball of blue wool drops to the sand and the wagtail moves a little further away, still watching her closely. She bends to pick up the wool but her right arm won't move. It's gone to sleep, she thinks.

‘Bad news travels faster than the sound of the drum,’ a voice reminds her.

‘Bad news does not wait for one to come back from the well,’ says another. They know already.

‘Go katikkiro. Fly to all the houses! Search all the compounds.’ The voices are forming a chorus. ‘Look for Joseph. Find Joseph.’

The wagtail cocks its head. It seems impatient, poised for action. She tries to stand, to follow, but her right side feels frozen. And my feet are wet. She is distracted. I must listen to the village women. They are trying to help me.

‘*Kugenda ku mulabale*.’

Ask the priest. Magician. Musamize. Mulaguzi. Mukongozzi. Call him what you will. But ask him. Go to him. Go to the *ssabo*. The temple. You understand? Dark faces closing around her, hands pulling, urgent. You need protection. Ask him for a *ddagala*.

A nsiraba.

Lukisa.

Mayembe.

Magic.

Spell.

Lweza.

Yirizi.

A charm.

Do you hear us?

‘Joseph has an amulet,’ I try to tell them. He wore it round his waist, a cowrie shell, on a thread. Once I found it under his pillow. I was angry with him.

‘Heathen!’ I called him. ‘Pagan!’

‘It’s just for luck, mother.’ His voice is careful, his face turned away from me. He is no longer a child, I see it for the first time and I am afraid.

‘Leave it, mother. You must never destroy your ddagala.’ Joseph said that. ‘I must hand it to my son and he to his son.’

Ah! Such pain! Waves of it, knocking me sideways, sucking me under. Leave me! Follow the namunye! Look! There, he was there. On the sand, the white sand. I said leave me. Can’t you hear me? Has he gone? Oh, katikkiro. My heart is breaking. Don’t let him fly. Find Joseph. Tell me Joseph did not die.

2

"'Here we go.' Marek patted the pouch attached to his chest and leapt from the plane. The green fields rushed to meet the plummeting pair. At two thousand feet the man felt for the ripcord and pulled. Nothing happened. He pulled again. Still the parachute failed to open. One thousand feet. He tried once more, knowing that it was already too late. The younger son of the Count of Zynofy was a brave young man. He was also a fatalist.

'Sorry old man,' his words were lost to the wind. 'This was not meant to be. You would have been safer in Zynofy après tout. Germans or no Germans.' And then he lost consciousness.

Man, cat and useless parachute hit the English grass at a speed no human could survive. Their more fortunate companions settled in billows of silk along the gentle slopes of the South Downs. Rajah, cushioned by his master's body, peered out. A little stunned, he watched the others loose their shrouds, bundle and stash the bright whitenesses inside their camouflaged jackets and run towards him. Would any of them care what had happened to him? He thought not. He scrabbled upwards and leapt free.

A dog might have licked his dead master's face, perhaps remained by his side to await his own fate. Rajah was driven by self -preservation. To shouts of surprise, and some alarm, he fled for the closest cover, a tangle of brambles in a shady hollow where his tabby coat defeated the brief search that followed.

'A Polish cat is very like an English cat,' decided the flight lieutenant. 'They certainly sound the same,' observed the navigator. 'And I suppose he will find food,' concluded the youngest and most sympathetic of the group. Then they were gone, heading for their rendezvous, their own survival being uppermost in all their minds.

Rajah let them pass out of sight, emerged from his hiding place and headed for a distant cluster of buildings. One of these looked remarkably like the barn at home where he had often found mice to supplement his diet. He would survive. Life would go on.

Next day..."

Lilia paused. What would happen next day? It had been a long day. Perhaps he could meet a kind little girl or boy? No, too soon. Some more tension was required, a little danger. An escapade. 'We cannot make things too easy for you,' she spoke aloud and then sighed. Episodes in *'The Many Lives of Rajah the Tabby Cat'* were her occasional contribution to a quirky column located towards the back of the local paper, usually inspired in some way by local or contemporary events. They provided her with almost the only supplement to the small pension she had earned from her years at the library, but she was finding it harder and harder to spin these small fantasies. Only this morning she had had to abandon one that involved Rajah meeting George V on his convalescence in Bognor in the 1930s. It wasn't only that she needed to research such matters as whether the royal family even liked cats, their predilection for horses and dogs being very well known. It was more serious. Perhaps it was because, since moving here from Brighton, her own life had become so dull and routine.

She looked across her living room-cum-study at the very large tabby cat that dozed, as usual, on a red satin cushion on the only good piece of furniture, a particularly beautiful carved mahogany armchair from India, which she had found at the Flea Market many years ago. What could happen next? This was wartime, although surely scarcely evident in rural Sussex, far from the horrors of mainland Europe. More planes flying overhead? A distant explosion? Hungry humans? No, the English would never eat cat, however desperate, however much it might taste like chicken. She sighed, still uninspired. Best to sleep on it. Something would occur, in time for the promised deadline. It always did.

'But oh dear, Rajah,' she pressed 'Save'. 'I have just killed off my father. Of course,' she continued to shut down the computer for the night, 'In fiction all is possible, indeed the author is all-powerful so far as the fates of his, or her, characters are concerned. In fact, I rather think that that is sometimes the major attraction of being a writer. It is otherwise a lonely and frequently disappointing occupation.'

She sighed. Rajah half-opened his eyes.

‘And perhaps, in view of what later ensued, he would have deserved it. However, in this case, I admit to feeling a little - stymied by reality. For he did not die, no indeed, or where should we be? Or, to be precise, where should I be, for you might well still exist, if somewhere else. As I am sure you would point out, if you could only speak.’

At this point Rajah extended his front legs, flexed his claws a number of times, jumped to the floor, stretched his entire body and padded towards the kitchen.

‘Which would be most helpful sometimes, I have to say, not to say more companionable,’ Lilia called after him. ‘As it is, I have to make up all your adventures on my own while you,’ she turned towards where her companion now sat purposefully near his empty dish, eyeing her through the doorway with what somehow could be read as impatience, ‘You actually do virtually nothing. And go nowhere. But I do love you.’

Lilia tried to be rational where Rajah, and his several predecessors, were concerned. She was very much aware of the absurdity of being overly dependent on a pet. But, at this moment, there was no one to see or hear her. Besides, appearances to the contrary, and all her cats had been male tabbies, no two cats were alike and each developed their own unmistakable ways of making their, admittedly limited, wishes known. Therefore, surely, each possessed a character to which one could relate.

‘I know, it’s dinner time,’ Lilia waited for her computer to enter sleep mode and switched off. She stood with some difficulty, rotated her shoulders a few times and walked a little stiffly to the kitchen. ‘And where do we suppose dinner comes from? Hmm?’ She bent down to stroke Rajah, who pushed his head hard against her hand, his whole body following in one long sinuous arch so that both of them were almost knocked off balance. ‘Oh my lovely boy, you do care a little for your old mistress, don’t you.’ She picked up his dish and glanced out of the window as she washed it at the sink.

The weather was changing for the worse. She looked across the small park that, together with the road and a line of beach huts, were all that separated her from the seafront. The half dozen palm trees were bending in the wind, their driest branches would surely have broken off by morning if there were a storm. Perhaps been blown as far as the beach. It had happened before. She became aware of the seed of yet another story beginning to germinate and stood still, awaiting the magic that never failed to amaze her.

Rajah wrapped himself around her ankles. She shook her head and reached in the drawer beside her for the tin opener. 'No, you're right, enough imagining for one day. I was about to have you whirled out to sea in a hurricane, but we'll stay in the warm for tonight.' She reached to switch on the radio to catch the headlines as she forked half the tin of tuna into Rajah's dish and wondered what to make for her own supper.

The July 7 bombings on the underground and bus were still top of the news even on this local station. The fifty two victims were being named, their individual stories told, and survivors were remembering their fellow passengers immediately before the blasts, their voices breaking with emotion. It was hard to listen for long and Lilia meant to switch off as soon as she had finished cooking and washed her hands. She was just putting the tuna soufflé into the oven when a final item of breaking news caught her attention. *'From West Bognor tonight: fishermen have saved an old woman from the sea. Her identity is as yet unknown. She has been taken to St Stephen's Hospital where police are waiting for her to regain consciousness. Anyone with any information is asked to ring the following number...'*

Lilia was looking forward to curling up in front of "Mastermind". It was the semi-final tonight and she was expecting to know a lot of the answers to two of the specialist subjects: the early years of the second world war, (before Russia, fortunately as it turned out, joined in), and Captain Cook's voyages. At different times she had researched both, for reasons professional, (the Rajah stories), and personal. So she tried to ignore the tiny twinge of concern.

3

'There we are. All tucked in.'

'We'? There's only me. And where? On my back, flat, between sheets, not moving, I cannot move. Am I dead? And are these shrouds, not sheets? And this face looming, is it checking, before closing the lid on my coffin, my life over? Did you not feel my breath? I CAN FEEL YOURS.

'That's me finished for the night, dear. Sleep tight.'

Now you're going. Whoever you are.

'I'll be back in the morning. I've got a clinic at 10 but I'll pop in and see you first, alright? See how you are. After a good night's sleep. And then I'll be back again, to see what we can do for you, after my clinic.'

Clinic? My clinic? Where was it now...

'Kamuli,' Stephen announces our arrival as he does every week.

'The road does not get any shorter.' Less than an hour from Iganga but how hot and dirty I feel already.

I look out at the short row of single-story wooden buildings with corrugated iron roofs that lines the dusty road. Among the throng of customers from the nearby African village or in from the bush, I can see women in bright saris flitting about on their errands. All the shops and businesses are owned and run by Indians. Through the open window I hear snatches of their conversation in a tongue from far away that I cannot begin to understand. Their glossy dark-haired children play cricket in the street, smaller ones perch on their sisters' hips. Some wave as we pass, and I smile but I have not come to see them, though they know who I am.

We turn down the track that leads to the village and park in the shade of the mango trees beside Mama Wanza's hut. I feel happy to be here where I know I am useful, where I have achieved something, and I feel a small rush of pride that I cannot deny. I want to open more such clinics.

'The line is longer than before,' says Stephen.

He's right. Women expecting babies, women nursing babies, calming sick children, sitting patiently, waiting to see me and receive what remedies I can offer: quinine, disinfectant, milk powder.

'Who would have thought it when we started?' The 'we' is automatic. Stephen is grateful to me for nursing his wife Grace through her difficult first labour. If she had still been living in Kamuli, she might not have survived. But I am also grateful to Stephen because without him, there would have been no introduction to Wanza and without Wanza there would have been no clinic. She understood the need and used her influence as a first wife and, once Mwangyengela agreed, the other elders followed.

'Everything is ready, Mama.'

I follow Wanza through the doorway, under the hanging bunches of neem leaves. She says they deter mosquitoes. The floor is freshly swept and there is new mud on the walls. I nod my approval of the pots of boiling water and clean folded cloths and the mats spread on the floor and sit in the one low chair that has been placed in the centre for me. Stephen brings in my bags and Wanza ushers forward her daughter, Leah, who bends in front of me with a basin of hot water. I wash and dry my hands carefully.

'Thank you, Leah.'

Her eyes meet mine for an instant and a shy smile flickers at the corners of her mouth. 'I ask my mother to call first patient, madam?'

Her English is improving weekly. She's a bright girl. No doubt she will have to go outside and ask Stephen to translate for a while yet but already she's a great help. She is fifteen, small for her age, still slender, but I can see she's outgrowing her uniform of white blouse and navy blue pleated skirt. I'm afraid she will soon have a husband and child of her own and give up her studies. It happens only too often.

'Yes. We have many today. I need your help. Do you think you can weigh the babies as I taught you last week?'

'Oh yes, Madam.' Her eyes light up and I watch as she gently takes the tiny baby from his young mother, lays him on a cloth in the scales, and adjusts the weights until she has achieved a perfect balance.

'Six pounds ten ounces,' she tells me.

Soon I shall trust her to keep the records as well. There are many tasks she could learn to do. After all, most of what I do is simple and what I teach is only common-sense. Good food, clean water, rest and hygiene. I don't need to mention fresh air as people are outside most of the time. I have given up trying to explain why personal cleanliness is so important since I caused such panic with my little slide show of the pictures of greatly magnified germs.

'Aiee! Mama mulogo! Ddogo. Ndwadde nganda!' The women watching started crying, wailing, backing away to the door. They clutched their children and looked at me as if I were threatening them with monsters or devils.

Wanza rushed in, too late to halt the stampede. 'They thought you were trying to poison them, do black magic.'

I was trying not to smile. Although I must say, those germs do look most alarming, it is just as well they are too small to be seen with our own eyes.

'Next time I'll start with a bit more explanation,' I told her, through Stephen.

'There must be no next time,' replied Wanza. She was not smiling.

'They have all gone running to the *mulabale*, the medicine man,' said Stephen. 'Now you will have to win them back.'

So I have given up trying to be scientific with them. As long as, God willing, my advice is successful, that's what matters. But I cannot help this next child. She is coughing and sneezing and she has a red rash on her body.

'It was on her face before but now it is gone from there,' explains the mother. 'I think soon it will be altogether gone.'

She is not worried and has only come because it happened to be clinic day. But I am worried. It is measles, I am sure, and, while waiting, the child has had plenty of time to give it to others.

'Keep her cool, out of bright light and away from other children,' I advise. 'And then we must wait and pray for her recovery.' I ask Leah to show her out the back way. 'And tell her if her daughter's cough gets worse, or she has trouble staying awake, or her ears seem to give her pain, to go to a doctor at once.'

It is an afterthought because I know that even if the mother could afford to do so and get her to Iganga it would probably be too late. Dr Sharma has even longer queues of patients at his clinic than we do. But I must tell her, because once I nearly left it too late. Joseph was three or four when he got measles. Penny and Colin must have been away or perhaps it was after they had left. If she had been there, Penny would have advised me. Edward was no help.

'Why is he crying like this?' I ask him.

'He must be hungry, he hasn't eaten all day and he keeps being sick. His stomach must hurt.'

'But why is he being sick? And listen to him, I never heard a child cry like that, so high pitched. It's not normal. And he's raging hot but his hands and feet are cold, so cold.'

'He's had fevers before.'

'He won't let me hold him. Look!' The small hot body arches away from me, as if irritated at being disturbed. Joseph's grey eyes, usually so eager and bright, are dull and unresponsive. 'Joseph, it's Mummy. Joseph,' I call him urgently. 'Come back to us. I love you, Daddy loves you.' Tears sting my eyes and fill my throat. 'Oh Joseph, please! It's not my fault you are ill.' I think we are losing him.

'What fancies you have, Rose. Of course it's not your fault. You are making yourself ill. I shall call a doctor.' Edward keeps his face averted, refusing to engage in discussion, as he always does when he is pretending he knows best.

Joseph was admitted to hospital for observation. Edward went off in the doctor's car with him. They said I was too upset to go. I fell on my knees in the dirt, wailing like an African woman. It was prayer of a sort and, God be praised, in a few weeks he had recovered.

This next young woman's face is pitted with the scars of small pox.

'Nursey, they are spoiling my life. What good man will want me for a wife? They say you can work wonders, nursey. Please make them disappear.' She starts to cry softly. I comfort her, pat her shoulder but what can I say?

'We all have our crosses to bear,' I tell her.

She is disappointed, a little angry. I watch her leave, thinking she will now put her faith in some useless traditional remedy.

Time passes as I weigh, measure, write records and offer what wisdom it pleases God to give me. There are more coughs and sniffles, which could be the beginning of measles. I repeat the same advice, despite knowing that it is almost impossible for it to be followed since the children of each mother sleep together in one hut. *'God's will be done,'* I think. But I cannot say it too often or people will see no point in coming to the clinic. And I do make a difference. I am making a difference. Could I wish for more?

4

Lilia did not want to get involved. Living at Number One she was used to, though far from content with, being treated as an unpaid concierge. Carers, meals on wheels, social workers come to persuade one or other resident to attend some lunch club or meeting, they were always ringing her bell to gain access to someone else. Often to Rose upstairs, they were always after her to join something. Sometimes they even tried to get her, Lilia, to mediate.

'Perhaps if you spoke to her, Miss Zynovsky…'

As if Rose would listen to her. And why should she? It was her life and Lilia had no intention of breaching the tacit understanding she felt they shared: help when in need without intrusion on privacy. Thus she was very grateful to Rose for occasionally feeding Rajah when she went away for a few days and had been glad to fetch in a few bits of shopping on the rare occasions when Rose had been poorly, alerted by her failure to draw back her bedroom curtains in the morning. Lilia still sometimes missed the distant company of the big house in Brighton, where she and her mother had lived in the basement for so many years, even after the Lipman family had moved out and rented it out as flats, and she did sometimes yearn for the youthful liveliness of the city itself. But, on the whole, she had become accustomed to living much more peacefully here, where everyone minded their own business and kept themselves to themselves in the best British tradition and she was by far the youngest amongst her immediate neighbours, despite being almost a pensioner herself.

'Surely, Rajah, there are times when one might be permitted to put oneself first?' Rajah had returned to his cushion where he was methodically washing his face. 'I mean, it's not as if we were close. Nor that she has ever shown signs of wishing to be, despite being willing to feed you from time to time and asking me to keep her spare key just in case. No, I am sure she prefers to be independent and is quite happy when she can spend her days over at that old beach hut of hers.' But there was the rub.

'You haven't heard Rose come back from the beach either, have you?' She sighed and noted the contact number as the announcer gave it a second time.

In the no man's land before the exclusive beachfront properties of Aldwick began, Lilia could see three fishing boats drawn up just above the high tide mark. She clutched her thin jacket against the wind and stumbled across the stones towards them. The sun had not set but the light was fast fading as black-bottomed clouds raced in from the southwest and the sea, alternately grey in the shade, green in the sun, drove in beneath them, pounding the top of the steep bank where the beach levelled off to a wide plateau. There was no one in the boats, but on the deck of one lay a blue woolly bundle attached to red plastic knitting needles. Lilia reached for the cold soggy mass. It seemed more likely that it belonged to an old lady than to a fisherman.

The wind was getting stronger. She clambered awkwardly up the beach, her hair whipping her face, her skirt tangling in her legs. At the top she straightened, then almost fell over as the shingle shifted under her weight, her ankle twisted and she cried out in pain. Damn. She should have just telephoned the hospital and given a description of Rose. It was quite obvious that she wouldn't still be down here in this weather. Lilia began to limp along the paved area towards the beach huts. There might be more of Rose's belongings she should collect, if she could find out which was her hut.

The only door that was unlocked belonged to the fourth hut from the end. It was ajar, an open padlock dangling from the latch. She looked inside, curious, for she had never been invited. There was a tiny table holding a two ring gas cooker attached to a gas canister, a small sink with draining board, a cupboard, a folding chair. Everything was in order and quite impersonal. But then she noticed the unwashed cup and plate in the sink and recognised the grey raincoat on a hook behind the door, a shopping bag on the floor under it with a newspaper, a loaf of sliced bread and some tins of food visible inside: signs of Rose's life in the hours before the accident on a day that she had surely expected to end like any other. We never know what might lie ahead, thought Lilia. She shivered, picked up the bag, threw the raincoat round her shoulders, locked the door and hastened home to call the police.

5

Rose lay on her back, her body scarcely raising the bedclothes, one thin arm attached to a tube suspended next to the bed, her hair spread around her head like a silver halo. She looked well, her naturally sallow skin faintly bronzed by the sun. Her breathing was shallow, almost imperceptible. The faintest frown appeared as from some distant dream and disappeared as quickly.

'Almost certainly she's had a stroke,' Staff Nurse Maureen Halliwell smoothed Rose's forehead and circled her narrow wrist with broad strong fingers as she felt the pulse. 'They did a CT scan last night. I expect they'll do another in a couple of days. Meanwhile we've just got her on aspirin.' She rubbed her thumb and forefinger together a few inches from Rose's ear. 'As you can see she's still unconscious. As far as one can tell. Here, sit down, hold her hand, talk to her, you never know.'

Lilia sat down on the chair beside the bed clutching her bag in her lap. She did not like to think of all the superbugs she might be in danger of taking home with her and the less contact with surfaces the better. But she took Rose's hand and gave it a slight squeeze. 'Hello, Rose dear.' She paused, uncomfortable at the lack of response. Nurse Halliwell nodded encouragement, the tight bun of greying hair on top of her head wobbling slightly. 'I've brought you some flowers,' continued Lilia, pulling them from the bag. 'Look, stocks, wonderful smell they have, I've always loved them, I hope you like them too. Oh, and I've brought your knitting.' She reached deeper into her bag for the now dry bundle and put it on the bedside table. 'I found it on the beach, in one of the fishing boats. It was wet but I managed to wash and dry it without taking it off the needles. I hope it's alright. Though I don't suppose you'll be wanting it just yet, will you, silly of me, I didn't think…Oh dear,' she looked up at Nurse Halliwell. 'I'm not very good at this. Babbling on. It's not as if we're close you see….'

''I'm glad she's got someone to visit, it can make all the difference to recovery,' Nurse Halliwell reassured her. 'Most recovery occurs in the first month. And the large motor functions should begin to return in the next two weeks if they're going to. But,' she lowered her voice, 'The first three days are really critical, when there's most risk of another stroke.'

'Well I…' Lilia tried to muster her defences against this further call on her better nature but the nurse continued.

'Do you know the name of her GP? It would help to have her history. If she's on any meds. Quite likely she's had TIAs – that's transient minor attacks – before, though she might not have noticed.'

'I'm sure I could find out – but she must have family,' Lilia protested. 'Surely the police…? I mean, I'm just a neighbour, and even that only for the last few years…'

Nurse Halliwell raised her eyebrows, acknowledging but not condoning Lilia's efforts to disengage. 'There's a story in the paper today. I'll show you. The police are hoping that'll help track down anyone who knows her. Mind you, it was written before you called in with her name.'

'Did you hear that, Rose?' Lilia raised her voice. 'You're hitting the headlines. We'll save you the cuttings.' She turned to Nurse Halliwell. 'Of course there'll be a follow up now.' She paused. 'I wonder if it will mention me.'

'There, I nearly forgot,' the nurse struck her forehead with the flat of one hand. The newspaper wants you to call. I said I'd pass on the number but they said you'd have it. Apparently they tried to get you at home.' She looked closely at Lilia, evidently curious.

'I write for the paper sometimes,' Lilia explained. 'The cat stories? That's me.'

'Really? Oh, I do enjoy them. Even though I'm more of a dog person myself, not that I have either. How interesting! However, must get on.' Nurse Halliwell pointed to the flowers that Lilia still held and reached out her hand. 'I'll put them in a vase.' She bent her head to the flowers and inhaled deeply then held them close to Rose and frowned. 'Can you smell them, Rose?' She turned to Lilia. 'We're not too sure about smell and taste.'

Lilia picked up her bag and stood. 'I ought to be getting back if I'm to look through her things, and ring the Editor.' She raised her voice. 'I'll come to see you again, Rose.'

Taste. What was that taste, a special taste, something I ate there, that day ...

"I ought to be getting back." That's what I said. But that taste, it delayed me, that morning, the same morning...

It is the best part of the morning, when the clinic has finished. I go outside Mama Wanza's hut and stand under the mango trees. Everyone who has waited is called together. Stephen fetches the harmonium.

'Our Father,' I begin. 'Which art in Heaven.'

Each week a few more voices repeat the lines after me, the simpler words at least. What does 'forgiveness' and 'temptation' mean to them? I don't know if Stephen gives any explanation in his translation. But I like to think it does not matter so long as the blessed words are spoken. In fact, sometimes it seems like a miracle. The Lord's Own Prayer arising to heaven from a clearing in the jungle in deepest Africa! Surely this is why we came here. I try to slow the pace, everyone always gabbles at this point. I used to as well when I was younger, we all did, as if it was a race to the finish. Now I want to prolong the moment.

'For thine is the kingdom, the power and the glory, for ever and ever, amen.'

There is a brief respectful silence and now it is time to sing. 'What shall we sing today?' I look around encouraging suggestions.

'Away in a Manger! Waynamanga! Manger!' there is a chorus from the children. Some of them have got hold of their baby sisters and brothers and are already eagerly rocking them. I don't want to disappoint them but we cannot sing the same songs every week.

'Not today, it is too far from Christmas,' I tell them. 'You remember, baby Jesus' birthday? How about "There's a Friend for little children"?'

They jump up and down in their approval. They don't know this so well but it can be sung with a fair deal of swaying. They sing, imperfectly, with great gusto. And then there is the new song, which, a few weeks ago, Stephen sang to the group. It comes, he said, from north Uganda, the homeland of his mother. I wondered whether I should encourage African singing in this way but, once Stephen translated – which, since no one else spoke the language of the Acholi, he had to do in two languages – I decided it was alright. Once again the older children grab a baby if they can and wait excitedly for Stephen to begin.

"If the chickens can teach
Their children to peck
And the birds can teach
Their children to fly
Then why can't you
My lovely baby, walk?"

The babies are now being dandled upright, their feet touching the ground. Some mothers stay close to make sure that none comes to any harm.

"If the winds can teach
The trees to move
And the mountains
Can answer back
Then why can't you
My lovely baby, walk, walk, walk."

'Walk, walk, walk,' the children encourage their charges. Toddlers proudly show off their newly acquired skills and older children without babies pretend to be toddlers. The adults laugh and clap and sing. There is such joy. I cannot help feeling this small glow of satisfaction.

We ought to be getting back. I promised Joseph we would go to Jinja and already I am afraid it may be too late. But Leah brings water and spiced plantain and we must accept. I sit down again and savour the perfect balance of sugar, salt and chilli on my tongue, feeling it stimulate the saliva that slides down my throat to help digest the solid starchy vegetable. I take a deep breath and relax. I'll take Joseph tomorrow.

6

On the way home Lilia stopped at the newsagents to buy the *Bognor Observer* and cancel Rose's order. The shop was also a sub post office and general store. *Prop. J. Ashling*. "*Only one schoolchild at a time*," warned the notice in the window. She went in, watched by the CCTV camera in the corner and the extraordinarily beautiful woman behind the counter.

J. Ashling had been a previous proprietor. Sarita Thakker looked as if she would have been more at home in a palace in Rajasthan or a Bollywood movie with her huge almond shaped eyes, aquiline nose and jet black hair swept high on her head. She wore tight jeans and a sweatshirt, a diamond stud in her nose, small gold rings in her ears and a jangle of gold and glass bracelets on her wrist. She had come from Kenya only a few months previously, following her marriage to the present owner. But she recognised Lilia and remembered Rose. Eyes narrowed, she listened to Lilia's story, rang up the purchase, handed over the change then turned abruptly.

'Bhavin!' she shouted. 'Come and hear this.'

A bear of a man appeared in a doorway, wiping his mouth on a small towel. He had clearly been interrupted in a meal. Sarita took the towel and made room for him behind the counter. He nodded affably at Lilia and then conversed rapidly with his wife. Lilia understood one word: '*Observer*'.

'You know Mrs McCormack was in East Africa long time ago?' he said. 'She told us one time just after Sarita arrived. Maybe she still has family there. You know what I am thinking? You should write this story, you being an author, right? And maybe we can help you. Give you some contacts.'

'Oh, but I'm not really a journalist,' Lilia began to protest but Sarita cut her short.

'You are her neighbour,' she said firmly. 'Better than a stranger. You will care about her.'

'We will be happy to help the press,' Bhavin joked, crushing Lilia's hand in his as she left. 'Being in the same line of business you might say, is it not, Sarita?'

Sarita raised her eyebrows enigmatically at Lilia. 'And you cannot trust the police to follow things up, that is sure.'

'Let us know what happens.' Bhavin saw her out.

'If you come up with something then you can certainly be the one to write about it,' Mike the Editor agreed as soon as Lilia had explained her access to Rose's flat and the need to search her belongings. He laid down that day's copy of the paper on his desk, pushed his glasses back above his much receded hairline and stretched his arms wearily before clasping his hands behind his head. 'Though I can't pay you much. Sometimes people leave notes to be found,' he went on, helpfully. 'They only tell people on a need to know basis. Even family. I've seen it quite a bit, with attempted suicides, disappearances, that sort of thing. Actually, family are often the last to know.'

'I'll have a look but it's not as if Rose was expecting anything to happen,' Lilia put the chipped mug of tea back on the desktop and aligned it carefully with one of the numerous interlocking white circles left by other mugs, or perhaps by the same mug on many occasions. She peered briefly into its heavily stained interior. 'God Mike, does anyone ever wash up around here? This mug is disgusting.'

'No one will stop you if you feel that strongly, Lilia my love.' He was looking at the ceiling but now fixed her with a fond, though weary, look. 'And I've got a lot more washing up at home if you fancy coming round. It's been a long time.' He leaned forward to take her hand but she recoiled instantly.

'This is business, Mike, and that's the worst chatup line ever. And I thought we agreed we weren't going anywhere.'

'You may have. I still miss you. Alright, alright,' he waved away her protests. 'So I did transgress. Briefly. But I regretted it, wholeheartedly. I wish you'd give us another chance. Neither of us is getting any younger. Ouch. Another great line. OK, forget it.' He glanced at the paper in front of him. 'See what you can find out.'

Lilia stood to leave. 'I certainly will though I might not want to put it all in the paper, if it's her private life.'

Mike raised her eyes to the ceiling again and sighed loudly. 'Oh God, here we go. Lilia on her moral high ground. You still don't get it do you, what one has to do to sell a paper?' Lilia ignored him, pointedly, until he continued. 'Anyway, I'm clearly in your hands on this one, so let's just agree for the present that maybe you'll find something that the police can follow up. And that just putting Rose's name in the paper might do some good. Someone might read it and remember something.'

'Fine. I'll be in touch.'

'A photo would be good,' he called after her. 'And don't forget we're available online. People read *The Observer* all over the world. Or they could if they wanted to.'

Rajah was lying in his usual chair, his paws drawn up under his chest. He looked up expectantly as Lilia walked in briskly, put her bag on the table and took Rose's key from the top drawer of her desk.

'Let's see what we can find, shall we?' She turned from him and walked back out of her flat and up the stairs to the first floor.

Rose's living room, which was directly above her own, always reminded Lilia of the succession of furnished flats in which she had lived with her mother during her childhood. The gas fire, the dark patterned carpet, floral covered three-piece suite with embroidered antimacassars, lace mats on every surface and under every ornament. But here it was the ornaments that took the eye. The line of elephants on the windowsill, the large giraffe in one corner and polished rhino in another, the elongated black warriors guarding the hearth. And the masks on every wall. Eyeless, wooden, yet apparently watching.

'Horrible things, aren't they?' she remarked to Rajah who had padded up the stairs in her wake and now sat watching as she riffled through the drawers of a small writing desk that stood in a corner. 'From Africa, you know, where the animals are really wild. You wouldn't like it one little bit….ah good.' She had found a folder marked 'Important Docs' in spidery ink handwriting. It contained Rose's National Health Service card with the name of her doctor, her pension book and one or two letters from banks and the Inland Revenue.

'You wait here, Rajah, while I go and find some things for Rose,' she said. 'I've never been in her bedroom before and it feels enough like an intrusion without -'

She broke off with a gasp on the threshold of Rose's bedroom. The bed was made, the dressing and side tables neatly covered with more lace mats. With no sign of recent use, the room would have been tidy but for the plastic carrier bags that almost covered the floor and bulged from under the bed. 'What on earth?' She picked one up and looked inside. Blue wool. She emptied it on the bed. Half a dozen identical small V-necked sweaters cascaded onto the candlewick bedspread. She picked up another bag. More sweaters. Every bag seemed to be the same. Hundreds of identical sweaters. She sat on the bed looking at them, nonplussed.

Rajah appeared at the doorway and cocked an ear as she spoke.

'Could they be for Oxfam?' she surmised, but very doubtfully. 'But then…' She stopped and began to think fast, with rising excitement. '*"Deckchair Woman Mystery Continues: Why was she always knitting?"*' It could be the title of her first article for the Observer. Mike would love it. The thought sobered her instantly and, after a minute's consideration, drew a notional line. Only if she thought it would help Rose would she reveal things about her that she could not have known without access to her private life. Meanwhile she would pursue her investigations. Why was Rose knitting just those sweaters? And keeping them? It seemed pointless, an empty ritual, almost like knitting the same sweater over and over again. Irrational.

'But we know better than that, don't we, darling? People always have their reasons. That's one thing I learnt doing all that wretched market research interviewing. Everyone has a point of view and usually one can discover it, so long as one is patient and asks the right questions.' Lilia tapped the side of her nose with an elegant forefinger as she considered how best to proceed. 'And there's more than one way to skin a cat,' she concluded. 'No offence, sweetheart. We must leave no stone unturned. But first I must find a few nightclothes and toiletries for Rose and pop them back to the hospital.'

7

There is someone sitting by my bed. Uninvited. An uninvited visitor. Asleep. Not much of a visitor! How did she get in? Who is she? Not a complete stranger. I do know her. I will place her, in a minute, if I concen... but this isn't my room! There's no wardrobe, no dressing table, this bed is too high and the bedside table too. Where am I? There is my knitting, but how did it get there on the bedside table, it should be – I should be knitting! I must get it finished, there's so little time, only a few days. Reach out, come on arm, stretch a bit, nearly there, now hand, no, that's not right, why won't my fingers - oh! Well that woke her up, whoever she is. And she's picking it up, my knitting, careful now, mind the needles, don't drop the stitches, I haven't time to –

'Sorry, dear, not much company am I? You were asleep when I arrived. It's good to see you moving a bit already. That nurse must be really pleased with you. It's a good sign you know. Here's your knitting, there I'll put it back, where you can see it, alright? But not too near this tea in case it gets spilled onto it.'

Not there, oh no not there. That's even further away. Here, near, I need it, I must have it.

'What is it now? Don't get upset! What are you staring at? Your knitting? Is that it?'

Yes, yes, yes. How many times?

'You were trying to reach it? Here you are then. I thought you were after the tea. Someone must have brought it while we were both asleep.'

But I can't hold it properly, my fingers won't, they don't -

'Don't cry! Oh dear, Rose, what can I do for you. How about a cup of fresh hot tea, yes? I'll go and find us both some more tea.'

'More tea, Edward?'

I am holding the teapot out to him I love breakfast time. A new day, the sun just clearing the tops of the tallest mvule trees and reaching the table. I raise my face to its warmth and close my eyes for a blessed moment against its brightness. It shines blood red through my eyelids. Joseph's voice calls from the far end of the verandah.

'Mum, can we go?' He is lying flat on his stomach, his top half over the edge of the step, long brown legs hooked under the bar of one of the low chairs where we sit at sundown. He has been trying to entice Blossom, the black and white mission cat, to leave off her mouse hunting and come out from under the verandah to play. He wants a dog like we had in Jinja but we have so far refused.

'It will just run wild when you are not here,' Edward told him.

'Then I can run wild with it when I am here,' Joseph argued. 'Oh please Dad.'

I will speak to Edward. Joseph needs company. Perhaps next year we can get him a dog. Next year, the next time Joseph will be home on holiday, it seems a lifetime to me, I try to banish the thought and look at Joseph, or what I can see of him, again. Not so long ago I would have run to him long since, afraid he would fall on his head. Break his neck. But now he would be angry. 'Don't fuss Mum.' How many times have I heard him say that? And so, I dare say, has every mother of boys. He tires of the cat, has rolled over, jumped to his feet and joined us before I can reply. His chair is rocking with the speed with which he sat down.

'Patience, Joseph.' Edward reproves him but, after yesterday, I am eager to please. I lean forward and pat his knee.

'Go and see if Mary has made the picnic. After we've finished shopping, I thought we'd go down by the lake.'

'Oh, super, Mum!' he has leapt up again and is leaning over the back of my chair, his curls, that are so like my own, falling over my forehead. I reach up to touch his cheek, he gives me a quick kiss on the palm of my hand and he's off. But at the corner of the house he stops and looks back.

'And can I swim? And can we take Nilu? Shall I telephone him?'

'Yes, yes, yes!' I am laughing. Today is his day. He disappears but almost immediately sticks his head back round the corner and grins at me. 'Thanks! And I love your new shoes.'

I have dressed up for our outing and he knows it. A pretty floral dress and newish, dark blue sandals. I circle one foot admiring the way the wedge and ankle strap flatter my leg. Edward seems not to notice, which does not greatly surprise me. He is frowning as he stands, smoothing his thinning sandy hair back from his forehead, and I am sure he is thinking of something else. I might ask, but not now, not today. I don't want to know. He pats his pocket to see if he has his pipe as he always does before going out. It is his comforter.

'I'd better go and see how they're getting on at the church,' he says, as if he does not go every day, at least once. 'They didn't get much done yesterday.'

So that's it. Of course. I offer him my cheek to kiss and he steps off the verandah and heads towards the far side of the compound. I watch his familiar gawky figure as it is swallowed in the shadows of the trees. Edward has somehow never grown into his tallness, he is ill at ease in his body, like an adolescent. Sometimes it irritates me, mostly I feel protective, as if I have another son.

What's worse is that he's never at ease in his mind either, always worrying away at some dilemma, never sure that he has made the right decision. I know that includes coming to Africa but then what would he do at home? Teach at a boarding school like Joseph's? We have discussed it in the past. But for the moment his path is set and he can be very stubborn. I have to give him that.

I sigh but almost immediately feel a smile on my face as I notice a familiar small black car nosing in through the nearby gates. It is my dear friend Father Thomas in his aged Morris Minor. The contrast with poor Edward could not be greater. Here is a man comfortable in his life, sure that it is being well spent. I rise to greet him and he holds my hands briefly in his before sitting in Edward's chair. I hear the telephone ring and someone picks it up. Joseph I think, making his arrangements. Very grown up.

'You're looking lovely today, my dear, if an old priest is allowed to make such remarks.' Thomas' face crinkles with the kindness that has helped me so much in the year since we came here. Sometimes I think I would not have survived without his advice and encouragement.

'A compliment never goes amiss!' I laugh, tell him about the outing with Joseph and am about to tell him what Joseph said when young Patrick appears from inside the house, bearing a note. He holds it on the flat of his hand, straight in front of him, like an offering. And is utterly solemn, bless him. I take it, equally solemn.

'Thank you, Patrick. And please can you tell your mother she can clear the table.' I smile as he walks carefully back the way he has come. He's a good boy of good Christian parents and we are lucky to have Peter and Mary to help us. But my smile fades as I read the note.

'*Come Bugiri. Kenario baby come quick*.' It is Mary's writing, she has translated the message from whoever actually made the call. I jump to my feet, I must get my bag, call Stephen. As I run into the house I stumble and the strap of one of my sandals breaks. I do not stop to change.

Joseph is standing in the hall next to the telephone table. He is trying so hard not to cry that he is angry with himself as well as with me. His face is red, his eyes narrowed and accusing.

'You promised. You promised.' He won't let me touch him.

'This lady needs me.'

'I need you.'

'She has lost lots of babies already.'

He wavers an instant, he has a kind heart, but then his eyes flick past me and he stiffens. 'Let someone else help her. Where's *her* mother?'

'Oh Joseph, I can't argue with you. She has called me, this very minute she is having the baby. She may die.'

'I don't care.' He flings himself away from me, knocks the telephone to the floor and, shouting, runs to his room. 'You care more about your ladies and their babies than you do for me.' His door slams and I stand there, hesitating, until Thomas places his hand on my arm. I hadn't known he was behind me but obviously Joseph had seen him.

'I'll talk to him, Rose. You get on your way. I came to tell you I'm going to Jinja myself shortly in case you wanted anything. Maybe Joseph would like to go with me. Just for the ride. And maybe an ice cream!'

'Oh Thomas, thank you. That would be such a relief. I'll be back as soon as I can.'

I have expected this call, anytime around now. Kenario is the third wife of Mutisya who, unusually, came himself to the Kamuli clinic one day to ask for my help. I gathered that he married her in a late, and what turned out to be a very brief, period of prosperity. He does not regret the decision and is fond of her. However, as he told me: 'A village blacksmith is not a rich man. I cannot afford a wife who is too weak to share in the work of the household. But,' he added, 'I do not want to send her back to her father though my other wives think I should. She is the daughter of my very good friend.'

I understand. Also that I am the last resource, for he has already spent money at the medicine man's for each previous confinement. My advice was that Bigogo and Gechemba keep Kenario in one of their huts and make her lie down as much as possible. They raised their eyebrows when I said that. As if they were not busy enough already with five children apiece! But they have done their best, I am sure. Kenario is not much older than their oldest children.

'Please see that there is boiling water and clean cloths,' I remind Stephen as we drive to Bugiri and I silently pray: 'Lord give me knowledge and strength to help this Thy child in her hour of need.'

Bigogo meets us outside Kenario's hut. She speaks urgently to Stephen. 'The baby started to come before nightfall.'

This is not too long. 'And is Kenario pushing?'

Bigogo looks at the sun and considers. 'One hour, perhaps a little more.'

Also not too long. I slip off my sandals and follow her into the half-darkness of the hut. Kenario is crouched on a mat, leaning on Gichemba, who meets my eyes, her lips set and her brows tight with concern. Now Kenario raises her eyes. They are wide and fearful although they brighten a little as she sees me. She holds out a hand and I go to her and take it, ready with reassurance. But then I see the small foot protruding from her body and I hope she does not notice my dismay. I place my bag on the floor, wash my hands carefully in a brass bowl that stands in a corner and kneel before her.

I have never delivered a breech birth successfully. I have seen such a baby born dead and its mother die soon after. At home, Kenario would have been in an operating theatre long since, the baby born, probably safely, by Caesarean. Gichemba says something to me. She places her hands close to Kenario's abdomen and moves them in a slow circle. Bigogo also speaks, she points at her co-wife, makes the same gesture with her hands and then raises one and points back over her shoulder. Before. Earlier. They have attempted to make the baby turn. I try not to look alarmed. No one does 'external cephalic version' at home anymore but we were told it happens here. Anyway, it has not worked.

Kenario tenses. 'Oh! Aah, aah, aah!'

The baby's knee is visible. I wish I knew how it lies inside her. As I wipe the sweat from Kenario's forehead, she has another contraction and the leg appears up to the knee.

'I must see.' I indicate. 'She must lie down.'

I put a folded cloth under Kenario's hips and get Bigogo and Gichemba each to hold one of her feet. She is, I am relieved to see, well distended. I think I can feel the other foot but there is another contraction and I wait as it pushes out the whole leg. I can now see the other foot.

'Breathe very deeply.' I demonstrate. It calms me too. I insert the fingers of one hand, feel up the leg from the heel and manage to straighten the knee before Kenario cries and pushes again. Now I can really assist. I guide the other leg out, hold both and, with the next contraction, pull gently.

'A boy!' we all exclaim as he emerges as far as his navel.

I make sure there is no pressure on the cord and we wait, at last with hope. I hear a murmuring chorus of encouragement and expectation and realise that I am part of it, although my words are different.

'Not long now, Kenario. One or two more pushes and you will have your son in your arms.'

But he is blue. I see Bigogo and Gechemba shaking their heads in resignation. I will not give up yet. I hold the tiny baby upside down, I slap his backside, I pray.

'Lord in Thy mercy take not this soul unto you. Give him life that he may bring joy to this world. Lord have pity on this mother who has known such sadness. Thy will be done. On earth as it is in heaven.' I don't think what I am saying, the words just keep coming

Kenario's eyes are fixed on her baby, her hands are clasped in front of her. Perhaps she is praying too.

'Amen,' I say.

'Amen,' I am surprised to hear the other voices. Not only Kenario, but Bigogo and Gechemba also. They have been listening all these months when I have visited and prayed over the baby growing in Kenario's womb.

The baby howls. His face turns red. The Lord be praised! I turn the little one up the right way, wrap him in a cloth, and give him to his mother. There is such joy and wonder in her face. I kneel and give thanks.

'How can we thank you, mama?' Mutisya is waiting outside the hut with a goat he has had slaughtered - for the children of the mission school he tells me.

'Thank God,' I tell him.

There is a moment's pause. 'This child shall be baptised,' he decides. 'We shall call him Christian.'

‘I’m afraid I could only find a machine,’ Lilia put two paper cups on the bedside table and held out her hand. ‘Let me take that while you drink this.’

Rose was staring straight in front of her. She clutched her knitting more tightly to her. ‘The sun is low,’ she said in a high, oddly girlish, voice.

‘Oh, it’s got a long way to go yet.’ Lilia glanced at the sun slanting through the Venetian blinds and checked her watch. ‘It’s only just after four.’ And then she realised. ‘You’re speaking! This is marvellous. I can’t wait to tell the nurse.’

‘He should be back.’

‘She, dear. The nurse is a she.’

‘He’s never this late.’ Rose’s voice rose as she tried and failed to get up. One of the knitting needles fell to the floor and rolled under the bed.

‘Hush!’ Lilia reassured her, bending with difficulty to retrieve the needle. ‘You’re upsetting yourself.’

‘Where is he?’ Rose laid down the knitting. She was near to tears.

‘I think you are having a bit of a nightmare,’ Lilia tried to sound calm. ‘I’m going to fetch help.’ She hurried from the room, leaving Rose leaning a little forward and peering anxiously ahead, as if trying to see something that was just out of sight.

8

'I can't see to knit anymore,' I tell Edward and peer into the gathering gloom. 'Shall we telephone and see if Thomas has got back from Jinja? I didn't realise he intended to be gone all day.'

'Now? They'll probably be preparing for vespers or some such ritual.' Edward takes a mouthful of his beer. 'Maybe they had a puncture or something. Let's give it a while yet.'

I slap at a circling insect and call out, 'Peter! Leta DDT!' and, when Peter has sprayed the verandah, tell him: 'We will have dinner in half an hour when Master Joseph is home.'

Lights are beginning to appear amongst the huts at the far side of the mission grounds, and I can see the shapes of bodies silhouetted against them. They have lit a fire and, from that, torches. A line of torches is emerging and processing towards the site of the new church. What are they doing? Edward is watching too, whilst pretending to be enjoying our nightly flying display as thousands of sparrows circle the treetops. It is wonderful against the orange sky, the dense chorus pierced by an occasional raucous cry of bigger birds. The last of the swallows are swooping and swirling low across the grass before finding their nests under the schoolhouse roof and, not long after, bats will appear instead. I am holding my breath, waiting as I do every evening for that brief, precious period of stillness that I love. But tonight it doesn't last more than a few seconds before it is rent by an unearthly squealing.

'Dear God, what is that?' I jump up and peer into the fading light.

'Oh, just a rooster being slaughtered, I expect.' Edward is making a performance of tapping out his pipe.

'It didn't sound like it.'

'Maybe it was a goat?' He is peering into the innards of the pipe and I turn to him with sudden suspicion.

'Why do you say you "expect"?'

'Oh I, ah,' Edward reaches for his tobacco pouch. 'I said they could have their ceremony.' He fills the pipe with fresh tobacco and tamps it down carefully in a way that always irritates me and tonight makes me want to scream. 'You know,' he goes on. 'For the foundation stone.' He lights his pipe at last and puffs vigorously. 'I told you how it was holding things up. Especially with those Azande carpenters we took on.'

'I thought we were trying to discourage these pagan customs.'

'Well yes, we are, of course.' His tone seems to me infuriatingly patronising. 'But there's no real harm in this, I feel. After all, it surely shows they know that this is an important place that they are building.'

And then he smiles at me and I can see it is with more hope than conviction. He wants me to agree but I can't. I am careful what I say however, because of course I sympathise with his quandary up to a point. Even Thomas says he finds it difficult sometimes to know where to draw the line.

'I can't help feeling it somehow *undermines* the building,' I say slowly. 'As if it belongs more to them than – well, to us. Though of course it is *for* them -'

'My dear.' Edward stands and puts his arm round me and we both look towards the line of torches that now encircle the church site. I want to shrug him off but I hear and feel how hard he is straining to reassure us both. Finally he says: 'But what if it is strengthening the hold of Christianity, deepening their belief through the practise of their traditional customs? Hmm?'

'Sometimes I don't understand you, Edward,' I say sadly. 'To me those are just words. Either you believe, or you do not.'

'Father John was here this afternoon,' he tells me now. 'Just before you got back from Bugiri. You know it won't be long before the RCs create a second diocese?'

I make no comment. I never like listening to Edward's disparaging of our Catholic colleagues and certainly not now. But he goes on anyway.

'Have you any idea how many new parishes they have opened since we've been in Uganda? Not to mention the convents, social centres, and hospitals. And they want to expand the secondary college at Mbale and start a rural trade school at Madera. But, you know, I'm quite sure they aren't always very particular over their conversion figures. Even with that *"in pericolo mortis"* distinction.'

Now he is really losing me and I stop listening as I hear something else, a low repetitive sound. I shiver. 'Can you hear those drums, Edward? What are they doing?'

Apparently he has not noticed but, as he listens, another drum, deeper and more insistent, joins in as if responding to the others.

'Quite catchy really,' says Edward, trying to make light of it.

They're talking to each other.'

'But what are they saying?' I know as well as he does that that is what drums do. 'What does it mean?'

He shrugs. He has no idea of course.

The shadows from the *mvule* trees are so long and deep it is almost as if the trees themselves have moved closer to the house. Edward used to make up stories like that when Joseph was little. 'See, even the trees are crowding round to listen.' Oh Edward, what happened to you, to us?

'Anyway,' he continues. 'It's no worse than a lot of Roman rituals, I'm sure. A few feathers maybe instead of white lace and incense.' He wants to change the subject. 'As I was saying, this *"in pericolo mortis"* thing. Thomas was telling me once, when we were having a bit of a drink together. Apparently, each diocese has to account every few months to Rome as to how many souls they've saved; baptisms, marriages, numbers in schools, that sort of thing. "Sacred Returns", they call them. But in the case of baptisms and confirmations they have to record if they are deathbed conversions, made in the fear of death. Neat, eh? I think it's meant to stop too much fiddling the books, over-estimating the numbers.' He chuckles.

I don't think it's a laughing matter and I don't let it pass. 'Trying to be more honest, you mean. Doing the right thing and letting God take care of the rest.'

Edward shuts up for a few moments and has the grace to look a little abashed. 'Maybe, my dear, maybe you're right. But apparently,' he starts again, 'They also have this 'second-generation' policy. They know that first generation converts may not be very devout, not get married in church and so on, but they overlook such lapses and count them as Catholics in the hope that they will nonetheless provide a more Christian upbringing for their children.' His glee at recounting his rivals' hypocrisy is turning into outrage. 'Who will in due course be fully practising Catholics. It's a battle, Rose. We got here first but, at this rate, they will overtake us. That's why this new church is so important.'

Ah, so there was a point to the diatribe. He is justifying the need for the ceremony but would still like my reassurance that he has done the right thing. I am thinking what to say but then notice how much louder the drums have become, louder and wilder.

Edward raises his voice. 'And then there's the school- we must be able to offer secondary education or it's no wonder people choose to become Catholics.' He pauses for my usual response at this point: *"hearts first, minds second"*, but, when it doesn't come, plays his trump anyway: 'People want what's best for them and their children, you have to admit that.'

A lone owl hoots close to the house. I whirl on him. 'It's completely dark. We have to find out what's happened.' I run into the house and telephone. Soon Thomas is on the line but what he says strikes terror into my heart.

'Joseph didn't go with me,' he said. 'I was delayed and he got a lift with the foreman of your builders instead.'

I am screaming, running to find Peter and Mary. 'Quickly, quickly, come both of you and help me look for Joseph.'

'Help me, help me! Quickly! Hurry!'

'You see,' Lilia was out of breath as she arrived back at Rose's bedside with Nurse Halliwell close behind her. 'She's speaking but

I'm not sure it's to us. She's not focussing on us, not really with us at all. What's going on, do you think?'

'Hmm,' said Nurse Halliwell, gently pushing Rose back onto the pillows and straightening the bedclothes. 'Unfortunately I'm not a mind reader. Helpful as that would be. So I'll just have to get her prescribed something to calm her down and give her a good night's sleep.'

Lilia stood. 'Then I'll go back to her flat to tidy up a bit,' she said. 'Give it a spring clean for when she comes home.' She meant to sound matter-of-fact. In fact, she was thrilled at the prospect of delving further into the mystery of the sweaters.

9

Lilia heaved the last of the large plastic sacks onto Rose's bed. Each contained the contents of at least half a dozen of the smaller bags. The floor was now clear.

'Three hundred and fifty five, give or take a few,' she said and sneezed. 'I'll have a good vacuum tomorrow morning.' She sneezed again. 'All this dust's not healthy. But right now, let's see what else we can find, eh?' She reached to stroke Rajah who was curled on the carpet near her feet. 'I must say I'm glad of your company.' She approached Rose's wardrobe and opened the mirrored door. The creaking hinge was loud in the silence. 'I do feel rather like a burglar.' She riffled through the clothes hanging on the rail and bent to examine the neat stack of shoeboxes beneath. Most of them looked decades old.

She started reading out the price tags. '"*Nineteen forward slash six.*" That was, nineteen shillings and sixpence, very nearly a pound. "*One pound, nine sh. eleven d.*" Which was nine shillings and elevenpence. Or 'nine and eleven' as we used to say. Only a penny less than ten shillings, for which there was a note which made it sound a lot more expensive.' She shook her head. 'I wonder when shoes cost that?' She picked up one of the boxes, removed the lid and a layer of tissue paper, and felt her breath catch in her throat.

The navy blue, wedge-heeled, sling-back sandals lying inside were almost identical to a pair that her mother had owned and she could remember trying on. She could picture it, her feet so small she could barely shuffle across the room, but, for Rose's pair now, her feet were far too big. She inserted just her toes into one and admired the effect. Sandals like this must have been in and out of fashion a few times since Rose had bought them and, apart from one broken strap, they were still in beautiful condition. Rose should have got it fixed, she thought, so she could have worn them again. She put them back carefully and reached for the largest box.

Once it had apparently contained Men's Size 11 (Tan) lace ups. Now it was full of yellowing newspaper cuttings. She laid them out on the floor. They were not in any obvious order, nor did they seem to have dates or a source.

Joseph: No New Leads Says Police Chief
Following weeks of investigations into the disappearance of Joseph McCormack, the eight-year-old son of Iganga-based missionaries, Jinja police superintendent Ken Jackson declared himself baffled. There are no new leads he told our reporter.

'McCormack,' said Lilia. 'Missionaries? And are those places in Africa?'

Joseph: Native Trackers Assist Police
Native trackers have been called in to help police in their continuing search for missing eight year old Joseph McCormack, son of Scottish missionaries.

'Rose doesn't sound Scottish, does she?' she addressed Rajah, who was investigating the suitability of the shoebox as a place to sleep. 'But maybe her husband was and then again, not all Scots do sound Scottish now I come to think of it.' She read on silently, with increasing horror.

Starting from his last known footprints in the mission compound, sadly obscured later that day by a fire, the trackers are scouring the bush in the immediate vicinity for signs of the lost boy and possible predators. Though unknown in recent months, leopards in particular are known to make sudden incursions in settled areas, particularly in summer when in search of food for their young.

And the young of other species are their favourite targets, thought Lilia. She was an avid viewer of wildlife documentaries and usually a determinedly dispassionate one, so she didn't think it sad when a cute little bambi got eaten by a lion or whatever, it was nature's way, the natural order of things. But, rightly or wrongly, it was hard to apply the same rationale where a human child was concerned, especially if that child might be related to someone one knew. She picked up the next cutting. Rajah had meanwhile given up on the box and, perhaps feeling dusty, now sat at a short distance washing his face.

Missionary Boy Disappearance: Police Divers to Search Lake Victoria.

Investigations into the disappearance of Joseph McCormack last week are now focussed on the lakeshore at Jinja where the boy is believed to have gone on the day of his disappearance. 'It is possible he went fishing and capsized,' said Police Superintendent Ken Jackson who is in charge of the investigation. 'I have requested the assistance of police divers from Mombasa. Joseph used to live in Jinja,' Lilia read on, aloud, '*with his parents Edward and Rose McCormack before the family moved to Iganga mission a year ago.'* This is our Rose, Rajah.' She looked up briefly and then back at the cutting. '*There are many crocodiles and hippos in this part of the lake.* Oh dear God.' She shuddered and clutched her throat, then sat a long time trying to imagine how Rose must have felt imagining her son meet either terrible end, before she shook herself and picked up the next cutting.

Spirited Away? Try Magic Says Missing Boy's Mother

Medicine men this week joined the search for Joseph McCormack the 8 year old boy who went missing from his Iganga home in August. 'My wife suggested to the police that they consult some of the local elders and wise men,' said Protestant missionary Edward McCormack. 'Of course we should try everything,' he added. 'And it is possible people will be more ready to talk to their own leaders. I should like to take this opportunity to thank the police for all that they have done to look for my son and support us at this very difficult time.'

'It doesn't sound as if he set much store on the results,' Lilia thought. 'More like he'd given up all hope of finding Joseph.'

The next few extracts added little to the story and indicated a growing feeling that indeed the case would not be solved, culminating in the closure of the police investigation four months after Joseph had disappeared.

'Oh goodness me,' Lilia unfolded several large glossy sheets. 'THE *PICTURE POST.*' She had long forgotten that the magazine existed, but now its once familiar layout exactly recreated the feeling of sitting in the public library on a Saturday afternoon while she waited for her mother to change her library books. And there was a date. March 1956. Perhaps she had read this very issue, this very article.

The top page was captioned ***"Beautiful Bujagali"***. It bore a large photograph of raging white water rapids on a wide river. Under it was a question: "***Swept away?***" Lilia again read aloud.

"*On 23rd August last year the eight year old son of English missionaries in Uganda vanished without trace after leaving his home near Lake Victoria. Picture Post sent its own reporters to investigate. The disappearance has baffled local residents and police who may be forced to call off the search. Could these raging rapids at the source of the mighty River Nile hold the answer? Rocks beside the stunning Bujagali Falls offer splendid views for photographers. But they can be treacherous. Jinja Sailing Club member Bill Garrett told us how he once slipped and almost...*'

Lilia stopped reading, unconvinced. 'It sounds to me like a lot of speculation,' she said. 'An excuse for a free holiday or to use some photographs maybe, especially since it was written after the case was closed. But do you know, Rajah, what I have just worked out?' Rajah cocked an ear in response. 'In 1955 I too was 8 years old. I am the same age as Joseph would have been. Would be,' she corrected herself. 'A good sleuth always keeps an open mind.'

Rajah stretched full length and, with slitted eyes, watched Lilia as she sifted through the few remaining cuttings, looking for the first report, when Joseph had just disappeared. She found it on the front page of the *Uganda Argus* of Thursday 24th August 1956, under a two-inch headline: ***"MISSING"*** and there was a photograph. Above the regimental white shirt and striped tie of a thousand British boys' schools, Joseph's wide clear eyes gazed into a distance far beyond the camera. His dark hair was severely pruned at the sides but revealed its natural state in the remaining shock of curls that spilled over his forehead. His mouth was slightly open, the top lip curled as if he had been told to smile but had not quite managed to before the shutter closed. He was also wearing a V-necked sweater. Lilia looked at the plastic bags and then back at Joseph's picture.

'Oh Rose,' she said. 'All these years you've been waiting for him to come home. Consciously or not I couldn't say, but you are surely remembering now. There must be someone out there who knows you, knows more about this.' She gathered up the cuttings and replaced them in the box with the exception of the photo of Joseph. 'Let's go, Rajah. I must write my first article.'

'She's still not speaking,' Nurse Halliwell greeted Lilia next morning. 'But look what she is doing.' She led the way into the cubicle where Rose sat, propped up in bed, knitting. 'Her manual coordination's almost normal. I shall have to try using knitting with some of my other patients. Rose, you've got a visitor.'

'Hello Rose, it's Lilia again, your neighbour. How are you, dear?'

Rose did not look up.

The nurse turned to Lilia. 'I'll leave you to it,' she said. 'I'll be around if you need me.'

Lilia sat in the chair at Rose's bedside. 'Look,' she pulled a copy of *The Observer* from her bag. 'I've written about you in the paper. Our nice newsagents, the Thakkers, suggested it, since you and I are neighbours and I write a little bit for the paper already. I'll read it to you. ***"Deckchair woman named: Does anyone know Rose?"*** That's the title. *"The elderly woman rescued from the sea on Bognor beach two days ago has been identified as Rose McCormack of Marine Villas, West Bognor. Mrs McCormack is still in hospital after suffering a stroke. Our investigations have established that fifty years ago Mrs McCormack was a missionary in Uganda with her husband Edward but so far no family or friends have come forward. The Observer asks for anyone with any information to contact the paper or to email Lilia Zynofsky c/o this paper."* That was the editor's idea that people should write into me, if they know anything. I do hope you don't mind. I only want to help you get better. I'm not just prying into your private life.'

Lilia hesitated. Methinks I do protest too much, she thought. I certainly intend to pry as far as I can and, as I cannot truly say whether or in what way this might help you, I fear my motives are not entirely altruistic. She reached into her shopping bag and pulled out a photograph. 'And Rose, there's something else. Look, I found it in some newspaper cuttings in your wardrobe. It was from an old Ugandan paper. I made a copy for you. I thought it might help you remember.' She sat on the bed beside Rose and held out the picture of Joseph for her to see.

Rose peered at it closely. Joseph's intent gaze cut through the fuzziness of the enlarged image. He seemed to be seeking attention, to wish to speak, with his upper lip frozen forever in its half-smile. He was beautiful. Lilia felt a lump form in her throat and swallowed hard.

'It's your son, Rose, isn't it. Joseph. Who went missing. I'm going to try to find out what happened.'

Rose's face was expressionless. She looked from the photo to Lilia and back again, gave the slightest of shrugs and returned to her knitting. Lilia put it back in her bag,

'But I'm not putting this in the paper,' she said. 'Mike, the editor, wanted to but I persuaded him to wait and see what else I can find out, or for you to be well enough to decide for yourself.' What she did not say was that Mike had also observed in an offhand sort of way that it would also enable her to spin out the story and prolong the suspense.

'And you accuse me of playing with people's lives,' he had remarked with bitter satisfaction.

'I'm going up to London,' Lilia said now as she had said then. 'Bombs or no bombs. To see what records I can find, of your life as a missionary. I'll see you in a day or two.'

10

It had been hard, however, not to feel nervous as the train left Clapham Junction and traversed the concrete jungle of South London towards Victoria. Lilia tried to follow the calm example of regular commuters who had had a few days to become accustomed to the threat. Yet the image of the mangled red bus refused to leave her mind. The London Routemaster was known around the world, surely as iconic as the World Trade Towers and, whoever was behind all the attacks, their ability to manipulate the collective psyche seemed almost scarier than the death and destruction itself. It was so very cold and calculating. Also, she often walked through Tavistock Square and might have today if it had not still been cordoned off by police.

However, once in the sanctum of the British Library, Lilia relaxed, found an empty desk and plugged in her new laptop. This had been a necessary extravagance since the Library, in its spacious new splendour and to protect its priceless contents, only otherwise allowed pencils for taking notes. Besides, it meant that she could readily edit information and even work on the train. She sighed with satisfaction as the silent company of serious scholars from around the world worked its usual magic and made her feel part of a vast curious organism, that sent out its tentacles through individuals like herself in order to recall distant events and places from every recorded perspective. There was hope for the human race, she thought, so long as any of us are interested in the experiences of other people and other times and went to collect the pile of books that she had ordered online from archives and collections in other parts of the city.

Much later as she travelled home she reread that day's notes.

Europeans began to hear tales of "the wonderland of Uganda" around the 1840s from Arabs who knew the country well as traders. They used to exchange firearms, cloth and beads for ivory and slaves, (slavery being a very old institution in Africa,) with the kingdom of Buganda, which had begun to expand from about 1700,largely at the expense of neighbouring Bunyoro, (where Rose lived). Bunyoro was the leading state in the previous two centuries. By 1800, Buganda controlled a large territory bordering Lake Victoria from the Victoria Nile to the Kagera River. It was centrally organised under the Kabaka, the king, who appointed regional administrators and maintained a large bureaucracy and a powerful army.

The first European to visit Buganda was John Hanning Speke, a British explorer, who in 1862 wanted to find the source of the Nile - which he did the following year at what are now known as the Ripon Falls at Jinja (where Rose was first based). He met the young Kabaka, Mtesa I, an intelligent man, "but," as Henry Stanley, who arrived a few years later, put it, "a Mohammedan." In November 1875 Stanley issued a call for missionaries through the letters page of the Daily Telegraph.

"I flatter myself that I have tumbled the newly raised religious fabric to the ground and if it were only followed by the arrival of a Christian mission, the conversion of Mtesa and his court would be complete... what a harvest ripe for the sickle of civilisation. It is not the mere preacher that is wanted here, (but) the practical Christian tutor who can teach the people how to become Christians, cure their diseases, construct dwellings... and turn his hand to anything like a sailor."

This challenge was taken up first by a Protestant missionary organisation (the Church Missionary Society, presumably the McCormacks',) and a couple of years later by the Pope. Stanley grossly underestimated the difficulties they would face, not to mention the cunning of the Kabaka. One of the sources puts this down to Stanley having "a Prospero complex, seeking a world where one can ignore the personalities of others."

Lilia stopped reading and glanced out of the train window as they raced through the last station before Bognor. Obviously, none of this was suitable material for the paper but Mike would enjoy hearing about it, she thought, and was almost tempted to invite him round to dinner so that she could share her deliciously righteous outrage at Stanley's cold certitude.

‘Or cynicism, him being a hack,’ she would have added provocatively. And they would have probably gone on over a second bottle of wine to disparage the efforts of missionaries generally and certainly the perfidies of colonialism, each of them harking back to their glory days in the sixties, when right and wrong were somehow so very black and white. But she didn’t miss Mike enough. He wasn’t the love of her life. Meanwhile there was just time to reread something else which he certainly would be able to put in her usual column. She opened another file on the computer in a folder marked ‘STORIES’ and experienced the same thrill of delight that she had felt earlier when she had first found its source in a story told to King Mtesa by Arab traders in 1881. She had elaborated a little.

THE KING'S FAVOURITE CAT

Once upon a time there was a good King who ruled over a beautiful land where everyone was happy and there was plenty of food for everyone to eat. There was so much food that the people gave what they did not need to travelling Arab traders. In exchange, the traders gave them fine silks to wear, spices to make their food taste even better and silver platters off which to eat.

One day a cat came to the King's court from a far off land and asked if he could stay. The good King welcomed the cat, who said his name was Rajah, and soon grew to love him. Rajah told stories of people and places that the King had never seen. He sang new songs that the King had never heard. The King began to spend much of his time singing and talking with the cat. He began spending more and more time with the cat and less and less with his people.

One day Rajah gave the King a book and taught him to read it. The King began to spend all his time reading the book. He no longer went out of his palace to see his country and his people. But Rajah did. He went wherever he wanted and the people did not stop him because they knew he was the King's favourite. And he did whatever he wanted and grew stronger and stronger as he did so.

First he ate all the eggs in the land. The chickens protested but, before they could tell the King, Rajah ate them. Then he ate all the goats and cows but, before the people could tell the King, he ate them too. So there was no one left to tell the King and one day Rajah ate him and became King in his place. Only then did he reveal his real identity.

'My name is the English.'

Lilia closed down her laptop as the train pulled into Bognor station. She yawned and sat up straighter to ease her aching back. All that research and a new story. It was a long time since she had had such a productive day.

11

'I've been reading about some of the early missionaries in Uganda,' Lilia told Rose next day. 'I never realised what hardships and difficulties they faced, what with the local rulers, the Muslim traders and, not least by a long chalk, Catholic colleagues who were more like enemies by the sound of it. Competitors anyway. Certainly not a good advert for Christianity!'

She stopped. Rose had again lapsed into silence. She had presumably been a devout Christian and Lilia did not want to upset her. Whatever her convictions now, she would surely not see inter-denominational rivalry as a matter of mirth. Lilia had thought of reading some of her notes aloud to see if they stimulated further memories and encouraged Rose to speak. But it was tricky. What would Rose make of Cecil Rhodes' view that *"Missionaries are better than policemen and cheaper"?* Or of the Reverend R.P. Ashe who, in 1894, wrote in his Chronicles that *"Asking missionaries to take no part in politics was much like asking them to take no part in religion.*" There again, maybe the situation was different by Rose's time, more settled perhaps, maybe Catholics and Protestants just got on with their proper mission, whatever that was. She sipped her tea, waiting to see if Rose would say something.

'It's a battle, Rose,' says Edward, not for the first time. 'We got here first but they are overtaking us. Even if they do cook the books over the conversion of souls.'

He must know that it's not true, it's not as simple as that. It varies from place to place for a start. But I don't think he wants to know. It's what keeps him going. It's why he's so desperate to finish building this church. And if I argue, he'll only start reeling off facts and figures. So I just say:

'They were mostly good men.'

'What's that, Rose?' Lilia put her cup down. 'Well of course, I never meant… I mean, I'm sure they were most sincere…'

Like Father Thomas. Dear Father Thomas. What would I have done without our conversations? Without your counsel and your consolation when Joseph went away to school. *'Have faith'*. *'It'll be alright, it'll be alright*.' If only Joseph had waited and gone with you that day to Jinja I know everything would have been alright.

Joseph did so miss living by the lake. He missed playing cricket with the other white boys and even some of the Indians. That Mehta boy, they had been quite thick the previous summer. Most of all he missed the Colmans. It was never the same for him once they'd left. We were all so happy to see them at that reception in Kampala. I hadn't wanted to attend. Joseph had just come home for the holidays. That very day.

'You go, Edward. Joseph and I want to eat ice cream in that new place.'

'It won't look right if you don't come with me. People will talk.'

'Let them.'

'And can we play table tennis? There's a new games room!' Joseph grabs my chin and pulls it so that I am looking at him.

Just like when he was little! I'd forgotten. Oh my darling son. We are rubbing noses. We've always done that too.

'I've been playing at school. I bet I can beat you now!'

'Oh yes? We'll see about - '

'You must come, Rose.' Edward's voice shatters our happiness. 'It won't be for long. Joseph can come too.'

'Dad!'

How I hate these affairs, all the important people and their wives, looking down on me. Which Edward says is stuff and nonsense but I know is true.

'Oh, we hear you're doing jolly good work with the women, jolly good show, well done, every little helps.'

This is one of the senior embassy chappies. He's probably younger than me for all his thinning fair hair and fattening belly. People go to seed quickly here if they're not careful. But he's the sort that was never really young. Born to lead. And here's his wife. Her medium length hair is held back with a black velvet Alice band but there the girlish impression ends. She is just like her husband, confident, upper class, well-fed, although fitter. It's all that tennis and golf she plays. She doesn't speak, she booms.

'I'll get up a little committee, Mrs McCormack. Raise a bit of cash. Have a whist drive, maybe a sale of work. *'Knitting for Africa'*. That would go down well with the Women's Fellowships back home as well, don't you think? I'll have a word with the Bishop. Ah, Ambassador!' And she's off.

'Mum,' Joseph tugs at my sleeve. He's been over at the buffet. Without thinking, I brush some crumbs of sausage roll from his shirt. He shrugs me off. He's not a little boy any more. 'Can we go now?'

Edward is deep in conversation with someone on the other side of the room. I start to take Joseph's hand, remember in time, and steer him gently by the shoulder instead. We join them.

'Colin! How wonderful to see you!' I am very happy to see him.

He ruffles Joseph's hair as he always has and smiles and Joseph smiles back. Colin looks quite a lot like Edward, tall and skinny, fair hair. But he is so much more relaxed, at ease with himself. You can see it immediately. He speaks to Joseph first.

'How's England? Have you been up to London yet? To look at the Queen?'

Joseph is nonplussed, and a bit bashful, but still very happy to see 'Uncle' Colin.

'Of course Kampala seems a big city to me now,' Colin tells him.

'How are you getting on up there?' I ask. 'Are you here for long? Is Penny here? Are Matthew and Mark coming home for the summer?'

Edward and Colin exchange looks and I wonder why.

'No, Penny's going to join them in England,' Edward tells me. 'And Colin's going a bit later, when their replacements are lined up.'

'There's Penny now.' Colin points to the doorway and I see her entering.

Tall, angular, 'handsome' people call her, too no-nonsense to be called pretty, she is smiling and obviously as glad to see us as we are to see her. Joseph and I go over to greet her, in fact Joseph runs ahead, knocking a few elbows of people holding drinks along the way and when I catch up she is hugging him...

It is later in our hotel room and Edward's sitting in one of the armchairs, puffing on his pipe. He doesn't smoke in public. 'Colin was telling me we should be teaching the local people to take the lead in everything,' says Edward. 'Don't you agree, Rose?'

He's eager, boyish, but entirely serious. I think of Leah in the clinic.

'Of course I do.'

'Colin's going to visit us on his way back to his mission. 'That'll be good won't it? Quite like old times.'

I'm sitting at the dressing table, rubbing cream into my face. 'Joseph will be pleased.' He is already asleep in the room next door.

'Colin was telling me how he has to 'be careful' when he goes out to the villages, "where fear and superstition still rule". His words not mine. Colin, of all people, who was always so good at getting out and about and meeting people.'

Edward puts down his pipe, stands and comes up behind me. He puts his hands on my bare shoulders and his eyes catch mine in the mirror. 'It makes me even more proud of you, my love. Driving off with only young Stephen to protect you.' He begins to caress me and I know what's on his mind.

But I want to be up early for breakfast with Joseph. I pick up my hairbrush and raise my arm so that Edward has to step back as I begin to brush my hair. Fortunately, he is easily distracted. Colin always had a great influence on him and is again uppermost in his mind.

'Colin said again today how it definitely gives us an advantage having women going into communities first, before men go in and do the church planting. You know, as Mary Slessor always said, women being less threatening than men.'

'I hope you are not suggesting I should climb trees and wear African clothes like Mary did!'

'Certainly not!' Edward chortles. 'That would give our colonial friends something to gossip about!' He seems about to embrace me again, but then his face grows serious. 'Do you know what else Colin said? Quoting Mackay all those years ago. Remember learning about Alexander Mackay, the pioneer, in our induction course? *"I feel that not one bit of work I've ever done has been wasted. In everything God has prepared me, til all has fitted together like a jigsaw puzzle to make a picture of work with Him in Africa."'*

'It does seem a shame Colin and Penny are being sent home,' I say carefully. 'Even Penny doesn't want to go, apart from being able to see so much more of the boys.'

But Edward isn't listening. He's staring into the mirror over my head like he's staring into space. 'It makes me quite envious, you know. To have all your life make sense like that.'

A shiver runs down my spine. Isn't that how we're supposed to feel? Or else why would we all leave so much to come here in the middle of nowhere, amid such strangeness? Why would we sacrifice our normal life, our children? Especially our children. Joseph will be gone again before I know it. How the days and weeks fly by... I should be getting on with that sweater for him to take back.

'What is it you're trying to reach?' Lilia had looked up to see Rose leaning perilously out of the bed. 'Oh, of course.' She passed what seemed to be a sleeve to Rose. 'I see you've started a new bit. Perhaps we should leave it where you can reach it. Though I think the nurse doesn't want you overdoing it.'

Rose counted the stitches on the needles and then began to knit furiously.

There are so few days before he has to leave. Colin is visiting, just for a night. He brought Joseph a present.

'A drum!' Joseph is thrilled. 'Thank you, Uncle Colin.'

'Here, I'll show you.' Colin sits next to him.

Two heads bent together, fair and dark, large and small hands taking it in turns, beating out rhythms. Colin looks up and smiles at me.

'Someone told me I must have been an African in an earlier life!' he says.

I can see he is proud of it. They say that about Thomas. That he actually is an African. Joking of course. And not because he has 'gone native', which most people seem to think such a sin. No, it's because he can speak all the local languages and gets on with everyone so easily. And of course he supports "Africanisation" of the missions. But not if it compromises The Faith. He opposes what the Catholics call "laxism". Cares about the means as well as the ends. Whereas Edward – well, I am dreadfully afraid that he cares more about the actual building of this church than about what it is for. What will he do when he has finished? Build something else perhaps.

Poor Edward, he's not very good with people at all, including Joseph these days. Like he made that swing for Joseph to come back to, as he had in Jinja. Joseph pretended to be pleased, but I know he thought it was babyish. The local children certainly use it more than him, while he just roams around the town or hangs about the workmen, watching them build the church. Which pleases Edward of course, especially when he's there too. It's good for fathers and sons to do things together.

'It's something to do anyway.'

Joseph? Is that you, my darling? Oh do stay, don't go running off. Why don't you play your drum for me. Make it talk like Uncle Colin showed you. Send a message – yes, that's it.

"The white man spirit from the forest
Of the leaf used for roofs
Comes up river. He comes up river
When tomorrow has risen high in the sky
To the village of us
Come, come, come, come

Bring water, bring sticks to the schoolhouse."

Oh, don't stop so soon. Play it again. But not like that! No, please, not like that. That sounds angry, frightening. I'm frightened. It's not Joseph playing, it's someone else. Joseph is not home and he should be. An owl is hooting, it is completely dark. I run into the house. 'Peter! Mary! Bring lanterns. Help me find Joseph.'

'Find Joseph!' Rose sat bolt upright.

Lilia leant over the bedside and covered Rose's hands with her own. 'I will try, Rose. To find out what happened to him. But it would make things a lot easier if you could tell me what you know. Rose?'

Rose had slumped back on her pillows, as if defeated, as if she knew it was a hopeless search. Her face twisted in pain, she held herself closely, arms folded tightly across her chest, and began to rock back and forth. Finally, with what seemed enormous effort, she spoke.

'Letters,' she said. 'Edward wrote so many letters.'

'And are they in your flat?' asked Lilia. 'Do you want me to find them?'

But Rose continued to rock, her eyes screwed shut, so Lilia patted her awkwardly for a few moments on one shoulder and then hastened home.

She found Edward's letters wrapped in a brown paper parcel in the bottom drawer of Rose's dressing table, written on both sides of a size of paper that she had forgotten. The sort that used to come in boxes tied with blue ribbon, together with envelopes that fitted through the smallest letterboxes. His handwriting was neat and regular but closely spaced and it would require quite an effort to decipher all the words. But she would not read them without Rose's permission, rewrapped the package and turned instead to reading the rest of her notes on the early missionaries. Then she wrote another article to email to Mike.

ROSE: The search continues

A few more clues have emerged concerning the identity of Rose McCormack, the elderly woman found a week ago on the beach at West Bognor, but so far no members of her family have been traced. Rose is still in St Stephen's Hospital where she remains bed-ridden but has some mobility and is beginning to speak a little. As her neighbour, I have established that in the late 1940s Rose went to Uganda as a missionary, where, together with her husband Edward, she worked first in the town of Jinja, by Lake Victoria, and then in the smaller town of Iganga. This was less than a hundred years since the first European had set foot in Uganda.

The first missionaries were sent by the Protestant Church Missionary Society, the CMS, to which I think the McCormacks belonged. The CMS were the first organisation to respond to a call for missionaries to go to Uganda that was published in the Daily Telegraph in 1875 by Henry Stanley, the American journalist who famously found the missing British explorer Dr Livingstone – and, when he did, is supposed to have said 'Dr Livingstone, I presume.' French Catholics followed two years later to be joined a further 20 years after that by British Catholics.

These early missionaries faced great hardships and dangers and many died of disease. One of the first, Alexander Mackay, took two and a half years to find a route there from Zanzibar, in the course of which he built fifty miles of road. He called himself an 'engineering missionary' and the local king admired his construction skills and called him 'mzungu-wa-kazi', white man of work. Mackay was less successful in combating what he called the 'terrible evils' of slavery, polygamy and witchcraft and the practice of human sacrifice. He also found himself in competition with Muslim traders who had long been in Uganda, and in due course with his fellow Christians, the Catholics. Britain made Uganda a Protectorate in 1894 to resolve the conflicts that had erupted into bloody wars and the king became a constitutional monarch sharing power with his mainly Protestant chiefs.

Even by the time Rose arrived in Uganda, it would still have been very difficult working away from the major towns. Another missionary, Colin Colman, a contemporary of the McCormacks who was surely acquainted with them, is on record as saying that when he went out on missions to the more distant villages he had to 'be careful because fear and superstition still ruled the hearts of many people.' I know readers will join me in the hope that Rose will recover her health and one day be able to tell us herself about her life in Africa fifty years ago. Whatever our differences of opinion and of religion, I think we would agree that missionaries like Rose and Edward, who sacrificed the comforts of home for the sake of strangers in a far off land, deserve our admiration.

12

As she closed the file and logged onto her email, Lilia marvelled at the ease with which she had managed to concoct a simple narrative from a history of events that, even from the single source she had so far read, were complex and subject to rapid shifts and reversals. She felt a little guilty for it was rather misleading, and a little more appreciative of the reporter's craft. Not that she would admit as much to Mike.

How many of those involved really welcomed the British stepping in and enforcing peace through the British East Africa Company, thereby obtaining a monopoly of trade? Presumably not the succession of Kabakas, who had played a long and clever game in the attempt to retain their kingdom in face of internal and external challenges, setting their opponents against each other, switching allegiance as, to the best of their knowledge, circumstances seemed to require. Surely not the Arab traders, who at one stage renewed war via an alliance with the neighbouring kingdom of Bunyoro, nor the Sultan of Zanzibar, whose kingdom had been such an important trading centre, whilst Egypt's hopes of controlling the upper reaches of the Nile were dashed by the arrival of General Gordon in the north. But then, of course, the "scramble for Africa" amongst European powers soon raised the stakes beyond the reach of any other players and Germany moved into Zanzibar and Tanganyika.

Nevertheless, many of the ordinary Baganda people might have been glad to see an end to the old regime, she thought, as they were surely better treated by the missionary factions competing for their souls. The French Catholic, Father Leon Livinhac, thought that *"These people, (the Baganda) have noble instincts that only need to be well directed,"* whereas, according to James Speke, the Kabaka "*took men's lives like those of fowls."* Lilia had read of one man being put to death by a minor chief merely for breaking a cask of beer. The Protestant chiefs too would have found their power enhanced under the new settlement and, in the end, constant fighting usually benefits a very small proportion of a population.

Moreover, it was true that it was the French Catholics that had actually suggested to the Pope that he should send some English Catholics, to stop missionaries being seen as government rather than religious representatives. The fighting factions had identified themselves as the "Bangareza" (English) and "Bafransa" (French) rather than as Protestant or Catholic, which must have made doctrinal differences even more difficult to clarify and spiritual matters somewhat secondary in what had become a many-sided power struggle.

'It rather recalls to me my own childhood,' Lilia told Rajah. 'In a very small way of course, when my mother was still trying to bring me up as a Catholic in honour of my missing father. I wrote to God, saying I would be a Catholic if he would send my Daddy home. I posted it up the chimney. But He didn't and in the end I was allowed to go to the Anglican Sunday School where my friends went. Needless to say, questions of belief were irrelevant to me at the time, as indeed they are now to my quest. I need to do some more research but where and how to begin?' she scrolled down her notes yet again and then abruptly stopped. 'Oh my goodness,' she exclaimed. 'How could that have escaped my attention?''

She had noted, but not registered, the fact that the English order of Catholics chosen by the Pope to go to Uganda had been the Society of St Joseph, otherwise known as the Mill Hill Fathers and "Mill Hill" now rang a rather large bell in her memory. In fact, it caused a powerful hot flush to steal through her entire body, a heat that was painfully laced with bitter regret and renewed jealousy. Hand to her throat, she googled the site.

'I thought so,' she said. 'They are based in Mill Hill, which, for your information, Rajah, is a district of North London and a stop on the Underground line. In fact, two stops I believe, on two different lines. More to the point it is where Daniel went to live. With his nice Jewish wife.' She spoke aloud, even though Rajah could not possibly understand and indeed had never met Daniel, not having been born at the time. Speaking aloud had always helped her to control her emotions.

Daniel Lipman had been the son of the Brighton house in which she had lived for many years, before and after her mother's death, and had been her first, and only true love, with whom she could have spent the rest of her life, had it not been for her increasingly dependent mother. Daniel had tired of waiting for her to sort out her conflicting loyalties, suspected her mother of dramatising her supposed sicknesses in order to retain her daughter's company and at last given in to parental pressure and married within their community. However, when his family had finally decided to sell their old home, not having lived there for years, and enquired of Lilia whether she would be willing to sell them the basement first, Daniel had made sure that Lilia got a good price, which enabled her to buy her Bognor flat and have a small nest egg besides. Over the phone, he had issued an invitation on behalf of his wife Sarah to come and visit 'any time'.

'So I am thinking,' she now said. 'That, so many years having passed, perhaps I might now be able to bear doing so. Especially as I have a very good reason. I shall email the Society immediately and ask if I may consult their archives. And worry about the Protestant records later. Although I am afraid it will mean you being on dry rations for a few days, Rajah darling,' she added. 'Auntie Rose not being here to feed you. I shall have to buy you one of those cunning feeding bowls that let down a certain amount twice a day. I know you won't like it, but Mother's got to work. Talking of which, just look at how many new messages have come in from the Observer! Honestly, you'd think I were a full-time employee.' She began to scroll down her inbox.

Mike had had forwarded dozens of responses to Lilia's earlier articles, all suggesting a possible remote connection to Rose based on surname, place or occupation. She scanned quickly through them.

Some members of our church were missionaries in East Africa...

My mother's cousin was a teacher in Kampala in the 1960s...

McCormack was my maiden name. My family came from Inverness...

Our neighbours come from Uganda. They are Indians who...

I live in Bognor and I remember an old lady who used to feed the gulls on the beach every day...

I had a colleague called James McCormack when I worked in the oil industry in Aberdeen...

My brother's wife used to work for a missionary society in London...

An Edward McCormack worked with my father ...

None of the messages contained details of obvious significance and it would surely take a very long time to check them out further. She wrote to Mike.

Mike: As you can see, I'm sending all this mail back again. Do you think you could ask an intern to scan it in future for anything that really seems relevant before forwarding? And I suggest send a standard reply of thanks to all hoping that they will keep reading my articles in case they think of anything else in the future.

Fwd. ravi@thinairfm.com to editorial@bognorobserver.co.uk
RE: Your article

And yet another's just popped up. I'm not even opening it. Please find attached my latest article: 'ROSE: The search continues.' Lacking any real news, it's mostly a rehash of some history. Hope it's OK. Am about to follow up various leads and will of course keep you posted. In haste as am suddenly inspired (Hooray!) to write another cat story which I will send in due course.
Best regards
Lilia

THE MISSION CAT

The mid-morning sun slanted across the verandah making a long rectangle of warmth, long enough for even a large cat. It was Rajah's favourite place for a snooze at this time of day until the family came and claimed the space for their coffee break. A pointless meal, Rajah had always thought, since all they ever ate were biscuits, sweet biscuits at that.

This morning, however, there was an earlier interruption. Rajah's ears pricked as they caught the faint rustle of dry leaves. He opened one eye. Outraged, he opened the other. It was Septimus, his black and white rival from the neighbouring Catholic mission. He was heading for the dark cavern under the verandah, which was the home of many mice and rats.

Why did that pesky cat have to come here all the time? As if there were not plenty of small animals and birds to hunt in his own compound. Rajah's tail began to twitch. Septimus did not know he was being watched. Rajah crouched, ready to spring. Septimus bared his teeth in a silent snarl.

The two cats met in a mid-air tangle of claws and fell to the ground in a kicking, yowling heap. The next moment they leapt apart, drenched by a bucket of water, and fled, howling, for the shelter of the nearest bushes. James, the small son of the house servants, ran laughing back to his mother in the kitchen.

Septimus and Rajah did not stop running until they reached the forest at the edge of the Protestant compound. It was dark under the tall trees. Birds flew from their nests cawing and chirruping warnings that enemies were approaching. A snake slid silently across their path. A passing band of monkeys paused in their treetop safety to hurl fruits and nuts at the two invaders. A mango fell on Rajah's head and the monkeys swung away, chattering with satisfaction.

The cats glared angrily at each other. Rajah was not hungry and did not want to hunt. He wanted to go home and sit in the sun. He turned tail and began to walk back the way they had run. Septimus followed him. Rajah could hear his soft paw steps on the sandy ground. Then he heard some other, slower steps. Another cat was following Septimus. A very large cat whose coat was covered with spots. Its coat gave it camouflage in the patches of light and shade where the sun filtered through the trees. Rajah's tabby coat was also good camouflage. But poor Septimus was a target. The leopard's wild yellow eyes were fixed on his every movement.

Rajah could have slunk off safely and saved his own skin. Septimus was in the middle of a clearing where there was nowhere to hide and no tree to climb. Besides, leopards could also climb trees. Brave Septimus faced the leopard, crouched and bared his teeth. He tried to make himself look larger and frightening but the leopard was not impressed. It approached with slow confidence. Septimus' eyes were dark with fear. Rajah crept around the edge of the clearing until he was behind the leopard. And then he snarled. It was not a very loud snarl but it was very sudden. The surprised leopard swung round but Rajah had already started running. Septimus took his chance and both cats ran faster than they had ever run before. And the monkeys, seeing a greater enemy, threw a storm of fruit and nuts until the leopard gave up the chase and slunk away.

'The enemy of my enemy is my friend,' thought Rajah. But, sadly, by the time Septimus next came hunting under his verandah he had forgotten this useful lesson.

13

Rose accepted the brown paper parcel, opened it, took her glasses from the bedside table, picked up the top letter and began to read, disappointing Lilia, who had hoped that Rose might indicate that she should read them for her. However, a minute or two later, Rose closed her eyes and her hand dropped into her lap.

'Shall I?' Lilia reached tentatively for the letter and when Rose did not respond, picked it up and began to read aloud.

"CMS Mission, Iganga
25th August 1955
My dear Rose,
I hope that you are as well as can be expected. I am sure the Frasers are looking after you at the mission. I am writing because I find it easier to express some things in this way but of course I shall telephone if there is any news. I am sorry I tried to stop you going to Jinja, although I am still of the opinion that we should let the police handle the investigations.

Father John came to see me today. He was unusually kind and sympathetic although he seemed a little preoccupied as if he had other matters on his mind. I think I told you that he had come to see me on - that day, with an invitation to the inauguration in Kampala next month of their new bishop. I shan't go of course unless... I shall stay here until there is some news. I keep going over and over that day in my mind. I find it hard to think straight without you to talk to. If only Joseph had come to find me down at the church I could have amused him until Thomas was ready to leave. John said Thomas is going to visit you tomorrow or the next day. Thomas is extremely distressed. The police questioned him again apparently. He keeps saying if only he hadn't delayed, had left for Jinja when he had said he would.

There was a large congregation today. Everyone here is praying for us.

Your ever loving husband
Edward."

Rose gave a deep sigh as Lilia stopped reading but did not open her eyes. Lilia folded the letter carefully and sat waiting for some further response.

I knew you needed me, Edward. But how could I think of that then? I had to look for Joseph and I could not understand that you could not see that. Let other people look after you for once I thought, though I had not imagined it might include Father John! I knew how intimidating you always found him. I expect he knew what you thought of Catholicism.

And I am afraid I did not want to be with you, knowing you would offer me no solace. I was so very glad to know that Thomas was coming to see me. I thought, yes, Edward, you pray for me with your 'large congregation'. That's all you can do for me.

Rose's head was bowed and Lilia was wondering if she had gone to sleep when she looked up abruptly.

'You want me to continue? Of course!' Lilia reached for the packet and found the next letter.

"26th August
Dearest Rose,

This will be brief as I am expecting Thomas shortly. He said he would deliver it to you personally.

Stephen has suggested that the police use some trackers he knows to see if they can find any more clues. I don't think he trusts the builders though I expect it is only because they are from other tribes. However, I have asked the police to question the foreman again. So far he is sticking to his story that he dropped Joseph where he requested, in the centre of town.

Rose, I must tell you that there are ugly rumours going the rounds. You may remember that young Brother Franz had taken to wearing just shorts and shirt a lot of the time and we commented that it was bit of a departure for the RCs and wondered what the Fathers made of it. Now it seems he has been having most inappropriate relations with some of the mission pupils. He has certainly been seen giving them rides on his motorbike, both girls and boys. And it seems there is more.

I only tell you because I am sure it will be preying on Father Thomas' mind since day to day supervision and pastoral care of younger staff is more his responsibility. He probably won't want to discuss it with you, especially at this time. I can hear his car arriving so will sign off.

In haste but with you constantly in mind,

Edward."

That was a good idea of Stephen's, engaging those trackers. To begin looking where Joseph must have started from soon after we had rushed off to Bugiri. But I don't think he distrusted the builders. His own mother was from a distant tribe. You never knew who was who, did you, Edward? Never talked to the local people properly. Were afraid of them really I think, when it came down to it. Yet another grievance I harboured against you, God forgive me.

I knew very well that Thomas was worried about the young Brother. Sometimes, when we were out for a stroll, Thomas and I saw him on his motorbike, wearing his shorts. Thomas did try to talk to him about it, but he wasn't sure that he was right to think it mattered. Gave him the benefit of the doubt. I never told you because I couldn't bear the way I thought you'd react. You'd laugh, I thought. Say 'What's all the fuss about? Normal men, and we all know what that means, wear them as a matter of course in this climate.' And it would have sickened me to see you gloat over another's spiritual dilemma.

Rose pointed to the packet of letters and nodded her head. Lilia picked out the third.

"29th August

My dear,

I confess I had hoped you would have contacted me by now. I expect John and Elizabeth will have told you that I telephoned when you had gone out with Thomas again. I was going to tell you that the trackers found nothing. That is, they found lots of Joseph's footprints, he was often down at the church after all, including some recent ones, and also the tyre marks of the lorry leaving for Jinja. But the crucial area, which would have shown whether or not Joseph got into the lorry, had been the site of a bonfire the night before, when they were having the ceremony I think.

I have to say that I rather think Elizabeth disapproves of you running around so much (her phrase). She said she is concerned that you are overdoing it. I must say so was I when I heard that you had gone to see a medicine man. It is so unlike you. I wonder who put you up to it.

In all these circumstances, I am not sure that it is true to say that no news is good news. There is certainly no good news here. Stephen tells me Franz is definitely accused of improper relations with more than one child; he heard it from one of the catechists. Worse still, Frantz is claiming that Thomas was aware of and turned a blind eye to it and that anyway he was only following Thomas' example because he, Thomas, also often gave children rides in the mission car. This is true of course, and included Joseph. I imagine you will know that Thomas is not to return to Iganga. I don't know whether John has asked Thomas to take leave or if it is Thomas' own wish.

All of this of course has no bearing on our loss and search for our dear son but I fear that it will prove something of a distraction in people's minds and perhaps in police activities also. Although I expect John will try to handle the matter himself if he is able. I do hope that you will find time to drop me a line and tell me how you are or ask the Frasers if you can use the telephone. Please put my mind at rest concerning your health and well-being.

As ever, Edward."

'As ever, Edward.' But nothing ever was the same. Hatred is a terrible thing. I always thought it should be one of the deadly sins. But I was close to hating you at first. Not for not taking enough care of Joseph. You thought he was going with Thomas as I did. And not even for being so obsessed with that wretched church that you didn't want to take a holiday that summer. If only we had taken Joseph to the coast as we had said we might. How could we have

thought he could spend his whole holiday hanging around the mission? Yes, I blamed myself too. I knew how he loved being by water.

No, it was because I thought you suspected Thomas. "No bearing on our loss"? Ha! I thought. You thought Joseph did not want to go with him. Preferred to go with the foreman. That it was nothing to do with having to wait for Thomas to be ready to leave. Although, being you, you might not have admitted it even to yourself. And I thought that because Thomas thought it. He said as much the day he came to be with me in Jinja.

'I think Edward blames me for Joseph going with the builder,' he says. 'He behaved most strangely when I went to collect the letter. Did not look me in the eye. I would have told Joseph to wait for me, you know that, don't you? I know you would not have wanted him to go with anyone else. But Rose, I did not even see Joseph. He sent me a message by one of the children, that he had found another lift.' Distressed? He is destroyed. Sobbing.

'Hush.' How can I comfort him, he who has always comforted me?

'It is only that he has heard about Brother Franz,' I say. 'Forgive me for mentioning it.'

He raises his eyes. Never before have I seen such despair.

'That was why I was delayed,' he said and buried his face in his hands. 'I have failed in my sacred duties, Rose. I have betrayed the children in our care.'

'I am sure you have always acted in good faith,' I start to say.

'No.' He looks up at me. 'I did not keep faith. I was trying to be – more modern. Up to date. I knew the younger men think me old-fashioned. And it is getting more difficult to find good men. I thought a little leniency – but it was laxity, unforgivable laxity.'

'God will forgive you. If there is anything to forgive.'

'Ah but Rose, what if losing Joseph is part of the punishment that I have brought on us? On you? What then?'

'But we have not lost Joseph,' I say. 'He has gone missing and we shall find him. I shall find him. Will you help me?'

He sits up straight. Looks hard at me. Puts his hand on my head and makes the sign of the cross. 'That I will, Rose. I will do all I can. Until...'

He is soon to go back to Mill Hill. He has asked Father John to release him. He must commune with God. Perhaps then he will take some leave with his family in Ireland.

'There are those who will see this as an admission of guilt,' he says. 'But I cannot care about that. God will know it is only an admission of failure.'

But he did care. I think he could not live with the knowledge that he could be even suspected of such terrible things. And I thought you were one of those who suspected him, Edward. Now I am not so sure and there is no way of telling. Perhaps you were just envious of my closeness to him. And to Joseph. Dear God, how we deceive each other and ourselves. There is the real sin.

Rose's eyes remained tightly shut and at some point she had put her hands together as if in prayer so Lilia rewrapped the parcel, put it in the drawer of the bedside table and quietly slipped away.

14

How long it is since I heard Edward's words. They break my heart and wrack my soul even though it is my neighbour's voice. I should try to let her know that I recognise her and show some gratitude, for she is being so kind, she is doing unto me as I would be done by. Unlike the one who failed me when I was so in need of love and understanding. Someone who should have known so much better....

'Rose, I really think you should try to rest. You will make yourself ill.' Elizabeth Fraser's thin face shows her disapproval despite her careful words. She is standing in the open doorway of the room I have been given at the Jinja mission that once was our home. The room was Joseph's but she doesn't know that.

'The police are doing all they can. Everyone is thinking of you. If anyone knows anything they will come forward. The DC made a special appeal at the Club last night.'

I continue to dress. 'We are going to visit the family of a friend of Joseph,' I tell her. I know she is getting impatient with me, wondering how long I will be a burden on her and I deliberately save the significant information for last. 'They are Indian,' I say casually pulling on my gloves.

'Really?'

I knew that would surprise her. 'Joseph was very friendly with one of their boys.'

'Ah,' she says, as if that confirms what she has heard about her predecessors at this mission.

For the Frasers, nearing sixty, civilised Jinja was a reward, an easy end to a long career in Africa. For us, I suspect it was a test, an introduction to see if we could cope. I was never sure if we had passed the test or simply been moved on where anything we might achieve would be progress. But either way, the church in Iganga was, of course, a perfect project for practical Edward.

'And Father Thomas is coming with me.'

'Why does everyone treat me as if I am ill?' Thomas is driving. Elizabeth has kindly lent us the mission car. We refused the offer of a driver. 'My son is missing. I am looking for him. Isn't that what any normal mother would do?'

We are heading down Main Street. There is the usual bustle of pedestrians and cyclists coming in from the villages to work. People opening the shutters of their shops and supervising the sweeping of the pavements in front. If it weren't the holidays there would also be children running to school, Europeans in one direction, Indians in the other. I remember how I used to walk with Joseph to school until he insisted he was old enough to go alone. He must have been six. So few years ago, yet it seems like another life.

'You are a good mother, Rose.' Did Thomas say that or is it what I wanted to hear?

'Left or right?' We are near the post office.

'Left, I think. It's just off Bell Avenue. Oh but stop.' I have had an idea. We are passing Drusilla's. 'Maybe Ann saw Joseph.'

Drusilla's is the only shop in town that is run by Europeans and the Williamses have just installed a machine selling soft ice cream. It faces out onto the covered walkway where there is even a small table and chairs for customers to sit and eat if they want to. Very European, we all think. Joseph was itching to try it. But Ann isn't there.

'I'm sorry, Rose.' It's her husband Bill. 'Ann's taken the children to the coast. I didn't see Joseph that day.'

I can see how awkward he feels.

'Good luck,' he adds.

It is not the most appropriate thing to say, but what is? I thank him.

The Mehtas live in a large bungalow on Busoga Road near the European area. I think they own one of the cotton ginneries out towards Bugiri. Thomas comes in with me and reminds me to remove my shoes at the entrance. Edward would never have thought of that.

'Joseph called Nilu that morning,' I tell Nilu's mother, Kamala. 'I said I would take them for a picnic by the lake.'

'But it was just after my brother-in-law's daughter's wedding,' she says. 'Nilu could not have gone with you. We had so many people staying. I am sure he would have told your son.'

'May I speak to Nilu?'

Nilu has left for school in India. 'Some of the family were returning after the wedding. We thought he might as well travel with them, especially as they planned to stay a few days in Mombasa before getting the boat. He likes it there.'

'So does Joseph.'

Kamala sees my disappointment. She has a kind face. I always thought I would like to know her better but it's just not done to mix socially with Indians. She gives us spicy tea and snacks.

'You know,' she adds. 'It was chaos that day. So many people and children everywhere. I hardly saw my own children. So maybe...'

'Maybe Joseph was there too?'

'It is possible,' she nods. 'But Nilu didn't see him. I telephoned to ask. I am so very sorry. Joseph is a lovely boy.'

'I thought they might have gone to the lake,' I say. 'We were going to have a picnic there and the police seem to think that is the most likely explanation. They think ...' I cannot say it.

She understands. 'Nilu would never go in the water. He knew it was forbidden.'

Except when I was there to watch them, I think, and feel a little guilty. But I believed you had to give children some freedom, let them spread their wings a bit. I am not therefore quite reassured when she tells me, 'Don't worry about that Mrs McCormack.' But I don't really think Joseph would go swimming alone.

We head for the lake. I want to find out how the police investigations are proceeding. It is a lovely day. A few white sails drift far out on the calm surface of the water. There would be many more if this were a weekend. There is a huddle of uniforms on the Yacht Club quay - the *"Whites Only"* sign presumably doesn't apply to the police - and a few spectators here and there along the road towards the pier. They are all watching some divers in the water. I shiver. Thomas touches my arm and I smile my thanks as I square my shoulders and recognise Superintendent Jackson, walking towards us, red-faced and sweating. The nurse in me thinks he should lose some weight, cut down on the booze, before it's too late. He touches his cap in greeting. I know he doesn't think much of missionaries, but at a time like this we Europeans stick together and, as it happens, he comes from the same small part of London as me. Somerstown, next to St Pancras. A poor area, so we never mentioned the coincidence again. He'll settle somewhere a lot smarter when he retires, I'm sure.

'I appreciate your supervising this yourself, Ken.'

'Least I can do, Rose. Nothing yet I'm afraid. That is...'

I help him out of his difficulty. 'No news is good news.' He looks surprised at my composure.

'We'll let you know the moment...'

'I know. Thank you.' I nod and turn to Thomas. 'Can we go for a drive?' I really don't think they'll find anything and it is hard to stand waiting.

'You don't want a drink? Some coffee maybe?' He indicates the Ripon Falls Hotel where, as usual, there are people sitting idly on the terrace, chatting, reading newspapers.

I shake my head. I don't want to be with other people. We head along Queen Elizabeth Way towards Owen Falls.

'We were here when the Queen, or perhaps she was still Princess Elizabeth, came to open the dam,' I tell Thomas. 'All the school children were given a packet of sweets and a flag to wave. Joseph,' my throat closes for a moment, 'Joseph was thrilled. He thought she looked straight at him! Edward was carrying him up high on his shoulders so maybe she did.' I sigh. Another happy memory. 'Let's go to Ripon Falls instead,' I say. 'I've never got used to the dam, Owen Falls was so lovely before.'

Thomas turns the car and we drive back and along Nile Crescent past the golf course. There is a sprinkling of players and, through the open window, I can hear the soft click of wood on ball, an occasional shout of triumph. For most people it is just another pleasant day. I feel happier when we stand high above the Nile as it begins its two thousand mile journey to the north.

'Does it really go all the way to Egypt?'

How many times did Joseph ask me that? Egypt seemed to him like another world, whereas I loved the feeling I always got of being connected through the mighty river to the rest of the world, imagining it flowing into the Mediterranean and mingling with all the oceans of the earth. Downstream, in the distance, I can see the railway bridge and a train puffing east to Nairobi and the coast. How Joseph loved that journey! Everything reminds me of him here. I know I am closer to him. I shall not go back to Iganga without him.

When we get back to the lakefront there is a commotion. Shouts from a diver, a sudden congregating of police and onlookers. 'Stand back!' I hear Ken's command as we park and run across the grass.

'Wait here, Rose. Please.' I let Thomas go ahead. My heart is pounding, my soul full of dread. I can see two of the policemen pulling something from the water. But Thomas turns and beckons me. It is a baby hippo, grey and swollen with water, already decomposing. In my utter relief I can spare a thought for this other mother that has lost her child. Hippos are good mothers, but I wonder how long they remember. Surely not a lifetime like us. But what is that policeman saying?

'Surprised the crocs didn't get it.'

I turn wild-eyed to Thomas. 'I never saw crocodiles here.'

'That's right.' Ken sees my terror. 'We chased them off long ago. They stay in the river. We're stopping now, Rose. But we'll be trying downstream this afternoon.'

'Maybe Joseph went fishing,' I suggest to Thomas as we walk back to the car. 'And the fishermen haven't got back yet, they might have stayed longer than they planned. Joseph used to love to watch the boats go in and out when we lived here.'

'I am sure the police have questioned all the fishermen.'

'Yes.'

Even I know it is a wild theory as it is unlikely any of them would take a white boy, especially on his own. But he might have been particularly friendly with one of them and I didn't know. I look out across the lake one more time, just in case. I feel I am missing something, some clue. Then I notice the ferry approaching from the far side. I turn to Thomas, excited.

'Maybe he took the ferry to Kisumu.'

'Rose.' Thomas is warning me. He thinks I am clutching at straws.

'Why not?' I say. 'Have the police contacted Kisumu? Oh, let us go there. It's just the sort of thing Joseph might do. He was getting so much more independent you know. It would be his idea of an adventure. Maybe he met one of his old schoolmates and they went together. He did have lots of friends in Jinja, you know.'

'Rose...'

'And he could be staying with this boy's family and maybe they don't have a telephone so he couldn't let me know. And maybe he doesn't like to make the journey back on his own. Yes I am sure of it. Please Thomas.' How can I persuade him? 'If you won't come with me I'll go alone. I'll be safe. I have my *ddagala*.'

Where did I learn this cunning? Of course he knows what a *ddagala* is, but he looks utterly shocked as I show him mine. It's round my neck, under my blouse. Smaller than Joseph's, a pretty pink.

'Someone I know took me to a *mulabale*. She said I needed protection.'

If only Thomas had said, *'It'll be alright,'* or *'Have faith,'* or offer to pray with me, I might have taken it off. Or I might have told him about Wanza and how she gave me hope. I might have tried to explain why I know I must keep on looking for Joseph. But he just looks sad, so very sad. Then he sighs and nods.

'I think she's right. For sure I'll go with you to Kisumu.'

15

'Another story!' Bhavin pointed to *'The Mission Cat'* in that day's paper. 'I don't know how you keep making them up.'

The plastic beaded curtain behind the post office counter swished as Sarita emerged from a back room. 'That's because you have no imagination,' she observed. 'How was your trip to London, Ms Zynofsky? Did you find out anything more about Mrs McCormack?'

'Not exactly,' Lilia replied. 'But I'm going up again tomorrow for a day or two to visit the headquarters of the Catholic Mission that was in Uganda. I'm not sure if they had missions in the same towns as the McCormacks, that is, in Iganga or Jinja, but there might be something relevant, some mention of the Protestant mission. The McCormacks were Protestants of course. And do call me Lilia.'

'Protestant, Catholic, it's all the same to us pagans,' Bhavin laughed but stopped abruptly, quelled by a look from his wife. 'Only joking,' he apologised.

'It's all the same to me too actually,' Lilia smiled at both of them to show that she was not offended, wondered briefly whether to add that there was rather too much religion in the world anyway, but decided that this might offend them. 'Anyway I discovered that the mission headquarters is really near old friends of mine so I can visit them at the same time.'

'We had an idea,' said Sarita. 'Bhavin knows someone, or knows of someone, a friend of his father, who was born in Iganga. I'm not sure exactly when but he's much older than us. We thought he might remember something.'

'You had the idea.' Bhavin smiled fondly at her. 'I only emailed him. I'll forward you any reply I get, Lilia. He lives in Leicester.'

'Well thank you.'

'We call Leicester "little India",' Bhavin continued. 'And practically the whole Indian population of Iganga have ended up living there after Amin threw them out. If my father's friend doesn't know anything, someone else will. You take care now up in London.'

London was, on the face of it, back to normal. Lilia tried not to think of the horrors being found underground as repairs to the tunnels began, imagining them all the same. Mill Hill East was at the end of an over-ground branch of the Northern Line. A taxi took Lilia along a ridge of high ground that climbed steadily from the station, was backed to the east by rolling fields, and fell away more steeply westwards down streets of large brick houses, each set in a well-kept garden. She asked the driver to drop her at a pair of ivy-clad gate posts to one of which was affixed a painted sign bearing the name: *'The St Joseph's Missionary Society'*, to the other an estate agent's board proclaiming the property *'FOR SALE'*.

Camera at the ready and trundling her overnight bag behind her, she climbed a long winding driveway towards the redbrick Victorian pile that was set in several acres of grounds. To her right was a wall of rhododendron bushes and other shrubs, on her left a field, where a grazing horse slowly raised its head and watched her pass. She arrived first at the gloomy rear of the building where an ugly modern block had been added, presumably when extra accommodation had been required. There was no sight nor sound of occupation now and no response when she rang the back doorbell. A little spooked by the silence, she followed an overgrown path around the side to the front of the main building and there was brought up short in a sudden flood of sunshine.

It was like entering a different world. As her eyes adjusted, she began to take in the stunning panoramic view far out over West London. The angle of elevation foreshortened the built up miles into an almost pastoral paradise, with trees burying the lower buildings and the warm afternoon sun covering the whole in a dreamy golden haze. The view might not have changed so very much in the last hundred or so years since the mission was built. Looking back at the building, she saw on each corner of the roof the statues of angels that reached out their arms to every part of the earth, while on the dome above the central porch stood a graceful white marble statue of the Virgin Mary, her arms outstretched, gazing down as if blessing the entire place and any visitors to it. The scent of roses drifted up from the gardens below, where several presently unoccupied benches encouraged rest and contemplation.

The St Joseph's Society had provided a pleasant launching pad for its new recruits, an anchor as they faced the trials of their far-flung postings and a haven of respite for those on leave. No wonder Father Thomas had decided to return there. But its training had not proved sufficient, it seemed, to keep young Brother Frantz on the straight and narrow; nor perhaps even Thomas himself, although, so far as she could tell, neither Edward nor Rose had ever suspected him of any wrong-doing. Lilia took a few photos and turned away from the view to keep her appointment with the archivist, wondering what if anything she would find out. She pressed the large old-fashioned bell at the central doorway.

Dieter Gershon was slight, bespectacled and about her own age, perhaps a little younger. He led her through a maze of long tiled corridors like covered cloisters, with walls covered in maps of the world and down narrowing staircases to his basement kingdom, where stacks of large cardboard boxes almost blocked the corridor. He apologised for the disorder.

'We are in the process of moving to Liverpool,' he said. 'You have come just in time.' He seemed sad.

'After so long,' Lilia commiserated. 'I noticed the sale sign. I suppose some builder will cover the whole place in nasty modern flats and houses.'

Dieter brightened a little. 'Planning regulations require that it continue to be an institution. Of some kind. We have had an enquiry from a Buddhist organisation.' He looked at her intently and she wondered if she imagined the note of irony, of gentle amusement.

She said, 'But Liverpool? It's a long way. Shall you mind? It's so lovely here.'

He spread his hands, gave the slightest of shrugs and turned to the business in hand. Gathering a few books from a shelf, he led her to a table beneath a shelf of bulging cardboard files all marked 'Uganda' and dated from the 1940s.

'I was posted in Uganda,' he said casually. 'In the 1970s and 80s, after the period in which you are interested. Under Amin. Not an easy time. Please feel free to ask me any questions you like.'

His face was inscrutable and for the first time that she could remember, Lilia could not at first think of any questions. She could not imagine what his life had been like, what horrors he might have known. She also could not think how to ask about the issue that preoccupied her: whether there would be any records of allegations of offences committed by missionaries against local residents, fearing that he might then, and understandably, deny her access altogether.

'Did you know Jinja or Iganga?' she asked at last.

He had spent most of his time in Kampala but having passed through Jinja a few times was able to give her an idea of what it had been like in his day. 'It must have been a very nice place in the 50s,' he said. 'It was a centre of the colonial administration, on the shores of Lake Victoria which is huge – the second largest in the world in fact - and it must have been a real hive of activity. Ships coming and going from Kenya and Tanzania and trains going all the way to the coast in the east and Congo in the west. But when I was there all of that had stopped and it was half abandoned and already rapidly decaying. All the Asians and Europeans had gone of course. I wonder what it's like now.' He confirmed that there had indeed been a mission at Iganga and several in the province, including one near Jinja, so that yes, she would be able to check the names of individuals attached to these missions for the years in question, although he trusted that any such information would not be publicised.

'Do you think there will be mention of the Protestant mission? And do you think it would have been the Church Missionary Society? In those towns?'

'I am almost certain it would have been,' he answered the second question first. 'Unless they were evangelicals but I don't think there were any there then, they came later. As for relations between the missions…' He laughed. 'I am afraid that they continued to be in a competitive rather than a cooperative spirit. We were of course seeking the same precious commodity, the souls of the local people. But individuals may well have struck up friendships.' He paused. 'You will find some sensitive material in your researches, Ms Zynofsky. I am sure I can rely on your humanity and commonsense. Your goal, as I understand it, is to try to locate friends and family of this elderly lady. I hope our resources assist you in this task.'

He did know of cases of abuse, Lilia thought. And perhaps he also guessed that she knew.

‘Even a little more understanding of the circumstances of missionary life would help me,’ Lilia assured him. ‘I can talk to Mrs McCormack and then maybe she will remember something important and even begin to speak more. So far she has said only a few words and much of that has been hard to understand.’

‘You will find correspondence, records of meetings, publications with photographs, and other documents including the so-called Sacred Returns, which are basically annual censuses of baptisms, confirmations, marriages and deaths for each mission.’ Dieter ticked them off on his fingers. ‘Obviously you can’t take anything away to read but I can make you a few photocopies and you will find summaries in some of these books. In fact, you may keep this book.’ He pointed to one. We have several copies and very few people ever come to consult them. You can make a small donation if you wish.’ He returned to his packing cases. ‘I’m here if you want me. We close at 6 and open at 10 in the morning.’

Lilia spent the next couple of hours sifting through the documents in the first few relevant boxes. Much of the material was correspondence, often letters to the Father General in Mill Hill from the Bishop of Kampala, handwritten or typed on flimsy, much folded paper. There were also minutes or reports of meetings of “vicariates” and “deaneries” in various places in Uganda, the agenda of which were mostly concerned with staffing matters – moving Fathers and Brothers between missions, allowing them leave, issues of pay and so on. There were details of schools, numbers of pupils and teachers and some *“sub secreto”* correspondence, partly in Latin, that she scanned without success for mention of Joseph. She was briefly amused by a reference to “Pluvius” wrecking part of the 1954 celebrations of the Order’s Jubilee celebrations in Kampala. Was he not the Roman God of rain?

In Rose’s province and in her time, the mid 50s, the Society of St Joseph had created a second diocese of Tororo and one of the Fathers at Iganga was briefly in the running for Bishop – could it have been Thomas she wondered? A third was established in Jinja in the 60s. A second church was begun in Jinja, and another opened successfully on a sugar plantation close by. There were many different tribes working there, and a high proportion of them were

Catholic. There was a technical college in Iganga where the Father was credited with doing a very good job, also a seminary to train native priests, and a convent of some order which at some stage provided nursing training. It appeared that the Catholics were doing very well, in the Iganga area especially.

There was, nonetheless, continuing anguish over the perceived need to compete with the Protestants, specifically 'the CMS', who were seen as being in cahoots with the Government. Certainly, in the nineteenth century they had been instrumental in persuading the British to stay in Uganda when the East African Company was all for quitting in face of the religious wars. The Government decreed that schools should provide "a proper education in British life and thought", which was of course difficult for the Italian and French orders: "Is there an RC contact in the Foreign Office?" asked one letter. Lilia read on quickly. The Catholics continued to feel insecure. In 1949 two new missions were set up 20 miles from Iganga at Namunyumya and Busowa "because the Protestants are making a big push for Busoga". There was an "urgent need" for more translations of religious books "because the CMS have them" and a need for an RC chaplain in a particular college, where Protestant staff were favoured, in order to keep it "suitable for Catholic boys".

It seemed overall that, through Catholic eyes at least, it was Edward and Rose and their Protestant contemporaries in nearby missions who were being more successful at this time. Over the years there were constant worries, due to lack of both finances and staff, that it would be difficult to maintain progress and, unless more mission stations and schools were opened, private non-denominational schools would fill the vacuum and Catholic converts would go to them. It was felt that parishes were too big so that, amongst other things, it was hard to supervise the "catechumens", the native lay readers, who were often responsible for "sub-grade" teaching in the local language. There even appeared to be difficulty finding enough priests for, in 1958, the Jinja church, by now named Our Lady of Fatima, still hadn't got a "superior".

Lilia was fascinated by these glimpses of ecclesiastical politics, a world she had never expected to enter, hadn't thought about, hardly knew existed. She found herself increasingly sympathetic to the dilemmas facing the senior decision makers, who were in turn of course accountable to Rome: there were mentions of “referring this matter to Propaganda”, which she discovered to be a department of the Vatican.

Who did the Protestants refer to if in doubt, she wondered. Unless they felt none, were more secure, being apparently more part of the establishment. So long as that remained. She reached for yet another box of documents.

16

Two hours later Lilia was sitting with Daniel and Sarah on their sunny patio after dinner enjoying the long light July evening with a glass of very cold champagne. A profusion of roses spilled from a trellis behind her, their perfume creating a heady mix with that of the jasmine that entirely covered a high fence in the garden below. It was so very pleasant to be out and in company.

'Here's to serendipity,' Daniel proposed the toast. 'And to the success of the strange mission that caused this happy reunion. Tell us more.'

Lilia did not intend to tell them much, particularly concerning the more sensational results of her researches. But she was tipsy and more than a little emotionally strung out by the sight of her first love still recognizable after many years, still very attractive in fact, but grizzled grey and with a softly rounded paunch blurring the handsome treasured memory. Sarah was a pleasant enough person and, on the whole, Lilia did not begrudge her what had apparently been a happy marriage, nor even the brood of children and grandchildren whose many framed photographs she had admired a short time before. It was her own indecision that had brought about Daniel's defection, induced by her mother's wailing pleas of helplessness were she to be left alone. Besides, she had never, in all honesty, felt herself to possess a thwarted maternal instinct and she really could not help noticing the contrast between her own still svelte figure and Sarah's very plump person. All the same, it was a situation in which she wished to appear at her wittiest and most accomplished.

'Well,' she said, 'The reason they built that ugly extension to their place up there was because in the 60s they started to train lay missionaries, so they needed accommodation for couples and families. Before that they were all priests or nuns - in separate establishments of course. But, surprise, surprise, that didn't stop them misbehaving. Not with each other, Daniel,' she added sternly as he tried to interrupt. 'Really, I found no mention of that at all.'

'They were, of course, all celibate,' suggested Daniel, raising an eyebrow and peering at her through his glass.

Lilia giggled. 'Supposed to be, anyway.'

'Ha! You see! Tell us more. Bloody Christians and their ulterior motives. Invasion, perversion, divide and rule. Leading to Empire, venereal disease and general rack and ruin. Whatever 'rack' might be.'

'Dan!' Sarah protested.

'Lilia doesn't mind, do you Lilia?' he retorted. 'She hates hypocrisy too or I always thought she did. Anyway, whatever else you can say about the Jews, they do not proselytise nor set out to conquer.'

'Except in the West Bank,' said Lilia.

'That's reclamation,' Daniel objected.

'Just don't let's go there.' Sarah raised her voice. 'You were saying, Lilia?'

'Well, they did have quite a few problems keeping the troops in order. Booze for one. And then paying for it when it became too much of a habit. You can imagine can't you, the young man alone in the long dark tropical evenings, no TV, at most the World Service for company or his much older white colleague, who is perhaps not even from the same country, does not therefore speak the same language, and who, though kind, is really rather dull. He hears his native colleagues and parishioners merrily carousing in the nearby village. If he is invited, should he go? Should he accept their hospitable offer of beer? Does he acquire a taste for alcohol that he associates with socialising and a feeling of well-being even though he cannot really afford it - unless he stretches the definition of masses, from the saying of which he is allowed to raise a little extra cash.'

'Were they?' Sarah interjected. 'Allowed to charge for saying masses? That's interesting, like selling pardons in the Middle Ages. Enterprising really.'

'Mmm. But what's even more interesting, I think, is that the underlying problem was that they were *supposed* to fraternise with the natives. I read this statement, made around the early 50s, something like: *"We all realise the day is past when the African will come to us, and the day has come when by every possible means we must go to the African."* You see? *"By every possible means."*

What can this mean? And how would you set about it?' Lilia accepted a refill of her glass and continued.

'For a start, what do you wear? I'm serious, honestly. Suppose that you are a young European Brother setting out to visit some of your pupils and their families out of school hours, that it is a Saturday, in fact, for you are encouraged to participate in "active ministry" at weekends also. Let us further suppose that it is a long way down hot dusty roads and that you will go by the mission motor bike – perhaps your Father Superior needs the car, anyway it is more economical and perhaps even, heaven forgive the thought, more fun on the bike. Do you wear the white robe, red sash and collar of your Order? Or do you dress like any other young European man in similar circumstances and wear khaki shorts and shirt? And, one hopes, a crash helmet, for the roads are full of potholes and the Highway Code no doubt unknown. But thereby you run the risk of losing the unique authority of your priestly dignity and worse, excite the unspoken suspicion that you are a 'broken-down European' or suspicious character. Bit of a dilemma?

'And then there is a further problem.' She was warming to her theme. 'Given the scarcity if not complete absence of public transport, do you offer or agree to give a ride to a young pupil or African colleague, who is returning home or perhaps just fancies a ride? What if the pupil or colleague is female? Although, as these days we are free to suggest, a male might in some cases be more of a temptation. You see my drift? And yes, a number of cases of inappropriate relations of this kind are documented, some resulting in pregnancies, some in marriage, with the young man in question then seeking a lay position.'

'Names are given?' asked Daniel quickly. 'And places? Details that are relevant to you?'

Lilia hesitated. 'Yes,' she admitted. 'But not to you.'

'Ah.' He was silent a moment. 'How about instances of paedophilia? I mean, there have been so many revelations recently involving Catholic institutions in various countries, some of them decades ago. That would really give you something to write about.'

'In the Bognor Observer?'

'Why not, if it pertains to your search for this boy.'

'I wish I hadn't told you about Joseph, no one else knows. And I'm not writing about that, not yet anyway. All I am saying, without naming names, is that these were problems that gradually emerged and were the subject of some sort of official pronouncements. One of those I found was written entirely in Latin - thereby making it effectively *sub secreto,* that was the term they used, to me at any rate - but for the telling exception of the word "shorts". Another edict, this time in English, decreed exactly when the red sash should be worn: until after Mass or breakfast, on Sundays and on feast days, at least until after last Mass, and on other occasions when a number of the order were gathered together for some purpose. I gathered that in some places at least things were getting a bit lax and the higher authorities felt the need to step in.'

'Including in this place? Iganga?'

'Yes.'

'Lax in more than the matter of dress?'

Lilia hesitated. She was finding Daniel's attitude hard to fathom and harder to deal with. Like her, he was quite drunk, but she didn't remember him being so aggressive nor in the least lascivious, if that was what it was. Maybe it was just the long-standing dislike of any religious evangelism that used to unite them. And religion more generally she recalled, though he had perhaps changed in that respect after his marriage. Whatever it was, she decided to continue. It would help to discuss her discoveries, hear some other people's opinions.

'There was one such case in Iganga involving a young Brother,' she said. 'And it was around the time Joseph vanished. And around the same time, a Father also left this Mission and returned to England. But I knew that already, from other sources. Some letters Rose asked me to read to her.'

'And you don't think any of this has anything to do with the boy's disappearance?' Daniel's tone was incredulous.

'I don't know.'

'What do you think Rose thinks?'

'I don't know.'

'What are you suggesting, Dan?' Sarah asked quietly. 'Murder? Surely not.'

'An abduction that went wrong?' Daniel waved his hands in the air, improvising. 'Could this Joseph have been a willing participant? Maybe he had already had some homosexual experiences at that boarding school?'

'Oh Dan.' Sarah put her fingers in her ears. 'He was eight. Don't listen to him, Lilia, he loves to shock.'

'OK, maybe he was so upset he ran away and maybe he jumped in the lake. I don't know. I'm just playing the Devil's Advocate,' Daniel was adamant. 'Sometimes the unthinkable happens. I wonder what his parents really thought.'

'Rose may yet tell me,' said Lilia. 'And I'm waiting for a response to an email from someone who used to live in Iganga. You'd think if something like that did happen, someone would remember.'

'I shall just pray that neither we, nor our children, ever have to face such a situation. And on that note I shall be off to my bed. Night you two.' Sarah stood and stretched and went inside the house.

'Won't be long,' Daniel called after her.

Lilia accepted her share of the remaining champagne and sipped it slowly. 'I should go too,' she said, without moving. 'It's been a long day and another one tomorrow. And I'll probably have a hangover.'

'Why didn't you ever marry?' asked Daniel abruptly.

'Because you broke my heart,' she thought but aloud she said: 'After my mother died, you mean? Oh, I suppose I got so used to being on my own, making my own decisions. And the literary types I was meeting by then were, are, a self-absorbed lot.'

'So you had some boyfriends?' She did not reply. 'But you have always lived alone.'

'With my cat.'

'I remember your cat. It gave me asthma.'

'I expect this one would too. I'm perfectly happy, really. You must come and visit one day. Both of you.' She inhaled deeply. 'That jasmine is absolutely wonderful. It must be lovely having a proper garden. We never had one in Brighton, did we, and I don't in Bognor either. I'll just go down and take a closer sniff if you don't mind.' She stood, swaying slightly and headed for a short flight of crazily paved steps that led into the main part of the garden.

'Be my guest.' Daniel's face was almost invisible in the deepening dusk and his tone non-committal. 'But mind the steps, they're uneven.'

She made her way slowly, testing each step with one foot before transferring her weight, but on the last she lost her balance and stumbled. Somehow Daniel was beside her in time to prevent her falling.

'I could see you weren't going to make it,' he said shortly. 'Here, sit on this bench for a minute.' He kept an arm around her and held her other hand in his as he guided her. Lilia held her breath willing these moments to last longer. Daniel still smelt the same.

'Sorry,' she said when she had sat down and he had retreated a little into the darkness. 'I didn't mean to do that, I wasn't pulling a Jane Austen trick. You know, in *"Persuasion"* when they visit Lyme Regis and she, whatever her name is, insists on climbing up on the Cob and falls into whatsisname's arms? Oh dear, once I would have remembered.'

'Why would I think you wanted me to catch you?' he interrupted and she realised her mistake.

'You're right, sorry, I was just burbling, must be the shock. Actually, it might have been *"Northanger Abbey"*? I always did get those two mixed up.'

'Maybe you are not as well-read as I used to think you were? You always had a literary allusion for every situation.'

'Did I? Oh dear, how pretentious and gosh no, maybe if I'd gone to university…what do you mean? ' His tone was more than scornful, it was bitter. 'Oh Dan, it's been lovely to see you again, don't let's fight. Let me just sit another moment and then we'll go in.'

'It's *lovely* to see you too, Lilia. You've still got that *lovely* red hair.' His tone contradicted his words

'Oh,' she said, touching it, uncertainly. 'I've had to dye it for years.'

'Why didn't you reply to my last letter?' he spat it out as if he could not contain it any longer.

'I did, I wished you good luck in your marriage, happiness in the future, something like that.'

'I wrote to you after that. Before I'd actually agreed to the marriage. I sent you a poem. A sonnet actually. I thought it might make you see sense, which I couldn't seem to do.' He laughed without humour. 'It seemed a good idea at the time.'

'I remember thinking it was very romantic,' Lilia said slowly. 'A lovely way to say goodbye. Terribly sad of course, though I knew it was my fault.'

He shook his head. 'Read it again, Lilia. I'll send you a link tomorrow.'

'I will when I get home although I'm sure I could find it, I kept all your letters, not that there were many, you living upstairs…' she stopped and clutched her throat. 'Oh Dan, what did I do?'

He shook his head. 'Just read it. But no need to look so stricken. It's a very long time ago. Goodnight,' he added a little more gently. 'I need to lock up.'

'Goodnight.' She pulled herself together, stood and brushed his cheek with her lips and went quickly ahead of him into the house.

17

It was nearly midday the next morning. Lilia had almost finished going through the boxes of documents without having found anything else of particular relevance, certainly no reference to a missing English boy from a neighbouring mission, and she could not decide whether this tended to refute or support Daniel's speculations. Either Joseph's disappearance had nothing to do with the departure of Brother Franz and Father Thomas and was therefore not an appropriate matter to include in the official records or it was the cause in some way, or at least had been suspected to be, and was too scandalous to include. Perhaps there had been a cover up and any records there were had been removed, even destroyed. How could one possibly find out? And even if there were any evidence to discover, what would she then do? She had not expected to enter such deep waters.

The intensive search of the previous two hours had helped distract her from thinking too much about the implications of Daniel's statement the night before. Could her life have been built on a misunderstanding? The story she'd always told herself, and anyone else who asked, a complete fabrication? She began to breathe more quickly, her heart was pounding quite painfully. She had never had a panic attack but wondered if she was about to. Also, the headache with which she had woken was beginning to return and she closed her eyes and rested her head in her hands with her elbows on the desk. She thought she might have even nodded off, when a slight cough roused her and she opened her eyes to find Father Gershon putting a cup and saucer in front of her.

'You looked as if you needed some coffee,' he smiled.

'That's extremely kind of you.' She sat up straight.

'It can be heavy-going sorting through this lot,' he nodded. 'Are you sure I can't help at all?'

'I think I've more or less finished, thank you.'

'Have you found anything very relevant?'

'Um, not exactly, no. So I'm just wondering what to do next. Of course I also have to consult the Protestant mission archives. But it's been really interesting,' she added quickly. 'As background information. On what it was like to be a missionary then. I am grateful to you.'

Father Gershon brushed this aside and pulled up a chair. 'You have understood some of the difficulties?' He sat a short distance from her.

She turned to face him. 'I think so. But -' she hesitated and then took a deep breath. 'I must ask you while I have the chance. I was looking for something more particular as I think you guessed. You see, Mrs McCormack lost her son. He went missing, in 1955 from the mission in Iganga. As far as I know he was never found. I think she may have even forgotten about it all these years but the stroke made her remember. And I've promised her that I'll try to find out. But there's absolutely no mention of it in your records.'

'It wouldn't have been a matter for our mission.'

'No, except that,' she told him of what she had read in Edward's letters and confirmed in the records. 'It's only circumstantial, I know,' she said before he could respond. 'And I have no evidence that the McCormacks ever blamed the Brother or the Father for their son's disappearance. And it's all so long ago and I certainly would not make any slanderous accusations. It's just that if the events were connected in any way and it was thought so at the time then I would pursue things differently. Or perhaps not at all as there might be no further need.'

Father Gershon stood and paced up and down in silence for several minutes. 'I have to say,' he spoke at last. 'That this is far beyond my small domain. I suppose there might be other sources, higher sources of information, if there had been a case, perhaps in Rome. I don't know. But I think you, or anyone, would have to be sure of the facts before you took that avenue. Perhaps you could look in newspapers of the time? Or colonial records?'

'Yes I suppose I may. Though I'm not sure how far I even want to carry this. Thank you for listening. I feel I have taken advantage of your hospitality.'

'I did find something I thought you would like to read. I'll just fetch it from my desk.' He returned holding a few photocopied sheets. 'I found an article I remembered reading in one of our magazines,' he handed it to her. 'It was written, most appropriately, in 1955 by a young missionary in Uganda. The author says he hopes it might save the reader, most likely another young missionary, some soul-searching.'

William More (grad. 1950), had written from *"the back of beyond": "an outpost of an outpost"*, where *"no two days are alike and very little seems within one's control." "I live by my wits,"* he felt, with very little idea what his congregation made of his religious teaching. *"Gave some simple instruction along the following lines: that Our Lord Jesus would arrive soon to pray Mass for us. He would worship God in our name and thank him for the good things we have received, pay the debt of our sins and ask for the graces that we need. He would give to God His Body and Blood and we should join with him in doing this and we should promise to God to keep his commandments. As usual, it felt like a series of shots in the dark."*

When he made his daily visits to outlying villages he was warmly welcomed. *"You have appeared. We are glad to see you. Thank you for coming to see us. How have you slept?"* and these greetings were interspersed with *"hummings on the appropriate notes"*. But he did not trust any promises made about following the Church's teaching on how to live one's life, to marry in church, one man to one woman, to study or to send their children to study the Bible. *"I know they mean nothing and they know that I know. Perhaps if I could keep at them and come back next week...Or if I could stay here in this little corner of about 50 square miles where I guess there are 1000 Catholics, 1500 Protestants, 30,000 or so pagans and a few hundred Moslems. But we would need another 5 priests for every one we have already."*

And yet his message was that he had *"learnt the hard way that nothing is truly set in stone and that all only truly makes sense when bathed in the glorious light of the universe that is the one true measure of God's creation."* After a very long day and a "bath" that consisted of pouring water over himself with a pudding basin, he was very glad to creep under a mosquito net into his camp bed but he still *"felt good, being in the heart of Africa, miles from anywhere. Trying to rise above that to the oneness of space and time – I fell asleep."*

Tears pricked Lilia's eyes as she finished reading. It was impossible not to be moved by the young priest's sincerity and joy in his work, even if she still could not really understand his point of view. She looked up at Father Gershon. 'Are you telling me this young man was more typical than those who – went astray?' she asked.

'I think so, yes,' he said. 'And I am entirely unaware of any cases that reached the limits you imply in this young boy's tragic case.'

'So I should exercise the benefit of the doubt in this case?'

'You could do so, yes. I would certainly be so inclined.'

18

Rose looked well, her cheeks the soft pink of her bed jacket, her hair neatly set in curls that framed her face. Lilia preferred Rose's usual more natural, and faintly girlish, appearance, but at least she was being well cared for. A vase of white roses sat on the bedside table. *'From the Editor of the Observer with best wishes for your recovery'* read the small card beneath. Mike was being uncharacteristically thoughtful.

'I've brought you some fruit, Rose.' Lilia arranged it in the bowl provided. 'Nurse Halliwell said it was the best thing, but if there's anything else you want…'

Rose did not respond. She looked at Lilia with wide bright eyes but seemed not to see her. Her face was calm but blank.

'We've been getting her up for a walk every day,' Nurse Halliwell had said. 'She's been reading those letters you brought in. And she still knits – in fact, she finished one sweater. And then immediately started another! She's going to need more wool pretty soon. But she doesn't talk. Not to us. Maybe you'll have more joy.'

'Have you missed me?' Lilia tried to sound cheery. 'I've been up in North London where the Mill Hill Fathers have their base, where they used to train missionaries. They were one of the Catholic orders in Uganda. Do you remember? You and your husband knew them in Iganga. Father John was one and Father Thomas, I was reading to you about him last time I was here? He went to Jinja to help you find Joseph?'

Was Rose's expression a little more attentive? If only one could know what she was thinking.

Thomas is trying so hard to help me find Joseph despite the swirling rumours, the pointing fingers, as if we are two criminals on the run. I am not sure which of us blackens the reputation of the other more. The Frasers are increasingly uncomfortable at having to put up with me. They know how much Edward wants me to return home. They think I am unhinged. Elizabeth wants me to see a doctor. How can a doctor help?

I am going to all the shops and cafes in Kisumu, asking if they have seen Joseph. I show them the photograph I gave to the newspaper. Joseph brought several copies home from school. It makes him look too pale, too serious, his hair is too short, but I haven't any other recent ones. I haven't many at all. I must ask Edward to send me them. Why didn't we take more, all those precious baby years? Where have they gone? If I had my life again I would grab each moment, hold it fast, fix it in my memory, before letting it pass.

Some of the shopkeepers have read about Joseph in the papers but no one has any news. 'No madam, sorry madam.' They are mostly sympathetic. And then one of them has an idea, a suggestion. 'Maybe your son go to Mwanza, madam. Try Mwanza.' I am doubtful. Tanganyika? We never went there. But then I think.

'That could be just why he would go there! A new place, a whole new country! And who knows, at that new school of his, maybe there was someone from there, Joseph surely wasn't the only pupil from Africa. Maybe he thought he could visit him, maybe he had telephoned him and arranged it.'

'You don't think he would have mentioned it to you?' Thomas asks, gently, carefully. I shiver suddenly, uncontrollably. I think Thomas believes he has upset me, he reaches out to comfort me; but I shake my head. It is not that. It is because I have realised how very little Joseph has told me about his life in England. Or have I not asked? Did I simply want him back as if he had never been away, as if life was the same as before? As if he would not leave me again? Oh Joseph. Joseph. When I find you I will tell you that we will not send you away again. I shall go with you to England. I shall tell your father we must leave here. We must be together.

We are crossing the lake again, just a few passengers in a small cargo boat, but it feels quite safe, the water is calm. I can see how easy you would have found it, my darling, a big boy like you, though you should not have gone without telling us, should you? You must have known how very much we would worry. Where would you like to live in England? By the sea, do you think? But not in Scotland, not near Gran and Grandad. I don't think we could bear the cold do you, darling? After so long in Africa. But of course we'll see them, you must go and stay with them sometimes. Maybe you will go to Edinburgh University like your grandfather and your father. I won't mind that, I promise. I know that big boys of eighteen have to leave home! I wonder what you will be. Perhaps a doctor? I know you are clever enough. How proud I shall be. A doctor!'

'Hush now, Rose,' Thomas says. As if I was speaking aloud! 'We're almost there.'

'A doctor, did you say? Do you want a doctor?' But Rose had stopped mumbling and appeared to have drifted away again.

I jump off the boat. I am suddenly sure that I am going to find news of you... but it is the same story as in Kisumu. I wander the streets by the harbour but no one knows anything, no one remembers seeing a small white boy on his own, and I am sure you would have been noticed here, if you had come. Mwanza is smaller than Jinja, less busy than Kisumu, there are less Europeans here and you wouldn't have known your way around. Now there is nothing to do but go back to Jinja and wait.

'Look, I took some photos of the Mill Hill missionary college.' Lilia passed them to Rose one by one. 'See, here is the approach to the college, it's almost like being in the countryside. And that's the building, you can just see it through the trees. And these show the building from the front, the old part at least. It's not unlike a church is it, a brick church, with that high tower and the statues on the roof. I don't know if they are saints or angels. And see on that lower dome, the white statue of the Virgin Mary. Isn't she lovely? And these I took from the front steps. Towards the west. Isn't it a wonderful view! Right out over London.'

So that's where Thomas went.

'I must return to England, Rose. To Mill Hill.'

We are in our Lady of Fatima's, it is still only half finished. We both feel freer here I think to commune with God because it's not to be run by the Mill Hill Fathers but by a Goan order, for the Indian Catholics. And it is opposite Joseph's school and the field where he learned to play cricket. It isn't a proper pitch but it's the nearest playing field to Main Street. He used to slip back in the afternoons after school was finished to practise with some of the Indian boys. It must be where he met Nilu. Joseph didn't know I knew but I used to find grass stains on his clothes and once I followed him just to see where he went. After that I went as often as I could to watch, though I never let him see me.

Thomas' search for forgiveness is beyond my understanding. He blames himself so much. *"Kindness which cannot refuse breeds lies".* He says it is a Lugandan saying. *"Too great gentleness makes the cricket bite you". "Trouble which is not revealed breeds in the mind".* I don't know if he means his own mind or Brother Frantz's.

'Frantz has gone to the college in Nairobi,' he tells me. 'There will be much more company, more Brothers from Europe his own age. I pray he will find his vocation.'

'I shall pray for you, Thomas.'

Thomas must have walked up that drive, stood on those steps, perhaps sat on that very seat and watched the sunset. Watched through all the seasons until the next summer. Our Lady, watching high above, did you comfort him? Did he climb up to be near you? Did he fall? 'We think he suffered a heart attack,' the Father General wrote to Father John. I think so too. But what caused it?

I wander the streets, alone now, where everything reminds me of my life with Joseph. Here is the hospital where he was so ill with measles. And there is the other where I started to practise my new nursing skills. Here is the theatre where I was such a triumph in South Pacific. Thanks to Babs, who would have liked the leading role herself.

'Give it to Rose,' she told the producer. 'You should hear her sing.'

What an audience we got! All those men who were in town to build the dam. It was like playing to the troops in the war must have been. And how Joseph loved it. He was one of the King's children. I can see him now, dressed in white with a little turban on his head and pointy silk slippers on his little feet. More Indian than Siamese, but very sweet. I never did another show. Edward was most unhappy, a missionary's wife making such a spectacle of herself. They are doing *Seven Brides for Seven Brothers* next. Babs is the star this time. She has asked if I would like to be the prompt but didn't press the point. I wrote to Edward.

"I am staying with Babs at the cantonment. She has just come back from Nairobi. Everyone has been returning from their holidays ready for the new school term. I know you never approved of her but I was a burden on the Frasers. And Babs was always a good friend to me. You can write c/o Sgt Roberts, King's African Rifles. There's no telephone at the house but I expect there is a number you could use if you really need to contact me. Rose."

Of course Edward comes to see me, tries again to persuade me to go home.

'School is starting,' he says first. 'And Sunday School.'

'Ask Stephen to teach my classes. He will like to do that.'

'And the clinics, Rose? Your patients?'

But I will not put duty to them above my son, ever again. I suppose that is what Edward is doing. Let him if he can. It is what he has always done. I fear that that is what I said. I did not mean to hurt him. I only wanted him to go. To leave me. I am not your keeper, Edward. We must each be answerable for ourselves.

'Our Lady, full of grace, hear me in my hour of need.' I spend a lot of time in Our Lady of Fatima's. 'Mary, Mother of God, who lost your own dearly beloved son, help me in my search, sustain me with your loving kindness that I may bear this... I will not say grief, say pain rather, say agony of separation, remorse for wrongs that I have done. Show me the way, through your knowledge of sorrow, give me peace from this suffering, heal my heart's affliction. Help me find Joseph. Amen.'

There are boys in the field by the school now, and it is so easy to imagine Joseph among them, stepping forward, bat in hand, to score a run, or with a hand shading his eyes from the setting sun as he leaps to make a catch.

'Howzat!' His friends cheer and clap. But he is not there.

One day the police stop looking, call off their search.

'The file is open, Rose,' Ken assures me.

But I know it is really closed. No one expects there to be any news. Everyone thinks Joseph is gone forever. Dead.

'He's not dead, Ken, I know he's not.'

I walk home the long way, by the station. Where I came to bid Thomas farewell. A train is leaving now. The last door slams and the guard's whistle blows. Suddenly I know I must leave too. Joseph is not in Jinja and I cannot stay here any longer. I know where I must go. I don't know why I didn't think of it before. Joseph left by train. He went to the coast. It was summer, he wanted to see the sea. And maybe he had arranged to meet Nilu, even though his mother knew nothing about it.

'The librarian at Mill Hill was stationed in Uganda,' Lilia continued, regardless of Rose's lack of response. 'He was telling me about Jinja, he knew it a bit though long after you left Uganda, he said it would have already changed a lot. I've written about it in the paper, in case anyone who lived in Jinja reads it and remembers. I know it's a long shot but…'

'Not in Jinja.'

'What? Not in Jinja did you say? Then where, Rose, where? Oh Rose, if only you could speak more.'

But Rose had closed her eyes and sunk back into her pillows with the photographs spilling from her hands and the smallest of smiles beginning to lift the corners of her mouth.

Lilia sighed. 'Well, I'm glad to see you well and apparently happy. But I really must go home to my poor lonely pussycat and write another little story for which I had the idea on the way back from London. I am sure it is no consolation to him at all that I have been more inspired lately in his absence than his presence. And I am sure he cares not a bit that I think I am beginning to understand the missionary enterprise.' And then, she thought, I will read my email.

THE BISHOP'S CAT

Rajah lived in a palace. It was really a big brick house but it was called a palace because it was the home of a bishop. It was on top of a high hill looking down over a beautiful city.

Rajah and the Bishop had lived in the palace for many years. Every day, while the Bishop was busy doing what bishops do, Rajah was busy catching mice. At the end of every day they sat together outside the palace and looked down at the beautiful city.

Every night before they went to sleep, and while Rajah washed his whiskers, the Bishop read to him from The Good Book. Rajah did not understand the words of The Book but he knew that they were good and that they made the Bishop happy. He was very happy living with the good Bishop, even though they were both growing old.

But as the years went by, and the Bishop and Rajah grew older together, more and more mice came to live in the palace. Rajah could no longer catch them all.

'You are too old to catch all the mice,' said the Bishop. 'I must find some young cats to help you.'

The young cats came from a faraway land. They did not know how to catch mice. 'Where we come from people feed cats,' they said. 'And we are hungry.'

'I must feed these cats,' the Bishop said to Rajah. 'And you must teach them how to catch mice.'

The cats did not want to learn to catch mice. They chased the mice and the mice ran away. But then the Bishop fed the cats and the mice came back. The mice were very happy. Even more of them came to live in the palace on top of the hill.

'What can we do?' the Bishop asked Rajah as he fed the cats. Rajah saw that the Bishop was not happy.

Then the cats stopped chasing the mice and the mice stopped running away and they all started to play games together. The mice chased the cats. They ran races against each other. They played 'Hide and Seek' with each other. Rajah saw that the Bishop was not happy even when he read the Book. Rajah was very sad.

And then one day the cats and mice put up a sign: 'The Young Mice and Cats Association: Join Here.' Cats and mice began to climb the hill from other parts of the city. They played games all over the palace.

'We cannot feed so many cats,' said the Bishop. That night he did not read from the Book before he went to sleep.

'I must do something,' thought Rajah and he began to write. He wrote all night.

You can always tell which cats have read The Book of Cats. They understand the rules. Life is not a game. Everyone must play their part. No one should try to be what he or she is not. Cats are cats and mice are mice. But coexistence is the greatest good.

19

Daniel had written. '*No comment*' read the message line. There was an attachment, nothing more.

'Better first email the story,' Lilia clung to the familiar. 'And perhaps I should check the rest of my mail first…' The computer mouse followed her indecision until her finger was braver. Two clicks and the words of the sonnet appeared on the screen. She read it quickly.

Since there's no help, come, let us kiss and part,
Nay, I have done, you get no more of me,
And I am glad, yea, glad, with all my heart,
That thus so cleanly I myself can free.
Shake hands for ever, cancel all our vows,
And when we meet at any time again
Be it not seen in either of our brows
That we one jot of former love retain.
Now at the last gasp of Love's latest breath,
When, his pulse, failing, Passion speechless lies,
When Faith is kneeling by his bed of death,
And Innocence is closing up his eyes,
Now, if thou wouldst,
When all have giv'n him over,
From death to life thou might'st him yet recover.
Michael Drayton 1563-1631

She read it quickly, half remembering, until she came to the second part which she read several times not wanting to understand. Dan was right, of course he was, he had chosen the sonnet for a reason. He was saying please, don't be so stubborn, throw me a lifeline before I am irrevocably committed to someone else. How could she have been so stupid? Blinded by self-righteousness and an overwrought sense of duty, bewitched even one might say into allowing 'Fate' to remove any element of choice. *There was still time to change her mind,* he was saying, *they could find a way.* Not goodbye, it's tragic, but life moves on.

Lilia slumped in her chair, her hands still on the keyboard, wanting to reply to him as she should have done all those years before. It seemed so clear now, so easy to imagine how different things could have been and cruelly ironic that making up scenarios had become her stock in trade, even if they were for other characters, mainly Rajah. She glanced across at him where he sprawled on his usual chair. He had seemed listless since her return, perhaps even a little thinner. She had promised him fresh chicken and fish to make up for having been left alone.

'You're not the best company today,' she said as she chopped up half a chicken breast, wiping tears from her cheeks with her sleeve. 'But I'm very glad you are here.' She returned to her email.

Dear Ms Zynofsky,

I have pleasure in responding to your inquiry. I was born in Iganga in 1954 at home. This was common for Asians. If it was during the daytime the GP (Asian) would leave his busy practice, (hundreds of Africans from the surrounding area would wait for hours), while he took off to birth the Indian baby. There was a CMS (Christian Missionary Service) at the Jinja end of town, not far from the main Post Office and police station. The CMS was kind of a hospital and my brother was born there in 1964. In the late 60s they did build a brand new hospital in Iganga at the opposite end of town. A lot of the new doctors were Korean.

My recollection was not many Europeans in town – I would see perhaps 1 or 2 white faces a week – when they came to our shop to buy toilet paper. Nobody else bought or used toilet rolls! I also do recall seeing nuns, from the CMS I suppose, and they were helpful to people in town.

The town was a bustling commercial place, lots of businesses run mainly by Indians – clothing stores, grocery, general supplies, radio/electronics on Main St. We lived on Plot 95, a corrugated iron roof and cement house, shop at the front and living quarters at the back. This was the typical set up. There were a few bars and a hotel - which looked a bit seedy. There was for a short time a cinema but it was not successful and was turned into a warehouse by the Indian family that owned it. They also owned mills for processing brown sugar/molasses. Other industry in the area was a timber mill and a cotton ginnery. A lot of cotton grew there. There was one Primary School that was used mainly by Indians – in the later days it was 30% Africans. But there were several other schools in the surrounding area and they would come to our school for the inter schools Sports Day as we had a huge sports field. You asked about a Technical College and secondary schools and I don't recall any. Most of the Indians sent their kids to Jinja or Kampala for secondary education.

I hope that this information is helpful. My memories are from a Ugandan Asian perspective and I was somewhat sheltered from the Africans as my grandfather was very protective. The only experience of Africans I had was the servants and workers at the store. In the late 60s the Indians were very suspicious of the Africans – there were no major crimes just petty thieves and burglary.
Yours truly
Jignesh Shah

Lilia replied immediately thanking Mr Shah for the interesting insight into life in Uganda at that time. However, as he himself said, it was from a very particular perspective and a child's one at that. A very unreliable narrator. She was amused by his understanding of the initials 'CMS', which was not such a bad description of missionary activities perhaps, but surely the nuns had been Catholic. She was quite shocked to hear how few Europeans lived in the town, surely not an easy place for a white child to make friends, especially in that short time after the move from Iganga. But it was plain that individual Europeans, whether missionaries or not, let alone events concerning them, had made no lasting impression on young Jignesh. It was like trying to see shooting stars, she thought, they always seem to occur where one is not looking, so at best you just catch a glimpse from the corner of your eye. Very frustrating. She decided that it was time to pull out all the stops and make the trip to Birmingham to look in the CMS archives, even though it would mean paying for somewhere to stay overnight and leaving Rajah again.

A few minutes later, Lilia wished that she had telephoned earlier as the cheerful woman in charge of the archive was not only available but willing to be very helpful. There were indeed records of the CMS going back for over a century. Many people had already researched them and there were not only published books but theses, a relevant list of which she could make and email. But in which years exactly was Lilia interested? Because unfortunately some of them were at present not in Birmingham. Lilia named her dates, adding in a few extra years just in case. The mid 1940s to the mid-1960s, she said. There was an ominous pause.

'Ah,' said the helpful voice. 'I was afraid you would say that. Yes those are the ones that are currently being held in CMS Headquarters, I am not sure why.'

'And that is where?' Lilia knew things had progressed too smoothly.

'London. Near Waterloo Station.'

'But that's wonderful news! Much more convenient for me. Thank you so much. I'll be there tomorrow morning.'

The archivist laughed. 'I'd better give you some contact numbers first.'

The modern purpose-built building of the Church Missionary Society, which was very near the Old Vic Theatre, housed quite a large library of books, including a whole shelf or two about African mission work, and very accessible photocopying facilities. The librarian on duty, a stern woman of about Lilia's age, who wore steel-rimmed glasses and her steel-grey hair in a tight pleat, was busy, seemed to know why she was there, gave her a quick tour, showed her to a desk and retreated into her office. This was separated from the library itself by a glass partition that still enabled her to oversee readers. Almost immediately Lilia began to find what she was looking for.

In the Annual Reports, which gave records of which missionaries were where when, she could see that Rose and Edward McCormack went to Jinja in 1946 and Iganga in 1954. There was another couple, Penny and Colin Colman, with them most of the time in Jinja who had been in CMS service for longer. Rose and Edward were marked as 'At home' in 1949-50 and another couple, John and Elizabeth

Fraser, also long-serving, replaced the Colmans in 1953. Rose was no longer listed after 1955, the year of Joseph's disappearance, so she had obviously never returned to Iganga nor to any other mission in Uganda, but Edward remained on the record until 1963-4 as did the Frasers. After that there were no missionaries listed at all for either station. Lilia went to find the librarian to ask why.

'It could mean the station was closed but much more likely that there were no longer any Europeans there,' she was told. 'And the records stopped listing African staff after 1946-7, there were too many after this time to keep track of statistically.'

Lilia nodded. There had only been one in Jinja, but eight for Iganga that last year. 'Do you have records of the families of ex missionaries,' she asked. 'That's what I'm really trying to do, track down anyone who knew the McCormacks at Iganga or Jinja. Would there still be details of people's applications, their addresses in this country? I know it's a long time ago.'

The librarian said stiffly that, if there were records of any family members, the Society would have to make the first contact and see if they were willing to be approached but then she paused, appeared to consider, smiled suddenly and added: 'And I can also make the same checks for surviving colleagues if you wish, in the circumstances.' She shook her head. 'It must be awful to end up old and entirely alone. Let me know when you've finished looking who you want me to chase up.'

Also listed for Iganga until the year before Rose and Edward's arrival were one, and sometimes two, European women, there were four different names that overlapped. There was a single man who seemed to have left in 1947, it wasn't clear how long he was there. On the whole there seemed to be more coming and going at Iganga than elsewhere and Lilia wondered if it had been a more difficult posting for some reason. Only Edward had stayed a long time. She began to feel some sympathy for him. First Rose lost her son, then she left her husband. To look for her son, yes, but with the result that she and Edward ended up apart, apparently for the rest of their lives; unless he had rejoined her after leaving Iganga. Was this normal? Even in such very abnormal circumstances?

Immersed in the records, she had not noticed how time had passed. She had planned earlier to go for lunch at a café she had noticed on the other side of the road and then return to consult some of the old newsletters and magazines that surely would include some report of Joseph's disappearance. However, a sudden flurry of people coming and going from the librarian's office and their urgent whispered conversations drew her attention. She tidied the documents with which she had finished into a neat pile and went to let the librarian know that she would be back in half an hour.

'I'm sorry but I think we are going to close.' The eyes behind the glasses were wide with what looked like fear. 'You haven't heard about the bombs.'

'More bombs? I mean, not the ones two weeks ago?'

'About an hour ago, you had better try to go home as quickly as you can.'

'Oh my goodness!' Lilia clutched her throat. 'Oh dear, I've left everything out, I really hadn't finished.'

'Give me the names quickly and I'll email you when I've had a chance to look at our records,' said the librarian. 'Then you may not need to come back.'

20

Three small explosions had occurred around midday within minutes of each other at Warren Street, the Oval and Shepherd's Bush Underground stations and an hour later on a bus in Bethnal Green. In the words of several terrorist manifestos, and as last time, in 'the north south west and east' of the capital. The various similarities to the bombings two weeks earlier made it immediately apparent that these explosions were at best intended as a reminder of those fatal events, at worst to replicate them. This much Lilia established as she left the CMS building and paused to watch the breaking news on the television behind the reception desk.

'All the lines those stations are on are closed,' the young man on duty told her. 'You might get on the Bakerloo at Waterloo and change but it'll be chaos. Best try a bus. Or a taxi if you can find one.'

Heading north on the Waterloo Road, Lilia soon found that a lot of other people were having the same idea. Every bus stop was surrounded by train passengers unfamiliar with bus numbers and routes. Lilia crossed the road and headed west at the first junction, in the approximate direction of Victoria Station, and found the right bus stop. But the busses were already so full when they arrived that very few people managed to squeeze on and some busses did not stop at all. She was trapped in the crowd with more anxious people arriving all the time, the majority intent on their own safety and escape, and not at all neighbourly nor concerned about weaker individuals. The arrival of a blue helmeted UN peace-keeping force would not have seemed entirely incongruous, or a contingent of the Territorial Army backed, as in the war, by the Women's Royal Voluntary Service serving tea and sandwiches.

Lilia was aware of a perverse pleasure in being truly caught in the thick of things, in experiencing the breakdown of order that one watched with helpless anger and pity on TV every day in cities torn apart by war or natural catastrophes. Living where she did, she was often more a spectator than a participant in modern day problems and preoccupations and had not felt particularly threatened by the previous attacks, really no more than by 9/11. Rather, she had thought that she ought to so feel, ought to be afraid of the fundamental changes in everyday life that they seemed likely to set in motion. All the same, after half an hour of being jostled back and forth and constantly outflanked by later arrivals in attempts to board busses, the concept of queuing having apparently been entirely lost, she had had enough and was contemplating a very long walk to Victoria, when a taxi happened to stop just where she found herself temporarily on the edge of the crowd. The door opened and the passenger leaned out.

'Any four people want to share to Victoria?' He reached and grabbed the nearest outstretched hands and Lilia was among these lucky few.

Victoria Station was extremely crowded and every train was packed so that she had to stand most of the way but she arrived back in Bognor by late afternoon, earlier than she had originally planned. She therefore decided to stop by the hospital and visit Rose before rather than after supper.

Maureen Halliwell gave her a hero's welcome and, having watched coverage of the crisis more or less all afternoon, she was well informed. The bombs had been meant to explode but only the detonators did, which accounted for the strange popping sound reported from every site. The failure to ignite was probably due to the use of a particular homemade explosive that has a short life, and the bombers had escaped. It was still unknown whether they were of the same group as those a fortnight before or were independent operators. 'I don't think you should go up there again,' she concluded. 'It's not worth the risk.'

'How is Rose?'

'Still in her own world, but knitting and reading those letters. Not talking to me.' The nurse rolled her eyes in mock self-pity. 'But right now she's asleep. I just peeked in on her. Go home, dear, you look all in. Come and see her tomorrow.'

Rajah had been sick in the middle of the kitchen floor but was now sitting upright close to his dish, obviously waiting to be fed.

‘Oh dear, poor boy. Maybe I’ve been giving you too much rich food? Let’s go back to Whiskas, shall we. You must be hungry. And cheer up, I don’t think I’ll have to leave you again unless my new friend at the library comes up with something. I’ll just check my email while you eat though I’ll be very surprised if there’s anything yet.’

The CMS librarian had not yet written but something very interesting had arrived a few hours earlier.

From ravi@thinair.com
To Liliaz@yahoo.co.uk
RE: Rose McCormack

Dear Ms Zynofsky,

I hope you will not see this as an intrusion. I have read your articles about a Mrs Rose McCormack, who having suffered a stroke, was found on a beach in a place called Bognor, which I see is in southern England. I replied to the paper’s request for anyone who might know her or her family to get in touch but had no response to my emails. So I googled your name, discovered that you are a published author and found this address.

I think that I may be related to Mrs McCormack but would like to hear from you before saying more as it is a very strange story and I do not want to betray family secrets unnecessarily. If you could give me a little more information about your Rose McCormack I will write again.

Yours truly, Ravi Makrani

From Liliaz@yahoo.co.uk
To ravi@thinair.com
RE Rose McCormack

Dear Mr Makrani,

I shall never cease to be amazed at the powers of the internet. And gratified to be listed therein - or is it on? As you will no doubt have noticed, my own few books were published a long time ago and I could barely buy a cup of coffee with the amount of Public Lending

Rights I receive these days. I am very glad to respond to your inquiry.

Lilia wrote most of what she knew about Rose and Edward, including the fact that they had one son, but she excluded Joseph's name and the fact of his disappearance. She said that she did not know much of Rose's life after leaving Uganda in 1955 but did say that she had left Iganga several years before Edward and that she had lived in Bognor for at least the last ten years.

I'm going to write another article later and will email it to you. It has been a rather exhausting day. I was in London and I daresay you have seen the news. If you are indeed a relative of Rose I should be most glad to facilitate communications, depending on her doctors' opinion as to whether she is presently in a fit mental state. I look forward to hearing from you further.
Yours sincerely
Lilia Zynofsky

'I wonder what will come of that?' Lilia logged off and turned to address Rajah, who was now washing his whiskers at her feet. She picked him up and took him onto her lap. 'I am letting Mr Makrani make the next move,' she explained. 'Since I would imagine that one has to beware of impostors in such cases, bad people who hope that there is money to be made, legacies to be claimed.' She stroked Rajah under his chin and, gratifyingly, he began to purr. 'But I can't expect you to understand questions of morality, can I? And I must say that life would be a whole lot simpler without them, if sometimes nasty, brutish and short. And you, my darling, are a lot quicker to forgive me for leaving you than many humans might be.'

21

Maureen helped Rose into the armchair by the window of the hospital room.

'There you are, dear,' she said. 'You've got a nice view of the garden.'

Rose wished she could see the sea. She pointed to the pile of letters on the bedside cabinet.

'Still reading them, are we?' Maureen handed them to her. 'Now don't go getting upset. Ring this bell if you want me.'

Rose began to read the letters that Edward had written in September 1955, a few weeks after Joseph's disappearance while she was still staying in Jinja. They consisted mostly of Edward's comments on her search - he thought she should leave it to 'the authorities'. *'I have just received a very kind letter from the Governor expressing his sympathy in our loss.'* He kept wishing that she would return to Iganga. He had turned up unannounced, using the excuse of bringing her a photograph album she had requested, and was then upset when she had refused to go home with him.

He also informed her that Colin would be passing through Jinja on his way home. *'You will be as glad to see him as I. I am sure you wish that Colin and Penny were still in Jinja'* and he passed on messages from others at the Iganga mission, including the school pupils and teachers. *'The girls are very sad that you are not coming back – I had to say 'yet'. Angela Nthamburi asked me to give a special assembly where some of them stood up and led the prayers, some of which they had written themselves. I am going to address the boys. One or two of them have come up to me and said how they hope we will find 'their good friend Joseph' soon. I don't know how well they knew him. All this helps to give me the strength to carry on. I hope it will you too. Edward'.*

Rose closed her eyes.

God is giving me strength, Edward, and that's exactly why I haven't given up looking for Joseph, unlike you, apparently - you don't know how well they *knew* Joseph? Is he in the past tense to you already? I suppose it hasn't occurred to you that Sir Andrew's letter is the official way of drawing a line under an unfortunate occurrence, moving on. You are so ready to believe the best of everyone, especially 'the authorities'. How can I come home and live with you and carry on as normal, as if nothing has happened? As if Joseph has simply gone off back to England to school, as he would have by now. Is that what you are pretending? You are a great one at pretence, to yourself I mean.

But no, I daresay you have already written to the school saying he won't be coming back, not now, not ever. Well, that's true at least, I will never let him go to a boarding school again. And I shan't pretend he's ill and needs me, I shall simply resign. They should never have sent us to Iganga, just when Joseph had gone to England. Jinja was the only home he knew. Yes, I do wish Colin and Penny were still here. Joseph would have run to them, he could have stayed with them anytime if that's what he'd wanted. None of this would have happened. *Where have I put that photograph album?*

The tea trolley roused her as the cheerful volunteer placed a cup on the windowsill.

'There you are, dear. That will perk you up. Bit early in the day for a nap.' She trundled off to her next client.

Rose took a sip and returned to the letters. She could not remember ever having read them. Perhaps she had started and then given up in face of Edward's dogged descriptions of his everyday life at the mission. There were two letters written in October and two in November. Evidently she had replied to none of them. Edward worried as to what she was doing, felt '*a little stymied*' by her silence. The church was '*progressing*', Peter was going to help canvass the better-off Protestants in town for financial donations, or perhaps, he had suggested, they would give items. The font, the pulpit and so on. *'In memory of their ancestors, a very good idea I thought.'* Angela was to get the older girls to make kneelers and Edward had decided to add woodwork to the curriculum so the boys could make pews. *"Even though some of the parents won't like it. But all work and no play...besides some of these lads won't make the academic grade even if we did ever manage to expand to highers and they certainly won't get in to Mwiri College."*

Then he told her at length about an initiative by girls at Gulu, a very good school, he reminded her. Apparently there were taking round the news of how important it is for girls to get education.

"*It was one of the Archbishop of Canterbury's main messages last May, if you remember. I think you gave a talk on it didn't you? These girls have even formed a society, the 'Society for the Promotion of Women's Education'. They raised money, got a lorry from the Community Education Department and got the DC to write round to the chiefs in the areas they had chosen to explain their coming! They put on a show, little plays, songs, some cookery and needlework demos. Anyway, when they heard about it, our girls wanted to do something similar, on a much smaller scale, but really no one is free to organise it"*. Rose knew what was coming. *"Very much up your street of course"*. Of course.

He asked if Mary could use her sewing machine, said she had offered to try her hand at a bit of needlework teaching. "*Perhaps then she'll feel up to taking on the Sunday School in your absence."* Later he told her that even Patrick had said he wanted to help teach the youngest children. "*It is so important to instruct the little ones at a simpler and more enjoyable level. I know they find my sermons very boring and Peter's even more so. I am afraid he went on for a whole hour last week! Some of it about tomorrow's return of the kabaka, about which there is a good deal of talk as you can imagine."* He also told her of the latest visit from his one-time rival, Father John, when they had discussed an article in The Times on the subject. *'And he told me that Thomas remains in seclusion at Mill Hill. He is much missed here"*.

Oh Thomas, how I missed you! But Edward had gone back to his main theme. "*Your Mothers' Union ladies miss you too. I am glad to say some of them have organised themselves to make the altar cloth, and then they plan a new MU banner, but no one has yet plucked up the courage to lead prayers or give a talk. Of course they still use our sitting room and Mary serves tea and I try to drop in, but I'm afraid the women from further away will stop coming without something that involves them more."*

Rose put down the letters, exhausted by their ancient demands. How hard Edward had tried to make her return. *'Pulled out all the stops'*, as people said these days. *Pressed all the right buttons*. But I didn't, couldn't, respond. I think I resented him being able to carry on as if nothing had happened, actually coming into his own by the sound of it, even making friends with Father John. Whereas I...what did I feel? That if I let go for one instant Joseph would finally slip away from me, and, if only I could keep the faith, he would return. And I did not just wait, go on waiting, surely I...yes, here it is...

"December 5th
Dear Rose,

I am very unhappy that you have decided to go to Mombasa, and without consulting me. I cannot think that it is a wise decision. And I have to say that there are financial considerations, although I am sure you will be welcome at the mission for the time being. It is also a pity that Colin will be unable to see you. He's flying home from Kampala next week as I may have told you. I'm expecting a brief visit any day. I think he would prefer to go slowly by ship but that's not the way these days. He's to have a parish in Sussex somewhere. Not looking forward to it, but putting on a brave face by the sound of things. I am very much looking forward to spending whatever time there is together. I daresay he will subject me to some soul-searching, as in our Jinja days. Shall be proud to show him the church at least. I am planning the consecration for early January. I had hoped you would be there.

Edward".

I don't care about your church, Edward. Is that terrible? And I will never come back to Iganga, never. As I told you when you came to see me. Face to face. Why won't you face up to things? *Don't be so timid*, that's what Colin used to say. Remember, when he was trying to persuade you to go and evangelise at the labour camp at the dam? I think that was one of the reasons they sent us to Jinja in the first place, because Colin already had more than enough to do.

Dear Colin. But I don't want to see him, not now. He will try to persuade me to return to the mission. He will think it is my duty and so will Penny. She didn't want to go back to England any more than he did, even though it meant she will be near her boys. But what do they know, either of them? Who would put duty before looking for their lost child?

22

'The police have just shot dead a terrorist suspect on the Underground,' Maureen informed Lilia as she arrived on the ward shortly after ten a.m. 'South London, Stockwell station? Apparently services on the Victoria and Northern lines have been suspended, so it's as well you didn't go to London today.'

'Oh dear what is happening to our country?' sighed Lilia. 'They are saying these are probably British men, boys I daresay, using explosives found in a stockpile in Leeds. They'll probably all have Yorkshire accents.'

'I don't care what they sound like, the sooner they are caught the safer we'll all be,' retorted Maureen. 'There's the biggest manhunt going on and it looks like they've already found one of them. Thank God we live in a well-organised country, say I.'

Lilia considered a reply to the effect that organisation wasn't everything if you thought of Hitler or indeed Saddam Hussein, as, quite likely, Iraq had been a lot better organised before the invasion two years previously, but she decided it wasn't the time to seem disloyal.

'I'll go and see Rose if that's alright.'

'Rose?'

Rose seemed to rouse at the sound of her name and picked up the letter that lay on her lap. She did not look up at Lilia.

'It's only me.' Lilia pulled up a chair next to her and touched her lightly on the arm in greeting.

Rose sighed and handed the letter to Lilia.

'Right, I'll be glad to read it. I'll just find my glasses.' Lilia scrabbled in her bag. 'Now, where have you got to? "*January 1956*". I've got some catching up to do. Maybe I could read the rest later? Here goes anyway. *"The church is finished and consecrated at last!* So *many people came that the Bishop, Peter and I had to repeat our sermons to the crowds outside. I think mine was rather good for once, the Bishop complimented me. I did try very hard to speak to the congregation in ways that they would understand, to reach into their hearts. Colin helped me prepare when he was here. I think he would have been satisfied with the result of his efforts.'*

Edward did try to change, and it was partly to please me. What was it he did? He went out of his way to do?

'*"February 14th*
Dear Rose,

Mama Ntate came to see Angela to ask for her help in persuading her husband to allow Leah to complete another year of secondary school and then try for nursing college. She says Leah wants this with all her heart. But Papa Ntate is afraid that if she has been to the town he will not be able to find a good man to marry her. I have agreed to go and see him when I can spare the time. We secured a small grant for the boys' school and some of the workmen from the church agreed to stay on to build it..."

Here he goes again. Perhaps if I wave her on she will get the message. Yes, that's it.

"Cedric asked me to..."

Further! Further! .

"1st March, I have been to see Leah's father."

Yes.

"Stephen came with me to translate. Success! Papa Ntate will even allow Leah to apply to Mengo after her year in Jinja. I told him that nursing is regarded in Europe as a noble profession, not at all demeaning. I told him about Florence Nightingale leaving the comforts of a very good home to go and nurse soldiers in the Crimea. I am afraid that he was rather intrigued to hear that Britain had fought a war against another Christian country in support of a Mohammedan one!

"He was still very doubtful about allowing Leah to go to the capital but I explained that Mengo is the very best hospital, the Government recognises it as such, and that girls go there from all over Uganda, many the daughters of the biggest chiefs. I said that, since it is a Christian hospital, the girls also spend much of their time in studying the Bible and learning how to live a good life. And finally, I said that you had studied there also. He reflected on all this

and then gave his judgment: 'Leah will bring honour on our family.' I wish you could have seen the happiness on Leah's face when her mother gave her the verdict. I hope you will be glad. It is hard to write without response, no longer knowing what is in your mind. I telephone sometimes to ask how you are, I don't know if they tell you.

Edward"

Rose sat very still, her eyes open though apparently not focussed on anything in particular. She seemed about to speak so Lilia waited silently, barely breathing, and at last her patience was rewarded.

'Leah helped me,' she said. 'In my clinic.'

'I just found out that you were a nurse,' nodded Lilia. 'From the CMS records in London. Although I didn't realise you trained in Uganda.'

But Rose was again silent.

'She can't go off to Kampala for months on end,' Edward objects. 'She has enough to do as it is, organising the women and children's activities.'

'She is wasting her talents,' Penny argues. 'We are desperately short of trained nurses and Rose already has all her wartime first aid experience. You shouldn't deny her the opportunity to make her full contribution to our work here.'

'I can't leave Joseph, he's too small.' I am excited but a little apprehensive.

'He'll be fine,' says Penny. 'With Matthew and Mark for company. It'll be good for him. And you'll be back at weekends.'

'Bye bye Mummy, see you Friday,' Joseph kisses me before running off to play again.

The classroom work is hard, though most of the other girls seem to prefer it to working on the wards. They're not so keen on getting their hands dirty!

'Tell us about your experiences in the war, Rose,' says the tutor. 'Among the bombed out ruins of London.'

'We often had to treat the wounded where they lay in all the dust and broken glass and buildings that could collapse at any moment,' I say. 'While we waited for the ambulances.' I am surprised myself at how brave I must have been. I don't tell them about finding the dead.

'I would like you to help organise some public health education,' the tutor says another day. 'To show people the importance of proper sanitation and hygiene. And at the same time we shall also try to make new converts or win back lost souls, people who have fallen away from Christianity.'

We have devised a little play about a hookworm sufferer, played by James, one of the dressers, who collapses at work and we, his workmates, persuade him to go to hospital. There, as nurses and doctors, we use a flannel graph to show him how the hookworms got into his body and how they can be prevented from getting in again. He drinks his medicine and goes back to work and tells his colleagues what he has learnt.

'Hallelujah brother, you have been given a new life, let us all go and buy shoes and then we will dig a latrine together.'

Our audience, a small crowd on a street corner, likes this bit! Especially, I think, seeing a white woman doing such dirty work.

One of the girls, this time it is Martha, steps out of the group. 'James has new life in his body,' she says. 'And if you follow the Lord Jesus he will give you new life of the spirit and eternal life with Him and his Father, the Lord God, in heaven ever after.'

'Onward Christian soldiers,' we all sing and march up and down accompanied by some of the crowd and James enthusiastically acts out how he has found Jesus. Overacts perhaps, he rolls about for quite a long time on the ground as if possessed, speaking in what sounds like a mixture of languages and calling on Jesus over and over to save him.

I am showing all this as best I can to everyone at the mission. Of course the boys love the marching up and down part best! As we stop Joseph salutes me solemnly as he has seen the soldiers from the barracks do. I pick him up and hug him tightly as he wriggles to be set down.

'And how many latrines have been dug?' asks Edward.

I don't know. 'But our church attendance has increased.'

'Hallelujah!' Colin applauds.

'I can't wait for you to start work in Jinja,' says Penny. 'Though I expect you'll find it hard at first.'

'It must have been hard nursing in Africa, what with the different customs and not everyone speaking the same language.' Lilia was wishing that she knew what was going through Rose's mind.

Rose looked at her intently for a moment but said nothing and then apparently drifted off again.

I made many mistakes, upsetting people, not understanding their point of view. I have got used now to patients wandering off if they feel like it. I am showing a European doctor round the hospital.

'Why are there so many beds in use but no-one in them?' he wants to know.

'That one's gone shopping,' I point to the beds in turn. 'She's gone to find firewood, and she's gone home for the day to look after her child.'

'And this one?'

'Oh she's gone to sell a goat.' He is not amused!

Rose smiled.

'What, Rose, what?'

Again Rose looked at Lilia as if considering whether to let her in on a secret.

'They had their own medicine too,' she nodded.

There is a Christian girl who had her first baby a few days ago and has come back to hospital because she is haemorrhaging. Her grandfather, a respected elder, has come with her. I walk into the ward and there he is praying for her recovery, and spraying saliva and well-chewed medicine, plant material I think, over her face and body. Of course we are treating her as well and she is recovering.

Here is another man, also Christian, who has been successfully treated for malaria but is suffering from the usual after effects – aching muscles, dizziness and weakness. He is far more worried about these symptoms than he was about the malaria itself.

'They are normal, not serious. You are getting better,' I tell him.

'I must go home and perform sacrifices,' he tells me as he rolls up his blanket. 'Only then will I be well.'

Rose sighed deeply just as Maureen came into the room.

'You must rest, Rose. Have a lie down. We don't want to undo the progress you've made, do we?'

She put her arm around Rose's shoulders and under her armpit, preparing to lift her, but Rose shrugged herself free and, a little shakily, stood.

'I wasn't just a 'missionary wife', was I?' she said.

Maureen looked at Lilia, puzzled.

'She was a nurse,' said Lilia. 'She actually trained in Africa. And then she ran her own clinic. Maybe more than one.'

Rose looked from Lilia to the nurse, nodded as if satisfied, and walked to the bed.

23

'I should go too,' Lilia hovered at the doorway after Maureen had left with her usual reminder about pressing the bell if in need.

Rose beckoned Lilia to come closer and took her hand. 'But was I a *good* nurse? A Christian nurse?' She whispered, her forehead twisted in concentration.

'I don't really know what you mean,' Lilia began carefully but Rose had closed her eyes tightly so she sat down quietly beside her and continued to hold her hand.

'It is not for us to ask why bad things happen to us, only trust in God and give glory to His name and He will give you courage and victory even over death,' I tell my patients. 'The day will come when sorrow and sighing shall cease and death shall be no more.' Did I know what I was saying? It didn't help me at all when I lost Joseph. But I did try again. I know I did.

Rose's face contracted as if she were in pain, then she opened her eyes, reached for the remaining letters and thrust them at Lilia who began to read.

'"July 28th 1956
My dearest Rose,

It was wonderful to hear your voice. Do believe that, had you called sooner, I would have cancelled my trip for the far more precious opportunity of seeing you again. However, too much is now arranged... I am only too happy that you are able to use your skills again ... There must be much to do as Kenya recovers from its troubles. I will write from Nigeria. And still be looking forward as I am now to visiting you after Christmas. I am overjoyed - if that is possible!

Edward

"August 7th
My dearest Rose,

It has been a most interesting visit so far. I believe I might be able to set up something similar in Iganga. The concept of 'malignant malnutrition' seems a most useful one and processing the groundnut locally would also provide more employment...Do you remember the talk at the British Museum where we met? November 1945. I was still in uniform. I found a copy of the talk the other day amongst my papers. How the Church in Africa is rooted in the villages and countryside, the old slogan 'The Gospel and the plough' still appropriate, despite urbanisation and the new aspirations of the young men who had seen service overseas in the war. 'The promise of a new social integrity lies in the betterment of rural conditions'. Anyway, my little - pipedream at present - is part of that.

Oh my darling, I can see you still, standing alone in a corner after the talk, near the tea urn and the first thing I said was..."'

'Could you possibly pour me some tea,' Rose interrupted, in a tone that sounded to Lilia like the clipped British of wartime films. She then continued in a London accent much broader than her usual careful way of speaking. 'He sounded that posh and I were right cross cos I thought he thought I was the waitress or something but then I saw he had his arm in a sling so I calmed down. He seemed to like talking to me…'

'It's such a relief not having to pretend to be a hero,' he says. 'I suppose it's because you were in the thick of things yourself.' Then he cocks his head on one side and looks at me, sizing me up so to speak. 'What brought you here, to this talk?'

'A girl like me you mean?" says I, on my high horse again. I thought he meant it was too clever for me, I was getting beyond my station. I soon put him straight!

'I often come here. I want to know more about the world. I'd sign up like a shot today if I didn't have me Mum to take care of.'

'You wouldn't say that if you'd been where I've been,' he says.

'Where's that then?' I'm still annoyed.

'In a POW camp in Burma. I can't tell you how good it feels to be home.'

'So you're not thinking of going for a missionary then?'

He shakes his head. 'I came here to please my father, he's a minister in Edinburgh but I think he always wished he had become a missionary himself so the next best thing is if I am. The speaker's a friend of his.'

Mum highly approves of Edward, 'A proper gentleman, he is. I'm leaving you in good hands Rose.' As if that was all she had been waiting for.

'Let's give it a go, Edward, now Mum's gone. I fancy Africa myself.' Rose looked startled at having spoken aloud and quickly nodded at the letters in Lilia's hand.

Edward had written about a Training Centre for young women who were engaged to be married to young ordinands or teachers. '*The girls are taught all branches of domestic science to fit them for home-making and looking after their husbands and children. They are then taught to teach others so that ...'* Rose waved this aside with impatience and Lilia read quickly with some paraphrasing. *"They assured me that life for Christian women, where they are the only wife, is much to be preferred."'* He asked her to think about where they might apply to be posted, *"in due course"*, and then she read the last line. "*Please be sure that I shall be devoting the 23rd to prayers for our beloved son,"* and Rose nodded, as if she remembered he had written this.

The next letter, from the beginning of September, brought "'*some very sad news I am afraid. John came to see me. He had heard from Mill Hill. My dear, Thomas has passed away, almost certainly by his own hand, although there was an 'open verdict'. He fell from the roof of the chapel. No one saw what happened or could say what he might have been doing up there. It happened on the 23rd August."'*

'The best Christian I have ever met,' whispered Rose.

'Edward seems to have thought so too,' said Lilia, whose eyes had skipped ahead. 'Listen. *"I have written formally to Father John, as from us both, to say how much we loved and valued him as a friend and fellow crusader for Christ, how he embodied, in fact, the very best of Christian virtues and had been a great comfort to us personally in times of sorrow. And I have asked John to forward this to Thomas' family."'* Was he trying to assure them that Thomas had not committed suicide? Lilia wondered what Rose thought.

Edward had sent a cutting from *'Outlook'*, one of the missionary sources that Lilia had herself intended to consult if she had not had to leave the CMS library so abruptly. It was about an old couple that he hoped they would emulate one day. *'"After 40 years service they still go to visit some of their old postings around the world, though they are both over 80."'* When they first were sent to Uganda they had had to walk all the way from the coast. 'O*ver 600 miles! As you'll see, one of Mr Stuart's achievements was helping to plan Budo College which had its Golden Jubilee this year (I was invited but did not go, quite a spectacle by all accounts) and, presumably before that was properly established, the then Katikiro, Sir Apolo Kagwa, had sent two of his sons to study at a college in Ceylon where Mr Stuart was then principal and other Baganda chiefs had then followed his example."'*

Lilia looked up to see if Rose was still listening. She herself found all this insight into a long lost world fascinating but Rose seemed to be waiting for something in particular. Her face became alternately sad and angry as Lilia read the final letter.

'"December 12th
My dear Rose,

I must repeat that I cannot support your proposed trip to India. You simply cannot rush off to another country on such slim evidence. A passing glimpse. In a big city. Where people come and go all the time. My dear, where would you begin?

Nor, I also regret to say, can I approach the Governor and ask him to contact the Indian Government. Perhaps if India was still under British rule some sort of informal approach might have been possible, but in the new circumstances I fear it would make him look foolish and embarrass the Indians in having to refuse. I am devastated at your consequent refusal to see me. I beg you to reconsider. Edward."'

'I had a visitor,' said Rose. 'At the mission in Mombasa.'

‘Who was that?’

Ali announces her. ‘Mrs Rose, there is an Indian lady to see you. Mrs ...?’

‘Mehta.’ The voice emerges from behind our cook and self-appointed protector. Kamala pushes impatiently past him.

‘Thank you, Ali. Mrs Mehta is an old friend, from Jinja.’ Ali retreats, grumbling a little, unconvinced. I don’t suppose we get many Indian visitors. ‘Kamala, how wonderful to see you!’ I want to hug and kiss her but am not sure it is their way. She sits beside me, accepts a glass of water from the still inquisitive Ali, turns to me.

‘I have some news. Maybe it is nothing but ...’

My heart stops. ‘Joseph?’

She looks at me sadly, then nods, as if reluctant to speak. ‘Nilu thinks he saw him. In Bombay. I was visiting Nilu in his school, he is not studying well, that is why I went. In fact, we are thinking of transferring him to a school in England. We were in a rickshaw going to Chowpatti Beach for an evening outing – like we do in Jinja, by the lakeshore – and suddenly Nilu pointed to a passing car. A big car, a limousine, I think you would call it. A rich person’s car. “That was Joseph,” he said. “Sitting in the back.” By then it was too late for me to see for myself. “Don’t be silly,” I told him. “Why would Joseph be here? You are imagining things.”

But he insisted. So much he insisted. So I told our driver to turn around and follow the car but it was going too fast and the driver soon was far ahead and out of our sight.’ She pauses, reaches out to touch my hand. ‘We were very upset, both of us. In fact, Nilu did not want to continue with our outing. We just went home. He made me promise to come and tell you all this as soon as I got back to Mombasa. I am on my way home to Jinja.’

Rose sat up straight and gripped Lilia’s hand more tightly. ‘A boy who was a friend of Joseph was sure he saw him in Bombay.’

‘I told you Joseph is alive,’ I scream down the telephone at Edward when he refuses to do anything. ‘I know he is and here is proof. Now I shall never see him. I hate you. Don't try and contact me again.'

Rose let go Lilia's hand and fell back on the pillow. 'But I didn't go to look for him.' Her face sank in misery, tears started in her eyes and rolled down her cheeks unchecked. She spoke aloud but it seemed as to herself, as if she were just realising something for the first time. 'And I lost all hope. They say I lost my mind. All I remember is living in a hut by the beach and the tide coming in and out, in and out… and after that a long, long blank.' Now she focussed on Lilia. 'Why didn't I go to India? Why didn't I just *go*?'

'My dear, Edward was right, surely? It would have seemed a very long shot, so unlikely? Rest now, I'll ask Maureen to come and see if you'd like something to help you sleep. I should go home and feed Rajah.' Lilia spoke in soothing palliatives but her mind was racing with this new possibility of what had happened to Joseph.

THE CAT WHO WENT TO SEA

Rajah, as his name suggested, lived a life of luxury and leisure. If he so chose, he sat all day on the velvet cushions of an exquisitely carved chair of Indian origin that was the pride of his mistress Wanda's otherwise somewhat shabby and certainly overcrowded basement flat. His food arrived at regular intervals and was of the most expensive brands, when not indeed fresh from the fish stalls on the seafront and cooked to a mouth-watering perfection on the ancient gas-stove in the tiny kitchen. In the minute conservatory, really more a lean-to, and within very easy reach, there was a daily-refreshed litter tray for his convenience. Most necessary on the days when Wanda spoilt them both with one of her wonderful fish curries.

So Rajah did not have to go anywhere or do anything and most of the time this was just what he did, or did not do. He made an occasional progress around the small backyard from which, before he became too fat, he had sometimes made forays into neighbouring domains, and which, very rarely, he was obliged to defend from rash invaders (they were inevitably much smaller, if fitter, and did not repeat the attempt). His only other obligation was to show a little gratitude and affection towards his doting mistress, or at least appear to show, for she had much experience and was no fool where cats were concerned. Rajah seemed as content as had been his predecessors, of whom of course, and unlike any human namesake, he had no knowledge. Surely his life would continue in this fashion until old age, or possibly gout, carried him off, forcing his mistress to transfer her affections to another. For some cat she must have, as a necessary, if not perfectly sufficient, companion in her straightened circumstances.

Rajah, had no reason, no good reason for a cat that is, to go missing, but, on one of those rare days when work had taken his mistress to London, missing he did go. Some people suspect the Chinese restaurants and some again the fur traders when their loved ones disappear, but such persons could not have even encountered Rajah if he had not chosen to leave his home and, again, tabby is not high in demand. Wanda made other enquiries. Imagine her surprise, given his sedentary and heretofore unadventurous history, when she heard from one of the fishermen that a tabby cat had been seen on the beach several days past lurking around the boats. Furthermore, that on casting their nets later that night, one of the crews had found this same cat hiding in the hold of their boat, whence, to their utter astonishment he, for from his size it was surely a he, had leapt overboard and swum to a passing cruise ship that was, it was believed, heading for the Orient.

Well, could that really be my Rajah she thought, because it is perfectly true that one tabby cat is much like another, however much their owner may like to think otherwise. But when he did not re-appear, even in a sadly deceased state, she began to think it rather likely that it was and to tell herself many stories of where he was and what was happening to him. Perhaps he had become, Dick Whittington style, the prized possession of some eastern potentate. Perhaps some empress – or Ranee – was even now petting and feeding him as she had done. On the whole Wanda did not wish him ill, whilst feeling a little piqued that he had appreciated her so little. So the months went by until one day, whilst on the seafront purchasing fish for a curry, she was handed a bottle.

"Seems to have a letter in it, addressed to you, Wanda," said the fisherman, whose name was Bill, though that is really irrelevant to the story. "Came in with the tide this morning."

Wanda took the bottle home, fished out the letter and read it aloud. This is what it said:

"Sweet mistress mine,
I went to sea
To see what I could see.
What did I find?
Where'er I roamed
Cold, hunger, cruelty.
No one cares for me like thee.
There is no place like home.
O! Hasten here
Please rescue me
Faithful I'll be
Forgive me dear.
Your loving
Rajah

c/o The Old Customhouse, Tawnipore."

One would like to say that Wanda packed her bags and set off in pursuit of her erstwhile companion, who had apparently seen the error of his ways but really it was impractical, as the reader will appreciate. The cost of a ticket for one thing. Quite beyond her means. Sadly, poor Rajah, by his own admission, made his bed and will have to lie on it. And it does not sound as if that is a velvet cushion, thought Wanda. One must forgive her that slight touch of schadenfreude. Anyway, what would she tell Ranee, who had settled in very happily on her velvet cushions after being rescued by the Cat Protection League from a life of hardship and neglect. It seemed unlikely that she would venture far.

24

'Of course I would never really do such a thing,' Lilia turned to speak to Rajah, expecting to see him on his cushion on the Indian chair, but he had walked to the kitchen and had his back to her. 'I'll be out to feed you in a moment,' she called.

She began to print the story and meanwhile checked her email where she found a message from the CMS librarian. Penny Colman had been contacted and was willing to speak to Lilia. There was a phone number and the first numbers sounded familiar. Lilia dialled, her hand shaking a little in excitement.

'Eastbourne 352258,' it was an old woman's voice but still firm and assured. Eastbourne, of course, what luck, thought Lilia, at most an hour's journey along the coast. She began to explain but Penny Colman cut her short.

'You may come and visit me,' she said. 'It is better to speak of some things face to face. You may come this afternoon if you wish. There is a good bus service.' The line went dead.

'Coffee,' Lilia said aloud. 'I need some coffee and a bite to eat.' She stood and walked towards the kitchen.

Rajah did not turn to greet her as he usually did.

'It's a pity you can't make it for me, instead of sitting there in a sulk.' She sighed. 'I've had a busy morning,' But then she noticed his shoulders heaving, saw him stretch out his head close to the ground and she knelt quickly beside him as he retched out the contents of his stomach, the sides of his body pumping like small bellows. 'Oh my poor darling, I must take you to the vet, except oh dear, it will now have to be tomorrow, first thing in the morning, I promise.'

She ate her lunch watching the news, which was still, as last night, showing a clip of the shocked passenger who had witnessed the point blank shooting of the suspected terrorist. He was clearly uneasy that so many shots should have been fired by the police into a man who was already pinned to the ground, or rather floor of the train carriage, yet his voice was low, his tone neutral. Lilia, herself feeling very uneasy and a little guilty about Rajah's condition, admired his restraint, as if he understood that desperate times sanctioned desperate measures, unless of course he had simply been told not to say too much. In the last two weeks one had become prepared to consider anything in this normally, and blessedly, peaceful island and much more appreciative of the ubiquitous CCTV cameras that had already enabled images of four suspects to be released. Clearly, much was happening of which the general population was unaware and for which they should consider themselves lucky.

But then the breaking news line announced the identification of yesterday's victim. He was a 27 year old Brazilian electrician named Jean Charles de Menezes with no connection to the bombings nor any criminal group, whose visa had expired two years before and who had presumably simply tried to outrun the authorities. Lilia switched off with heavier heart, put a little food in Rajah's dish just in case he should feel hungry and set off to catch the bus to Eastbourne.

Penny Colman lived in a retirement home on the seafront, not far from where the Downs reared precipitously above the southern end of the promenade, where began the South Downs Way, along which one could walk as far as Winchester. Frail in body, she was stooped and walked with a stick, her eyes were as sharp as her tone had suggested and there was little wrong with her hearing. She motioned Lilia to sit opposite her on the other side of a small table, which held a tray of tea and cake, where the late afternoon light fell full on Lilia's face but cast her own in shadow. She indicated that Lilia should pour the tea with the slightest of gestures. It was easy to see her in joint charge of a mission, making things happen in the most unpromising circumstances, easy to understand that she would have been irked by the wasted potential she saw in Rose and make it her business to see that it was developed to the benefit of all concerned.

'Becoming a nurse there was the making of her,' she told Lilia. 'She really blossomed as she never could have at home. She was much more suited to the life than Edward. Or so I thought.' She frowned, even now disapproving. 'It was terrible for them of course losing Joseph, but it helped nobody, her running away like that, and harmed more than a few, Edward included. He was only in his forties when he died, you know, in Iganga. I don't suppose he looked after himself very well.

'And she completely let herself go in Mombasa. She moved out of the mission and set up what you would today call a 'drop in centre' right by the beach for the displaced young men who had been fighting the British and were afraid to go home. I suspect they were looking after her as much as the other way about in the end, judging by the state Edward found her in when he went to take her back to England. She was in a mental hospital near here for years and years, you know that was what happened then, especially to women. Drug them up and lock them away. We used to visit her quite often, Colin especially. But when they moved her to Bognor I didn't keep in touch. I seemed to have enough to do with my family and I wasn't getting any younger…perhaps you think me selfish, cruel even, but I always thought she was cruel to Edward.' She paused and then smiled, a little ruefully, thought Lilia. 'Although one should not judge and it was certainly through all his suffering that Edward then found the strength and wisdom to do God's real work. God moves in mysterious ways, as it is said.'

'Edward was naturally more a man of action, I gather?' Lilia was trying to understand. 'Building things, like the church. Developing the school. I've read some of his letters, Rose gave them to me.'

'His letters?'

'To Rose, after Joseph went missing, for about a year he wrote to her in Jinja, then Mombasa. They were nearly reconciled.'

'Ah yes, then. We were already back here by then. I was thinking of later when…' she stopped and shook her head. 'It's all so long ago. Look, I have something for you.' She stood with difficulty, hobbled to an old-fashioned roll-top desk and from one of its inner compartments extracted a small, faded photograph album. 'It belonged to Rose and Edward, he left it here when he stayed with us in case she ever wanted it again.' She spoke quickly as if to discourage any questions. 'Take it to her, it sounds as if it might mean something now and perhaps even give her some comfort.'

The pages of the album were crumbling at the edges and slightly stuck together where the adhesive paper corners that held the photographs had become bent or detached. The photos themselves were black and white and small save for one of Joseph pictured sitting on a rock in the sea. "AGED 2. MOMBASA" Lilia read the caption handwritten beneath. This photo had been enlarged the fill the whole page and, somewhat garishly, tinted. But he was beautiful nevertheless, with a shock of dark curls around his face, beaming at the camera, his head protected by a wide-brimmed floppy hat, his eyes a little squinted against the sun, and his feet dangling in a pool, a fishing net in one hand. There were others of him as a baby on the lap of a very young Rose, with a serious pipe-smoking Edward, standing fair and gangling over his little family; as a toddler pushing some sort of wooden truck; sitting on some steps with a couple of African boys, all three bare-chested and without shoes, and, aged about five, with his parents standing outside a wooden building with another European family, a couple and two slightly older boys.

'That's me, and Colin my husband, God rest his soul, and our boys, Matthew and Mark. We were together in a mission in – '

'Jinja, I know.'

'Of course you do. I must say your detective work is impressive. It's very good of you to take the time.' Again she seemed to be considering saying something further but changing her mind.

'What do you think happened to Joseph?' Lilia asked.

'It was most likely that he drowned in the lake,' said Penny without hesitation. 'I had left Africa by then but that's what everyone at the time thought, from what I gathered, including Edward. It was certainly what the police thought.'

'Yes, I've read the news cuttings. And I suppose it was unlikely that a child of Joseph's age travelled alone to Mombasa as Rose thought?'

'No, that was possible, children did travel on the train without their family, my boys did once, to stay with some friends in Mombasa one summer, though of course we made sure there was someone keeping an eye on them. But I didn't think that's what Joseph had done. You see,' she hesitated and then spoke as if with reluctance. 'I knew Rose used to take him to play in the lake. No-one else did, it wasn't healthy, never mind any other dangers, crocs and so on, and I absolutely forbade my two to go. But she said Joseph loved the water so much, a real water baby she called him. So long as he never went on his own, she said.'

‘But he might have.’

‘Yes. So, you see, it really was the most likely explanation.’ Penny took Lilia’s teacup, saucer and plate and stacked them with her own, as if to conclude the interview. ‘Otherwise I am sure more people would have supported Rose in her search, would have pursued other possibilities.’

‘Rose thinks he went to India,’ said Lilia. ‘A friend of his, an Indian boy who was at school there, told his mother he saw him in a car.’

Penny looked up sharply. ‘Now that is impossible.’

‘Rose has never stopped blaming herself for not going after him,’ Lilia told her. ‘Nor forgiven Edward for not letting her.’

‘Ah,’ said Penny and sighed deeply. She looked troubled and Lilia waited for her to say more but her face was set, her eyes downcast.

‘It’s extraordinary how little you have changed,’ Lilia glanced again at the photograph as she closed the album and put it in her bag. Penny’s hair, though now white, was cut in the same no nonsense short style with the same slight wave across the front and her lean, angular face had sagged little with age.

‘I never took much trouble with my appearance,’ she brushed this aside and suddenly spoke more urgently. ‘Keep in touch, Lilia. I’ll come and visit Rose if you think it would help her recover. You’ve got my number. And I’ll ring you if I think of anything else.’

25

'I'm going to visit Rose,' Lilia patted Rajah, who, for once, was sitting on the sofa beside her rather than on the Indian chair. He had just polished off a late and large breakfast of lightly poached coley fillet, following their visit to the vet. 'I won't stay long I promise. And then we'll sit outside in the sun together and take it easy. That will make a nice change, won't it? For me, anyway.' She stood to carry her coffee mug to the kitchen and was immediately followed by Rajah, who sat expectantly at her feet.

'Are you really hungry again?' she reached down to stroke his head. 'You must be feeling better, my darling. I'm so happy there's nothing really wrong with you. But I'm not sure I should feed you again yet. We don't want to have to go to the vet again, now do we?' Rajah wound himself around her legs and purred. 'Oh, you charmer. Maybe just a little bit then. You know,' she said as she scraped the last of the fish into Rajah's dish. 'If you'd gone running off to India I would have tried to find you, however much it cost.'

Rose was overwhelmed to receive the album. 'I thought it was lost for ever,' she said softly, slowly tracing Joseph's two year old face in the fishing photo with one finger. She bent to kiss him. 'We're looking for you,' she said. 'Mummy will find you.'

Lilia was alarmed. 'There are pictures of Iganga,' she thought to divert her. 'Penny knew nothing of them, of course. I wonder if you'd recognise any of the people? It would be nice for me to put some faces to names.'

Rose frowned. 'Iganga?' she said. '"The place of spirits?"' She shivered and began to turn the pages over and back, peering closely at the photos and mumbling softly. Finally, she began to point to them one by one and spoke more clearly and with increasing confidence. 'Stephen. He helped me run the clinics. Peter Kyasi, the main African priest and Mary his wife. And that is ,' she pointed to a small and solemn boy who was standing very straight for his picture to be taken. 'Patrick their son. Younger than Joseph. Too young for him to play with.' She put down the album suddenly and lay back in her chair as her eyes began to flood with tears. 'That's all he wanted, Joseph, someone to play with. That's why he went off to Jinja.'

'Oh Rose, hush,' Lilia tried to comfort her, an arm around her thin shoulders as she sobbed. 'You mustn't keep blaming yourself so. You'll make yourself ill again.'

'Go to Africa!' Rose said suddenly, sitting bolt upright and shrugging Lilia off in the process. 'Go to all the same places. Pick up the trail. And don't give up.' She turned to Lilia as if it was all perfectly clear.

'I don't think you are quite well enough…' began Lilia.

'Not me. You! On my behalf. As my representative. You know where to go and in Mombasa…' She closed her eyes and frowned briefly before opening them again. 'Bamburi Beach, that's what it was called. Ask for the Hindu Cottages.' She gazed past Lilia, remembering. 'It's such a beautiful long empty sandy beach, fringed with coconut palms, you hardly notice the few buildings there are.' She smiled faintly. 'That's where I found him, wandering …'

'Joseph?' Lilia hardly dared speak.

'Of course not Joseph!' She was irritated. 'Selim. And after Selim came others. All frightened to go home. Afraid of what they had done or not done. Afraid of what harm they would bring to their families if the government caught them. They were fighting against us you see, against the British. As if I cared. My lonely boys. My crazy boys.' This time her smile was sly. 'Or that's what people thought. But then did you know,' she fixed Lilia with a look that was almost accusing. 'Did you know that an American psychiatrist, I can't remember his name, thought that runaway slaves must be mad. He said running away showed that they had 'drapetomania', a serious mental disease that could only be cured by recapturing them and beating them into submission! I found that out at the mission, when I thought I needed to study up the subject if I was really going to help. After that I didn't bother.' She looked away, and then spoke so softly that Lilia had to bend closer to hear.

'Maybe we were all crazy together, sitting by a fire wrapped in our red blankets, singing to the moon, always with the sound of the surf breaking on the coral reef a mile from shore. I told my boys "*Suffering comes in and out with the tide but one day the sea will wash away all our sadness.*" And they told me they could see water between me and Joseph. They said "*Maybe Arabs took him, like they take so many people.*" They wanted to help me. But "*No, no,*" I cried, I could not bear to think that, so then they said "*Then maybe he's gone home, missus, back to England. You should go home missus, Kenya bad place for you.*" But I knew Joseph hadn't gone to England. England wasn't home for him.'

'My, those photos have really got you going!' Maureen's smiling face peered round the door. But then she noticed Rose's far away expression and the tears that were welling again in her eyes. 'I don't think you should stay long today,' she said to Lilia. 'Whatever it is, it's upsetting her a lot. '

'Two more minutes,' Lilia said softly. She leaned forward as soon as the door closed. 'Rose, might Joseph really have gone to India, somehow, do you think?'

The tears began to course down Rose's soft cheeks. 'I threw away my ddagala,' she said. 'I went out on a boat and threw it into the ocean,' she raised an arm as if to demonstrate. 'In a great arc it flew, far into the Indian Ocean.' Her eyes seemed to be following its path before swivelling abruptly to look at Lilia. 'You should never throw away your ddagala. Joseph told me that. And you must never give up hope.' She grabbed Lilia's hands in hers. 'Promise me you will go.'

On the way home Lilia stopped at the Thakkers' to buy some milk. When they heard that Rose wanted her to go to Africa they were all in favour.

'Uganda is fine,' said Sarita. 'You won't need to go to the far north and west where there is trouble and we have a contact – well, Bharat does, a cousin – '

'Now why am I not surprised?' laughed Lilia.

'Indians are taking over the world,' Bharat grinned. 'But very quietly.'

'As for Kenya,' Sarita continued. 'Well, it is true it is not very safe for visitors but all my family is there in Nairobi, my brother, sister, uncles and aunts…you could stay with any of them. They will look after you. I can call them now.'

'But - ' began Lilia. 'I can't just, I mean well, there's my cat for a start, I can't just leave him, can I?'

'Sarita loves cats,' Bharat assured her. 'We will look after him, don't worry about that.'

'It's extremely kind of you both but I really have to think about it,' Lilia said firmly, whilst thinking that a trip to Africa in any circumstances was a very exciting prospect.

Sarita was closely watching her face. 'Lilia, why does Rose want you so much to go? Does she think she has family there?'

Lilia returned her look for a few moments before making up her mind. 'There's something I haven't told you, haven't written about in the paper,' she said. 'And I would still like to keep it out of the news.' And then she told them about Joseph and then she started making her plans to go to Africa.

Mike persuaded her to go out for a farewell dinner at what had always been their favourite Indian restaurant and refused to let her share the cost. 'I don't understand why Rose wants you to go so much but I do know you well enough to know that once you make your mind up you stick to it.'

Lilia looked down and pretended to study the menu. Mike wasn't being critical on this occasion though he might have been. He certainly didn't know that it was this unappealing characteristic that had ruined her life. Changed it utterly anyway.

'I've promised, that's all,' she muttered. 'Though I don't really get it either, what she expects me to achieve.'

'Ah well, anyone would find a trip to Africa an attractive proposition. I wish I were coming with you. But I have thought of a way I, or rather the paper, might help.'

He said he had found a small pot of money that he reckoned he could 'push in her direction', if she could write a few general interest articles from Africa, so long as she didn't mind him editing them as he saw fit. 'It's called 'Development'. We've developed a bit of a following of the Rose story, it's helped the old paper's circulation. People like a crusade, it's what they think newspapers should do.'

Lilia pretended to believe him, whilst being sure that he was actually just being generous and kind, which made her feel good in a way that she would have to examine later. Meanwhile she just teased him. 'And it has been all without compromising one's integrity a bit.' She raised her glass.

'Hmm,' he retaliated swiftly. 'Despite having caused an interesting change in some of the writer's attitudes.'

'Meaning?'

'Missionaries? Religion? You are mellowing, Lilia.' .He raised his glass to hers. 'And I suspect you haven't told me half the things I should have been told, never mind the things I do know that haven't been included in the articles. And we'll have to see about how to wrap it all up when you get to the bottom of the mystery, if you do. When you get back anyway.' He put down his glass and took her free hand. 'But take care of yourself, you hear? A bit more of that tough old bird I used to know. And keep me posted.'

On her last afternoon Lilia went to say goodbye to Rose. She found her wearing a floral print dress, with her hair newly set. She said little but her eyes shone and she was clearly excited.

'Doesn't she look pretty,' Maureen observed, with professional pride. She had bought a cake to celebrate and was cutting it into slices. 'We'll have her out of here in no time. Once you are back home, that is.' She looked slyly sideways at Lilia. 'But not without an appropriate care package of course.'

'Of course,' Lilia agreed, feeling she had missed something.

'Only teasing,' Maureen clarified. 'No one would expect you to do it all, dear.'

That evening Lilia received another message from Ravi Makrani.

To Liliaz@yahoo.co.uk
From ravi@thinair.com
Dear Ms Zynofsky,

I am almost sure now that I am related to Rose McCormack but would really prefer to tell you my story in person. My work takes me to the States via the UK quite often. Can we meet? Perhaps in about a month?

Yours truly
Ravi Makrani

Lilia clicked on 'Reply'.

Dear Mr Makrani,

I am preparing to go to Africa, where I hope to contact people who knew both Rose and Edward McCormack, following some success here in my research into mission records. I'm happy to say that Rose is mostly now much better, speaking quite clearly and it is very much her idea and wish that I make this trip. Perhaps this will also help us establish whether or not there is a connection with your family. I appreciate that you do not want to betray secrets. Neither do we. My researches were actually prompted by old news cuttings about a family tragedy that I decided not to mention in my articles for the time being. I look forward very much to our meeting in a few weeks. As you will, I am sure, understand I shall not yet inform Rose.

Regards
Lilia Z.

She forwarded this exchange to Mike.

See how I trust you now, she wrote. *Publish it and I'll never speak to you again. Attached is what you can publish for now. Thanks for a nice evening. See you in a few weeks.*

The tough old bird.

Then she turned guiltily to face Rajah, who was busy washing all traces of fish from his whiskers.

'It's just for two weeks, darling,' she said. 'Or possibly three. After all it is summer, most people have a summer holiday and you will still be able to sit out in the sun without me.'

And Rajah continued to wash his already spotless face.

ROSE – A happy ending?

I am delighted to say that my research into missionary records has led to contact with a one-time colleague of Rose McCormack, the elderly lady who was almost drowned on Bognor beach a fortnight ago, and of her husband Edward when they were all in East Africa in the 1950s. Now well into her 80s, this lady now lives in Eastbourne and plans to visit Mrs McCormack very soon. Naturally everyone hopes that this will aid her recovery and help bring about a happier ending to a story that so nearly began with a tragedy.

At the request of Mrs McCormack, I am now making plans to visit East Africa to try to track down some of Rose's other one-time colleagues. I will be the guest of relations of Bognor newsagents Bhavin and Sarita Thakkar and I am most grateful to them for helping me with all the necessary arrangements. Uganda has only recently emerged from civil war and, whilst now largely peaceful, it may be hard to travel about since transport links, as I wrote in my last article, are not as good as they were in Rose's time. Kenya is a beautiful country for a holiday but not an easy place to visit. The capital city Nairobi has the largest slums in East Africa and unemployment, especially amongst young men, is high. The coastal city of Mombasa was the last place where Mrs McCormack worked as a missionary nurse. She spent some time in the mission in the city and then a number of years further up the coast where it appears that she worked mainly with displaced people. This was just after the Mau Mau uprisings against British rule when the country was still in some disarray.

It seems that the work took such a toll on Rose's health that, after her return to England, she spent many years in a Sussex nursing home before coming to live in Bognor. I look forward to sending you first hand reports of life in Africa today as I follow in some of the footsteps that Mrs McCormack took over fifty years ago.

26

'I suppose you are going to tell me it was all about oil,' Lilia spoke to the dark curly back of the taxi driver's head, as he negotiated the slip road onto the M4 on the way to Heathrow

It was Friday 29th July, and it had just been announced that police had that morning in London arrested two of the four main suspects from the 21 July attempted bombings, following another arrest two days before in Birmingham. The fourth man was currently being held in Rome and police were still looking for other suspects and had arrested numerous other people in the course of their investigations. Lilia had, perhaps somewhat rashly, but almost certain that her driver was a Muslim, wanted to make her sympathies clear.

'I have never been a fan of American foreign policy,' she had said. 'And I have always wished I had gone on that first huge demonstration but I didn't have anyone to go with. Not that it made any difference, of course, Britain still tagged along after Big Brother.' She had added that, whilst she fully accepted the argument that the invasion of Iraq had been a mistake and was largely to blame for the London attacks, she had kept an open mind on Western motives at the time.

The driver nodded. 'Oil, yes.' His strangely light green eyes met hers briefly in the rear-view mirror. 'And America's plans to dominate the world in the 21st century.'

'You're going to tell me some conspiracy theories.'

The green eyes hooded as he considered. 'Let me tell you some facts only. There is a paper written in September 2000 called "*Rebuilding America's Defences*." It says that, because Iran is just as big a threat to America's interests, there should be a large American presence in the Gulf even if Saddam Hussein is not in power in Iraq.'

'"*This is America's century*."'

He shook his head. 'It is more specific. It calls for - what were the words? - a "*worldwide command and control system*", led by America rather than the United Nations. It talks of the creation of

U.S. "*space forces*" and the development of biological weapons that could target specific genotypes.'

Lilia swallowed a small but deep lurch of fear. 'Science fiction,' she suggested with more confidence than she felt. These things were perhaps not far at all from present capabilities.

'And it also mentions the desirability of "regime change" in China.'

'Oh dear God,' she closed her eyes. 'World War III.'

He smiled slightly, relented a little. 'Perhaps some of it was, how do you say, a dream, a fantasy. But,' his tone again became urgent. 'It talks also about "key allies", such as the UK, as "*the most effective and efficient means of exercising American global leadership.*"'

Lilia looked out at the passing peaceful fields of England in high summer, where the squat towers of Windsor Castle rose above a bank of oak trees in full glorious leaf. She sighed deeply.

'And what does this have to do with 9/11 and the war on terrorism?'

'Did you know Bin Laden could have been arrested in late September 2001? Two of Pakistan's party leaders negotiated his extradition to Pakistan. And on ten occasions US forces were not given permission in time to attack identified Al Qaida and Taliban leaders. Their complaints are on record. And also that, in July 2001, a former Pakistan foreign secretary was told by American officials that "*military action against Afghanistan would go ahead by the middle of October.*"'

'No I didn't. I know that the U.S. supported the Taliban for a while because they thought that a stable government would enable the construction of oil pipelines from the old Soviet Union.'

'Yes. But then the Taliban refused to accept US conditions. So, in November 2001, US representatives told them "*Either you accept our offer of a carpet of gold, or we bury you under a carpet of bombs*".' He paused. Lilia said nothing. 'It makes 9/11 look like an excuse for attacking Afghanistan, does it not? Oh, and by the way, the report says that transforming the US into "*tomorrow's dominant force*" would take a long time unless there was "*some catastrophic event – like a new Pearl Harbour*".'

‘You have a good memory,’ commented Lilia. ‘Even people who read these things soon forget.’

‘I am from Afghanistan. I was a teacher.’

‘Ah.’ Lilia was silent for a moment in homage to his greater moral authority, if not the veracity of his opinions. ‘So what is your theory about the shooting of poor young Mr de Menezes?’

‘I have two questions,’ said the one-time teacher from Afghanistan. He paused as he overtook a convoy of articulated lorries from the Czech Republic. ‘Would anyone involved with the plot return to the scene the very next day? And was it really necessary to shoot? Some of the witnesses do not appear to have thought so.’

‘There could have been other reasons why he failed to stop when challenged?’

‘As was later discovered.’

‘He could have been a failed asylum seeker?’ Lilia thought she saw a flicker of fear in the driver’s eyes and relented. ‘Or a common criminal.’

‘Perhaps,’ he seemed encouraged and then spoke increasingly quickly. ‘And the four young men on the video on the 21st – do they look like terrorists? They look like just ordinary blokes. Many people carry rucksacks. And did you know that one of the supposed suicide bombers on 7th July has turned up alive?’

‘No, I didn’t.’ Lilia hoped her tone made plain her disbelief.

They had reached the airport turn off. A large jet whined low over the motorway. The driver laughed briefly. ‘I don’t believe it either. But it is what some of my colleagues are saying. Young guys on the rank. Excitable young guys. British Muslims. They are living – what did your government call it in that report just recently?’

‘Parallel lives. And they are constructing a parallel reality.’

‘It is dangerous, no?’ he stopped the car at the departure building. ‘It is difficult to communicate with people who live in a different world.’

27

Lilia stayed the first night in Uganda at the Imperial Botanical Beach Hotel near Entebbe airport. It was not safe to drive to Kampala after dark. She woke to a view over palm trees and lush grass that sloped down to the shore of Lake Victoria. Its grey still waters disappeared into a misty distance. From the balcony she could hear strange bird songs and the hum of a lawn mower. A bird with a long neck, (a stork?), stood in its nest on top of a nearby palm. White uniformed members of staff occasionally criss-crossed the paths between the hotel buildings. As she watched, the sun grew strong enough to cast shadows on the ground and to find reflection in the ripples that lapped the small stony beach.

The bedroom furniture was heavy, highly polished with inlaid designs of different wood. She slid a finger down a scroll of leaves and flowers round the mirror of the dressing table and thought how out of place her small plastic bottles of cosmetics looked. There should be a cut-glass scent spray, perhaps a single jar of Pond's Cold Cream. She walked to breakfast along wide half-panelled corridors, imagining elegant companions in light linen suits and dresses, echoes of their easy laughter muffled by the soft carpet.

The dining room recalled photographs of the restaurants in old London department stores, tables covered with immaculate white cloths and set with silver and plain English chinaware. Only a few were occupied. A lone African man in a dark suit, reading a newspaper, a group of three white men in shirt sleeves, each with a sheaf of papers, engrossed in discussion. One at least had an American accent. At home Lilia might have been able to place them all, guess their purpose. Here she could only wonder.

The hotel must date from at least the immediate post Second World War period, she thought, if not before. Rose and Edward could have stayed here, but she doubted if they had. Even then it would not have been cheap and it was not for the colonial life style that they or any other missionaries had come. She felt a moment's guilt that her own introduction to the country should be so pleasant but quickly determined to enjoy a day or two of luxury before her search began. A waiter approached. She smiled.

'Full English breakfast please.'

Roger the taxi driver was intrigued to have a passenger newly arrived from London and just as keen as his London colleague to discuss politics. He passed Lilia an open copy of the Weekly Observer, which, but for its tabloid size, looked very like its Bognor namesake.

"*Bombs blow lid off UK's religious strain. Londoners shaken but not stirred after terror attacks*," read the Special Report, by a Ugandan journalist on a Master's programme in London. "*The bombs might have struck the body, but they have not hurt the spirit of the city*," was the conclusion.

'What is it like there? Is the journalist correct?' he asked.

'I don't live in London, but yes it seems so,' she said and thought how generous was such an attitude. A touch of *schadenfreude* would have been quite understandable in someone coming from a country that had suffered so much more over so many years. She closed the paper.

The front page was devoted to a report on the result of the referendum earlier that week, when voters had been asked whether they wanted to amend the constitution to allow a multi-party system to replace ageing President Museveni's one party 'Movement'. "*Do you agree to open up the political space to all those who wish to join different organisations/parties to do so to compete for political power?*" Selecting a tree symbol had denoted "Yes", a house "No".

'Museveni should go while he is still loved like Mandela,' said Roger. 'He was a leader of the National Resistance Army, a guerrilla force that overthrew Amin. With help from Tanzania. But he's been President too long. Although the women still like him. But I did not vote,' he concluded. 'All politicians are the same.'

They were approaching the city. Low-rise buildings at the centre of cultivated smallholdings began to appear amongst the banana plants and palm trees. Stacked in front of many plots there were piles of red bricks for sale, the colour of the earth, manufactured, if not right there, then surely not far away. Yet more surprising, and sign of equal industry, there were, at quite frequent intervals, large groups of brand new armchairs and fat matching settees, sitting, entirely unprotected from the sun and dust, in front of the workshops where they were made, but where presumably there was then no room to display them. There was the supply but where was the demand? All Lilia could see was the occasional man or woman disappearing up a track under the trees with large bundles on their heads or balanced on the handlebars of their bicycles. As attentively as she looked and noted, most of what she saw remained a mystery, many outward signs but so few clues to the hidden life of the people around her.

The settlements became denser, housing shops the dark entrances to which were festooned with clusters of multi-coloured bowls, buckets and bottles. Chicken food. Tools. *Singo's Drum Maker. Hima cement.* A small restaurant and take away. A barber's shop. *Dora's Salon and Bridal Centre for modern hairstyles and gowns*, with a painted placard of a wedding couple, the bride in a long white dress, the groom in a dark suit. And just beyond this was a large hoarding depicting smiling young people holding books and vowing to *Put Their Future First*, with *Stop AIDS Now* in smaller letters beneath.

The shops began to be obscured by a dense row of makeshift stalls, many heaped with vast piles of green bananas. Others held large bunches of much smaller yellow bananas, and unfamiliar vegetables - sweet potatoes and yam, Roger told her. Sheaves of sugar cane leant between the stalls that were tended by women in brightly coloured dresses or wraps, their heads swathed to match, with children playing amongst them. Clusters of bicycles, each firmly in the charge of its owner, mostly young men, congregated in every available space. Radios played everywhere, African music vying with American soul, hip hop and reggae. Smaller streets flashed by on either side, their red mud surfaces deeply rutted, lined by yet more stalls, selling yet more fruit and vegetables. It seemed a market more of sellers than buyers and certainly not an easy way to make a living.

'I could take you to a place where you will get a view over the whole city,' offered Roger.

But first he needed to get some more petrol. In fact, he needed some of the fare up front to buy it and was clearly pleased that Lilia did not dispute the fact. The Lonely Planet Guide had warned her that tanks were kept as empty as possible to prevent car thieves from getting far.

They drove up Kololo hill through wide avenues lined with flowering trees, where large detached houses sat back from the road behind high fences and hedges, each gateway with its own armed guards. Some were embassies or the headquarters of aid organisations, those unmarked were presumably the homes of the rich. Roger parked at the top.

'Kampala is built on seven hills. Like Rome,' he said. 'Perhaps not so beautiful as Rome.'

In one direction Lilia could see over gently undulating hills to a distant Lake Victoria that stretched hazily to the horizon. In another she looked across a valley that was bounded at the far end by hills of equal height. Red roofed buildings nestled below amongst dense vegetation. In the foreground she could distinguish palm trees, narrow evergreens shaped like Mediterranean cypresses, delicate trees with their branches faintly tinted with opening blossom, larger trees fat and heavy with thick glossy leaves.

'It is very beautiful,' she said. 'I didn't expect it to be. I've always thought of Africa as dry and dusty.'

'Uganda is the garden of Africa; they say it is always like an English summer.' Roger pointed to the top of each distant hill. 'There is the Anglican cathedral on Namirembe, the Catholic cathedral on Rubaga. And behind us, where you cannot see, is Kibuli hill on top of which there is a mosque. And of course, in town, there are also Hindu temples.'

'It is a garden where all the religions flourish,' commented Lilia. 'Although I believe it was not always so.'

Roger laughed. 'You are looking over a battleground. A hundred years ago Protestant Bagandans on Namirembe attacked the Catholic faction on Mengo hill over there, which resulted in the first Catholic cathedral being burnt to the ground.'

'Oh really?' Lilia took out her camera. 'I read about that. You do wonder why Christians fought each other. In the circumstances.'

'Why do Muslims fight each other? In the circumstances.'

'Yes indeed.'

'Why can't all the religions come together?' Roger spoke with sudden ferocity and, surprised, Lilia turned to him.

‘I am a Bahai,’ he told her. ‘We believe Abraham, Moses, Krishna, Jesus and Mohammed were all incarnations of God. Also our founder, whom we call Baha’u’llah, who was a Shi’ite Muslim born in Iran. Also his son. All these are the Day Stars of God, symbols of His divine unity, who, over the ages, have progressively revealed the nature of the one and true religion. We have a beautiful temple but it is out of town. Perhaps I could take you tomorrow? We can make a whole tour of the city. And perhaps you have some pens or pencils you could bring for our Sunday school?’

Roger turned away from Lilia and spoke into the shafts of the declining sun. ‘*Whoso maketh the slightest possible difference between their persons and their messages hath disbelieved in God and betrayed the cause of his messengers.*’ He held out his hands like a preacher, a prophet. Then he dropped them to his sides and sighed. ‘Baha’u’llah was of course frequently persecuted and exiled for these teachings.’

‘The world would certainly be a better place if more people believed him….’ began Lilia, but then she jumped as Roger again stretched out his arm, this time to point at the sky behind her.

‘We must go quickly. Mukasa is making a storm.’

‘I beg your pardon?’ Lilia noticed the swelling black clouds for the first time.

‘The god of the lake. It is going to rain. Very hard.’

28

The terrace of the Speke hotel was wide and sheltered. Over the past half hour it had gradually filled as parties of khaki-wearing, camera-carrying guests returned from safari trips, drenched in the minute it took them to run indoors from their four by fours. Most were European or American, a few Indian and Japanese. Lilia ordered some tea and sandwiches from the young waitress and watched in amazement as dense vertical sheets of falling water fell to the ground a few yards from her table. It was like being behind a waterfall.

In the park across the road the boughs of the biggest trees soughed up and down like monster waves in mid ocean, alternately cowed low and fighting back against the weight of water. The view was increasingly blurred, any sounds from the hotel drowned by the downward crashing and upward splashing. The traffic had stopped and no one remained on the street. As she ate, Lilia planned the rest of her day. She must sort out some onward transport to Jinja, write an article and check her email. Then a long hot bath before dinner. Or perhaps take the bath first.

'More tea, madam?'

'My name is Joy,' proclaimed the badge on the waitress's cerise uniform shirt. She was neat and pretty in a short black skirt, her hair closely braided. The black bow tie could have looked comical on another person, yet it somehow enhanced the gentle intelligence of her expression and wide generosity of her smile. She was eager to talk. Lilia liked her at once.

'Did you vote in the referendum?' she asked her after a while.

'Oh yes,' said Joy. 'I voted for Museveni. He has brought peace.'

She was a Bagandan, born in the capital.

'I was thinking of visiting the tombs of the Kabakas tomorrow,' Lilia told her. 'Perhaps you could tell me more about them.'

'They are pagans,' Joy dismissed her ancestry. 'There are just some old women looking after some shrines. The clans take it in turn. They believe the Kabaka was God. Though often the kabakas were the most violent of men. I am a Christian, a Catholic.' Her father was a policeman, she had been to college.

'I have tourism qualifications, a college certificate,' she said. 'But, as you see, I am still only a waitress. I have already been here three years. I work long hours and do not earn very much. I wish I could travel, work abroad. Perhaps Madam knows someone in London…' Her eyes held Lilia's for a pleading moment and then she looked down.

Of course Lilia would have liked to help her. If only she could. But it wasn't that simple. 'I'll have a think,' she promised, smiled too broadly and saw the hope drain from the girl's face and the mask of politeness return as she withdrew. Joy was clearly accustomed to disappointment. No doubt she would try again. Perhaps her next customer would be better connected.

Lilia leafed quickly through the rest of Roger's paper. She wondered whether to do her own vox pop opinion survey on the referendum for her next article but remembered Mike's caution. 'General interest is OK, as opposed to strictly about Rose,' he said. 'But nothing too abstract or heavy.' Anyway she didn't know enough about the political situation here herself. Then she noticed a small article on an inside page written by a Spanish Catholic missionary, based in Northern Uganda.

The Father had recently been in London, at the time of the failed bombings and had received several calls from Ugandan friends urging him to return to the greater safety of Gulu, the Acholi capital. He was even more surprised when these were backed by his parents in Madrid for, as he wrote:

"Gulu is supposed to be a dangerous place. It suffers sporadic attacks and ambushes from rebel forces and it is also the focus of child night migrants who trek in to sleep in its streets in order to avoid kidnapping by the Lord's Resistance Army. In fact, at this very time, two Canadians are nightly making a parallel trek into the centre of Toronto to highlight the plight of such children and next Sunday (31st July) Gulu walks will be held around the world. I keep on wondering why Gulu roads are full of potholes, the streets are not clean, every day you hear sad stories, there are plenty of displaced folk and desperate children…and yet I love living in Gulu! And

when I find myself working alone, the song 'Bedo Gulu yomo iya' (living in Gulu makes me happy) rings in my mind."

It could have been written by that other young Father, fifty years ago, thought Wanda, whose article Father Gershon had given her to read in the magazine at Mill Hill. There was the same joy and valour in circumstances that surely would have daunted most people and that Lilia very much wished to understand. 'How I would love to meet this young man, perhaps write about him,' she thought. 'And he might even be able to put me in touch with a Catholic colleague in Rose's town.'

A soft cough roused her. It was Joy, trying to catch her eye, hoping for - what exactly? Lilia turned her head slightly, unwilling to rebuff more hopeful requests, but Joy simply handed her an envelope and walked straight to another table. .

'Thank you,' she called after her and turned the envelope over. '*No need to RSVP*' was scrawled on the back. She slid a finger along the flap and opened it. The thick card inside cheered her immediately.

Narendra Thakkar
CEO Globalgoods Uganda
Requests the pleasure of the company of
Miss Lilia Zynofsky
At a Reception
7pm Saturday July 30th
Sheraton Hotel, Kampala

She put what she hoped was a generous tip on the table and went off to investigate the hotel's internet facilities.

29

The reception was in a conference room of the Sheraton Hotel in the park opposite the Speke. The rain had stopped and Lilia walked there, incurring the unspoken disapproval of the receptionist, who had suggested calling a taxi. She picked her way through a fleet of taxis and limousines depositing their well-dressed chattering occupants at the porticoed entrance. Narendra, who was, he told her, Bhavin's cousin, met her as she entered a large wood-panelled room that was already half full of chattering groups of guests. A tall, softly spoken man, Narendra was Managing Director in Uganda for the multi-national company that was hosting the event and therefore, he apologised, very busy that evening.

'I hope you will come for dinner with my family another day,' he said. 'Let me introduce you to someone who will look after you.'

Charles Parker was a middle ranking attaché at the High Commission. Lean and elegant with longish fair hair, he hailed a distant waiter, took a glass of wine from the proffered tray for Lilia, downed the rest of his own and took another for himself. He listened politely while she told him why she had come to Uganda and offered to advise her if she wanted to check colonial records once she got back to the UK. He advised most strongly against her idea of visiting the north of the country.

'DO NOT,' he said. 'As I'm sure our website puts it in large bold capitals. Far too risky. Write about this, much more where it's at. Appearances to the contrary, perhaps. And do call me Charlie. It makes me feel famous.'

Lilia laughed briefly and then asked: 'What is it all about? Something to do with development? I see one of the speakers is from the Commission on Africa.'

Charlie eyed her briefly, one brow raised and then shrugged his shoulders. 'What it's always about. What it's always been about since the beginnings of the empire. Of human time perhaps. Trade. Except that instead of ripping people off directly, we now have to work through their governments. This is off the record of course. I'm not quite ready to retire.'

'You must attend a lot of these occasions.'

'Sometimes I think it's all I do. Ssh. It's time for the speeches.' He nodded his head in the direction of the front of the hall where a few people had assembled on a small dais. An imposing grey-haired European woman in a flowing blue-flowered dress looked vaguely familiar. The room fell gradually silent.

'I am delighted to welcome first Baroness White, who as you all know has a long-standing interest in Uganda and is a member of our Board of Directors,' Narendra led a short round of applause as he gave her centre stage.

'I am very happy to be back in Uganda where I have so many friends,' the Baroness smiled graciously around the room as if including all those there.

Lilia placed the fruity confident voice: ex-minister of the Major and possibly Thatcher Governments, with some sort of responsibility for foreign affairs or development. How one forgets people who were once in the news daily, she thought. Fascinating to see one of them obviously still very active in a new role and, in the Baroness's case, as a member of the House of Lords, presumably still in a position of some influence, if no longer on the government side.

'I know that all of us share the same aim in coming here today and that is to express our commitment to the long term prosperity of this beautiful country, and indeed East Africa and Africa more generally,' continued the Baroness. 'We have this common aim. We also have *A Common Interest,*' she paused to allow the slight titter of recognition to run around her audience. 'I use the title of the recent report by the Commission on Africa deliberately. I am honoured, truly honoured, to be sharing a platform tonight with one of the Commissioners who has contributed, I am sure with great wisdom, to this excellent report.' A slight, bearded, grey-haired man, sitting on Narendra's left, inclined his head in appreciation of this tribute.

'James Mkono, economist and advisor to the President,' whispered Charles.

'I have read the report in its entirety with great interest and admiration and…'

'Agreement?' suggested Charlie in a low voice.

‘Whilst I shall try not to pre-empt what my co-speaker may say, I feel that some things bear emphasis if not repetition.’ The Baroness launched into a catalogue of inequalities between the West and Africa, each presented with the same arresting rhetoric. ‘We live in a world of great wealth shared by unprecedented numbers of ordinary people. Yet in Africa millions of people live in poverty and squalor. Where unprecedented medical advances have wiped out many of the diseases that used to afflict the developed world. Yet in Africa four million children under the age of five die each year, two thirds from illnesses that cost very little to treat. We have developed drugs that can control the advance of AIDS, surely one of the most devastating diseases ever known. Yet in Africa where 25 million people are infected, these drugs are not generally available.’

‘What is it about official speeches that makes them so mind-numbing, however worthy?’ thought Lilia. She struggled to pay attention. The list continued.

‘We subsidise the production of unwanted food at a cost of almost a billion US dollars a day, while in Africa hunger is a key factor in more deaths than all the infectious diseases together. Where the internet….yet 40 million children do not go to school. Where scientists can map the human genome yet … Where rich nations … globalisation…. global justice…’

Was it a deliberate ploy, Lilia wondered, to lull the audience’s critical faculties so that they would scarcely remember what was said and be unable to raise any significant challenge? She stole a glance at her companion, who was nodding gravely at each new fact. She was sure he, a veteran of many such occasions, would have an interesting, or at least amusing, view on this. Watching him furtively, she began to notice a pattern in his reactions. Without change of expression, his movements were perfectly calibrated to the tone and cadence of the speaker’s voice. He’s learned how to appear to be paying the utmost attention, she realised, without perhaps actually listening at all. Maybe most of these people in the room were similarly skilled in which case – as if he had understood her conclusion, Charlie caught her eye and winked. It was ritualised behaviour, almost religious in its coordinated response to words, and perhaps to shared meanings of those words, but to what end, she wondered? With what effect? Would such a speech, such an event, make any difference in the real world? Was it meant to?

'The eyes of history are upon us,' the speaker was surely on the home stretch. 'If we do not act to remove these injustices, to reduce these inequalities, to end these scandals of unnecessary deaths from hunger and disease, future generations will ask how could we have known and done nothing? We must halve world poverty by 2015. Allow me to quote an Igbo proverb, which prefaces the Commissions' Report. '*Not to know is bad. Not to wish to know is worse.*'

But still she hadn't finished. 'We also have a strong vested interest in so doing because, as we all understand, a fairer world will be a more peaceful and a more secure world. The company that I represent here today is eager to lend its weight to such endeavours. Yes we have to remember our duty to our shareholders, we want to expand our markets, we have to make a profit.' Here Charlie nodded so vigorously that Lilia took a quick drink to cover her smile.

'But we believe that this is compatible with, part of, and indeed dependent on, the wider development agenda. And finally, let me underline what I believe was the starting point of the work of the Commission, the majority of the members of which were from this continent. It is a point with which I am in utter agreement. Africa must drive its own development because if it does not create the right conditions for development then, however much support it receives from outside, it will fail.'

'Does she mean corruption?' whispered Lilia under cover of the ensuing applause.

'More or less,' Charles affirmed. 'Actually, less of a problem in this country than in some of our neighbours. Museveni's been quite tough on it. In the past anyway. She also means security for foreign investment, undertaking not to nationalise, measures to reduce social unrest, that sort of thing.' He stopped clapping. 'Now this should be interesting. He knows what he's talking about.'

James Mkono had stood and taken centre stage. He started with a joke. Several jokes in fact.

'Someone once sent me a list of definitions of capitalism,' he surveyed his audience. It is a rather long list so I will give you but a few examples. I hope no one will take offence.' He cast a benign smile around his audience. 'Under traditional capitalism: You have two cows. You sell one and buy a bull. Your herd multiplies and the economy grows. In American capitalism you have two cows, sell one and force the other to produce the milk of four cows. You are surprised when the cow drops dead.' There was hearty laughter across the room. The Commissioner continued.

'Under French capitalism you have two cows and you go on strike because you want three cows.' This evoked laughter amongst the Europeans, or most of them. 'In Britain you have two cows but both are mad. No longer of course,' he turned graciously to the previous speaker. 'And Hindus with two cows,' he smiled briefly at Narendra, 'Simply worship them. There was no African example but this is the one that I believe used to be the most applicable: what we have too often had is 'Real capitalism'. We don't have any cows and the bank will not lend us the money to buy them. Why? Because we don't have the cows to put up as collateral. To those that hath shall be given. The rich get richer.

'We have had real capitalism and we want traditional capitalism. To continue the cow metaphor: did you know that in Europe every cow has received almost two dollars a day in subsidy and this is double the average income in Africa? And Japanese cows receive almost four dollars a day.' He paused to allow these facts to register. 'We want to have a level playing field. We want to be players not spectators. In the same league and not for ever condemned to fail in the first play offs. Our football players are of course amongst our proudest ambassadors but theirs is not the sort of wealth that must be created for all our citizens. And can be created.

'Ladies and gentlemen, many of you are too young to remember the days when so many African countries were achieving independence from their colonial masters. I recall it vividly. I was a very young man then. There was such optimism. No one was worried about Africa's future. For Africa has great natural riches. And in those days the average income in sub Saharan Africa was twice that of South and East Asia. Now life expectancy, that barometer of economic health, is 17 years higher in India and Bangladesh than here, where it is 46 years and falling. What has gone wrong? And what is to be done?'

Maybe I could write about this, thought Lilia. He's talking about the time when Rose, or at least Edward, was here. Anyway, Mike will be interested even if he does have to edit most of it out. She listened carefully and wished she had a notebook.

'See what I mean?' said Charlie when the Commissioner finished speaking. 'Come on, I'll introduce you. Have a question ready.' He steered her firmly across the room.

'Commissioner, you say that the solution to Africa's current economic disadvantage lies in a combination of trade, debt cancellation and aid,' began Lilia. 'I appreciate that you could not go into great detail in your talk but I wonder if you could elaborate a bit on the last. I think a lot of basically well-intentioned people, like the readers of the paper I represent, are somewhat sceptical as to whether - '

'You are talking about issues of governance,' he waved a hand, though not impatiently. 'Eradicating corruption and inefficiency.' He nodded. 'All this is important and steps are being taken, will be taken. However, there is another side to aid: the conditions under which it has been given in the past. The strings attached, as one might say.'

'To the self-interest of the donors, perhaps?'

James Mkono laughed. 'You might say. Although I could not.' Lilia laughed with him but he was instantly serious.

'Aid works,' he assured her. 'We have examined the evidence. And it need not be for ever. Look at South Korea. Look at Botswana. What is needed is a big initial push over the next fifteen or so years. Perhaps you should read our report and then come and talk to me.'

He reached into an inner pocket and withdrew a business card.

'One last question for now, Commissioner, if I may?' An article was shaping up in Lilia's head and she intended to write it that night. 'You talked of capitalism and level playing fields. Is it, do you think, in the nature of capitalism to think long term and help weaker players? Is there really ever going to be, as it were, one team?' She was rather proud of the phrasing and unprepared for the reaction.

James Mkono withdrew his hand and pocketed his card. His face was an expressionless mask. 'Read the report,' he said. 'I'll get one of my staff to send a copy to your hotel. Perhaps you have never heard that adage of civil servants: where there's a will there's a way. And I would draw your attention to our comments on the role of independent and professional journalists. Good evening.'

Charlie had been eavesdropping. 'Good try,' he grinned. 'But whatever he really thinks, tonight we are indeed all in Team Africa, paddling the same canoe, etc. etc. You could still follow it up though. Offer him a profile piece, not too controversial.'

'Unfortunately I don't think the paper I'm writing for would be that interested. A twin town might be more in their line. Anyway, I ought really to be heading out of town. I need to get to Jinja. Tomorrow if possible. I don't suppose you know what time the busses go?'

'I'll do better than that,' Charlie waved to someone across the room. 'I'll get you a lift. And then stand you dinner if you'll join me. My wife's at the coast with the kids and I'll only drink myself into a stupor if I'm on my own.'

'Will that event help Uganda's development?' Lilia asked Charlie as they waited for their food in the very upmarket Chinese restaurant near the Sheraton. It was quite crowded, their fellow customers of every ethnicity and chattering loudly in a babel of different languages. 'Or will it just enable the company to make even more money on the backs of the poor?' She took a sip of wine.

Charlie looked genuinely thoughtful. 'Actually,' he said. 'The climate *is* changing. People really do recognise 'a common interest.' So, a bit of both is the answer and very glad I am too.'

'Really? I mean, you're not supposed to have opinions are you, political ones that is.'

He nodded. 'Officially my job is to get the best deal for UK plc. But the reason I wanted the job in the first place was because I wanted to Make a Difference.' He laughed and sat back, waving his wineglass to encompass the room. 'And all this of course, exotic places, meeting interesting people.' He raised his glass to Lilia.

'So a rather missionary-like motivation then,' she said. And I should point out that I've come to regard that as a compliment. In some cases at least.'

'Lord no!' he threw back his head and guffawed loudly, momentarily silencing the diners at adjoining tables. 'Peoples' souls are their own affair, I've always thought.' He lowered his voice and she had to lean closer to hear what he was saying. 'There are more than enough missionaries of the old sort still coming here. The place is crawling with them, driving around in their four-by-fours, setting up rival schools, competing for influence. See over there?' he nodded to a table of middle-aged white people on the other side of the room. 'Americans,' he said. 'Evangelicals of some description. Give me self-seeking businessmen any day of the week.'

IN ROSE'S FOOTSTEPS
A Wonderland?

I am in Uganda, the country where Rose McCormack, the old lady who suffered a stroke on Bognor beach some weeks ago, was a missionary 50 years ago and which Winston Churchill called 'the pearl of Africa'. Back in the 1840s Europeans thought of it as a 'wonderland', when they first began to hear tales from Arab traders of its great lakes and mighty kingdoms. A century or so later, at its independence from Britain in 1962, around the time the McCormacks left in fact, the future looked bright, as it did at that time for the continent as a whole, and it was surely partly due to the efforts of missionaries like them in the fields of health and education. Yet today most people, if they think of Uganda at all, probably think first of AIDS and then of the atrocities committed under the rule of ex- President Amin. Can the source of the Nile with its fertile earth and equable climate regain its reputation? Many people in Africa think so. James Mkono, economist and adviser to President Museveni, is one of them.

Tonight in Kampala, as a guest of Navin Thakker, a cousin of Bognor newsagents Bhavin and Sarita Thakker, I attended a meeting addressed by Dr Mkono in his capacity as a member of the Commission on Africa that has recently published its weighty report: 'Our Common Future'. Convened by Tony Blair, most of its members were African. The report argues convincingly that the correct mixture of fair trade, debt cancellation and aid will turn the tide of underdevelopment and begin to restore Uganda's fortunes, and indeed those of Africa as a whole. Many Observer readers may have become sceptical about aid and the dreadful term 'compassion fatigue' has entered the language. We have all heard of wastage, misguided projects and resources siphoned off to fund the lavish lifestyles of those in power. So I asked Dr Mkono how he could be so sure.

'We must eradicate corruption and inefficiency,' Dr Mkono agreed. 'But we do need more resources, money, investment, and Africa itself cannot provide it all. An additional 75 billion dollars a year is needed, provided in two stages. And in the first stage, we

propose that two thirds of this should come from aid from rich countries, a third from African governments. Aid does work,' he assured me. 'Thirty years ago Botswana was one of the poorest and most aid-dependent countries in the world. Yet today it is classified as a middle-income country.' Let us hope that in thirty years at most Uganda can become another success story.

James Mkono also spoke out against Amin. As a student leader he famously argued against the expulsion of Uganda's Asian community in 1972, foreseeing the terrible effect this would have on the country's economy. Under President Museveni they were invited to return with their property restored. I have been invited to visit one result of this successful policy: a once-again thriving sugar factory near the town of Jinja. This will be the subject of my next report.

30

The road to Jinja cut straight through Mbira Forest. Outside the city it was more or less empty of other vehicles and Lilia had a clear view ahead as it undulated gently into the distance. The earth verges stained the painted side markings pink and here and there spilled onto the tarmac as if trying to reclaim the lost ground. Occasional clearings in the dense vegetation revealed small clusters of rough thatched huts, where people sat or in the shade or went about their business, goats were tethered and dogs roamed freely. When she felt she was unobserved, Lilia took photographs from the moving car. So much was strange, her impressions so dense and quickly changing, that she did not trust her memory and was sure she would want to later consult a record, however imperfect and incomplete. Suddenly the car began to judder and slewed violently to the left.

'Puncture,' her driver, Moses, informed her tersely. 'Madam must get out while I fix it.'

'No problem,' said Lilia and prepared to stand and wait. She watched idly as, effortlessly, Moses jacked up the car and began to unscrew the nuts. He was tall and strongly built. As if feeling her scrutiny, he turned and spoke over his shoulder.

'Maybe madam would like to take a walk in the forest, take photos,' he suggested.

'Really?' Lilia felt her eyes widen. 'Is it safe?' she added and was instantly sorry. She was very grateful to Kiran Somani for lending her his car and driver while he was away on a business trip, but she did not feel at ease with Moses. She had decided to maintain a polite distance for the time being.

He laughed with what could have been scorn and his tone was certainly amused, if not patronising.

'No danger here,' he said. 'Plenty of 'nature trails' for tourists. But don't go too far, maybe half hour maximum.'

Lilia walked first up a wide track. At one point, a four by four bumped past, its passengers an equal mix of white and African and she wondered if they were the new style missionaries Charlie had talked about. She then turned right onto a smaller path where the sunlight barely filtered through tall trees raised on massive roots, each as thick as a normal sized tree. Clouds of small butterflies hovered in its beams like dust and settled like blossoms on the undergrowth. Birds surrounded her though she could not see them: she could hear the variety of their calls: cheeps, chirrups, flutings and snatches of more ambitious songs. Once or twice she heard loud rustling in the branches above and wondered what bird could be so large. And then she saw a face. A monkey! In fact several small, greenish monkeys that peered at her before swinging lightly away high overhead, her camera clicking blindly after them.

'Africa,' she said aloud. 'I'm really here.'

Before she turned back, Lilia thought she had better have a pee while she had the chance and having no idea when there might next be a proper toilet. She crouched near the safety of the path but behind a screen of bushes where dry leaves made a thick carpet. Almost at once she became aware of being stung, then noticed with horror the tiny ants swarming up over her feet and ankles and backed off hastily, stamping and brushing at her legs. One much larger black ant clung on and, by the time she had managed to flick it away, it had drawn blood.

She stared at the welling drop in horror and realised how ignorant and vulnerable she was. What exactly had bitten her? Was it poisonous or could it carry infection? Should she ask Moses to get out her suitcase so that she could find the small first aid kit she had brought? She settled for spitting on the small wound and pressing it with a piece of clean toilet paper from the small wad she had thought to take from the hotel and stuffed into her bra. I will cope with this country, she thought grimly, as she headed back to the car. Then she screamed. She had almost trodden on what looked like a small black snake. Watching her feet very carefully she hurried back to the car.

'You have a problem?' enquired Moses who, evidently having completed the repairs, was lounging on its bonnet, chewing on a stalk of grass.

'No, no, I'm fine,' gasped Lilia. 'Just out of breath from running. I think I saw a snake.'

'Really?' he spat out the grass and his eyes narrowed as he stood up. He straightened his shoulders, as if preparing to do battle.

'Yes. It was this long, shiny, black, with sort of segments…' even as she said the word she realised how unsmooth and snakelike it sounded. 'Actually I've just realised it had legs, lots of legs.'

Moses clapped his hand to his head and laughed. Much more than was necessary, thought Lilia sourly.

'Heh heh! It was a millipede. A giant millipede. Oh ho!' he continued to laugh and shake his head as he got back into the driving seat. This was clearly a tale to be retold. Another stupid tourist, frightened of their own shadow.

'It was certainly very big,' Lilia responded frostily and got into the back of the car. 'I'm going to put up my feet for a bit.' She was going to have to scratch and spit on them a while yet.

Moses became sober, as if reprimanded, and she wondered if that was what she had intended. They drove in silence to the end of the forest before she relented. He might be afraid she would complain to his employer and she didn't want him to lose what must be quite a good job.

'Have you worked long for Mr Somani?' she asked.

Moses was thirty and still single, he told her with a little further prompting. He had completed tenth grade, done a short course in mechanics and begun one in forestry before this job had come along. A small house in the grounds of the sugar factory went with it so, though sometimes bored, he would need to have something much better lined up before he quit. 'Such as a rich lady,' he laughed briefly, catching her eye in the rear view mirror. Meanwhile there were many single girls at the factory and, when he had time off, he could go and stay with his mother who kept a shop in a nearby town. He gave her to understand that, but for chauffeuring her, that was where he would be headed right now. Lilia realised that she would have to give him a very good tip in recompense.

'Which town?' she asked idly.

'Kamuli. A small town. Nothing for tourists.'

Lilia relaxed back into the soft leather seat, closed her eyes and soon began to doze. It was some time before she again looked out of the window to see that the trees had cleared and that they were approaching some sort of settlement. A line of wooden shacks connected by a covered veranda appeared on either side of the road.

'Where are we?' she said. 'Do you think we could get a drink? I'm thirsty, aren't you?'

Moses smiled broadly and nodded. 'This is Lugazi,' he told her. 'My friend has a café here.'

An hour later, with the sun overhead, Lilia was again finding it hard to stay awake. She was back in the front seat sitting next to Moses and did not want to find herself leaning on him. His voice roused her. He was pointing ahead.

'Jinja,' he said. 'Owen Falls. Shall I stop the car?'

The road passed over a huge dam, the falls a comparative trickle at its lower side and only the width and speed of the river higher up gave a hint of the power harnessed beneath. There were few pedestrians and, as she walked over the bridge, Lilia felt curious eyes upon her from every passing vehicle. Moses picked her up at the other side.

'Amazing,' she said. 'Not beautiful like the falls must have been but still amazing.'

'I can show you beautiful falls, 'said Moses. 'You want to see, the road is soon here, before we reach town. Many Europeans come to Jinja to see them, to go rafting on them.'

'Really?' she said doubtfully. It did not look like a tourist spot.

Bujagali Falls was actually a series of smaller falls where the Nile divided round a small island and swept together again in a mighty confluence of competing currents. Lilia and Moses clambered down a grassy slope and stood where the rushing water foamed white across its whole width. Clearly there were many rocks beneath.

'It is too late for rafting today,' said Moses. 'At this time of year there is only one trip a day. You can book in town.'

Lilia stared at the relentless white torrent, wondering if she dare, thinking how quickly she would be swept away should she fall in. She remembered the *Picture Post* article and decided she had been right to suspect its accuracy. Even a daring small boy would have had more sense than to venture near the water here.

'Hallo!'

She turned to see a young man hurrying toward them.

'If you give him five thousand shillings he will swim over the falls,' Moses told her.

'You're joking.'

'He does it every day,' Moses assured her. 'There are always one or two young men here. It is how they make a living.'

Lilia paid and watched the young man walk a little upriver, pick up an empty plastic jerry can and launch himself into the water. He waved as he passed them, was buffeted to left and right as he descended and was then carried far out to the middle of the broad river beneath the falls, where he was swept along by the powerful current. How would he get back to shore? Lilia wondered tensely, before noticing the boat that had already set out from the bank a little downstream. So several people benefited from this enterprise.

'You come in good time. President Museveni wants to make hydroelectric dam here also,' Moses informed her.

'Oh no! It seems a great shame,' Lilia sympathised, but she had misread his feelings.

'Uganda needs electricity,' he said curtly. 'It is more important than tourism.'

31

'I have to take some letters to the office,' announced Moses as they approached the town. 'I will take you first to a hotel where you can have lunch and I will pick you up later. I think you will like Jinja Nile Resort, it looks over the river. It has swimming pool, gym. It is just off the road here.'

Lilia had been reading the guide, which listed three big hotels, about five medium and another ten or so cheap guesthouses, mostly catering for local students. 'It's a bit far from town,' she said. 'And too expensive.'

'You are not a rich lady?' He sounded disappointed.

'Certainly not,' she laughed. 'I am on a tight budget. I thought the Crested Crane sounded good.'

Owned by the Ministry of Tourism and used to train staff in the tourism industry, it was a wide, white two-storied building of simple modern appearance, set back from the road in pleasant grounds. Opposite, further from the road, there was another large building surrounded by green fields. The hotel had none of the splendour of the hotel at Entebbe or the Speke but still, thought Lilia, it must have been there in the 50s. The McCormacks would certainly have known it. She felt a rush of excitement that she was getting nearer to them.

When Moses returned, he was not alone. Mr Kumar held out his hand.

'Welcome, Miss Zynofsky. Kiranbhai has asked me to look after you. I am the office manager.'

He looked well past retirement age. Small and slight, his thinning black, surely dyed, hair was brushed carefully over the top of his head. His eyes, magnified by round wire-framed spectacles, looked sad.

'It's very kind of you. Of him.'

'I trust you are comfortable?' he spoke with old-fashioned precision. 'I would ask you to stay at my home,' he ran his hand over his already smooth crown. 'But my wife is in Mumbai with our son and his family. She does not like to live here.' He sighed then brightened. 'We make a tour, yes? And I shall try to answer all your questions.' He ushered Lilia to the car, opened the back door for her to get in then settled himself in the front next to Moses.

'To the source of the Nile,' he commanded without looking at him.

'The dam?' asked Moses. He seemed a little aggrieved, perhaps, thought Lilia, because he was no longer in charge of their itinerary.

'Of course not. Although,' Mr Kumar conceded, 'some say the source is truly there. Not that you are old enough to remember the Falls, Moses. They were magnificent,' he informed Lilia and sighed again. 'But that is progress. No, no, we will go to Ripon Falls, also somewhat of a misnomer since they are almost non-existent. I remember when they were blasted away to provide a steady flow of water for the dam. But there is a wonderful view there.'

'Have you lived here a long time?' asked Lilia. Mr Kumar might be a better guide than she had hoped for.

'I was born here. That was my secondary school opposite your hotel. Of course we had to leave in '72.'

'When Amin…'

''Yes yes. I went with my family to India. But when President Museveni invited the Asians back and the sugar factory started up again Mr Mukeshbhai, Kiranbhai's father, asked me to return. I have now been here ten years, but I still remember it as it was before. It is not at all the same place. Although,' he seemed to be reminding himself, 'The Source of the Nile viewing place is perhaps better now. More developed.'

They turned onto a narrow track that wound down through trees and parked by a small wooden building, a sign saying '*Gifts and Curios*' visible through the bright pink flowering bushes that climbed around the entrance. Two young African women came out to greet them and beckoned to Lilia as she got out of the car. Mr Kumar was clearly prepared to wave them away but Lilia stopped him and entered.

Herds of wooden animals, elephant, giraffe, lions ranged on the floor along the walls, reminding her of Rose's living room. Smaller models stood on tables, together with carved soapstone dishes, chess sets and more miniature animals. Bright beaded jewellery hung on stands and in display cases. Lilia chose some bangles for Sarita, a deep blue necklace for herself and, as an afterthought, some amber beads for Maureen Halliwell. Nothing was expensive.

'I'm sorry I can't carry more,' she told the women and rejoined Mr Kumar. She followed him down the uneven steps of a path that emerged into an open grassy space. Below, in either direction, stretched the wide clear water of the River Nile. On the far shore, a red earth track led up to a circle of round stone huts with conical roofs. A few small boats were moored by a jetty and cormorants sat proud on the topmost branches of nearby trees, preening or peering attentively down into the slow moving water. Lilia gasped in delight.

'It's beautiful.'

Mr Kumar nodded, pleased, and pointed to the left. 'That way around the corner is the lake,' he said. 'Unless you regard this narrow stretch as also the lake. And that way, past that bridge, is Owen Falls which you must have seen when you arrived.'

'So the Nile flows that way.'

'For two thousand miles.'

'Is that the railway bridge?' asked Lilia.

'It is. Or was. There have been no trains for many many years. Since 1972 or soon after.'

'The railway is still shown on the map in my guide book. And the station.' And Rose would have travelled that way to Mombasa, she thought.

'Perhaps it will run again one day. I do not suppose I shall be here to see it.' His tone did not reflect the melancholy his words suggested and, as he turned to Lilia, his expression was joyous. 'Let me show you something else.'

The temple was a short walk away. In its grounds was a bronze bust of Gandhi, donated by the Indian Government to commemorate the fact that some of the Mahatma's ashes had been scattered there.

'I come here as often as I can,' said Mr Kumar. It was not hard to guess why.

As they drove back into the centre of town Lilia reflected how strangely at odds it appeared with the guidebook's description. Where were the tourists to fill the hotels and clubs and bars that it listed? There were several tourist shops and signs advertising trips to

Bujagali, Mbira and other places but only a few white backpackers ambled down Main Street. Perhaps it was the wrong time of day, the wrong season? But there were hardly any local people either and very few bicycles or motor vehicles. Surely there should be more signs of purposeful comings and goings? She looked out at the lines of wooden, two storey buildings and the pavements shaded by arcades supported on fading blue and white painted pillars.

'It reminds me of a film set,' she said. 'For a western. The wild west of cowboys and Indians.' She stopped, embarrassed, and tried to explain. 'It seems very quiet. Empty.'

Mr Kumar was not at all offended. 'That's what my wife says,' he said and then smiled coyly. 'Once it was full of Indians.' He paused as Lilia acknowledged his little joke. 'All these shops,' he gestured along the street. 'They were owned by Indians. When we walked along here we knew everybody. It was so lively, busy, prosperous. And in the evenings everyone went walking to the Pier, to the lakeside and we saw all our friends, and relations. I thought it must be the best place in the whole world. It was a wonderful place to grow up.'

'Could we go to the lakeside? I think you know why I have come here?'

'You wish to visit the sugar factory? I can arrange that for tomorrow.'

'Yes, but I'm also investigating the disappearance of an English boy, back in the 1950s. Many people thought he drowned in the lake. His mother now lives in the same town as me, where I write for the local paper. She's my neighbour and she's very old now and I've promised…'

Mr Kumar did not remember anything about the disappearance of an English boy. 'We didn't mix with the Europeans,' he said. 'And I would have been very young then. Maybe my older brother would remember something, but he is living in England. We will go to the lakeside but these days it is not a good place to go. Turn left at Bell Avenue,' he instructed Moses. 'Look,' he pointed up the next turning on the left, a smaller street lined with large bungalows. 'That is where we used to live when I was a boy. Iganga Road. It is the way you will go tomorrow. Plot number 22. Now it is a nursery school.'

'I thought the Asians got their properties back?'

'Some did. But,' he shrugged. 'I live in a flat in a building with the other Indian employees. It is better. We'll go right on Oboja. Down to the Sailing Club. You can go there if you like for a drink, though there is no longer any sailing. Kiranbhai wants to start it again. And the golf course. You will see.'

The stretch of shore between the sailing club and the pier was certainly no longer a place for leisurely promenades. It had been entirely taken over by a line of small broken down shacks, cobbled together from pieces of corrugated iron and odds and ends of wood. On the bare earth in front of each shack there congregated a small crowd of people preparing food, cooking, smoking, or just sitting. Half naked children stood with their thumbs in their mouths, solemnly eyeing the visitors. By the end shack, a jaunty blue and white sign, proclaiming *'Jinja Sailing Club Uganda'*, was attached to a sagging landing stage. A small jetty, lined with lifebelts, provided a roost for yet more cormorants.

'Someone told me this was once a really busy port,' said Lilia.

Mr Kumar nodded. 'You used to be able to take a ferry to Kenya or Tanzania from that pier.' He pointed along the lakefront. 'And there was a rail siding to load cargo boats with sugar and other materials. Up there,' he pointed to a large derelict building set back amongst trees, 'That was a very nice hotel where people could sit and look out at the lake. Before independence it was only for Europeans. Your neighbour would have known it.'

'I'd like to have a closer look.'

'You may of course. But I wouldn't go into the building. It might not be safe.'

Lilia walked up a once gravelled driveway that was almost entirely carpeted with weeds and climbed a few broken steps to a wide terrace in front of the hotel building. Here and there were scattered a few twisted remains of wrought iron tables and chairs, looking back there was a wide view of the lake and, from this angle, no sight of the straggle of hovels on its shore. She might have been looking out to sea. It was easy to understand how the young Joseph would have loved it here, how it might have reminded him of holidays at Mombasa. Had he been unable to resist going swimming that fateful day? Might the police and everyone else have been right all along? She could almost hear the ghostly whispers of long departed hotel guests who would surely have sat here gossiping while the search went on and Rose alone refused to give up hope. And there would have surely been at least one malicious soul, there always was, who said what others were thinking and blamed Rose.

'Fancy letting that child swim here as if we didn't all know it wasn't safe!'

'And then,' another was emboldened. *'Leaving him on his own while she went off playing at Florence Nightingale among the natives.'*

'What sort of mother does that?' There were several of them now, heads nodding in unison over their cocktails.

'Miss Zynofsky!' Mr Kumar's brisk voice sent the ghosts packing. 'Let us return you to your hotel.'

The road ran parallel to the lakeshore. To their right, long drives curved away through overgrown lawns to the colonnaded entrances of large low houses, fit for Hollywood film stars - and of about that vintage, thought Lilia. One or two had cars parked outside though they still looked neglected, but most were apparently uninhabited. To the left of the road, sloping down to the water, was an unkempt expanse of rough grass where large, sinister looking black-backed birds with very long legs stalked purposefully, their powerful beaks dipping periodically in search of food.

'They are maribou storks,' said Mr Kumar 'And that was the golf course.'

Lilia could just detect the mounds and hollows that must once have been so carefully sculptured and tended. She took photos to left and right of the road, again imagining the carefree scenes of luxury and leisure that had once existed. But she felt the full force of Father Gershon's observation that Rose would surely find it very hard to recognise the Jinja she had known. She was finding it rather unnerving herself. How rapidly whole worlds could disappear! What she could see were as much the ruins of a civilisation as the stone columns and mosaics that marked the cities of Ancient Greece or Rome. It had happened before, it had happened in living memory and it would happen again.

'But things are coming up,' Mr Kumar assured her, cheerfully, in apparent understanding. 'You will see when you visit the factory.'

Back at the Crested Crane, Lilia had commandeered the only computer in order to write and send an article and check her mail. There were two messages: one from Sarita saying that Rajah was fine but never seemed to have had enough to eat, was he usually so greedy? To which a slightly worried Lilia responded that no, he wasn't, and please could Sarita always leave a dish full of the new dry food recommended by the vet. She sent her love to Rose and asked Sarita to tell her that she was in Jinja, had seen some of the sights and was moving on tomorrow. The other message was from Ravi Makrani.

'Your mention of a family tragedy makes me almost certain it is our family. If you cannot email please telephone when you can on this number to arrange our meeting.'

Lilia wrote back saying simply that she would contact him a few days before returning to England so that they could agree the necessary details, puzzled as to what connection there could possibly be with Rose. More likely, she thought, it was with Edward who might have had a brother or sister, even an aunt or uncle, with some sort of Indian relations. Anglo-Indian relations. Well, she would find out soon enough, she just hoped they were nice people who would care about Rose for herself and not for any money they might think she had. She sent a copy to Mike, briefly described her spooked observations of the rise and fall of civilisations, and promised to send the article within the hour.

She was just beginning to write, whilst musing about how strange and sad it would be if after all these years Rose were invited to go to India, when she became aware of a figure hovering outside the room, beyond the slightly open door to the corridor.

'Nearly finished,' she called over her shoulder, swivelled in the chair and stood to leave. It was only then that she saw Moses, his hand raised as if to knock. 'Did you want to use the computer?' she asked doubtfully. He was not a guest, he had said he was staying with one of the office workers and she had given him some money for a meal.

'No, madam – Lilia,' she had asked him to call her that. 'I -,' he stopped, looked away, looked her full in the eyes and as quickly looked down at his feet.

These, she now noticed, were now no longer shod in boots but in smart light slip-ons. In fact, he was smartly dressed altogether in a short sleeved white shirt that skimmed slim-fitting fawn trousers, rather than the army style khaki shirt and trousers he had worn earlier. She felt suddenly scruffy, bedraggled after the long day of travelling and sightseeing. A bath had been next on her agenda.

'Yes?' She took a step back, feeling disadvantaged further by his height. He filled the doorway, shifting his weight from one foot to the other. He kept fingering the keys he held in one hand whilst clenching and unclenching the other. He looked up then down again, then shrugged and half turned as if to leave.

'I thought you might want to go somewhere this evening,' he said, dismissively as if she had already said no. 'I could take you to some of the places the Europeans like to go, the other end of town. Hear some local music, have one or two Nile Specials. The local beer. It's very popular with tourists. Mr Kumar doesn't know these things.' His lips twitched with something between a smile and a sneer.

Lilia thought quickly. It would be interesting, she liked listening to the world music programmes on the radio, and she hadn't been to any kind of nightclub in years. Nor had she been invited out on any kind of date for a very long time, let alone by a young and very attractive man. But she needed Moses in his official capacity for some time yet and it would not be a good idea to compromise their relationship, whatever it was that he had in mind.

'Oh that's really thoughtful of you,' she said casually. 'I'm sure it would be most enjoyable. Except I am really rather tired and if we are going to the sugar works in the morning…besides I have to do some more work, write something for the paper that is helping pay for my trip. Earn my living.' She was overdoing it and he probably knew it, had already retreated, his eyes expressionless, his body tense in what she was trying too hard not to make appear rejection. 'Maybe another night?' she tried to smile.

'Whenever you like, madam.' He touched a non-existent cap in a half salute, turned swiftly and walked away.

IN ROSE'S FOOTSTEPS
A Lost World

I am in Jinja, the town on Lake Victoria, where Rose McCormack, the elderly woman found on the beach at West Bognor almost three weeks ago, was a missionary for almost ten years in the 1940s and 50s. Today it seems a sleepy place on the shores of Lake Victoria, which is the second largest lake in the world. But in Rose's day it was a centre of the British colonial administration and a bustling hive of trade and commerce.

Jinja was a stop on the East African railway line that stretched from Mombasa on the Kenyan coast in the east to the borders of the Congo in the west, and cargo and passenger ships linked its port to others in Kenya and to Tanzania on the southern lakeshore. Today there are no trains, though there is still a station and a bridge, and no ferries. No boats sail from the Jinja Sailing Club and the golf course is overgrown and a parade ground for giant storks.

My guide is 65 year old Haresh Kumar who was born and educated in the town but forced to leave in 1972 by the then President Amin, together with the entire Indian community. Mr Kumar returned to work for the large Somani Corporation about 10 years ago when Asians were invited to reclaim their property by the present President Museveni. There are still relatively few Indians here and Mr Kumar's wife prefers to remain in India.

I have visited the wonderful viewing point at the Source of the Nile where the greatest river in the world flows from Lake Victoria two thousand miles north to Egypt and the Mediterranean. It is a stupendous sight and I felt very privileged to be at the place that the famous Victorian explorer David Livingstone suffered so much to look for - and in fact, died without finding. I have also seen the famous Bujagali Falls where braver souls than I can take a white water rafting trip. Apparently young backpackers come from all over the world for the experience although I did not see any. I did see the very brave young local man who, for a small amount of money, regularly throws himself into the rapids with nothing but an inflated car inner tube to support him. Anyone who wants to experience the more organised trip for themselves had better hurry:

like two other sets of falls near here, Bujagali is due to be dammed to produce more electricity to meet the needs of this now rapidly developing country.

What would Rose think if she came back? I wondered. I have not yet found the Church Missionary Society premises where she would have lived but I have seen the houses once inhabited by her fellow countrymen and women. Large mansions along the lakeshore, they must once have been the scenes of a very pleasant life of ease in Uganda's perfect climate. Today they are mostly empty, faded, ghostly places set in overgrown gardens: once fit for film stars I thought, a little fancifully, but of a film that stopped running a long time ago. The Jinja that Rose knew as a young woman is a lost world, its inhabitants, like her, long scattered to the four corners of the earth.

32

It was the next afternoon and they were driving on to Iganga after visiting the sugar factory. Moses' mobile rang as they reached the outskirts of the town.

'Yes sir. Of course, sir. No sir.' It sounded like a business call. He was clearly taking instructions. Lilia hoped it would be brief as, single-handed, Moses continued to navigate around the parked trucks and children playing at the side of the road and the dogs and goats wandering across it.

'It's for you.' He passed the handset in time to avoid a bicycle, heavily laden with green bananas that had wobbled into their path. 'Mr Kumar.'

'Lilia? How are you? Did you enjoy the visit to the factory? I hope you will write about it for your paper, Mr Somani will be pleased. I am calling because I have just been speaking to my brother in England.'

Lilia inhaled sharply. 'Does he remember anything?'

'He certainly remembers 1955 quite clearly.'

'And?' She felt a surge of excitement.

'It was the year the kabaka returned from two years exile in London. Everyone was talking about it. Hoping it would bring greater peace. He had been plotting against the Government you see and …'

'But about Joseph, the boy who disappeared?' Lilia could not contain her impatience any longer. 'Doesn't he remember anything about that?'

'I am sorry, no. He said maybe he was on holiday at the time. But you see, Lilia, the Indian community was really not so well integrated with the Europeans, or the Africans for that matter. We had our own life, in our own community, so many social gatherings, events, it was a wonderful life…'

'I'm sure it was.' Lilia tried to hide her disappointment. 'Thank you very much anyway for trying, and please thank your brother for me next time you speak. And I have made some notes for an article, I'll send it to you if it is published.'

'There was one further thing he remembered.'

'Yes?'

'He used to play cricket after school with his friends. You know how crazy the Indians are for cricket.'

'Yes?'

'And he remembers there was a white boy used to play with them some days, who was the son of missionaries. He doesn't remember his name but …'

'It could have been Joseph.'

Moses stopped the car outside a two storey cement block that many years before had been painted pink. '*Welcome Hotel*' proclaimed a board tacked over the entrance, on either side of which straggled dusty pink hibiscus planted in old oil drums.

'Mr Kumar says you must stay in the best hotel in town.' Moses' face was expressionless as he opened the passenger door. 'I do not know how long it is since he came to Iganga. This is the only hotel.'

'I'm sure it'll be fine.' Lilia got out. 'So long as I have clean sheets. And you must stay here too.'

She walked towards the hotel entrance but Moses did not follow. She turned and saw his frown.

'I'll pay of course.'

He shook his head. 'I can stay with my mother. She is waiting to see me.'

'Oh yes, of course she is.' Lilia hesitated. 'How far away is -?'

'Kamuli? Maybe an hour.'

'Then…'

'Then I can come back at night?'

'Yes. Could you? Please? I can find my way around the town in the day on my own but …'

'You want me to stay at night with you.'

Was he being deliberately provocative? Lilia met his narrowed eyes without smiling.

'I should be much happier if you were also in the hotel.'

'You are afraid.'

'If you like. I am the only white woman in town, I imagine. So yes, I do feel a little…vulnerable.'

He paused, appearing to consider, no doubt enjoying the power she had conferred upon him.

'Then yes, I will return.'

'Thank you. And if you want to return to Kamuli again tomorrow I can wait here for you.'

Lilia progressed slowly along Main Street, the focus of attention and followed by a growing crowd of curious children. They were shy but persistent.

'Hey mama. Mama mzungu.' The bolder ones called softly after her amidst muffled laughter.

She was not sure how to respond, felt faintly threatened. When she turned they scattered like birds, before again creeping closer as she walked on. There were about twenty-five of them, ranging in age from the mid-teens to toddlers. Lilia decided to act as she would at home.

'Shouldn't you be in school?'

'School closed, mama. Holiday, mama. School tomorrow.'

Lilia nodded, smiled, and was wondering what else to say when she felt a slight tug at her camera strap.

'Hey!' she addressed the culprit, a very small boy whose minder, a girl of perhaps eleven, who was also carrying a baby on her hip, immediately cast down her eyes to avoid Lilia's challenge.

'My brother say you take pictures mama,' she said softly. 'You take our children pictures.'

'Of course, of course.' Lilia gushed relief at being given a way to relate to them, to please them.

She took their photos separately and together, and jumping up and around her, faces bright with laughter, clenched fists raised in triumph. She showed them the results, amidst great hilarity and some surprise.

'I'll send them to you if you give me an address,' she offered and they inclined their heads from side to side in appreciation. But maybe, they suggested hopefully, she had some pens to give them? They seemed content, however, with the sweets that she had brought from the factory. As she distributed them, the taller children reached to touch her hair, and after she had finished, the smallest fought off fierce competition to hold her hand. She felt like Gulliver, caught in a web of gentle caresses and demands.

'What is your name?'

'Where you come from?'

'Why you come our town?'

'I am looking for the mission.'

There were only blank looks.

'A church maybe? And a school?'

'She is going to our school!' An excited ripple ran round the group and hands again reached out to touch her. 'We take you! We show you!'

'Head teacher he lives there, mama,' said the girl with the baby, shifting it to her other hip. 'Mr Kyasi, he help you.'

The headmaster was digging the garden in front of a pleasant bungalow, situated in a large compound that was secluded from the road by a line of tall trees and hedges of flowering shrubs. Several larger single-storey buildings, linked by a deep wooden verandah, edged the further side of the grassy space and, at the far end, Lilia could see a big brick building that, from the cross over its entrance, appeared to be a church. Mr Kyasi straightened as the noisy group approached, laid down his spade and came to greet them, a tall, bespectacled figure, his hands outstretched to calm the clamour. Half a dozen of the younger children abandoned Lilia and, calling his name, ran to meet him.

'Children, children!' He stooped to touch each lightly on their heads and they fell back in respectful silence as he shook Lilia's hand. 'Thank you, all of you, for bringing me my guest. I will see you tomorrow. Come, Mrs - '

'Zynofsky, Lilia Zynofsky and it's not Mrs.'

'Patrick Kyasi.'

33

Lilia leaned back in the low cane chair on Patrick's verandah and placed her glass on the table beside her. Soon she would ask if she could take some photographs, perhaps look inside the house if it did not seem too impolite. For the moment, she just tried to absorb the knowledge that she was in the very place that Rose must have sat with Edward, with Joseph, looking out at the same trees, perhaps the same buildings, and at the church that Edward had been so desperate to finish building. And that her host was the young boy who had lived there at the same time.

'I've seen your photograph,' Lilia told him. 'With your parents and the McCormacks, in an old album that just came to light. I could send you copies if you like.'

Patrick looked doubtful. 'Sometimes one's memory alone is better but still, I should like to see my parents as young people, thank you.'

'I also have this photo of Joseph.' She gave it to him.

He looked at it closely, shook his head and handed it back. "I don't remember his face,' he said. 'But let me tell you what I do know. This was the mission house, where Mr McCormack lived. I lived,' he indicated with a wave of his hand, 'in a small house behind here, with my parents of course. It was pulled down when the government took over the schools after independence. Over there,' he pointed to the other buildings, 'Was a girls' junior secondary boarding school and a small boys' primary school that Mr McCormack gradually expanded into a junior secondary boarding school. I was one of the first pupils. The first boarders used to stay in this house with him and he made me a monitor to help look after them. My father was the pastor of the church and this was where I went to school, where I returned to teach and, as you see,' he touched his grey hair. 'Have remained for many years. I am beginning to feel my age, it is hard work teaching. But our country is short of teachers of experience. Because of AIDS.' He was silent a moment, then brightened. 'So Mrs McCormack is still alive? She must be very old.'

He did not remember Rose clearly. 'There were several English ladies when I was small, they used to teach at the girls' school,' he explained. 'Mr McCormack taught mathematics and science. Mrs McCormack maybe also taught there but by the time the McCormacks came most of the teachers would have been African. My mother used to run the Mothers' Union after Mrs McCormack left, so I expect Mrs McCormack did it when she was still here. It was mostly the missionary wives who did these things. Also I think it would have been Mrs McCormack who started the Sunday school – the missionary before the McCormacks didn't have a wife - and my mother used to help her. I liked going there, it was better than staying in the long church service like we had to do before! We used to sing songs and once I was Joseph in the nativity play. We even took our play to some other villages – Busembaga, Bugiri maybe, I know we went as far as Kamuli...'

'Kamuli? My driver's mother lives there, he's gone to visit her.'

'Ah well, I don't suppose anyone would remember our play now! But someone might remember more about Mr or Mrs McCormack.'

'Do you remember Joseph at all? I know he would have been here only a few weeks that summer.'

'He let me play on his swing. I do remember that. His father had made one for him, and I remember how much I wanted to sit on it, but my mother wouldn't let me until Joseph said I could. He taught me how to work myself higher, you know putting your feet out and back, out and back.' Patrick demonstrated, his legs too long to fold back under his chair. 'I didn't know how to do it at first. But he was three or four years older than me, he didn't really want to play with a little boy like me. I don't suppose I could even catch a ball at that age!' His eyes crinkled with laughter before he again became serious. 'And I do remember the day he disappeared. I had to go over to the church for Mr McCormack. That was when it was still being built. I think that was one of the reasons Mr McCormack was sent to Iganga, to get it finished. I remember it standing there big and empty, without even a roof, for years and years. Shall I show you? We are quite proud of it.'

As they walked across the grass to the church, he pointed out another building to its right.

'That used to be a medical facility, a clinic. I had all my vaccinations there. I think I remember Mrs McCormack being in the clinic.'

Lilia nodded. 'She was a nurse. I heard from someone who used to live here that there was a hospital here.'

'A hospital? I don't think so. Although yes, I suppose you could say - there were a few rooms where patients were sometimes kept overnight, longer I suppose. Sometimes their family members slept out here on the grass. I'd forgotten that. But it wasn't for long, just until the big government hospital was built at the other end of town. I think there would have been only one or two nurses and a visiting doctor. Most of the daily care and treatment was done by what they used to call dressers. Young men mostly, I remember one of them well. Stephen, he was here many years. He helped me learn to read.'

'I've seen his photo as well,' Lilia said. 'Is he still living?'

Patrick Kyasi sighed deeply. 'No. He was killed by Amin's soldiers. He was part Acholi – from the north of the country. Many of his people were killed. Here we are, Miss Zynofsky. Here is our church.'

He opened the door to a large brick built circular building with a conical roof of corrugated iron and a large square porticoed entrance. Lilia walked past him into the quiet dark interior. It was almost undecorated with plain white walls, a simple altar table, rows of wooden benches and a single strip of faded carpet up the centre of the grey stone floor. Yet it had the calm solemnity of a House of God and was clearly cared for.

'All the inner furnishings were donated by different families,' Patrick pointed to the wooden cross above the altar, on which hung an unmistakeably African Christ, and a pulpit and font, both adorned with carved animals and flowers. In front of each sitting place was a hassock, each with a different tapestry design.

'The work of our ladies in the Mothers Union,' he explained, as Lilia fingered one admiringly. 'They have to work hard to keep ahead of the ants. My wife, God rest her soul, was always darning them. But look behind you, this is our most prized possession.'

Above the western entrance where they had entered was a large round window of coloured glass, through which the afternoon sun streamed in beams of many coloured light. At its centre was the figure of an African man holding a small goat or sheep under one arm, his other raised in blessing. It was simple compared to most of the stained glass windows that Lilia had seen in Europe, but here it looked the more beautiful for being set in such humble surroundings.

'It is most unusual for a parish church in East Africa,' Patrick told her, her gaze still fixed on the marvellous sight, his entire person bathed in its multi-coloured light. 'It took the people a long time to save the money but Mr McCormack was determined to have it. I remember watching him count the money. "Nearly there," he would say. "One more push." The patches of colour on Patrick's face danced as he laughed. 'It was of course much more than 'one more push'. But in the end he got his window and he got the Bishop to come and consecrate it. That was quite a day… It was not long after that he died. I didn't tell you that, did I? He died while still in office.'

'I did know that. The person who found the album told me. She was a missionary in Jinja with the McCormacks, before they came here.'

'And she too is still alive,' Patrick marvelled. 'Mr McCormack cannot have been very old, though of course he seemed it to me.'

'It was in 1963 or 4,' Lilia told him.

'Then I was about twelve or thirteen and he perhaps was in his middle or late forties. Such a long time ago.' Patrick was silent for a moment before shaking his head as if to clear it . 'We removed and hid the window for safety all the time President Amin was in power. A lot of soldiers were based at Jinja and they often drove past on a shooting spree.'

'It's really wonderful,' said Lilia. 'I'm glad Edward had time to finish it.' Was it Edward's memorial to Joseph, she wondered? The lost lamb, safe in the arms of the Holy shepherd? It seemed very likely. She shivered. 'Tell me about the day Joseph disappeared.'

'You are cold. Let us go back outside. I will show you the school rooms.' He led the way but stopped just outside and turned back to look again at the church. 'On the day that Joseph disappeared, Mr McCormack sent me with a letter for the builders' headman. I had never been inside the church since the builders had started work again and I remember they were sitting around on the ground just inside there, smoking and drinking, arguing maybe, I didn't understand what they were saying. They weren't from round here most of them and I was quite afraid of them. My father said some of them were bad men. I think he meant they were pagans. And he did not smoke or drink himself. Anyway, as soon as I gave the headman the letter, they all jumped up and started working. I remember feeling very surprised and pleased with myself! Very important.' He smiled at the memory.

'And the other thing I remember was late that night. I woke up to hear Mrs McCormack outside our house, calling for my parents to go and help her find Joseph, and there were drums. That's what I remember most, her shouting, screaming almost, and the drums and being afraid. They left me alone in the dark. They thought I was asleep and I lay there, listening to the drums and being afraid.' He was silent for a long moment and then reached to touch Lilia's hand. 'It is all a long time ago, Miss Zynofsky. A very long time. So many terrible things have happened since that time. Since Joseph disappeared.'

'Yes, of course,' said Lilia. 'I know. And it does seem very unlikely that I will find out what happened to him. But I have to try because I think Rose has never given up hoping that Joseph will return. All these years. Can you understand that? Sometimes I think I do.'

'Hope is eternal. Where there is life, there is hope. Perhaps the opposite is also true.' He paused. 'You must know what St Paul says: "*And now abideth faith, hope and charity, these three. But the greatest of these is charity.*" Which is often translated as love. The first epistle to the Corinthians, chapter thirteen.' He paused.

'It is a good thing that you are doing so much for another, for Mrs McCormack. It is a form of love. I am sure you know that the second, and second most important, Commandment is "*You shall love your neighbour as yourself.*" But you know, I was always very sorry for Mr McCormack. You perhaps do not know that Mrs McCormack went away when Joseph disappeared and never came back?'

Lilia nodded. 'I gathered as much from the mission records. And the same old colleague of the McCormacks told me. She said she had always thought it was wrong of Rose.'

Patrick nodded as if in agreement. 'My mother used to tell me how she sometimes felt that she was the real missionary's wife, because she had to deal with all the people who used to come to the house to see Mr McCormack.' Patrick's tone became more insistent. 'He was a good man, Miss Zynofsky. He helped me 'to say for myself'. '*Okweyatulira'* we say here in Uganda. It is a special stage between baptism and confirmation. To profess the faith oneself, to understand what one is taking on when one becomes a full Christian. I should not be here as I am today were it not for Edward McCormack.'

As they walked towards the schoolrooms, the lengthening shadows of the great trees cast by the rapidly setting sun seemed to pursue them, as if determined they should not escape their cold embrace. Lilia shivered again, feeling the influence of past events catching up with her. But whether she would have felt the same had she had no knowledge of them, or whether it was mere superstition, she could not say.

Before dinner she wrote again to Sarita, describing how she had met Patrick and asking her if she could visit Rose and tell her. She also outlined some of what she had discovered from Patrick about the church and the work of both the McCormacks, but emphasised that, for Rose's sake, she needed time to think about how much to write in the paper and therefore not to tell Rose more than she seemed to wish to know.

I have written instead another general interest article about a visit to a sugar factory. Well I found it interesting. You could show Rose that. Please could you ask Bhavin to tell his father's friend that so far I would say Iganga has gone downhill if anything since his day. The hotel where I am staying is certainly seedy. The town is still bustling I suppose but surely more ramshackle than it was fifty odd years ago. However there are, as you see, internet facilities so I shouldn't grumble. And do thank Mr Shah again.

Another thing to tell Rose please: my escort in Jinja, whom I met through Narendra, to whom I am also extremely grateful, has a brother in England who he contacted and who thinks he played cricket with Joseph. 'A white boy, the son of missionaries.' Rose will like to hear that though not perhaps what Patrick the school teacher said, and you all probably think, that it is all so long ago - and that I am on a fool's errand.

Tomorrow I am hoping to go to my driver's village or town, Kamuli it's called. Another long shot but it was one of the places where Rose used to go to hold a clinic.

Logging off now. It's getting dark, which it does very quickly here of course. I am missing the long summer evenings. Dinner and then straight to bed. Not much night life here as you can imagine. Or not the sort I'd want to find. Cannot imagine living here for years on end like all those good missionaries.

Love to Rajah. And to you both with many thanks as ever. It's good to have you there.

Lilia

IN ROSE'S FOOTSTEPS
Not Just A Load Of Humbug

Still in Uganda, I am visiting some of the places known to Rose McCormack when she was a missionary here 50 years ago, hoping to meet people who knew her and also to report on matters of more general interest.

How many people know how much work is required to produce that staple of our diet, the humble bag of sugar? Today I found out when, just north of Lake Victoria, I visited a sugar factory that was founded in the 1930s by the grandfather of the present owners. The Somani family was forced by then President Amin to leave Uganda along with all the other Asians back in 1972 and by the time they were invited to return by President Museveni in the 1980s, sugar production had ground to a halt. I was told how all the machinery was rusted up, overgrown and undermined by ants and beetles and how impossible it had seemed to get it all operating again.

But today, shuddering conveyor belts again transport the raw sugar cane direct from the lorries that bring it in from surrounding farms, on to the powerful shredders, into huge steaming vats and a succession of gleaming steel revolving drums, all with temperatures closely monitored by the engineers. In another building, some of the product is made into a variety of brightly coloured cellophane-wrapped boiled sweets and toffees, mostly for the local market. And, in a side building that is connected to the main factory, the discarded sugar waste is converted into electricity that in turn helps power the entire production process.

'We are in the process of expanding output with the ultimate view of powering the surrounding township and perhaps even selling to the grid,' Process Control Manager David Mbeke told me.

It was in the township where most of the workers live that I realised that what I was seeing was 'sustainable development' in action, that is, economic activity that is in harmony with the local environment and people, rather than putting profit first. For the factory is the powerhouse of a thriving community with pleasant streets of houses with gardens, a primary school, a hospital and a social centre. Not to mention a guesthouse with attached restaurant, where I could have stayed had I wished. There is even a Christian meeting house. The one time head of the Somani family, though himself Hindu, welcomed both Catholic and Protestant missionaries as a helpful influence amongst employees, who came from many different tribes and parts of the country.

This is in effect, a model village on the lines of Bournville, which was built in the 19th century for their British employees by the Cadbury family who were inspired by their Quaker beliefs. As I looked round, I could not help thinking how much Rose, and especially Edward, her husband, would have approved. He took a great interest in the development of projects that would benefit the whole community. Best of all, and unlike its nineteenth century counterpart, the Somani township is located at the source of its primary crop, rather than thousands of miles away. It thereby benefits the growers of the crop and their dependants and the economy of the country of origin rather than the foreign settlers, traders, middlemen and their home economies as in previous eras. Perhaps one day we shall be able to buy Ugandan sweets in our supermarkets and corner shops. Lake Victorian humbugs anyone?

34

The small dining room behind the bar was as quiet and respectable as any Bognor guesthouse might be, thought Lilia, not that she had stayed in any. The other guests eating there were a family of four, whose two little girls stared at her until their mother sharply reproved them; two young couples who were only interested in each other; and a few single men, who, perhaps just passing through, ate quickly, downed their beers and left. Moses had not appeared by the time that Lilia had finished picking dubiously at a plate of grey chicken and rice but she had felt no need of his company. She was obviously perfectly safe and she wished she had not asked him to return that night.

Her room was on the second floor at the back of the building, away from the main road. It was clean enough with newly ironed sheets but it had some very strange features. The enormous wardrobe had a clothes rail at least six feet from the floor and the towel rail in the adjoining bathroom was situated right under the shower head so that any towels put there would get wet. The rail was also far too high. She squinted up at the neon tube in the centre of the bedroom ceiling, around which buzzed a haze of moths, flies and mosquitoes, all intent on self-destruction, and wondered why the two wall lights, situated near the ceiling, were so far from the bed. Not that she could have used them as they had no bulbs. It was as if the fittings had been installed by a giant with no idea of their intended function. She decided to go to sleep as soon as possible for it had been a long day. She set the alarm on her watch, put it on top of The New English Bible on the bedside table, switched off the light and got into bed.

She was just beginning to doze when loud voices that sounded very close roused her. She sat up quickly and looked at the door to see if it had been opened but it remained shut. She got out of bed to lock it, just in case. The same thing happened several times; very loud voices, sometimes followed by the banging shut of other doors, all sounding impossibly close. Why was everyone so noisy, she thought irritably, so inconsiderate? She got up at last to investigate and discovered that there were no solid landings between the floors of the staircase, only metal grilles, which reverberated and transmitted every sound straight up the central well as efficiently as if that were their purpose. She had vaguely noticed that the staircase looked more like a fire escape on her way up, but had not realised the effect that this might have. After a further half hour of this torture she switched on the light, awakening the suicidal insect crowd, picked up the Bible and found the passage quoted by Patrick Kyasi, here written in modern form. Her own secondary school head teacher had read it out in morning assembly every few months so she knew it almost by heart, yet had never really thought about it.

"There are three things that last for ever: faith, hope and love; but the greatest of them all is love. Put love first." A few verses earlier she found St Paul's definition: *"Love is patient: love is kind and envies no one. Love is never boastful, nor conceited, nor rude; never selfish, not quick to take offence. Love keeps no score of wrongs; does not gloat over other men's sins, but delights in the truth. There is nothing love cannot face; there is no limit to its faith, its hope and its endurance. Love will never come to an end.'* For these lovely words she could almost forgive Paul his attitude to women, who, according to the next chapter, should not be allowed to speak in meetings but, if there is something they want to know, ask their husbands at home. *"It is a shocking thing that women should address the congregation."* No wonder there was such opposition in the Anglican Church to the ordination of women.

The trouble with love though, she thought, like many elegant theories, is putting it into practice. Especially when, as in her case, it makes competing demands, which, at twenty-one, she had been too young to resolve. A mother's love is surely most like Paul's ideal. But not in her case. Mothers were supposed to sacrifice themselves for their children, not the other way round. If her mother hadn't been so unreasonably demanding, there would never have come a point where her future life would depend on her understanding a stupid sonnet. She and Dan would have had children, whom she would have loved, and by now, like Sarah, she would probably have been a grandmother too, rather than a lonely old woman trying (again!) to sort someone else's life out and in a horrible alien place. Lilia had chosen anger tonight, it was less destructive than self-pity. But there was no control over her dreams.

Daniel, that's no way to hold a baby, under your arm like that. You are supposed to support its head. Be careful, you'll drop her! I'll take her but I must put on some clothes first... why can't I find anything to fit? Why is everything too small? I can't suddenly have got so fat. Oh there, that dress, you used to love me in that, there it is hanging in my wardrobe! I can't reach it, why is the rail so high? I can't concentrate with all that shouting. And I must brush my hair, I look awful. Who keeps banging the door? Is that my face in the mirror? It looks like an old woman. It is me. I'm frightened. Daniel, help me. Why are you holding that goat? Where is my baby?

She woke to find the light still on and a grey dawn filtering through the scanty curtains. She fleetingly recognised bits of several recurring dreams that had haunted her over the years, before the growing daylight sent them back into her unconscious. The high clothes rail was a new one, as was Daniel holding the goat, which was obviously inspired by Edward's church window. She felt exhausted and wished she were at home where she could start the day with a cup of tea in her own kitchen with dear Rajah. But this is no time to be faint-hearted, she chided herself, just when I am making more progress than I had expected, and she got quickly out of bed to investigate the curious shower.

Moses was sitting with two other men at a table in the corner of the dining room when she entered. He nodded but did not approach until she had finished breakfast.

'My mother says I must take you to visit her,' he said. 'I told her why you are here in Uganda and she says she can perhaps help you. Of course, it is up to you.'

Lilia smiled at him, resolved to be more friendly. 'That's very kind of her,' she said. 'I should very much like to meet her. In fact, I was thinking of asking you to take me there. Patrick Kyasi mentioned it yesterday as somewhere people might remember the McCormacks.'

'Mr Kyasi? The headmaster? He is still here?'

'I met him yesterday at the school.'

'Our school used to go there for sports competitions,' said Moses. 'He presented me with a medal one year. I was very good at running.'

Lilia glanced sideways at his long lean body and muscular arms that effortlessly guided the steering wheel. He was like a coiled spring, ready for anything, wasted in this safe domesticated role. What could he have achieved given more opportunity? What would he have been if Europeans had never come to his country? His lips curved in a faint smile and he shifted his weight, straightened his shoulders. He knew she was looking at him. She turned her eyes quickly back to the road ahead.

'Let's go there first,' she said on an impulse. 'Just for a short visit. I'd like to see the school with children in it. They were on holiday yesterday. And I am sure Patrick would be very happy to see you again.'

Patrick was about to take morning assembly.

'Come and meet the children, Moses,' he said. 'It is good for them to meet someone who has got on in life. Tell them they must study. It will be better coming from you. And Lilia, if you have brought more of those sweets the children were telling me about, you are very welcome to distribute them.'

He led them out of his office to the compound where the children were sitting quietly in neat rows. The sun was still low and it was cool under the tall trees and many of them were wearing sweaters. Blue sweaters. The same blue as those that Rose knitted for Joseph. Edward must have made it the school uniform. Lilia wondered if she should suggest to Rose that she send all those sweaters here.

After the children had been sent to their classrooms, Patrick rejoined them. 'Last night I found the sermon Mr McCormack gave when the church was consecrated,' he told Lilia. 'At the time I thought it was so very good at reaching out to the different parts of the congregation, which is not an easy thing to do, even now. If you can spare the time, come back to the church and listen. I should like to do it justice in the proper setting. And you will see why I hold Edward McCormack in such esteem.'

'I will stay with the car,' said Moses.

'No one will touch it,' Patrick assured him. 'But as you wish.'

Patrick climbed the steps to the pulpit, stood a moment with his head bowed in prayer and then spoke, his voice deep clear and powerful. *'"Dear Friends and Brothers in Christ, I am full of joy at being able to address you today in this our lovely church. It has been many years in the making, due mainly to the determination of the people of this parish that it be truly a fitting house for God.*

'"This happy day owes much to the labours of those who have come from many places far from our parish, some of whom have still themselves to see the Light and allow Jesus into their lives. For these, and all other such souls, we pray to God to help us, his servants on earth, to help them acknowledge his power and presence in all the corners of the earth and throughout creation.

'"*My friends,"'* Patrick continued. *'"Consider the beehive that hangs in the tree waiting for the wild bees to swarm into it. I say to you, let us become like that beehive and receive the Lord Jesus as the bee to dwell in it. Then He will bring us his honey and our lives shall be full of sweetness. And I believe this church is like that beehive too, for it is full today of those who have worked together to do his work, as bees work together to make their honey. This is the true spirit of Christianity that knows no difference between men and women, wherever they may come from, whatever country, whatever walk in life, this is the love of God that passes all understanding.*

"'Love is the greatest of the three great guiding principles by which Christianity teaches us to live our lives. Those of you who know your Bible, and there are many of you here today, know that St Paul travelled to many distant places to take the Word of God to the people living there. It is in one of his letters to one of these peoples, the people of Corinth, in Greece, that he explains these three principles. They are faith, hope and charity, or love as we may translate it, and the greatest of these, he tells us, is love. In those days it was often difficult, even dangerous, being a Christian, much as it was in this country not so very long ago. We all know of the boys at the court of the kabaka, who chose martyrdom over renouncing their Christian faith. Some white men like me also laid down their lives in their mission to bring the good news to Uganda.

"'I know that some of you here today must sometimes feel like those early Christians, far from the centres of religion in our towns, far from the loving support of other Christians. It is hard to be the only Christian

in your family or your village. Hard to hold to the faith that you are in the right and everyone else is wrong. Hard to hope that you may one day, by the grace of God, persuade them to join you in your faith. Some of our priests and catechists, whom I can see before me, often face a lonely task in doing God's work. Remember, you are like the forked stick that holds up the bananas in the garden. The owner of the garden has put you there because he wants all of the fruit in your village to be his, and, if you were not there, the fruit might fall to the ground and be spoilt. Although, unlike bananas, it is never too late for human beings to rise from the ground and be made good, be made sweet again.

'"But I say to you, let us all be like those sticks that hold the bananas. Let us stand firm. Let not the ants of doubt gnaw away and eat at our faith. Let not the worm of decay enter our hearts and destroy our hope, whatever sorrows we may suffer, whatever hardships endure. And let us remember that the sweetest fruit is not the one with the smoothest skin and that God sees through our outer skins to the truth in our hearts. God loves a pure heart. Let us be more like Him.

'"Oh God, we are Thy cooking pots. Give us the fire and the water that we need so that the food for Thy children may not be spoiled and thy children go hungry. In the name of the Father, the Son and the Holy Ghost, Amen."'

'Amen,' echoed Lilia automatically and heard another deeper voice speaking in unison. She looked over her shoulder to where Moses stood just inside the doors, his head bowed, his hands raised together as in prayer.

Patrick joined her and they walked slowly down the aisle towards Moses.

'Thank you,' Lilia said. 'I see what you mean. How Edward must have tried so hard to find metaphors, word pictures really, to which his congregation could relate and understand his meaning.'

'It is what we all need to do more often,' Patrick responded. 'If we are not to destroy the world with our conflicts. Goodbye, young man,' he held out his hand and shook Moses' warmly. 'Come and see us again. The children liked you. And goodbye Miss Zynofsky, please remember me to Mrs McCormack. I am sure you are helping her just by looking for Joseph.'

35

Kamuli's main street was a shorter version of Iganga's, lined by single and double storey cement constructions with corrugated iron roofs that housed the usual variety of shops and businesses. Their contents spilled onto the roadside. Moses stopped the car by towers of gleaming aluminium saucepans without handles, stacked in a diminishing order of size that began with ones surely big enough to feed a small village. A boy of about twelve sat on an upturned bucket reading a book. He jumped up, his face breaking into a wide smile when he saw Moses.

'Hey, uncle, I didn't expect you to come here again so soon!'

Moses cuffed his ear affectionately. 'I can tell that. Or you would be paying more attention to your job.' He turned to Lilia. 'Michael is supposed to keep the animals away from the merchandise but he's always got his nose in a book. Where's big Mama?'

'Making your dinner, what else?' A deep voice sounded from the doorway to the shop. The speaker was a well-built woman of perhaps sixty, dressed in a long cotton robe printed with trailing green vines, her head in an elegant wrap of the same material that enhanced her imposing height. She held Moses close to her before stepping forward to welcome Lilia.

'Come through,' she said, leading her through the dark interior of the shop into a living space behind. 'Sit outside in the shade.' She indicated some plastic chairs by a table under a banana tree in a small garden behind the house. 'I will make us some tea and Moses can watch the shop. It will do him good to sit still for once, all this driving around he does. It is time he settled down with a nice girl and made me some more grandchildren. As he has heard me say many times.'

'Miss Zynofsky?'A soft voice startled Lilia as she sat waiting for Moses' mother to reappear. She turned to see a thin elderly woman walking briskly up the garden path, wearing a plain white blouse and dark skirt and thick-lensed glasses.

'Leah Ntate.' She shook Lilia's hand, smiling broadly. 'Adeke told me she was expecting you.'

Before Lilia could reply, Moses' mother reappeared. 'Here you are, Miss Ntate, bursting in on us the back way as usual.' She placed a tray holding a bunch of plantains and three steaming cups of tea on the table and clasped Leah's hands in her own.. It was obvious that the two women were old friends.

'How goes it with you today, Adeke mama? Did you pass a good night?'

'But for the creaking of my bones. How goes it with you?'

'Well, the Lord be praised. So here is our visitor come from afar.'

'Leah has news for you,' Adeke sat at the table and began to cut up the plantains, between sips of her tea.

'I know your name,' Lilia had been thinking. 'You were the girl Edward McCormack helped become a nurse.'

Leah laughed and slapped her thighs with her hands. 'I was a young girl ripe for marriage,' she said. 'But the Good Lord sent Nurse Rose to show me a different path.'

'I have read letters written by Edward to Rose, when he went to see your father to ask him to allow you to stay at school. I can't believe I am actually meeting you.'

'It was a very long time ago.' Leah nodded. 'But I remember so clearly the impression Rose made on me, how much her kind of medicine had to offer. In those days, many people used to keep to the old ways. Some people still do.' She glanced briefly at Adeke. 'They went to the hospital to see if white medicine would help them but if it did not, or not quickly enough, then they would go back home and use the traditional methods. I remember a girl in the next village, she was about my age, and we were quite friendly in school. She was expecting her first baby. But the baby did not come, after many hours it did not come, and as you can imagine she was in great pain. So her husband took her to the hospital where a doctor came and operated to remove the baby which was already dead. And then the girl was not recovering, she was speaking like a mad woman, I know now she must have been delirious with a high fever. The doctor started to give her medicine, but the husband insisted on taking her home to make a sacrifice.'

‘What would that have involved?’

‘They would have put her bed in the centre of the family compound and all the family would have gathered round and called a *mulabale,* a medicine man, what white people call a witch doctor. Then they would have sacrificed a goat as everyone danced around her, the contents of the goat’s gut and its blood would have been smeared on her body and her bed and then they would have eaten the rest of the goat.’

Lilia’s head was beginning to ache. Shimmering slivers of sunlight cut through the banana leaves and flickered from the faces of her companions. She reached for her tea and gulped it, closing her eyes to shut out the glitter, but then black after-images like gesticulating fingers traced shifting patterns on the blood red of her eyelids. She forced her eyes open and shook her head to try to clear her vision.

‘You are disgusted, Lilia.’ Leah misunderstood. ‘It is not so different to what we can read in the Old Testament. Let me tell you the rest of the story. The girl did not recover. She might have died anyway, but Nurse Rose believed that if her people had had more faith in white medicine and left her at the hospital, or perhaps brought her earlier, then she might have survived, and her baby. So she was determined to take her medicine to them, to win their trust. One of the places she started to come to was my village and she held her clinic in my mother’s house. My mother was my father’s first wife, and he trusted her judgment in many things. I used to help Nurse Rose. She taught me how to weigh the babies, take temperatures, keep the records and explain to the women what she wanted them to do. I was very happy, I knew that it was what I wanted to do with my life. Nurse Rose said God was calling me.

‘I missed her very much when she left, many people did. Many good friends she had, many people she helped. When she lost her son, one whole village converted because she had saved one of the headmen’s sons: “God has taken away one Christian soul from this world,” he said. “Let there be one hundred more.”’

‘What did you think had happened to Joseph, her son?’

Leah did not reply for several moments. Then she said. ‘Next day my mother went to her house, in Iganga. She said she would take her to a *mulabale* and ask him to make a divination, to intercede with Nyasaye. With the Creator and Giver of all things. He is also called Nkalaga the Protector who takes care of people. People have different names for him, Adeke calls him Jok.' She waved her hand dismissively. 'I think some other women went too, I don't know exactly what happened but, when my mother returned, she made what you would call a shrine under a big tree in our compound. For some time I remember there was a picture of Joseph there that she had cut from a newspaper. She used to pray there every day, make offerings.'

'Was it this picture?' Lilia reached into her back and handed Leah her copy of the picture of Joseph.

'Oh dear God,' Leah cried softly. 'It is the same. Poor little child.' She passed the picture to Adeke and Moses.

'So your mother did think he was dead?' asked Lilia.

Leah looked away and it was Adeke who replied. 'For many people, traditionally, including where I come from, there is not such a difference between the living and the dead. Or between human beings and the rest of creation. Nature. Everything is connected. If we do not live our lives correctly, then powerful forces of nature can make bad things happen. But if we pray and make sacrifices, then God can change these forces, command them to act in a different way.'

Was this what Rose believed? Lilia wondered. That, whether or not she was responsible in some way for Joseph's disappearance, if only she now 'acted correctly' she would in some sense keep him alive? Even find him? Lilia felt she almost understood but her head was pounding too much for her to concentrate.

'Excuse me,' she said. 'I need to get something from the car, some aspirin. I've got a bit of a headache.'

'Moses will fetch it. Moses!' Adeke disappeared into the house carrying the dish of plantains with her.

'Perhaps you should lie down,' Leah reached across and felt her forehead. 'You feel a little warm.'

'I'll be all right in a moment. Oh, thank you, Moses,' she took her bag from him as he emerged from the house and sat down beside her. She reached in to find the small plastic purse that contained all her medicines and, rummaging for the box of paracetamol, she found also her malaria tablets, packaged in dated foil pockets like contraceptives. What day was it? It was hard to keep track here. She realised she had forgotten to take one again and surreptitiously swallowed two together, making a greater show of swallowing two paracetamol with the water that Moses had also fetched. She smiled firmly at Leah.

'I'll be fine now. So then you became a nurse?'

Leah nodded. 'Yes, soon after that my mother started telling my father he should let me go to become a nurse and I went to Kampala, to Mengo Hospital, a big hospital and training school that was founded by the Church Missionary Society. It was where Mrs McCormack also went. We were taught to be good Christian nurses'

'Rose said something about being a Christian nurse,' Lilia remembered. 'Actually about not being a good one. She was still not speaking properly, I didn't really understand.'

'I can tell you what she meant. In fact, I can remember exactly what they taught us,' said Leah. '"*Remember that Christ sent out his disciples 'to preach the kingdom of God and to heal the sick' and the Church has always been a pioneer in caring for the sick. In London there are still two great hospitals, St Bartholomew's and St Thomas's, set up hundreds of years ago by religious bodies to care for the sick poor.*

"But our medical work, our nursing, is not like the fisherman's bait, to lure people into listening to the Christian Gospel. We believe that, like Christ, we are spreading the Christian message as much in our work of healing as in any sermon. We, like Christ, care for the whole person, in body, mind and spirit. By 'health' we mean wholeness, completeness and, for us, there is no completeness apart from God. For the Christian nurse, nursing is active prayer, it is eternal love in action, as we work with God to restore the sick to completeness in God."'

'Dinner is ready.' Adeke summoned them inside before Lilia had time to reflect on how exactly Rose might have found herself deficient according to these teachings. Leah's explanation was much more - mystical, one might say, than she had expected. Moses was already seated at the table. Lilia began to eat despite feeling increasingly sick.

'Have you told Lilia about the meetings you used to have after the clinics?' Adeke asked Leah after a few moments. 'Prayer meetings. To convert the heathen, like me.'

Leah shook her finger in smiling reproof. 'Nurse Rose used to finish her clinics with some hymn singing and prayers. We joined in as well as we could. And when I started work here I used to do the same. It was how I met Adeke. She used to take her first son there.'

'Boas, God rest his soul.'

Sharp pains gripped Lilia's stomach. She took a deep breath and turned to Adeke.

'Is he…?'

'My brother died of AIDS,' Moses informed her without raising his eyes from his plate. 'Michael is his son.'

'I'm so sorry.' Lilia swallowed back the bile that had risen to the back of her mouth.

Adeke patted her hand. 'It is some years past,' she said. 'And I thank God I have Michael. Do you remember?' She turned to Leah and laughed. 'When you persuaded me to join the Mothers' Union? To learn to be a good Christian home-maker? I was a member for some time. But I am afraid I was a troublemaker. I used to say we women know enough about home-making. What we need is a Fathers' Union! '

'Oh my friend, such a shameless old pagan you are!'

Lilia pushed back her chair and stood up. 'Excuse me but where is the bathroom? I feel really sick.'

36

Lilia woke with an acute pain in her stomach. She was lying on a low narrow bed in a white-walled room that was lit dimly by a small window high on one side. Somebody had removed her outer clothing and covered her with a thin sheet. She thought she was going to be sick again and attempted to sit up but fell back instantly on the pillow. She had never felt so giddy. She decided to roll sideways instead and, relieved, saw the bowl on the floor beside the bed. As she retched out what felt like the very last contents of her stomach, Adeke came in with a glass of water and a cloth. She helped her back into bed, supported her while she sipped the water, and put the cool damp cloth on her forehead.

'I'm so sorry,' Lilia whispered. 'I'm sure I'll be fine soon.'

Adeke looked sceptical. 'Perhaps,' she said. 'But you must stay here until you do. I have sent Moses for some medicine and Leah said we should call her when you woke.'

There was a soft cough at the door. Moses bent his head to clear the doorframe as he came in. He was holding a plastic carrier bag and a small twist of paper, which he handed to his mother. Adeke untwisted the paper and poured its contents into the remains of the water, put one strong arm under Lilia's shoulders and raised her slightly.

'Drink this,' she said. 'It will help your stomach. Slowly, slowly,' she added as Lilia choked.

'It's very bitter,' Lilia spluttered. 'What is it?'

Moses shook the bag. There was a slight rattle above the rustle of the plastic. He reached inside and pulled out what looked like a very large runner bean made of dark wood. 'The fruit of the 'sausage tree,' he said and shook it vigorously, making a sound as of small stones knocking together. 'Made into a powder. Shall I grind some more, mama?' he addressed his mother, who nodded.

He went out of the room and Lilia heard him begin to pound the beans or whatever they were. The rhythmic thudding gradually became more muffled, which was presumably because the bean pieces were becoming smaller – or was it because...

She woke next to find Leah bending over her.

'What's wrong with me?' she asked. 'It happened so quickly.'

'It is early to tell,' said Leah. 'We will see how you are in the morning.'

'But I should…'

'You should sleep,' said Leah firmly. 'But I will help you to the bathroom before I go. And you can please Adeke and swallow some more of her medicine. It certainly will do you no harm.'

The room was dark when Lilia shuddered awake. She was intensely cold and her teeth were knocking uncontrollably together. There was now a blanket over her feet so she pulled it up and wrapped it closely round her, but still she could not stop shivering. She then tried lying on her back with the pillow over her front and the sheet over her head, and finally, she remembered that the bowl at her bedside stood on some kind of mat, so she put this on top of everything else and managed to fall asleep.

It was still dark when she next awoke, two or three hours later, drenched in sweat, her body on fire. She had a desperate urge to find water. Outside, next to the latrine, she knew there was a full bucket. She must reach it and pour it over herself before she was entirely burned up.

'You should have called me,' Adeke said. 'You were lucky Moses found you before you had been lying there long.'

'Moses?' She had a dim memory of strong arms lifting her, carrying her and putting her back into bed. 'Oh dear, I'm being such a nuisance. I'm so embarrassed.'

'Hmm. I think we will not worry about that. Here, drink this. You were sick again in the night.'

'I feel a bit better now, perhaps I could get up and Moses could take me back to the hotel. I have to send an article to the newspaper. I need a computer.'

Adeke pushed her down. 'Later, later. Michael will help you. Hush now.' She smoothed the hair from Lilia's damp forehead. 'For now you must put yourself and your health first. Why do you care so much about your neighbour and this boy? Do you have no husband, no family of your own?'

'Only a cat. I live with my cat,' Lilia said, knowing how odd and unimportant that must seem to Adeke. Would she be able to make her understand how important he was to her? She wanted to tell her life story to Adeke, but somehow she couldn't find the words, seemed to be slipping away again. It was very difficult to stay awake. I am like Rose was, she thought, locked in my body with the world beyond my control.... *I see Joseph, a dancing shadow on the horizon, feel him looking at me, his lips slightly parted. Is he calling me or mocking me? Does he want me to find him? Or does he mean to stay forever tantalising, tauntingly out of reach? It is Daniel who approaches me, again and again he comes close enough for me to touch, and I turn to him, but do not, cannot reach out. So he leaves, hurt, angry, looking over his shoulder, daring me to follow. But I am tied fast, a line to my heart, its hook digging deep, my life ebbing away and I am sucked dry, cast out in the end like an outgrown toy.*

'Dan! Don't spit on me!'

She felt that she had spoken aloud and became conscious of griping pains in the region of her heart. She opened her eyes to find Adeke holding her hands, chewing and in the process of leaning forward and spitting a thin stream of brownish coloured saliva onto her chest. She recoiled, horrified, and then noticed the vacant expression on Adeke's face. It was as if she were in a trance.

Adeke began to sing softly, not in words, or not in words that Lilia could recognise, and it sounded like an interchange of voices, a complex conversation pitched on the very edge of, or in a shifting space between, sharpness and flatness. Lilia felt a tingling like an electric current coursing through her that seemed to link her to the other woman, to be enticing and pulling her away from her own body's normal patterns and preferences. Pockets of resistance gathered and gave way one by one until she felt she must follow this power, wherever it led. She was being drawn into, dissolving into, something larger, wider, higher than herself, but she wasn't afraid. She felt free and infinitely powerful, part of the song, a voice in the sublime symphony.

The sun was streaming through the small window. The square of light inched across the room and still Lilia lay, motionless, without desire or emotion, without pain or sensation. Slowly she became aware of sounds; birdsong, movements, and voices. Leah came in and sat on the bed beside her. She was holding a cup of gently steaming water that gave off an aroma like a forest after rain. Lilia raised herself on one elbow.

'Drink this,' Leah held out the cup. 'It is just a mixture of herbs that Adeke has prepared. Your body is in shock.'

'I feel much better.'

'Yes, but I fear it will not last. Come, gather your strength for the next battle. I will stay near you while Adeke rests. She looks worse than you this morning. I suppose she has been dancing all night.'

Lilia drank, staggered to the latrine and bathhouse, brushed her hair and then felt exhausted. She lay back in bed as a violent wave of shivering took hold. Leah nodded as if satisfied, covered her with the blanket, brought another, sponged her forehead and called Moses.

'I am going to the dispensary,' she said. 'Keep her covered. She must sweat.'

Lilia lay shaking as violent spasms seized her, coursed in roller coaster waves through her, left her gasping in brief respite, then raced back to pitch her again into a heaving whirling maelstrom that seemed to threaten to tear out her insides, to pulp her brain into a jelly. She was powerless, swallowed in a moaning, groaning darkness rent by violent flashes of unbearable brightness. At last, and with great relief, she felt gentle hands still her and hold her safe.

'Don't be afraid. It's just the malaria taking its course.' Leah's face hovered over her as she struggled to the surface.

'That is not all that ails her.' Adeke's voice came from the other side of the bed.

'She must take all these over the next three days. Promise me you will see that she does or I will insist on taking her to a doctor.'

'She must stay here.'

'I want to stay here,' Lilia held out a hand to each of her guardians. 'And I will take the tablets.'

All day Lilia drifted in and out of consciousness, either Leah or Adeke waking her to swallow tablets and the herbal mix. Towards evening, she again began to feel ill. Leah had gone home. Adeke appeared to have been waiting for this moment. She pulled a chair to the head of the bed, sat behind Lilia and took her head in her hands. Lilia noticed that she had put a bracelet of shells on her left wrist. Moses came in.

'Did you find an *adangdang?*' Adeke asked him.

'No, mama.' Moses sounded annoyed.

'Or an *atin bul*?'

'Nor that.' Moses laughed suddenly. 'I have no *bul* at all.'

Adeke seemed surprised, and then she laughed too. A full deep laugh that welled out of her as she looked at her son. 'Silly boy. It is time you did. At least you have not forgotten all the old ways. Now go and fetch your sausage and see if you can be of some use for once.'

'Mama,' Moses again looked cross, resistant.

'We can use it as an *aja.*'

'I know,' Moses hissed, glaring at his mother. 'I know what you want me to do. I just don't think we should.'

Lilia's idle bemusement dispersed. She froze, twisted her head free of the hands that had begun to massage her temples. A ripple of unease disturbed her unquestioning trust in her host.

'What are you doing?' she protested. 'Please let me sleep.'

'Hush,' Adeke began to hum. '*Oreme. Oreme.*' She again took hold of Lilia's head, forced it gently onto the pillow and began to make circular motions with her thumbs under each of Lilia's ears.

Moses returned with the large pod and shook it experimentally. 'You must not resist her,' he told Lilia and looked at Adeke with sudden pride. 'My mother is an *ajoka.* She is a ministrant of …'

'Don't say it!' Adeke interrupted him swiftly, sharply. 'Only the initiate can say her name!'

'Oh mama!'

'Atida,' Adeke spoke with reverence. 'Atida. But you can call her *min jok*. Mother of God. Now begin.'

And she began to hum, and then to intone the words of what was clearly a prayer as Moses accompanied her with rhythmic shaking of the rattling seed pod.

'Awer' Omarari, do,
Awer', Omarari, do, do.
Omarari, wek' kol' obedi.
Awer', Omarari, do,
Awer', Omarari, do, do.
Omarari, wek' kol' obedi.

I sing then, Omarari,
I sing then, Omarari.
Omarari, let thy wrath cease.
I sing then, Omarari,
I sing then, Omarari.
Omarari, let thy wrath cease.'

37

Over the following two days, Lilia suffered alternating chills and sweating, extremes of temperature that were interspersed by long periods of sleep. She stopped being sick and began to eat and to sit up and enjoy company. She managed to dictate an article to Michael about her visit to the school and church, including the story of Edward's determination to collect the funds to construct the stained glass window. Michael knew someone in town with access to the internet, so she asked him to send the article both to Mike and to Sarita with a note asking her to read it to Rose.

Adeke's 'treatment' was at first supplemented and then supplanted by story-telling and singing. Often both Moses and Michael were present as Adeke told of the customs and history of her ancestors, before her own parents had moved to Busoga in search of work.

'The Lango homeland is to the north of here, in 'Bukedi', what the Bagandans called the land of nakedness. Our people did not wear any clothes apart from a sort of apron.' She demonstrated with her hands. Michael and Moses exchanged grimaces. 'But long ago, maybe two, three hundred years, some say more, we came from a country called Ogora, to the north east, perhaps near Mount Agora. We used to come down in every dry season to hunt and then return, but in the end we stayed because there was too much fighting in our homelands. The Lango were known by all as fiercesome fighters -'

'There are more than sixty words for warrior, based on the way they usually killed a man,' Michael interrupted.

'You listen well, little one.' Adeke laughed. 'One day you will tell your uncle's children all my stories for I fear he has never listened.'

'I'm listening now,' said Moses.

'Well. So, sometimes the fighting was caused by raiding. One people trying to steal cattle or slaves from another. Sometimes it was because there wasn't enough water for all our cattle. Everyone needed to be near a river or lake. Usually we were on good terms with our neighbours, the Acholi; many of our customs are similar, also with the Langudyang and Langulok. But then there was a great famine and the Madi began to push in from the west and we lost one great battle, so the Acholi had to make alliance with them in self-defence and we had to move on….there are many stories. But after that we were always on the move, always migrating, to better hunting and better pastures. We met Arab slave traders, who betrayed our hospitality...that is another story… and gradually we came closer to where the British had begun to establish contacts, in Buganda and Bunyoro. So then it was not long before we came under their government. And we began to lose all our customs and to fight also amongst ourselves, village against village, as if we had forgotten that we were one tribe…' Adeke's voice trailed away. She seemed lost in her thoughts.

'Tell her about the rain-making,' Michael said eagerly.

Adeke did not seem to have heard.

'Please.'

Adeke still looked into the distance.

'She's done enough remembering, Michael. It's not just stories.' Moses rubbed the boy's head affectionately.

'I know, it's our history.' Michael brushed him off and went to stand beside his grandmother. 'I like to hear it. Please, *Tato*.'

At this, Adeke did look up. She put her arm out and drew Michael close to her. 'Then, *Okwaro*, you shall hear it.' She closed her eyes and leaned back.

'Long ago, when my *papo,* your *kwaro*, was a boy, there was a great festival held every five years. It was known as the *ewor,* or *aroron,* the festival of honouring the aged and the men of old. But its main purpose was to instruct the young men in the arts of rain-making. The *awobi*, the initiates, were divided into four groups named after the elephant, the leopard, the rhinoceros and the buffalo and they had different songs. When they had all gathered, the old men led the young to a traditional sycamore tree under which they sat and taught the duties of citizenship, the lore of hunting, the art of fighting , the traditions of our race, and finally, the mysteries of rain-making, together with the rain dances and the songs belonging to their group. The young men had to sleep under the tree for three nights, only their teachers were allowed back into the villages. Just before dawn each day, each group sang its own bird song. My father's was the crested crane, he used to sing it to us sometimes. At the end of three days the old men ritually washed the *awobi*, and there was a ceremonial killing and eating of a certain kind of ram.

'The actual rain-making ceremony was usually held in April. The old men and the *awobi* gathered with their spears, one each, and the old men consecrated the spears with the special sacred rain spear of which there are only ever a few in existence. This is the ceremony of *agat*. Do you remember, Michael? *We overcome this wind,'*

'*We overcome*,' responded Michael.

'*We desire the rain to fall, that it be poured in showers quickly*.'

'*Be poured*.'

'*If our grain ripens, it is well.'*

'It is well.'

'If our women rejoice, it is well.'

'*It is well.'* Moses deep voice joined that of Michael, at first hesitantly but with growing assurance.

'*If the children rejoice, it is well.'*

'It is well.'

'If the young men sing, it is well.'

'It is well.'

'If the aged rejoice, it is well.'

'It is well.'

An overflowing in the granaries.'

'Overflowing.'

'May our grain fill the granaries.'

'May it fill.'

'A torrent in flow.'

'A torrent.'

'If the wind veers to south, it is well.'

'It is well.'

'And then the men all sat in orderly rows and prayed to *Min Jok,* and asked for her assistance. They danced the *awara, or* bell dance, and sang the appropriate animal songs for that year, and the women danced other dances, while the sacred spears were stuck point down into the ground so as not to frighten away the rain. On the third day…'

Lilia found herself drifting in and out of sleep. The rituals had been complex and passed down through many generations and it was hard to follow the details. Probably, she reflected, even Adeke knew only a fraction of the original, especially as she was a woman. She thought she heard that, if the ceremonies were unsuccessful, some tribes would sacrifice an old man, the rainmaker. But not the Lango, who, in Adeke's father's youth, consulted a particular *ajoka* named Angwech, whose reputation as a priestess of Atida had spread throughout the tribe, even to those in the most remote areas.

'In 1918,' continued Adeke. 'There was a terrible drought and ambassadors came to her from all over the district to bring her gifts, and receive the sacred water from her pool. They said that almost always she was successful.'

'Oh grandma,' said Michael. 'I wish you could be a rainmaker and everyone would bring you gifts.'

Adeke smiled. 'Angwech did not do it for the gifts,' she said. 'In fact, once she refused to accept the gifts because she said the rain had already begun and sure enough, when this particular deputation returned home, they found that she had spoken correctly. She did it because she had the power and her people needed it. And that is how I wish to be. Now go and fetch your old *Tato* a drink. It is not only old men who deserve some respect.'

'And later,' Lilia told him. 'When I have had a sleep, I should like to write another article about your grandmother and her powers so that people in England will learn that there are other ways of understanding the world.'

'Perhaps you could help us write a book,' said Moses suddenly. 'So that people here can learn about their own history.'

'I should be glad to do what I can.' Lilia smiled at him. 'And maybe you could involve the children at the school. Some of them must have older relatives they could talk to.'

'You write a book?' Adeke teased Moses. 'How you are changing.' But she looked very happy.

IN ROSE'S FOOTSTEPS
Magic and Medicine in Modern Uganda

Adeke, named after the number adek, three, since she was the third daughter of her father's third wife, is an 'ajoka', a medium, a seer. Among her people, the Lango, the most competent and renowned medicine 'men' have always been women. The Lango God is called Jok and, like the wind, is omnipresent but invisible. Jok has many manifestations, the oldest of which is Atida and female, who has, or had, for Jok is always manifesting in a new place, a shrine under a sacred banyan tree north of the River Morolo, where an aged woman sat and gave prophecies, particularly on matters of hunting, fighting and the rain.

Jok Lango's speciality is sickness, except epilepsy and demoniacal possession, and, when consulted, an ajoka may chew the root of the oreme and spit on the patient: a gesture that it is easy to misinterpret! Interestingly, oreme means 'health', hence the greeting 'Oreme?' 'Are you well?' or 'I give you health.' Oreme is also sacred to Jok Nam, a manifestation of the late nineteenth century, who deals in 'ekwikwu', possession, which suggests that the complaint increased around that time, which apparently often happens when a tribe comes in contact with a more advanced people. The most recent manifestation in 1916 was Jok Omarari, whose speciality is bubonic plague, which he is believed to bring and from which, through incantations and song, he is entreated to avert a fatal outcome.

I was treated in all these ways, as well as with preparations from various plants, the properties of which no doubt have analogies in western medicines. What was wrong with me? I do not know, and I shall be very careful from now on to take regularly the malaria pills prescribed by my NHS doctor. But perhaps Adeke was right in thinking that I was also suffering from a malign influence on my 'tipo', my soul or spirit. The tipo is absent in sleep, and its wanderings and encounters with other tipo, causes our dreams. I certainly feel so much better now than I have done for a long time.

The cult of Jok Omarari reached another tribe, the Acholi, where he was named Jok Marini in a curious confusion with the name given there to the British King's African Rifles, who were then recruiting in the area – and thought by some to have brought the plague. But it is important to know that the ajoka were no charlatans, accepted only the most nominal fee, and dealing as they did - or is it 'do'? - with a range of inquiries, play an important role in their society as a sort of priest, physician, psychiatrist and social worker rolled into one.

Over the past centuries, the Lango, the Acholi and other tribes in the surrounding regions, have been constantly forced to uproot and migrate, often due to conflict over water shortages and famine. It seems to me remarkable that so much of their knowledge and customs survived so much upheaval, but very sad that little is likely to withstand the more recent pressures of urbanisation and globalisation. Adeke told me a saying of the Bantu, the predominant racial group in this region, and indeed in the whole of southern Africa. 'You can take a feather from a bird, but when you get home that will not make you fly.'

Lilia wrote also about meeting Leah, about how she had also diagnosed and treated her malaria and how she had known Rose and Edward and was thankful to them for helping her to become a nurse. Surely, thought Lilia, it would help Rose just to know that, after all these years, she was still remembered with such respect and affection and she wished she could be there when Sarita read this to her.

38

Moses was already sitting in the car with the engine running. Lilia kept hugging Adeke, Leah and Michael over and over again, knowing, but finding it hard to believe, that she was unlikely ever to see them again. She could of course write and she had taken some photos but how she would miss them! I have never, she had realised some days before, been part of a household with more than one person, a dependent one at that. And it is decades since anyone looked after me when I was sick. Michael had gone to join his uncle who was showing him how to change gear.

'I'm so sad to leave,' she told Adeke and Leah. 'But at the same time I feel happier than I have in years.'

Both women nodded and exchanged a look of satisfaction.

'Don't forget to take the tablets,' Leah wagged a finger.

'And listen to your *tipo*,' added Adeke.

When they drove back through Iganga, it seemed impossible that it was only just over a week since she had been there and met Patrick at Edward's old school. She still felt weak, light-headed and occasionally dizzy and Adeke had insisted that Moses get permission from Mr Kumar to drive her all the way to Nairobi.

'The busses don't stop for hours and even when they say they will have a toilet, they often don't. You will not like to be in public by the side of the road, especially in your present condition.'

Lilia had also spoken to Mr Kumar, who was very disappointed that she would not be returning to go on a safari to one of the Somanis' lodges at Murchison Falls in the north or Queen Elizabeth Park in the west. She promised to try to return one day. Out of Moses' hearing, Lilia said that, if he, Moses, had lost money by being away from work so long, she wanted to reimburse him. She was shocked to hear how little that would be. But Moses was very happy at the prospect of a long drive, especially after being in Kamuli for so long. He switched on the radio. African music filled the car and Lilia was already tapping her feet to it when he started to flip through the stations. He settled on one playing Marvin Gaye.

‘OK?’ He was drumming the rhythm on the steering wheel.

‘Oh, I remember this. Very much my era. “*Yeah, yeah, I heard it through the grapevine*.”’ She sang to him and he nodded in appreciation and joined in.

‘You like hip-hop? Reggae?’ he asked her at the end of the track and began to change stations again.

‘I’d like to buy some CDs,’ she said. ‘Of African music, Ugandan music. Like your mother was singing.’

‘I have a friend…’

‘Who has a shop in the next town!’

Bugiri was an uninspiring place and what Lilia was beginning to recognise as a typical ex-Indian township; a string of low concrete and iron constructions set back some distance from the roadside. But Moses’s friend, Amos, was pleased to see them. His stock of hand-labelled CDs was ranged on a few shelves behind a plain wooden counter. A small, broad-faced man, he stopped smiling and looked perplexed at Lilia’s request.

‘I don’t think there are any commercial recordings of traditional women’s songs,’ he said. ‘There’s no market for them.’

Moses laughed. ‘I’m not surprised,’ he said. ‘Play her some modern Lugandan band,’ he said. ‘She’ll like it.’

The first track started slowly with what could have been a glockenspiel or xylophone and a soft drum. A gradual rhythm developed, guitars and flutes joined in and together sustained an effortless, yet insistent and achingly optimistic paean of what sounded like praise to the lush country through which they were travelling. It was very long and built up such a momentum that Lilia simply could not stand still and listen. She began to tap her foot, then to sway her hips. Moses nodded, pleased.

‘Turn it up,’ he told Amos and began to dance. ‘Gently, gently,’ he told her. ‘Keep your movements small small, move from inside,’ and, when she looked puzzled, gestured quickly to his lower abdomen. ‘Let your body feel the music and follow its rhythms, especially the drum.’ He laughed. ‘It is the traditional way.’

She concentrated. At first only her pelvis moved, rotated almost imperceptibly, then she discovered how her legs would follow its rotations and her feet took steps as their extension, not through conscious choice. The same began to happen with her upper body, her arms, and finally her hands. It required deep control but it felt wonderful, was mesmerizing. She turned her back to Moses and found him close behind her, not touching, never touching; but she could feel his breath on her neck and wished that she could move closer and mould her body to his. She desired him. It was a very long time since she had made love and she had not expected to want to do so again. She moved carefully a little further away from him, hoping he had neither guessed nor been offended.

'Enough, my friends,' Amos switched off the music. 'This is a shop not a night club.' He smiled at Lilia. 'Soon you will dance like an African woman.'

Lilia smiled back. 'Find me some more like that,' she said. 'I have to take it home with me. But you,' she turned to Moses. 'Should record some of your mother's songs.'

They ate matoke and stewed okra and drank cold beer at a small bar before continuing towards the Kenyan frontier, playing the new CDs all the way. Some tracks had a reggae type beat, very like Bob Marley, another recalled Paul Simon's '*Graceland*' album, '*Banka*' was like funky fairground music, and evoked a carnival atmosphere. The voice on '*Ngugumuka*', it was unclear of which gender, seemed to resonate with regret and loss across a steady backing of drums, with flutes scaling crazily around and behind other unidentifiable instruments and heart-stopping brass stepping forward here and there into the front line. Maybe, thought Lilia, these are only songs about individual love as they usually are at home, but they sounded like the expression of the collective soul of an entire people. She decided not to ask Moses for any translation, especially the tracks called '*Doctor*' and '*Waiter*' which were probably much more mundane.

'Look!' Moses pointed suddenly to the side of the road. He stopped the car, switched off the music and wound down his window. 'Take a picture,' he whispered.

Lilia was just in time to see a large bird step behind a bush. She reached for her camera and leaned across Moses to focus on where it might emerge. She was very conscious that her breasts were almost touching him. The bird's long beak emerged from behind a tall mound of orange earth, followed by its dark blue head and long crimson neck. She snapped quickly before it again withdrew.

'It's a hornbill,' said Moses. 'Let's follow him.' He opened his door quietly and got out. Lilia joined him in the long grass at the roadside.

'Oh dear,' she felt instantly dizzy. 'Maybe I shouldn't have had that beer. I think I need to sit down.' She took a step towards the orange mound.

Moses grabbed her arm. 'Not there! That's a termite nest. Wait.' He went to the car and fetched a blanket from the boot. 'Sit here.' He spread it on the grass. 'Sometimes I have to sleep in the car.'

Lilia sat down and, resting her head on her knees for a few moments, began to feel better. She raised her head and watched Moses break a branch off the bush, strip it of its leaves, and with a small knife from his pocket, whittle the end to a point.

'My sacred rain spear,' he said solemnly.

Lilia smiled at him. He looked very young and earnest, quite like Michael in fact. She looked around at the trees from which hung nests of weaver birds as numerous as if they were its natural fruit. A monkey with her baby on her back ambled across the road a short distance ahead. A herd of apparently unattended cattle with enormously long curved horns looked up briefly from their grazing in the grassland on the other side of the road. She sighed with contentment.

'I feel I could stay in Africa for ever,' she said. 'It's so beautiful.'

'You wouldn't like it if you lived here.' He was scornful.

'Maybe not. But I shall miss your mother and Michael – and Leah – so much. Your mother is wonderful.'

Moses smiled at this. 'But crazy.'

'She's not.'

'You believe in magic? I'll show you how crazy it can be.' He took off his sandals, stood up and held one in each hand by the inner edge and placed them toe-to-toe and sole to sole. 'Watch.' He threw them in the air with a twisting motion of his wrists. They fell on the ground, parallel and a short distance apart.

'*No danger; hunting will be safe*.'

He picked up the sandals and repeated the action. This time the right sandal landed at a right angle to the left.

'*I will kill game.*'

'What *are* you doing?'

'Divination by sandals. A very skilled business.'

'Do it again.'

The sandals landed with the heel of the right on top of that of the left.

'*I will kill a female animal.*'

'Let me have a go.'

'All right. But since you are using my sandals and not your own you must hold them by the outer edge.'

The sandals landed parallel but the left one had flipped over so that the sole was uppermost.

'*A satisfactory flirtation. The one on its back is the man.*'

'You're making it up.'

Moses held up his hands to protest his innocence. 'Try again.'

This time it was the right hand sandal that had flipped over and it lay at right angles to the left.

'Ah,' said Moses thoughtfully. 'That means *respect to your mother-in-law*. Or perhaps *beware of an accidental meeting on your journey*. They are very similar.'

'I really don't believe you.'

'It's true. I told you it was crazy.' Moses picked up the sandals and sat on the blanket next to her. 'Have you ever been married?' he asked suddenly.

'No.' Lilia picked a blade of grass and chewed it for several moments. 'We have a saying,' she said at last. '*Once bitten, twice shy.*'

Moses cocked his head to one side, considering. 'Is that why you are shy?'

'I'm not, that is…'

'But you have been bitten,' he said softly.

Lilia met his eyes for a long moment and then looked away. 'We should be…' she began.

'Marry me.' Moses knelt in front of her with a quick fluid motion. His voice was serious, urgent. 'Be my *bul.* My wife.'

Lilia stood quickly and stepped off the blanket. As she did, she felt the strap of her sandal break. She stooped and fiddled with it briefly, then, feeling giddy, stood with her hands covering her face, trying to think, to decide how to deal with this unexpected change in the situation. Except that she knew it shouldn't have been entirely unexpected. She had encouraged Moses to open up to her, whilst pretending to herself that her feelings were wholly platonic. Like an aunt's. She had been thoughtless, unkind, cruel, unless…could she do it?

'Oh, Moses,' she began, without knowing exactly how she would continue.

Moses stood also and reached out his arms to her. 'Take me to England.'

Lilia's mind stopped racing. A vague vision of herself living somewhere in Africa with Moses became a series of much sharper images of Moses in England. Moses wandering aimlessly along the seafront attracting suspicious, if not hostile, glances from passers-by. Moses lying around her flat all day, watching TV and interrupting her writing. Perhaps, at best, Moses working as a taxi driver, taking ladies even older than her to Sainsbury's. Moses meeting Rose - that was the one part that was conceivable, they would probably get on very well. But still, it would not do, it would never work. Especially if she retained the suspicion that a passport to England was a stronger motive than any feeling for her. It had to be that; she was simply too old for him to find her desirable for more than a very short time. She looked at him sadly.

'You wouldn't like it there, really you wouldn't. It's cold and…'

His face closed as it had that other time in the hotel at Jinja. But this time it held a suppressed anger that made her afraid. He picked up his stick and held it high in the air and she tried not to cower, but then he tossed it carelessly aside, placed his sandals on the ground, parallel and quite far apart, and looked straight into her eyes. She flinched but returned his gaze. He pointed to his sandals.

'*No danger. Go on your journey in safety.*' He slipped his feet into the sandals, picked up the blanket, stepped into the road and then pointed to where a small beetle scurried across his path.

'*Proceed with your journey, as you will find beer at the end.*' He laughed without humour. 'That I will surely find.' He met her eyes briefly. 'And we have another saying. If your sandal strap breaks at the beginning of a journey, you must return home, as to continue will bring disaster.'

39

The sky began to darken almost as soon as they had set off. Huge spots of rain hit the windscreen and made dark patches on the dry road ahead. Within a minute the entire surface of both were wet and Moses switched on the wipers. There was a clap of thunder and an instant downpour.

'I made too much,' he said without humour, as he leaned to peer through the rivulets of rain that coursed down the glass between each sweep of the blades. A few miles further on there were road works in progress, diggers and bulldozers abandoned in the deepening mud of what would be a second carriageway. The workmen huddled in makeshift tarpaulin shelters at the side of the road, together with pedestrians and cyclists caught out by the sudden downpour. Wide trenches were rapidly filling with bubbling red water and would be death traps, Lilia thought, should they skid on the slippery mud-splattered asphalt. Moses drove as if he did not care if they did.

At the Kenyan border there were long lines of people waiting outside the wooden buildings housing passport control. Lilia queued, sodden and shivering, with a busload of travellers that included a large party of young British students who, she gathered from their loud chatter, had just finished working on some project and were also bound for Nairobi. Moses, in a separate queue of bus and lorry drivers, made more rapid progress and she could see him having some sort of refreshments in a café. She hoped it was not more beer. Behind the sheds, she found a filthy toilet, for the use of which she had to pay two men who claimed to be its attendants. It was a bad introduction to a new country. She hoped she would not again become ill.

Once they were back on the road, she began to doze until about an hour later when the car stopped in a busy street of shops and cafes. The sun was shining.

'Kisumu,' announced Moses. 'We stop half an hour. You will like that place.' He pointed to the Hotel Natasha and disappeared down a side street.

Several of the tables in the café attached to the hotel were occupied by European backpackers, who eyed her casually and then looked away as she made her way to a corner table. She felt ill at ease, stranger than when she had been the only white face but was, however, relieved to see some very English dishes on the menu. She ordered a plain omelette and chips and, while she waited, fished out her Lonely Planet Guide to find out about where she was.

Apparently, Kisumu was, since 2001, a city, Kenya's third largest, once a very busy port on the eastern shore of Lake Victoria, and now again its fortunes were improving. There seemed plenty to attract the visitor, several good hotels, a better nightlife than Nairobi, a nice campsite by the lake, with thatched cottages also available, and boat trips to nearby islands. It seemed a shame to be just passing through and seeing none of this as it was so unlikely that she would ever return, whatever she had told Mr Kumar. She envied the youngsters taking their 'year out' of work or study to travel. There was a "cyberstation" marked on the map, just around the corner from the hotel and she remembered that Michael had said there was some email waiting. In case her hosts in Nairobi did not have internet access, she went off to find it as soon as she had finished eating.

Sarita had written several days ago. Rajah was ill, she thought, as he only seemed to go outside to use the garden as a toilet and she had had a few messes indoors to clear up as well. *I don't mind but I am worried about him*, she wrote. *What should I do*? Lilia was seized with guilt for having left Rajah in uncertain health in the first place and for not having checked her messages more carefully. For having been too wrapped up in her new life to think of the creature whom, despite her denial, she loved more than anyone. Blinking back tears, she wrote back to say that, if Sarita possibly could find the time, here were the vet's contact details and please could she take Rajah and let the vet do whatever he thought necessary. *Please ask him not to spare the expense*, she begged, *and to start as soon as possible*. She added that she thought she should be back within a week.

Moses was asleep in the back seat when Lilia returned to the car. There was a strong smell of beer as she opened the door. Moses stirred, half-opened his eyes and sat up yawning.

'Long drive ahead, mama. Driver tired.' He swung himself out of the car and stood near her, stretching his arms and flexing his shoulders.

Lilia skirted him swiftly, got into the back of the car and closed the door. 'OK, when you're ready. Do you want coffee or something?'

Moses accepted the money for Cokes for both of them and she hoped it would be sufficient to keep him awake. She herself soon nodded off and woke as they were driving high along the side of a vast valley, in which rose strange dark peaks and hillocks like slurry tips in a giant's disused coalmine. A mirage shimmered in the distance, or it could even have been water, a lake, tinted pink at the edges. She did not want to ask Moses where they were, or even to stop so that she could take a photograph, but he did stop after a while at a large lay-by that was already quite full of cars and busses. Built onto the side of the road on a rickety wooden platform, its broken slats revealing the vertical drop below, was a viewing platform. "*Great Rift Valley*" read the sign. "*6000 kms long from Mozambique to the Dead Sea.*" There was a map and a direction indicator, including to Lake Naivasha somewhere in the distance straight ahead. *"An area not to be missed"* according to the Guide, yet she would have only one or two photographs to remind her that she had been close.

Moses was chatting to a man draped in a patterned red blanket who, as soon as she turned towards them, advanced, shook her hand and hustled her along the lay-by to a group of stalls all selling similar blankets of different designs. They were very attractive, even the asking price not expensive, and it was noticeably colder here than in Uganda or Kisumu. Lilia travelled the rest of the way to Nairobi wrapped in her red and black tartan Masai blanket, wishing she had not so hurt and offended Moses, regretting that she would now be glad to be out of his company.

It was almost dark as they entered the suburb of Westlands with Moses taking directions on his mobile from Bhavin's sister's husband. Preethi and Ashok lived in a modern apartment in a large three sided four-storied red brick block, the entrance to which was gated and guarded. The guard was armed and hostile, until he saw Lilia in the back. He waved them through and Lilia buzzed the apartment bell. A man's voice answered and, a minute later, Ashok opened the door.

'Please go on up,' he said. 'It's on the second floor. I'll fetch your luggage from the car.'

Lilia took some notes from her purse and passed them to him. It was all the Ugandan money she had left, worth about thirty pounds.

'Please can you give it to my driver,' she said. 'I'm not used to tipping.'

She turned and waved briefly to Moses, walked away through the brightly lit foyer and glided silently upwards in the softly carpeted lift.

40

Preethi was waiting for Lilia at the open door of the apartment. Unlike her brother, she was small and slim, and as pretty as the sound of her name suggested. She had just got home from the travel agency where, she said, she worked long hours. Her five year old son, Shrai, who had spent the day at his grandmother's, clung to the skirt of her pink cotton Punjabi dress. She showed Lilia to a bedroom, which, being full of toys, was obviously usually Shrai's.

She brushed aside Lilia's protests. 'Please stay as long as you like,' she said. 'We like to have visitors.'

Ashok joined them and handed to Lilia what, to her dismay, looked like most of the money she had given him. 'It was far too much,' he assured her. It was of course too late to protest.

'I am sure you will want a bath and to change after your journey,' said Preethi. 'Any dirty clothes you can just leave in the bathroom and the servant will wash them in the morning.'

When Lilia rejoined them in the living room, another young man had arrived. It was Preethi's nephew Amit, on holiday from his studies in the States. He was playing on a handheld computer game, with Shrai sitting close beside him on a low white sofa giving advice. Amit asked what she wanted to do while she was in Nairobi.

'If you want to go on a safari I can help you arrange it,' said Preethi. 'It's the best time to go to Masai Mara, to see the wildebeest running. Although that means it's very booked up. But I can try.'

'I could take you on a tour of downtown now,' offered Amit. 'I've got a car outside.'

Preethi and Ashok exchanged glances. 'It's getting dark,' said Preethi.

'Oh, Auntie, I'll be careful. People have to go out. Back in time for dinner.' He was already on his feet, jangling his car keys, Shrai having taken over the game and pretending not to mind at being abandoned so soon.

'You don't understand what it's like here now. You know why we moved into an apartment.' Preethi's voice rose as she turned to her husband. 'Tell him, Ashok.'

'Your aunt is right,' Ashok said firmly. 'You mustn't take chances. Especially with our guest.'

'Oh all right then,' Amit grumbled. 'Tomorrow? I'll come by at ten. And take Shrai too. Okay, Shrai?'

Shrai looked up adoringly at his cousin and then quickly to see his mother's reaction.

'So long as you drive slowly.' Preethi smiled, stood up and hugged her tall nephew. 'Now go on home to your Mummy before she starts worrying.'

'Why did you move here?' Lilia asked, later that evening. They had had dinner, watched Sky News, (the family of the young Brazilian man shot as a suspected terrorist by the Metropolitan Police was demanding an inquiry), and, while Preethi cleared away the dishes, Lilia had told Shrai a story, having declined an offer to play on his Gameboy. He was now asleep on the sofa with his head in his father's lap.

Preethi looked doubtfully at her husband.

'Why not?' he said. 'She's used to London. Preethi doesn't want to scare you,' he explained.

'It was a few months ago,' said Preethi. 'We used to live in a lovely house with a garden. I had just been to fetch my father-in-law from the temple. The *askhari,* the watchman, opened the gate and closed it behind us as we drove in. And that was the last we saw of him. As we walked to the house, three men leapt out from the side of the porch where they were hiding beside some bushes, grabbed both of us, forced me to unlock the door and pushed us inside. Then they tied up my father-in-law on a chair and held a gun to his head. They wanted money, gold, any portable valuables.

'I begged them not to hurt Bapuji, he's nearly eighty, and gave them all the money and jewellery I had in the house, which wasn't very much. People don't keep much at home these days. The robbers were still threatening both of us, but I kept saying that was all I had and finally they said they were sorry they had to rob us, but they were unemployed. I said I understood and they left. I don't know how I kept so calm. Often people get killed anyway, even when they do cooperate.' She seemed about to add something but thought better of it. 'So we were lucky.' She smiled brightly.

'What happened to your watchman then? Did they kill him?'

Preethi sighed and shrugged. 'Ashok thinks he let them in, that he knew them. I hate to think that, he was with us for years.'

'Maybe they had threatened to kill him if he refused to let them in or gave them away. Who knows?' Ashok sounded bitter. 'You can't trust any of them anymore. So that's why we moved here. Preethi's sister Neeta, Amit's mother, is also moving to a secure block soon.'

Preethi clapped her hands. 'Enough!' she turned to Lilia. 'Would you like to watch a DVD? We get all the latest films before they've finished showing in the Bombay cinemas.'

Lilia was tired. It had been a very long day. She hoped Moses had found somewhere safe to stay and was not drunk or sleeping rough in the back of the car. 'I think I had better go to bed,' she said.

Amit came to collect Shrai and Lilia next morning as promised and they drove downtown on a busy dual carriageway, modern houses and apartment blocks to their left, a long open green area to their right. They turned left at a roundabout just before another park into a grid of narrower streets, high-rise offices and expensive looking hotels. There were very few Indians or Europeans amongst the pedestrians. Amit parked immediately opposite a row of lower buildings housing shops, an insurance business and a travel agent's.

'Mummy's work,' Shrai pointed to "*Rhino Travel*" as they crossed the road.

Preethi had managed to book two nights in a lodge in Masai Mara National Park, starting the day after next. Shrai was thrilled.

'Two double rooms,' said Preethi. 'I thought if we all go, Ashok and Amit could share. Shrai has never been there.'

'Five years old and never seen a lion?' Amit teased him.

'We still might not see any,' cautioned his aunt. 'By the way, Lilia, we have been invited to Ashok's cousin brothers' for dinner tonight. You too, of course, Amit, if you want to come.'

There was steady traffic on both carriageways of the wide road as they drove back out to the suburbs. Shrai was asleep.

'I'm really looking forward to the trip,' said Lilia.

‘It would have been a shame to come to Africa and not go on a safari,’ Amit nodded. ‘Masai Mara’s stunning, at the right season especially. You won’t believe there could be so many wildebeest. And zebra. You can be surrounded by them, as far as the eye can see. When I’m at college it makes me homesick imagining it. I’ll be glad when my course is finished and I can come back here. Uhoh, what’s this?’ He braked hard as they rounded a bend in the road to find a long line of stationary cars and lorries.

A passenger from a lorry near the front of the line soon came walking back along the line. Half a mile ahead there had been an accident, he said. Could be a long delay. Amit handed Lilia a bottle of water and then pushed back his seat and stretched out his legs. But, after a few minutes, several men joined the first man on the central reservation and, after a brief discussion, fanned out into the offside lane of the other carriageway and began to direct the oncoming traffic aside and to wave the waiting vehicles across the central reservation to take its place.

‘Crazy Kenyans,’ laughed Amit as they bumped over the grass, sped past the pile-up on the opposite carriageway and back onto their original path. ‘But so much quicker than waiting for the police to arrive and sort it out.’

41

Ashok's three cousin brothers and their families lived in separate parts of a large house which stood within a double perimeter of high barbed metal fences. There were guards at each electronically operated gate and a large sign told the outside world that *Ultimate Security Systems Inc.* guaranteed the safety of the residents and offered a phone number in case anyone else wanted to be similarly well protected. The guards had rifles, smart uniforms and sprang to attention before allowing the car to pass through. The windows of the building were barred and there were additional metal grills fitted at the front door and foot of each internal staircase.

The family had gathered in the oldest brother's apartment since it was the most spacious. Assorted youngsters sat in a large den watching TV on a big plasma screen. Ashok joined the men in one sitting room, while Preethi ushered Lilia to sit with the women of the household in another. Preethi had told them nothing of why Lilia was in Nairobi, except that she knew Bharat and Sarita in England. Lilia sat and smiled, sipped a fruit juice, and let their gossip wash around her, the frequent English words a reasonable guide as to its content. Occasionally she asked them to translate.

There had been another armed break-in, not far away and very similar to that suffered by Preethi. Another lucky escape, especially since the husband had managed to run to the neighbours to post through their letter box a big bag of cash that he had just brought home from his business, while his wife and mother were held captive. The neighbours were too scared to open their door but had called "the vigilantes" so the robbers had fled empty-handed. Much less lucky was the young girl, about to be married, whom, in yet another instance, intruders had disfigured for life by throwing acid in her face. Lilia's neighbour, a woman of about forty, who wore a white sari, had said nothing throughout. She simply listened and looked sad.

'Do you live in Kenya too?' Lilia asked her.

‘I live here,’ responded the woman. ‘I have one of the apartments.’

‘So your husband is one of the three brothers?’

‘There were four brothers,’ said the woman. ‘Until last spring when my husband was killed. He was at his office, he gave them all the money there was, but still they shot him.’

After dinner Lilia joined the younger set watching *“Friends”*. She was tired of answering the same questions repeatedly, well-meaning and polite as they were. Yes, she liked Africa. Yes, Uganda was indeed, it seemed, ‘coming up’. Yes, she would like to visit East Africa again and see more of the tourist sights. She discovered that very few of the older generations either expected or wanted to leave Kenya and they mostly thought that, at least since the terrorist attacks, they were no worse off than people living in the UK. They were keen, however, for the younger generation to leave if they could through study, work or marriage. Meanwhile, they were focussing on the imminent visit of a respected guru who was here to open a new temple, of which there would now be thirty in the city.

‘So expensive, it was,’ Preethi told her in the car going home. ‘All donated by different families,’ she waved her hand to include her own. ‘Maybe we can take you there tomorrow evening, don’t you think, Ashok? Ashok? What’s the matter?’

Ashok kept glancing in the mirror as he drove. Lilia, who was sitting in the back, with Shrai curled up asleep beside her, looked over her shoulder. A car had driven up extremely close behind them. Ashok accelerated and moved into the outside lane, but the other car followed him and, despite their increased speed, remained as close. If Ashok had braked there would have been an instant collision. Preethi looked from her husband’s grim face to the lights of the following car, gasped and clasped one hand to her mouth as if to stop herself screaming. They were approaching red traffic lights. They stopped, their pursuers stopped behind them, a third car pulled up on their left. The lights turned amber and Ashok accelerated immediately, cut across the nearside lane and the path of the third car and sped away down a side road. He continued to drive fast, cutting through smaller residential streets until they reached home.

Preethi was too upset by what was almost certainly an attempted hijacking to go downtown to work next day. She slept late and Lilia watched cartoons with Shrai, while mentally writing to Mike. She didn't expect him to put any of it in the paper, it having nothing to do with Rose. But she did have a title.

'PARANOIA AND PRIVILEGE: A High Price to Pay for Prosperity?

I am staying in Nairobi where, for many people it is impossible to live the sort of life that in the UK we take for granted. You cannot walk anywhere and are at risk of robbery and hijacking when driving, as I discovered for myself last night when the car in which I was a passenger narrowly avoided this fate. You must park in a secure area. At home, you must not only lock your door but also have guards for your building and/or compound, which ideally should have crash-proof metal gates. All windows should have bars. Indeed, internal staircases should also have grilles that can be locked at night when the occupants are upstairs asleep, and internal rooms that have any items of value should be lockable. It is better if the whole household does not go out at once. Burglar alarms and intercoms are a useful additional feature but not to be trusted: off duty police might be moonlighting armed burglars.

The more layers of security you can erect between yourself and the outside world the better since no one system is failsafe. You are very fortunate if you can trust those you employ to clean, feed, guard and drive you to closed shopping malls or private beaches. Anyone who thinks such warnings are exaggerated may wake up to find themselves peering down the wrong end of a Kalashnikov - as happened to one newly arrived NGO worker I heard about. Two Kalashnikovs in fact.

I am fortunate to be a guest in the home of a young well-to-do couple, an apartment in what is becoming a typical gated community, part of the cocoon that the middle classes are erecting between themselves and an increasingly hostile and dangerous society. The often luxurious houses and apartments are conspicuous demonstrations of wealth that may serve to reassure their owners that life is better here than in the UK or India. But clearly they must also fuel envy and discontent in the poor African population, including those who work in them as servants. I have noticed a kind of controlled hysteria, especially in some of the women who are often cooped up all day with their potential assassins, which became entirely understandable when I heard of some of their experiences. Everyone seems to have a story to tell ...'

The telephone rang and Preethi appeared in a dressing gown, pale and drawn.

'Amit has invited us all there tonight but I said I really don't feel like going out, so he's going to collect you and take you out somewhere first. Actually, he's invited you to stay there as well but otherwise I know he'd bring you back...'

'I think that's a very good idea,' Lilia hoped she did not sound too relieved. 'You need some peace to get over last night.'

'If you are sure...and I don't think I want to go on the safari either. I'm very sorry to spoil our plans.'

'It's quite alright.' Though disappointed, Lilia was hardly surprised. 'I'm not on a holiday after all.' She went to pack her things and Amit arrived about ten minutes later.

42

Amit's family lived in a large bungalow set in a pleasant garden, with one guard, a cold-eyed tribesman from the north, who, according to Amit, was a much better deterrent than hi-tech security systems. 'A killer, no doubt about it. So long as we pay him enough.' Nevertheless, his mother Neeta confirmed that they would be moving quite soon, 'Especially after last night.' After tea and various spicy snacks, Amit said he felt like a nap and Neeta suggested that Lilia might like to do the same as it would be an hour or two before Amit's father came home to dinner. Lilia asked if she could check her email first.

From ravi@thinair.com
To Liliaz@yahoo.co.uk

I hope you are enjoying your travels. Any clearer idea of when you will return to the UK? Ravi

From Liliaz@yahoo.co.uk
To ravi@thinair.com

Expect to be in Nairobi a couple of days more at most and then I want to go to Mombasa for a few days before I return. Will let you know. Looking forward very much to meeting you and hoping for some good news.

Regards
Lilia

From mcolman@btinternet.com
To Liliaz@yahoo.co.uk
Dear Ms Zynofsky,

My mother Penny whom you visited recently asked me to write on her behalf. She wishes to post you something that is relevant to your research and hopes you have a safe address. She says it is very important that you receive and read it as quickly as possible. Please let me know at your earliest convenience and I will ensure that this item is posted by the fastest means.

Yours truly

Mark Colman

On the point of clicking the 'reply' button Lilia stopped to think. She had been planning to ask Preethi to book a hotel for her in Mombasa, preferably on or near the beach Rose had mentioned. She did not want to presume on any more connections of the Thakkers and, now that the safari trip was cancelled, there was nothing to delay her departure. She googled the telephone number of Rhino Travels and made her arrangements and then replied to Mark Colman, giving him the address of the hotel.

She then wrote a quick note to Sarita giving her the same information and hoping that Rajah was no worse – she did not like to ask again if he had been taken to the vet – and then started to write to Mike. She was feeling very pleased that she had achieved so much without assistance and would not need to burden her new hosts for long. She would relax now for a day, perhaps do some sightseeing or shopping if someone would take her, otherwise simply enjoy the comforts of this very nice home.

It did not seem long, however, before she heard Neeta's voice calling. Surely it was too soon for dinner? She saved her message as a draft and went to open the door. The sun having now set, it was too dark to see clearly down the corridor outside. She groped unsuccessfully for a light switch and began to feel her way along the wall, while her eyes became more accustomed to the gloom. Neeta's voice called again. It was full of fear.

'Don't hurt me, please don't hurt me.'

Lilia stepped carefully closer along the polished wooden floor. Directly opposite was the corridor where the family had their bedrooms. The two corridors met in a small hallway that gave on to the living area where the lights were on.

'I will open the safe but I need to get the key.' Neeta was now very close; it sounded as if she might appear in the hallway at any moment.

Male voices rose in sudden argument and Lilia flattened herself against the wall. At that moment she saw a door open at the far end of the other corridor and the silhouette of Amit appear and approach. He noticed her and held up a finger to his lips. With the other hand he held a gun. As he reached the hallway, he raised and held it with both hands at arms-length and wheeled swiftly to face the scene in the living room. A shot was fired, Neeta screamed and rushed forward to catch Amit as he clutched his leg and fell. As he hit the floor, he tossed the gun aside so that it slid towards Lilia. She moved swiftly, bent to pick it up and came face to face with a young African man. Fortunately, he was the more surprised and she had a precious moment to hold it out in front of her and aim it at him, while Amit pulled himself back against the wall and Neeta crouched silently beside him.

'Back,' she gestured abruptly to the intruder, knowing that she was acting like a character in a film. The situation seemed just as unreal and she felt no fear. 'Back,' she said again.

'Get the gun, idiot,' another man, still out of Lilia's sight, shouted angrily.

The young man edged nearer, his eyes wide in terror, his hands slowly reaching out towards her. 'Give me the gun,' he whispered. 'Give me the gun.'

She fired once; he fell doubled up to the floor. She rushed forward, shooting wildly as she turned past Amit and his mother into the living room, in time to see a man run out of the front door and away down the drive.

'Lilia, leave him. Keep this guy covered,' Amit shouted. 'I'm calling the police.'

The would-be robber was moaning and trembling, holding his stomach. Blood began to trickle through his fingers.

'I won't move, don't shoot,' he looked up at Lilia. He was very young, perhaps eighteen or nineteen. He looked at Neeta. 'I'm sorry, missus, I'm sorry, I've never done this before.'

'I'll fetch a towel to stop the bleeding,' said Neeta, her eyes meeting Lilia's over the young man's head. 'He's in a worse state than Amit. We should call an ambulance.'

The young man started to cry. Lilia crouched beside him. 'What is your name?' she asked.

'Jacob,' he said. 'Jacob Lwanga.'

'I'm sorry I hurt you, Jacob,' said Lilia. 'I was scared.'

‘Me scared too, missus.’ Jacob closed his eyes.

They all stiffened as they heard the siren approaching. A police car, blue light flashing, tore up the drive and three tall policemen leapt out and rushed into the house. Two took up positions with their guns pointed at Jacob, the third motioned Lilia aside.

‘The other one escaped,’ Amit told them, standing with difficulty and leaning against the wall.

‘He shoot you?’

Amit nodded. ‘I’m afraid we shot this one.’

‘We think he needs to go to hospital,’ added Lilia.

The policeman looked at her, unsmiling, inscrutable. He stepped over to Jacob and with one heavily booted foot rolled him onto his back. The towel was soaked in blood.

‘Hurting bad?’ it was more of a statement than an enquiry but Jacob nodded, his eyes, full of fear, following the tall policeman.

‘Yes sir. It hurting bad.’

The policeman looked away. ‘OK,’ he addressed his two colleagues. ‘Give him some pain killers.’

43

Lilia lay in the huge old-fashioned white bath at the Nairobi Club, the events of the last few hours rotating relentlessly through her mind. They had all had to go to the police station to give statements but a court appearance was unlikely. Self-defence was the obvious conclusion. She wished it felt more like an excuse and knew she would never forget the pleading on Jacob's face as he approached her and his terror as he looked up at the policeman. Probably he knew what was going to happen to him, would have heard of other such instances of summary execution. Amit had told her that often the police themselves turned robber because their wages were so low that they supplemented them with crime and, when one of them was caught, chose to close ranks and prevent further implication of their colleagues. But Jacob seemed too young to have been a policeman. Perhaps he would have died anyway of his injury, which made her his killer and the cause of the grief that somewhere in this city his family might now be suffering If they ever found out what had happened to him. Perhaps he was one of the many young men who came to the city to look for work and were lost in the violent poverty of its underworld.

Through the open window came the hum of traffic, the maelstrom of *matatas*, busses and lorries rendered benign by distance and by the foreground sounds of a lawn mower. She could see two men rolling the turf of a cricket pitch, in front of a white wooden pavilion like those on village greens and in school grounds all over England. She slid deeper into the water, her feet still far from the liver-spotted chrome taps under which she could read the name of the bath's manufacturer: *Messrs Josiah Booth of Derby*. It must have been shipped out a hundred years ago to this newly burgeoning corner of the empire. At two metres long, it would have been large enough for the tallest coffee farmer. She thought about the generations of out of town visitors lying here as they made themselves fit for city company. Did they miss these comforts, miss England, she wondered, however good a life they had here?

Amit's family were moving to stay with relatives, they were unlikely ever to return to their house. His father, who had returned soon after the police arrived, had offered to bring her here where he was a member, assuring her that she would be safe and would feel at home. How right he was. In the light of a grey dawn, she had been able to see a low Edwardian-style building, half covered in creeping foliage, with a porticoed entrance supported on slender white columns and flanked by flowerbeds. The foyer was a mixture of gleaming red brown wood and green padded plush armchairs and sofas. A wide carpeted staircase that curved up to the right was watched over sternly by photographs of the founders and their ladies. It could have been the setting for an English period drama, Howard's End perhaps.

Everything spoke of continuity, as if the intervening decades of rebellion, independence, bloodshed and social upheaval had passed it by. The middle-aged woman and younger man on the desk had surely attended an older school of hotel management, their demeanour a soothing blend of gracious helpfulness and unassuming restraint. Anything they could do to help… they murmured. She would like a taxi to visit Amit in hospital later, she said, otherwise she would be leaving for Mombasa the day after as already arranged.

The water was growing cold. She wrapped herself in a towel, went through to the bedroom, drew the curtains, lay on the bed and pulled the heavy white cotton sheet up over her head. The early morning mist had cleared and the sun was high and bright. She needed her eyeshade but had not yet unpacked her case. Half an hour later she gave up trying to sleep, got up and went down to a large sitting room, where identical dark brown leather settees were arranged around low tables, creating separate spaces for members and their guests. At one end of the room a carved screen divided off a small area set with dining tables and chairs, at the other a large TV screen was fixed to the wall. Halfway along one side was a fireplace of baronial size and style, ready laid with logs, while the fourth side gave onto the club grounds through a number of French windows, presently closed. There was a terrace, although no one sat there, it was, perhaps, chillier than the sun made it appear.

Her only companions were a very old white man with a very long white beard, who sat by the fireplace reading a newspaper as if he had not moved for fifty years, and a couple of African businessmen who sat quietly conversing in a corner near the television. A white-coated waiter appeared from behind the screen and she ordered coffee. She was holding a few sheets of headed club note paper taken from her room, planning to write about the robbery. She would email it later to Mike - together with the earlier draft about how dangerous it was living here. Other people would see it in context and people who knew her would be more concerned for her than for some unknown African burglar. Maybe eventually she would forgive herself. She had to do something...

'Madam?'

The waiter's voice cut into her dream of Moses begging, approaching with outstretched arms, fixing her with Jacob's terrified eyes, his expression turning to horror as she pulled the trigger. She tried to throw away the gun but it stuck fast to her hand and her fingers squeezed tight and would not release their grasp. She woke to find the sheets of notepaper screwed in her clenched fists.

'I'm sorry, excuse me,' Lilia sat upright. 'I didn't get much sleep last night, I was dreaming.'

'Bad dreams, madam, we heard what happened to you.' He was surely as old as she if not older, his hands a little shaky as he bent over the table to set down the heavy tray.

'Did you? Oh!' Lilia found herself suddenly in tears at this unexpected understanding.

He averted his eyes and concentrated on pouring coffee and milk from silver pots into a gold-edged white china cup. 'Drink coffee, madam, and I will fetch you breakfast also. And we will light the fire for you.'

Lilia thanked him, sniffed loudly and blew her nose. The old man with the beard looked over his paper, frowned, rose to his feet with difficulty and the help of a stick and shuffled out of the room, while one of the African men stood and turned up the volume on the TV. It was the latest news of the London bombings and the shooting of the suspected terrorist at the Oval underground station. *"Police have now admitted that the young Brazilian student was not running and did not jump the barrier as first claimed. Members of his family are due to arrive at Heathrow airport later today to pursue their demand for an inquiry. The Commissioner of Police has agreed..."*

Lilia took her coffee to the fireside and stared into the collapsing kindling wood pyramid of the newly lit fire. How could the police have got it so wrong? What had happened to the usual safeguards? Of course, everyone was angry and afraid, including the police, so many people knew it could have been them in those carriages, or on that bus. But still it was less understandable than the police-turned-robbers here. Was nowhere safe anymore? On 21st July it was a miracle really that no-one had been hurt in all the chaos and crowds. She looked around the room and out through the tall windows to the cricket pitch beyond and for a few moments wished intensely that she were back in her blessedly peaceful corner of England, where this world still more or less existed. Should she abandon her quest and go home? She had achieved so little and caused great harm, killing one young man and hurting Moses. But Rose wanted her to go to Bamburi beach, to complete the journey she had herself made. Lilia sighed. She would go, she would not give up at this last hurdle and besides, she remembered, the parcel from Penny, whatever it was, might already be on its way.

44

Lilia stood at the top of the short flight of steps that led down from the hotel grounds to the beach and surveyed the scene with some disappointment. The tide was high and the sea so full of weed that she did not fancy swimming and there seemed to be nowhere to sit in peace on the beach because it was one long string of stalls of traders who, the moment they spotted her, called out to come and buy. Resolutely ignoring them, she descended the steps and walked to the water's edge. Under the coconut palms in either direction she could see other hotels, each guarded by rows of wooden sun-beds pointing seawards like gun carriages. "*Such a beautiful long empty beach, fringed by coconut palms, you hardly notice the few buildings,*" was how Rose had remembered it. Well, there still were palm trees, she thought, though surely many had been cut down, but only the sight and sound of the surf breaking in a long white line on the coral reef far out from the shore could be unchanged. That would have continued, more or less constantly, through changing tides and weather, down all the days and months and years since Rose had come here, and whether or not there was anyone here to pay it any attention.

She walked north along the beach, looking for the Hindu Cottages where Rose had stayed, until the hotels finally petered out and there were no traders, only an occasional figure sitting under the trees, which made it feel unsafe to continue. She decided that she must ask exactly where the cottages were and go by taxi tomorrow. On the way back, she passed an elderly white woman arm- in-arm with a dreadlocked young man, her servant perhaps. Then she noticed a grey-haired white man sitting on a hotel sun-bed with a pretty young African woman massaging his shoulders, and two middle-aged white women walking with two elegant young men, who wore western clothes with a red Masai blanket draped stylishly over one shoulder. She was very glad that she did not have Moses at her side, probably already looking as impassive as they did, maybe exchanging with them covert glances of camaraderie.

She had an early dinner in a glass-walled dining hall that looked out onto a swimming pool and an outdoor bar, where a music group was setting up their equipment. As she ate, the sky darkened and began to fill with stars and the other tables were gradually occupied. There were a few European couples, none English as far as she could tell, and many more Indians and Africans, both couples and large family groups. She was the only person who sat alone and, despite her earlier conclusions, she could not help thinking how idyllic the evening would be if there were someone with whom to share it. But she firmly discouraged the young waiter, who was eager to talk and left before the evening entertainment had begun. That night she slept badly in her pretty little white cottage near the beach.

Next morning she felt a little better. She stood on her balcony, looking out over the other cottages, and the grass and shrubs between them, and listened to the distant roar of the surf and the cawing of the crows in the palm trees. There was no one about. The sun had just reached the top of a smaller date palm and she felt its flickering warmth through the gently waving fronds, traced its early morning sparkle out across the low ripples of the ocean to the protective coral reef. She decided to go for a swim before breakfast.

At the foot of the steps, a middle aged man was setting up his stall of wooden animals and sandstone ashtrays and chess sets.

'Jambo,' he smiled.

'I'll come back later,' she promised. 'When I have some money with me.'

The tide was lower than the day before and someone had collected seaweed into piles along the sand. A few solitary Europeans jogged along the water's edge, where some fishermen prepared a boat for launching. Half way out to the reef, sailed a dhow, its sail gracefully unfurled in the shape of centuries past. Lilia threw off her wrap and waded into the shallow water that was as astonishingly warm as the air outside, like no sea in which she had ever swum. I shall enjoy myself after all, she decided, as she floated on her back and gazed back to shore. After breakfast, I shall lie on one of those sunbeds under those picture postcard palm trees, forget everything else and read a book.

Very few of the sunbeds were occupied and there was a pleasant out of season feel to the place, or perhaps most of the guests had gone on one of the safaris advertised in the hotel foyer. Lilia took her time covering herself with sun cream and repositioning the chair so that she was partly in the shade, and generously tipped the young attendant, who appeared unbidden with a mattress for the bed and a luxuriously large towel. After an hour or so spent dozing more than reading, she went for another swim in the sea and then ordered coffee from one of the white-clad waiters who hovered at a discreet distance. Then she went back as promised to the stall by the steps and bought a chess set and a line of black wooden elephants. No one had heard of the Hindu Cottages.

Returning to her room, she discovered a fridge containing bottled water behind a wooden façade under the dressing table and determined to find a shop later and buy some alcohol. She felt pleasantly tired and lay down on the freshly made bed. This is just what I needed, a proper holiday, she thought, before falling asleep.

She was woken by a tapping at the door.

'Parcel for you, madam.'

It was a pretty young woman dressed in a neat turquoise suit that identified her as one of the receptionists from the front desk. She was carrying a bulky brown package with a UK postmark. It was from Penny.

'Could I order lunch in my room?'

'Of course, madam,' the young woman smiled. 'I will see to it myself.'

Lilia tore open the padded envelope and extracted a dark blue, hard-covered note book that was battered and bent with use.

'Foolscap size,' she thought. 'Strange word. And stranger still how these things come back to you.' She opened the front cover of the book, her heart throbbing, wondering why Penny had thought it vital that she read it as soon as possible.

At the top of the first page was written: *"The Journal Of Edward McCormack, Iganga Mission 1954-64"*. Lilia recognised Edward's writing. Squeezed above it as an apparent afterthought was a title in capitals: *"SEEING THE LIGHT"*. She sat on the bed, leaned back against the pillows and began to read.

45

The journal began on 4th September 1954, which was two days after, Edward recorded, his and Rose's arrival in Iganga. They were in charge for the first time, he would have to make monthly reports to his superiors in the CMS in London, he thought it would help to keep a more frequent record. The first few pages - Lilia skimmed them quickly - were full of details of repairs to the buildings of the mission school, meeting its teachers, all African, organising classes, timetables, supplies of materials. The costs of everything were carefully noted in the margin. Then she noticed Rose's name again and read more carefully.

In early October Rose was *'still very depressed'* about Joseph's departure for boarding school. *'Fortunately'*, Father Thomas soon became her comforter and frequent companion, although Edward had suspected his motives at the beginning. *'I thought he was here to spy on how many pupils and what facilities we have,'* he admitted to himself. But, apparently largely thanks to Thomas, Rose soon began to show an interest in her medical work in the mission clinics, vaccinating the children of the area, providing a first aid service and other care, especially ante natal, with the help of a visiting doctor and Stephen, the dresser. Over the next couple of months she extended these activities further afield and, by the following spring, seemed well settled in a number of new roles that included setting up a branch of the Mothers' Union and re-starting a Sunday school. This was all interesting, thought Lilia, but more or less familiar. She turned the pages quickly. "*TUESDAY 22ND AUGUST 1955.*" That was where she must start. She read with a mixture of excitement and dread.

"Breakfast on the veranda with R and J. Much excitement because they were planning to go to Jinja. J needs a haircut about which he is less keen! Even R agreed he can't go back to school looking like a girl. He looks so like her with his curly dark hair and brown eyes, though he'll soon be taller. I hope she doesn't go into a depression again like last year. I think the school is good for him,

he's much less of a mummy's boy, more a little man. Went to the church. As yesterday, not much happening. The men sitting around in their tribal groups, sullen. The same problem. Katana says they must have their sacrifice. It's something they do all agree on. Every big building should have one. Then they will work 'quick, quick', make good strong – columns he meant, and beams – he knows all about how to make them he says, so we can have a proper tiled roof, not thatch that will need replacing every few years. He showed me the tree trunks they have begun to cut. I tell him he must get good timber, he must go to Veljibhai's at Jinja and fetch it. I will give him the money. 'But the ceremony?' he says again. 'Katonde too busy for small small things. Is why we make sacrifice, he happy, make all things good.' I knew what he meant. Katonde is far away in the sky, that's why they pray to all these other gods and ancestors, to look after their daily affairs.

'The Lord God is never too busy to listen to us,' I told him. 'To answer our prayers.' Quite pleased with myself for using this opportunity to witness. I still find it so difficult. Colin would have been proud of me, casting my net in a very rough sea. Spent some time measuring up with K and going round inspecting, trying to whip up a little activity, and then I said I would go home and think about it and let him know before sunset. Came home, discovered (from Mary), that Rose had been called away to a confinement, that Joseph was v disappointed but that Thomas was going to take him to Jinja instead. He wasn't around so I went off to the school for a while to see if anything needs fixing before the new term begins.

Alone here later in my study I did pray for guidance but as so often I found it hard to make out God's will from my own. The church is for Him but would He want it at any cost? Just then Mary announced Father John who had brought us an invitation to their new Bishop's inauguration, for the second diocese, and I found that my mind was made up. I took it as a sign that we must have our church, and, after the usual pleasantries, I told John of my decision about the foundation ceremony. 'And it is surely in line with current thinking, reaching out, being more inclusive and so on.' This conclusion came to me as a revelation in the telling.

Very relieved, a problem shared as they say ...but still a bit uneasy. John perhaps not the best confidant. Half wish it had been

Thomas with his 'It'll be alright, it'll be alright,' then I'd really have felt reassured. Of course, T might not have agreed (too 'lax') but then he might have had another solution. John, (when will they make him a bishop?) as ever much more difficult to fathom. Makes me uneasy at the best of times, as if I were sitting on the wrong side of my own desk, and of course he barely sipped his tea and disdained the sinful pleasure of a digestive biscuit so that I felt I couldn't eat either! What did he say? Eyebrows raised, that non-committal tone. 'According to a somewhat loose interpretation one might say?' Reminded me of my theology tutor at Edinburgh, almost as if I should be standing in John's presence - as he is rumoured to demand of young priests. Really made me nervous.

'There are many ways to skin a cat,' I said.

'And many paths to God.'

Check. Rebuke. Slap in the face. Of course it was a much more appropriate metaphor. Maybe I was becoming lax in my determination to get this church finished? Though I was, am, pretty sure that, in my place, John would have made the same decision and maybe for the same reason. If he supports me in advance he won't be able to criticise me later if, or rather when, the news leaks out. Still he didn't let me off the hook. He stood to his full gaunt height, looming over me of course, smoothed down his (already immaculate) white cassock, straightened his red sash, inclined his head very slightly to one side and gave me that small cold smile.

'Let us not be too, shall I say, Jesuitical, on this matter.'

'Heaven forbid!' I stood up too and made to shake, or more likely briefly clasp, hands. His hands are always as cold as his smile. But my torment was still not over! Blow me if he didn't close his eyes, raise his right hand and make the sign of the cross! Heaven forgive his theatricality! Like a cat with a mouse. Point scoring. Sometimes I wonder if we worship the same God (joke).

When he'd gone, I chose my favourite pipe and a piece of paper, drew a picture of a goat (as close as I could manage), on a sheet of paper, signed it and called Patrick to ask him to take it to Ketana. Impressed on him that he must put it in K's hand. He went off very solemnly, holding it flat on his hands as if it were an offering, which I suppose it is in a way. Then I lit my pipe and wrote the above.

Now going out on the veranda with a beer (well-earned I think) to wait for R and J."

Little knowing, thought Lilia that his life was about to change. She shifted slightly, the journal was a little heavy.

"WEDNESDAY AUGUST 23RD

A most terrible time that began yesterday evening. Joseph has disappeared. He did not come home. I can hardly bear to read my light-hearted meanderings of yesterday. As in another life. Rose and I had been sitting enjoying the usual nightly flying display when there was a sudden squealing. Of course I guessed what it was, though it sounded quite unearthly, some poor goat had met its end, if for a very good purpose and with every due observance of pagan propriety. Rose was alarmed, not entirely calmed by my explanation, and she never did settle after that, kept dropping her knitting, jumping up to look into the growing dark for any sign of Joseph, brushing off any of my attempts at conversation.

When the drums started I became nervous too, despite knowing more or less what they were up to with their torches circling the fire. Soon there would be chanting, I thought, let them get it over with and then, praise God, we would soon have our church. But it was spooky with the mvuli trees casting the deepest shadows over everything, as if they really did contain the spirits of ancestors overseeing the rituals, as at least some of the people down at the site believe. And when it was truly dark, even I could no longer pretend there was nothing wrong. Joseph should have been home long before.

I called Thomas first but he hadn't seen Joseph since morning. He had offered to give him a lift into Jinja but then Joseph had sent a message not long after saying he was going with Katana instead. Then I called the police and the new young fellow McAndrew arrived with a native sergeant. He took details and then went off to contact Jinja and organise a search, while the African officer went to question Katana. I hope not too roughly. Katana was a little intoxicated but, it seems, he consistently maintained that he did indeed give Joseph a lift, but that he dropped him on the outskirts of town and did not see him thereafter. He says Joseph said he would get a lift back with Thomas, about which Thomas knows nothing.

I myself searched all night with the help of the less inebriated or mesmerised men from the site, who still had their torches to guide us. Drum messages were sent to other villages and Peter and Stephen organised bands of well-wishers from the town to cover the surrounding area. We have found nothing. No clue. Rose ran around half the night, with Mary and Thomas trying to keep up with and look after her until I called Dr Gohil to come and give her something to make her sleep. She is still sleeping. I cannot. I write this instead, trying to recall any detail that might be of use. Peter to lead prayers later.

Lilia began to recognise details from the newspaper cuttings and letters. She skimmed the next few pages which recounted the early days of the search and the breaking news of the Frantz business.

"Thomas came on his way to Jinja. Was shocked at his appearance. He looks a broken man. Utterly distraught. Tried to reassure him we don't blame him at all. Tried to pray. Called R but she was out with T – 'again', said Elizabeth. She is v worried about R. Not eating, up most of the night. She told E that one of 'her women' had taken her to a medicine man, which of course E found most disturbing. As do I. But R is full of hope. Wish I could be…R does not call and I don't like to call her again. Feel so alone, although everyone is being v. kind. Spending a lot of time at the church. Good progress there at least."

There were more descriptions of events about which Lilia already knew. Edward's readiness to accept the worst became more explicit and she could understand Rose's disaffection. On September 4th he wrote that he thought that the police were still searching the lake. *"I think that drowning is still their preferred theory, what with the strong currents there… I should not despair but really cannot any longer feel much hope. Cannot help but think Rose's continuing optimism is blind, hysterical even."* But then she began to feel more sympathy for him. *"Joseph's picture on my desk. Five years old with R on the beach at Mombasa. Happy days."* And then, after he had failed to persuade Rose to go back with him to Iganga, there was something about the little service at the girls' school that he had not included in his letters. The girls had written *"little prayers asking Jesus to take care of Joseph, wherever he is, and bring him back safely, but how heaven is a better place and Joseph is a lucky boy if he is there so we shouldn't cry too much. Found it very hard to remain dry-eyed myself. If only I could feel such simple faith."*

A knock on the door signalled the arrival of lunch. As she went to open the door, Lilia wondered again why Penny had sent the journal. Perhaps she had wanted her first to understand Edward's point of view and then decide, before returning home, whether Rose should read it.

46

Lilia took the tray of food onto the terrace and continued to read. She immediately recognised an issue from her Mill Hill research that had made quite an impact on her at the time. It had, in fact, helped inspire one of her stories.

"Must record something which, despite everything, made me smile. John and I were discussing the influx of young men to the cities and I said that that was where the Young Men's Christian Association is important, providing a social centre and healthy activities above any particular creed. I rather thought the benefits of this organisation self-evident. John admitted they do some good work, but then said it is however 'highly dangerous' because it encourages freedom from any religious creed, 'perfect freedom of thought'; he quoted Ephesus I ("We, though many in number, form one body in Christ") and concluded with a ringing statement that we are privileged to be a cell in the Mystical Body of Christ. There was a bit of a silence after that before we returned to more mundane matters! No idea that he felt so desperate: we seem to be chugging along here quite well. Or is it my lack of vision?"

So Edward was beginning to doubt his reliance on 'mundane matters' to achieve his mission, thought Lilia, but was he so much to blame when the early missionaries had also been such practical men? November 10th 1956 was the eightieth anniversary of Stanley's call for missionaries and there had apparently been a commemorative edition of '*Outlook*'. *"Just read an article on one of the pioneers: the Rev. A.B.Fisher, now 88 years old and living with his wife in Eastbourne,* (*where Penny lives now,* thought Lilia, *what an odd coincidence*) *who arrived in Uganda in 1892 and had helped invent the 'biscuit tin' bible, which just fitted into the then standard size tin for biscuits, thereby protecting it from white ants.*

'In 1892 there were 200 Christians, one church, no schools and no African clergy,' he says. 'And yet I am still alive!' What a life of achievement. His favourite text: 'For the earth shall be filled with the knowledge of the glory of the Lord, as the waters cover the sea.'

Habakkuk 2:14. Inspired. But briefly. Cedric to see me about funding for another classroom for the boys: do I think we qualify for a government subsidy?"

Then Edward was again racked by doubt. *"November 23rd. Peter's just read 'Outlook'. Says all most people in Uganda think about now is money and getting a good education. Progress just means bigger hospitals and going to England to get a degree. This is not why the early missionaries came and suffered such hardships and even death. They came to bring the word of life. People must not forget this vision. Only then can we avoid the moral breakdown that is threatening the country. Stirring stuff. John would approve. P thinking of making it his subject for next Sunday. Wish I wasn't so hopeless at expressing my feelings. More than that. Feeling my feelings. Knowing what I believe. Church now being plastered".*

In December he recorded that Rose had gone to Mombasa and *"I must"* be glad she had had the sense to stay at the mission since *"Mau Mau may have been overcome (a special supplement of Outlook) but surely the country is still not so settled as Uganda. She seems to think Joseph may have gone there. Cannot argue about that but have written expressing concerns."* And then Colin Colman had stayed overnight. *"What a treat, though it gave him more chance to have a go at me! Liked what he saw of things here, says I've got my hands full which is a compliment. Sat and prayed together for Joseph. Better than trying to discuss it. C very concerned about Rose's mental condition but reassured me re the situation there – says he's heard that the policy of the villagisation of the Kikuyu is working. Also (and ironically, see later) that the Revival Christians were amongst the most brave, refusing to renounce their faith, whatever the consequences."*

This was new, thought Lilia, interested, even if it were a digression. It seemed to have something to do with Colin going back to England. *"I think he is very hurt that they want him to take a break and doesn't really know why. He has won so many converts, he says, and in a much more difficult area than Busoga. And I can see why: when I took him round, everywhere we went there were immediately smiles and laughter. Joy. It simply wells out of the man and infects everyone around. Not the British way. Not sufficiently rational. Not according to the book. Colin says you have to communicate in ways and concepts people understand. Discussed St Paul, who clearly says that there is nothing wrong per se in speaking in tongues but it is more important to 'prophesy' i.e. speak for the purpose of edifying others in ordinary language that they will understand.*

'For if the trumpet give an uncertain sound, who shall prepare himself to the battle?' Corinthians I, 14:8). C said maybe he's been letting the African love of the spectacular (something they share with the Corinthians apparently) take over too much in services, too much clapping, visions, confession of sins, etc.) but that he has always tried to keep close to the scriptures, never had any intention of encouraging a break away from the Church. It occurred to me that his is the opposite of my fault, I have always stuck too literally to the printed Word. Which to some of my parishioners might as well be 'tongues', I suppose.

He must have immediately striven to overcome this, Lilia realised, for the next entry, January 7th 1956, was the day of the inauguration of the new church, when he had given the sermon that Patrick had read out,. She skimmed a few more pages. Father John was now concerned about *"Mohammedan efforts to establish influence from the Mediterranean to the source of the Nile which is 'not unrelated' to the continuing unrest in Sudan.*" There was *"a growing desire for self-government elsewhere – Tunisia and Morocco expected to become independent this year."* John also saw a general lack of piety, of going through the outward motions, concentrating on practical projects. *"'Some prefer bricks to souls,' he said, 'perhaps finding the former more pliable.' Not getting at me, I am sure, though am only too aware of this weakness in myself."* According to the Mombasa mission, Rose was still out and about all day every day but did not confide in anyone, though they were taking as good care of her as possible.

Then in March came Edward's account of his 'mission' as he called it, to persuade the father of the girl who used to help her, Leah, to let her stay at school and then study nursing. *"Very impressed by the man's natural authority and wisdom, almost wasted in such a small sphere of influence. There is surely hope for the future of the country with people such as him as leaders,"* he had recorded and added *"Left thinking how much could be done, must be done, to develop the rural economy."* Hence the groundnut project, remembered Lilia and sure enough, she smiled to herself, Edward had indeed begun to make his plans. After more practical details about the new classroom and how to involve his woodwork class, (making desks and chairs), she found another entry following yet another call to Mombasa.

"Rose a little better – has asked if she can do some work in one of their medical facilities. Very glad. They say they will try to find out if she would like me to visit. Am resigned to the fact that she won't return here. Do not know if she is still actively looking for J. One should not give up hope and yet there is surely also virtue in bowing to one's fate? Do feel so alone, especially in the evenings. Spend a lot of time in the church. Remember J there. So many mornings of those few weeks he was with us we used to go down there together."

Edward did suffer, thought Lilia and Rose must have known. She turned a couple of pages to an entry in late July where she had relented at last. "*Rose has telephoned and wants to see me! So very glad. Feel a new man! But I cannot cancel my trip at this late stage. She says she understands. She's mainly working with the mentally ill. Rather concerned but said nothing. Her choice I gather".*

It was mid-afternoon. Lilia realised that if she did not go shopping now it would be too late. She marked her place in the journal with a scrap of the envelope and was about to close it when she saw an entry at the foot of the page. *"September 1st. Returned from Nigeria to the terrible news that Thomas has committed suicide. Or so one assumes: it was officially an open verdict. On the anniversary of Joseph's disappearance, so there has to be a connection. Had no idea he blamed himself so much for letting Joseph go with the foreman. Did he suspect him too? I do not think we shall ever know. Shall write to T's family. Such a good man…"*

So was that Edward's final view and the reason he had not believed in the Bombay sighting? Though he had made enquiries, she checked the December entry, from the Bishop, who advised most strongly against approaching the Governor, and from the Mombasa mission, which said that Rose was still in a very frail mental state and, like him, felt she was clutching at straws. Mrs Mehta had said she did not herself see the boy that her son thought was Joseph, and the policeman in charge, Ken Jackson, said there was not enough evidence for him to request action from the Indian police. Rose had always blamed herself for not ignoring Edward and going to India. Would it have been better if he had told her what Stephen apparently, and perhaps he himself and Thomas also believed? That the man – she checked the first page of the journal - Katana - was responsible for Joseph's disappearance. She closed the journal and made hasty preparations to leave.

47

A taxi dropped Lilia a mile to the south at a small covered shopping mall where she looked first for an internet café. She wrote to Mike adding an account of the robbery and shooting to the earlier draft article.

From Liliaz@yahoo.co.uk
To editorial@bognorobserver.co.uk
RE The last post
Attachment Article W/E August 28.doc

Dear Mike: This might be my last epistle. Expect you'll be surprised at some of the content which accounts for a slight delay in my return. I was of course very shocked but am beginning to feel better and in a couple of days or so will find out re flights home. Meanwhile enjoying being a beach bum near Mombasa and hope to find where Rose once lived. Let's hope for a really good news story soon after my return if this Ravi Makrani really is family.

Best regards

Lilia

PS Also just started reading Edward McCormack's journal that the ex-missionary whom I visited in Eastbourne belatedly sent me. OBVIOUSLY(?!) will tell you more in due course.

There was no message from Sarita but she sent her a short email anyway to tell her where she was and another to Penny's son to say that she had received the journal and was in the middle of reading it. Meanwhile, she was thinking. Why would Ketana have abducted Joseph? She quickly googled 'white slave trade'. Oddly, nothing came up though there was plenty of apparently substantiated evidence of continuing slavery, especially in the Sudan and Mauretania. Presumably there would have always been a demand for a rare commodity like a young white boy. No wonder that Rose couldn't bear to think that that had happened to her son, although it would have been another reason to go to Mombasa, through which some of the trade must have passed. But Rose had not discovered anything here, had ended up instead trying to help other mothers' lost sons and had again apparently rejected any suggestion that Joseph had been kidnapped.

Back out in the mall, she bought a large bottle of white wine and some fruit, again drawing a blank when she asked about the Hindu Cottages, and then, as she passed a shoe shop, she saw them: navy blue wedge sandals with an ankle strap, very like the ones she had found and coveted in Rose's wardrobe and which had reminded her of her mother. Perhaps it was a good omen. Some kind of African music was playing inside the shop and she thought of Moses and his proud disappointment at her rejection as she entered. Perhaps she could still make amends, if only for the loss of her intended tip, and send him some money. No, he would be offended. Better send a regular amount to help Michael through his education. She had considered joining one of those schemes advertised in the papers before, £15 a month they usually asked for, but how much better to help someone she knew, especially since his family had possibly saved her life.

The sun was still quite high in the sky so Lilia decided she would walk back to her hotel along the beach. The hotels directly below the shopping mall appeared much grander than hers, newer perhaps. She cut through the palatial Sun 'n' Sands Resort, that had a huge irregular-shaped swimming pool with a swim-up bar on a central island and a circling waterway along which guests drifted on inflated plastic rings. No one challenged her right to be there, her skin colour sufficient passport and, feeling much more sympathetic to the hustling beach traders, she bought a painting of a dhow sailing into a rosy dawn for Rose, a purple kanga to wear on the beach, which could double as a throw when she got home and, on impulse, a rather beautiful wooden carving of a man and woman intertwined for Mike. She would have to wait for an appropriate occasion to present it.

She passed more hotels with water slides, paddling pools and fountains, all protected from the beach by flights of steps and watchful *askharis*, and then she reached a rundown plot, with a lower wall and unwatered grass and no watchman. *'PRIVATE PROPERTY*

OF THE HINDU ASSOCIATION MOMBASA' read a peeling sign. She had found Rose's place.

She climbed the few steps and, under the palm trees, saw square patches of concrete where small buildings might have stood. One remained, small, white-painted with a green tiled roof and, in front, a big shaded terrace area where there were a few picnic tables. Rose's house? Or maybe hers had been one of the others that had been demolished. She peered through the dusty windows and made out a primitive kitchen and a room with three beds under yellowing mosquito nets. Rose's 'boys' might have slept there sometimes, or perhaps out under the trees, depending on the tolerance of Rose's landlords. Lilia sat on the steps of the terrace and looked across the grassy space towards the sea. A few small monkeys skipped away and clambered chattering up the nearest palm. Crows scavenged the dusty grass for picnic leftovers. This place must have been quite isolated in those days, she thought, but probably safer than now. She tried to imagine a young Rose, wearing a Masai blanket, sitting by a fire and 'singing to the moon' with her circle of homeless young men. But at a dead end, and, by her own account, hopeless.

It was 'happy hour' at the hotel when she returned, with free beverages and cake served by the pool. This time she chatted to the young waiter, whose real name turned out to be Sanigo, though his lapel badge said 'John'. He was a Masai, one of a family of six girls and four boys. Two of his brothers were also in work, one as a policeman and one as a game warden. He was looking forward to getting leave in a few weeks to take his turn herding the family's cattle. His eyes shone as he told her that he loved being out alone with them, though once he had nearly been killed by a lion. He told her that after dinner he would be dancing with some other Masai warriors and she promised to go and watch. But first she wanted to write a last story.

A CAT'S LIFE

In all his lives Rajah had been a good cat. Wherever he lived, he looked after his house and its compound and kept it free of mice. Most of the time he lay in the shade under the floor of the verandah of his house and slept, or appeared to sleep. But he was not lazy and no-one had to give him food. Whenever he heard the noise of sniffling or of squeaking, he was wide-awake and ready in an instant to pounce or give chase.

But now he had come to live in a new house and compound where there were very few mice so that his family began to feed him and he had nothing to do but lie all day in the shade under the verandah and sleep. He became very lazy indeed, never went on patrol around his new house and compound, and, even when he began to hear the noises of sniffling and of squeaking, did not get up and pounce or give chase. Only if a mouse, thinking he was asleep, came too close did he reach out a paw in warning.

Then one day, as he lay as usual under the verandah, he heard different noises, the noises of many voices and of scraping and of digging. They were very loud noises and he could not sleep at all. The next day there were different noises, the noises of chopping and of sawing, of hammering and of voices shouting. On the third day the hammering and sawing stopped and some of the voices started singing. Rajah still could not sleep and at last went to see what was happening in his compound.

The men who were singing were sitting under the trees at the edge of the compound. The men who were shouting were standing around a hole in the ground, a big square hole with a wooden floor. Some of the men saw him, pointed at him and gave chase. Rajah ran but one of the men pounced and Rajah was caught. Then all of the men climbed into the hole, stood on the wooden floor and started to sing a different song. One of the men opened a gap in the floor and the man who had caught Rajah threw him into a dark space below and closed the gap.

The men sang all day. They played drums and danced all night. Rajah lay in the dark space and could not sleep. No-one gave him food and he was hungry. The next day there were many noises of hammering and sawing. The next night Rajah slept but he was very hungry. The third night he was so hungry that he could not sleep. Even when the noises stopped and the men went away he could not sleep. Then he heard a different noise, the noise of sniffling and of squeaking, very close to him in the dark.

Rajah reached out a paw but the mouse started to run. Rajah chased after it and pounced but the mouse had run through a hole in the side of the dark space. Rajah had not seen the hole and it was not very big but it was big enough for hungry Rajah. The mouse ran on and so did Rajah. It was a very long hole and at the end of it Rajah found that he was under the trees. The mouse ran on but Rajah turned back and saw, where before there had only been the hole under which he had been thrown, now stood a large wooden building.

Rajah ran home where his happy family fed him. Then he lay down and went to sleep, but he was ready, should he hear any sniffling or squeaking, to wake and chase any mouse that strayed into his house. Lucky cat. It was the start of a new life. His ninth.

48

Lilia finished writing to find her tea grown cold, a wind stirring the tops of the palm trees and black-bottomed clouds rolling in from the south eastern horizon. There was no one else around. She missed Rajah's silent company, his solid warmth on her lap, the feel of him winding around her legs as she fed him. She had just decided to find out how to call home to ask Sarita how he was, when a sudden gust of wind snatched a sheet of paper from her lap, plastered it to the trunk of the nearest tree and threw a handful of stinging sand in her face. She saw Sanigo running towards her.

'Better go inside, madam,' he advised. 'A storm is coming.'

Bent close together in the wind, the swishing fronds of the palm trees sounded like a disorganised band of snare drums. From the top of the steps to her cottage Lilia could see the traders hastily packing up their stalls, chasing paintings and kangas that had escaped along the beach. She closed her door against the disorder but, as it was still warm, left the sliding door to the balcony ajar.

The sound of the palm trees had already changed to an urgent clacking as each, bending more and more violently, attended to its own survival. An agitated group of magpies swooped down to ground level and up again, as if afraid to land and Lilia saw the cause of their concern: a flapping black plastic bag wrapped around a tree. A few crows watched from a safe distance and, perhaps deciding it was inanimate and certainly not one of their own, flurried into the shelter of some nearby bushes. A smattering of large raindrops sent Lilia back into the comfort of her room. She opened the bottle of wine, lay down on the bed and took up Edward's journal.

"January 15th 1957. Informed that I must start holding parish meetings as part of the 'Uganda Diocese Mission', the first since 1938. We have a booklet based on the Epistle to the Romans as our guide. Am I fit to teach? Does Christ still dwell within me? Lord, give me strength to stand firm and serve you with all the talents that you have vouchsafed me."

Fortunately, he wrote a week later, much of the outreach work was to be carried out by local lay people and, by February, Stephen was *"proving himself an excellent leader*." There was also a 'Mission-over-the–air' which made *"most effective use of the wireless to take regular messages to every parish."* In March there were preparations to take fifty parishioners to Kampala in Holy Week for two days of meetings in the stadium. *"I am needed to drive,'* wrote Edward. *"Many people saying they have found new direction to their lives, new purpose. Perhaps it is enough to serve them."* At the 'huge' rally in Kampala in April, where many people had given public witness for the first time of their renewed faith and commitment, Edward observed that it was *"Difficult not to be affected by the joy so evident on every face. If I have ever wondered why I have come to Africa, what is my real task, then this should be the answer."*

Still 'should be' not 'is', thought Lilia, and noted his apparent relief at coming *'Back to earth. Teaching. Career counselling. Trying to see every top class boy for half an hour alone. Repairs to the mission house. The ants have been at play as ever*." Stephen was not satisfied however, it seemed, and was talking about going out together over the summer to as many churches and villages as possible. *"To keep up the momentum of the mission. I have said I will think about it although I am fairly certain the answer will be no. I cannot face it. Gold Coast independent as 'Ghana'."*

Instead he began to think of making a trip to Kenya, partly inspired it seemed by a report in 'Outlook' of the *'artificiality and squalor of life' in Nairobi, post Mau Mau. Overcrowding, lack of family life, homeless children. Uganda is a blessed place in comparison. The CMS hard at work there again, calling for women workers in particular. Wondered yet again what Rose is doing. Surely someone would tell me if there were bad news."*

The following month, July, he had read a report about a missionary family working in a hospital near Mombasa. *"I wonder if Rose knows them. A picture of their house servants and another of their two small sons with their friends the son of the headmaster and the son of the carpenter-instructor. All four in shorts and barefoot, holding hands, smiling. So very like Joseph in the old days, before Iganga, before we sent him away. So much easier when they are little."* He had gone to Kenya, paid a dutiful visit to some boys' training centre and then tried and failed to see Rose. He had stayed very near to her, but someone at the mission *"advised me most strongly that to try to see Rose might upset her recent precarious balance"* and told him about her *work with homeless young men, many of whom have mental health problems. It sounds very risky to me. The mission has given her a very small grant but will review the situation every six months.*

"September. Another year begins. I feel some renewal of strength, it was good to get away." Stephen was extremely enthusiastic about his summer's achievements. *" 'The basic principle of Mission is to preach to all men at all times by all means,' he told Peter and I after service yesterday. 'And preaching does not mean delivering sermons to the converted.' Oh dear. Peter had just delivered a particularly weighty example. 'We must proclaim Christ to the unbeliever, by word of mouth, as did our Lord Jesus Christ himself with his disciples. We must recover this calling or our mission is finished.' I can see I am going to be under continual pressure to go on safari next time with him."*

January 1958 saw Edward wrestling with the annual accounts. *"Most of our financial support now comes from Government –they need us to meet the urgent need for more educated Africans in every sphere. But whence the staff? Many conundrums. Easy to feel overwhelmed. One has to do what one can in one's sphere of influence. No doubt the RCs feel the same."*

Then in April he agreed to accompany Stephen to a Revival Fellowship meeting in Kampala. *"At least two hundred 'saved ones' in a hall near the cathedral, more than two-thirds men, the women sitting together in one block. People getting up and speaking informally one by one of depression, worry or fears and how the Lord had given them the victory. Stephen read the story of the feeding of the five thousand. A further exposition from a 'brother', developing the theme that there is no desert with the Lord, for with Him there is always food and drink. All interspersed with the singing of the 'theme song', which must have been sung about fifteen times in an hour and a half. 'We praise you Jesus - Jesus Child of the Lamb – Whose blood cleanses –We praise the Saviour.' No one person in charge, but things seemed to happen in quite an orderly fashion.*

Stephen stayed behind with one or two of the men whom he knew and I went off to see the Bishop. He said that one has to say that these people on the whole are the only members of the Church in Uganda who have personal experience of the Lord and are leading lives consistent with that. I said I was pleasantly impressed to hear so much sincere commitment and there was no unpleasant emotionalism."

Lilia reached for another drink and noticed how dark it had become. As she switched on the bedside lights, a torrent burst from the sky and she knelt up on the bed to see whether she should close the door. The grass between the hotel buildings was rapidly turning into a sandy swamp and the sloping paths becoming streams, but the rain fell vertically onto the balcony and was not coming into the room so she relaxed again.

Edward was enjoying himself! He was on a *"mini mission"*, together with Stephen and two other members of the congregation on a three-week safari of some outlying parishes. *"Wonderful to be away from the daily round. Our first stop was for five days at the end of a long track made by cotton lorries, the church a small mud thatched building with a garden of maize in front. The floor covered with dry grass for the people to sit on. Morning Prayer with a sermon, a different subject each day. One of the brothers read from Acts 3:19-20 and spoke of the need for repentance and release from the soul-sicknesses which afflict so many of us. He said it is like taking an ox to auction and returning with the money: if we take our sins to the cross they will be blotted out and in return we have peace. Afterwards, we gave out booklets to those who stayed and could read and sat around under the trees discussing.*

Later we visited homesteads and talked to the families living there. Stephen scored a great success with a woman who practised witchcraft. She destroyed all her instruments and asked him for books so that she can read and understand and have faith in Christ. It was the most striking of many other similar occasions as we moved onto other villages. What also struck me most keenly was their kindness and hospitality: they often touched me with great gentleness and, I have to say, love in their eyes. Stephen says many of them had heard that I had lost my son and lived alone and wanted to show that they shared my pain. Not to have any descendants is almost unthinkable. Who will pray for me when I am gone from this world? It is so good to meet people outside of my usual roles, as equals, as friends. Determined to learn more Lugandan this winter as it's the most common language and we have translations of the Bible etc. Kitchen Swahili no use up here."

He wrote to Colin with a long account of his trip. *"I know he will be pleased – and no doubt wish he was still here and doing the same,"* and kept to his resolve about learning the language. *"We have agreed to speak no English at mealtimes. Patrick finds my efforts a great joke."* Lilia wondered if Patrick remembered. Edward, typically, had been inspired to further reflections. *"What a labour of love it is to render the word of God to people in their own language, many of whom have had no previous written literature. Read about an American who invented a written language in Liberia, translated the Bible and then went on to write many books in the language. There is such a hunger for books, to learn more of the world. Apparently, he found a great interest in the story of the Titanic: it provoked long fireside discussions as to why men would die to save their women and children!"*

Lightning began to flicker in the distance, followed, after some minutes, by distant rumbles of thunder. Father John was worried about the growth in nationalism. In November Guinea had become independent. *"People more interested in joining political parties than going to church."* Apparently Catholics had been joining the Democratic Party, Protestants the Uganda People's Congress and there were fears that the old evils of heathenism, disease and ignorance had been replaced by nationalism, materialism and a 'nominal' Christianity, *"the same evils that brought war to Europe,"* noted Edward.

The lightning was brighter, the thunder louder, closer, and John was very pessimistic indeed. "*'We have been building on sand,' he said the other day. Moreover, he seems to think it is partly their own fault for too often taking the easy option, following the rituals without enquiring as to their converts' true understanding and motivation. New education laws will probably mean they'll have to introduce lay teachers – if they can find them. They have finally got a priest for Our Lady's."*

The lights began to flicker and, for a couple of seconds, went out altogether. Lilia began to feel apprehensive. It was now very dark outside in between the flashes of lightning. She felt isolated and tried to be distracted by Edward's March accounts of tribal violence in Rwanda and a trade boycott of non-African shops in Uganda, though not in Iganga. Edward had actually taken more interest in a report by the London-based CMS Secretary, who was of the opinion that in these changing times they should be "*'ready to experiment'. He specifically mentions going more frequently on tour! Feel I am definitely doing the right thing (thanks to Stephen). Am now greatly looking forward to the August safari."*

Underlining this shift in the balance of faith between him and his old adversary, in June he described how John was *"again in black mood following some meeting where they discussed a report on the recent rise of paganism: the law forbidding sorcery is lax, all the paraphernalia of herbs and charms are publicly on sale in markets. 'Religion is for the bazungu,' is the slogan. 'Let us stick to our customs and the nation will stick together.' I get the feeling he has almost had enough. While I feel I am at a new beginning."*

A lump rose in Lilia's throat, she felt absurdly happy for Edward, dead so long ago when she was just a carefree teenager in love, and privileged to be able to read this account that had probably never been meant for anyone else's eyes. She read on, no longer noticing the flickering light and the approaching electric storm.

"On the road again! Staying this week in the pastor's guesthouse, a small white washed thatched cottage next to his own, situated at the end of an avenue of fig trees. Separate round hut for the kitchen. What looks like an enormous basket on stilts with a thatched top: the millet granary, enough to last the family a year. Further off a little thatched bathhouse and behind that a fenced-in path leads to the neat little pit latrine hut. Our cottage very well set up too. Windows wired against mosquitoes, two cushioned Oxford chairs, two wooden, and a table with an embroidered cloth. A jug of flowers, a jug of freshly made orange juice. For our ablutions: a table in the corner with a basin and a covered bucket of water. A

bar of Sunlight soap which, I suspect, was bought especially for us at great expense. I always use the local stuff at half the price.

Today we went with the pastor to two of the smaller churches in his huge parish, thirty miles away. Impressed greatly by one young boy who, when asked what Christianity meant to him, replied that it meant 'he must not go into the spirit hut in his homestead.' Brought it home to me what our people give up on conversion, what pressures they may be under from their family and friends. About to have dinner with the pastor's family: can hear the drum summoning us. Rain expected tomorrow: the frogs are beginning to mutter. The Southern Cross shining brightly tonight. At peace in deepest Africa. More than I ever hoped for."

The lights went out. At the same time there was a blinding sheet of lightning, followed almost immediately by a painfully loud crack of thunder. Lilia jumped but read on by the intermittent flashes. It was as disorientating as trying to decipher a drinks menu in a strobe-lit club. But Edward's mood had so abruptly changed that she was not sure that she was getting it right.

"8th August. Stephen is taking me back to the mission in the morning. Am in shock. Writing this to hold myself together. Today began as the day before. A service in the church and then we were introduced to all the elders of the congregation, the schoolteachers, other special visitors, leaders of the local villages, Christian and non-Christian. Stephen and I were discussing school and church matters with a group of these, Stephen interpreting for me as necessary. Again some expressions of sympathy about Joseph. An elderly man who was rather deaf suddenly turned to his neighbour and loudly asked 'Is this the white man whose son was...' but I did not understand the end of the question. What I did see was its effect: an instant and very uncomfortable silence."

In the next lightning Lilia saw a movement at the open balcony door. Petrified, she waited for another flash, which revealed a long arm reaching slowly inside. In the next she saw a small head and another arm reaching towards the top of the dressing table, which stood between the bed and the door. She held her breath and then jumped as there was a knock at the cottage door.

'Candles, madam,' she recognised Sanigo's voice with relief. 'I've brought you some candles.' As she moved quickly to open the door, there was a flurry of movement on the dressing table and her glass was knocked to the floor.

'Someone was in the room,' she said quietly and pointed.

Sanigo leapt to the balcony, then laughed and pointed. By the light of a candle they could just see the monkey clinging to the tree, clutching a whole bunch of bananas.

'Dinner as usual,' Sanigo said as he left. 'Perhaps by candlelight.'

Her heart still pounding, Lilia re- read the last few lines. Is this the white man whose son was - what? *"Stephen said something then rapidly brought the meeting to a close and we left. When we got back here I had to force the reason from him. The word I did not understand was 'sacrificed'."* A chill crept down through Lilia's body. 'Truth is stranger than fiction', she whispered over and over again. Similar things, coincidences, magical-seeming and certainly unconscious connections, had happened to her before in her writing but nothing as horrific. So this was why Penny had sent the journal.

"It is September, what day I do not know. Stephen prays with me morning and night. I cannot go in the church. I cannot bear to see it. Monument to my pride and folly and not to the glory of God. Dear God, I thought I was living my life in Your service, but surely You have long since turned your face from me. How could you accept our praises in a place founded on such evil? My only son. The God of Moses was never mine and You would not have asked it. Though I believed I would have made any other sacrifice.

"Stephen is also in agony. He knew from almost the beginning, but could not say. Thought the pain of not knowing better than the truth. Again and again I tell him he was right. All the fault is mine. I pray that in time he will find peace of mind but what worth have my prayers? No sin can be worse than mine. Surely there can be no forgiveness for me. I have asked the Society to find a replacement, I must go. They know only that I am sick. Have granted me six months home leave, to be extended if necessary.' Can I ever return? But where will I go? What do with my life? I can see no future. I begin to understand Thomas' final decision."

The lights came on and, noticing the time, Lilia hurried to dress for dinner. Whatever else Edward had written, and there were still quite a few pages, could wait. She needed to be with other people.

49

'The Old Town?'

The matata's conductor nodded and Lilia found a seat in the already packed minibus. It was the next morning and she had thought she should see where Edward and Rose had spent their last days together in East Africa. It was a pilgrimage, now that the search was over. She started to climb the winding path up alongside the mouldering Portuguese battlements that surrounded Fort Jesus, with the wide port entrance to her left and the open sea ahead. She passed an old man resting on a bench, with both hands clutching a walking stick in front of him.

'Arre,' he called.

'Arre,' she responded, thinking it to be a greeting and sat on a bench a little higher up. She took out the journal and found the passage.

"October 1st 1959. God in His wisdom gave me a purpose. Rose is ill and must go home and I will take her. One of her 'patients' brought her to the mission here in Mombasa. So far as they understand, she had taken to walking naked on the beach, eating whatever rubbish she picked up, talking to herself. A doctor has diagnosed psychosis: these are apparently common signs, even amongst Africans. In the circumstances, it is almost as if it were an infectious condition, but surely it cannot be so. She is currently on tranquilliser drugs, which I must see she takes. She shows no sign of knowing who I am and I shall not attempt to tell her. I have brought her to a hotel in the Old Town where neither of us will embarrass the CMS. Waiting for flights. After some soul-searching, I have written to Colin and Penny asking for their help. Did not know to whom else to turn, though I will not depend on them long. No doubt the Society will offer some temporary accommodation. Have only told them of Rose's sickness.

"LATER: Rose 'escaped'. I found her nearby, wandering naked on the ramparts of Fort Jesus. Fortunately her clothes were nearby and I persuaded her to take her tablet. We sat for a while looking

out at the Indian Ocean. Memories of family holidays. The 'nonsense' she talks sadly made only too much sense. She kept pointing out to sea. 'He's over there, he's over there. Take me there. Won't someone take me there? Please? Someone?' Lilia looked out sadly over the sea where Rose had wanted to go to find Joseph. Edward had had good reason by now not to do as she begged. She stood to climb higher into the sunlit morning.

'Arre, stop,' the old man had followed her. 'Not safe,' he pointed ahead with his stick. 'Not go alone.'

Lilia stopped and looked from him to the path ahead. In a broken down corner of a tower a shady figure lurked. Further up, under a small tree sat another man and yet another passed them and looked back, appraising.

'I see what you mean,' Lilia turned back. 'Thank you.'

'Gusalalbhai Thakker,' the old man shook her hand. 'You go in the fort, many tourists go there.' He indicated the main entrance as they descended the path. A sign advertised a special exhibition: '*ENVOY OF PEACE FROM CHINA*.' A wooden box was labelled '*ANTI CORRUPTION SUGGESTION BOX*.'.

'Thakker? I know some Thakkers in England.'

The old man's face creased into a smile. 'Many many Thakkers,' he said. 'Like Smith.' He stopped smiling. 'Both my sons are in England, in business.'

'Have you lived in Mombasa long?'

'All my life,' he nodded. 'In that house there.'

Lilia looked across the small roundabout where the matata had dropped her. It was an ancient house of several storeys with high covered wooden balconies clinging to its façade. Perhaps also of Portuguese origin, it must be part of the conservation area of which she had read. It certainly looked in need of renovation.

'Is it safe to walk that way?' she pointed ahead where more old balconies overhung the road and a red banner of Liverpool Football Club hung between them. .

'To the Old Port? Yes. There are many tourist shops now. But keep to the main road, the side roads are still full of Arabs. When we were young it was not so safe. Our parents told us not to go there. The same thing I told my children.''

'Why?'

‘Kidnappers,’ he said. ‘There were cases.’ He raised his stick in farewell and returned to his bench.

So Joseph might have been abducted if he had got as far as Mombasa. But he hadn’t. All the time he had been buried close to his home, under the foundations of the new church. Lilia walked to the Old Port and sat on a wall looking across the harbour that for centuries had been a haven for traders from many countries, bringing precious silks and spices to exchange for equally valuable cargoes of ivory, mahogany and slaves. She read the rest of the journal, written when Edward had gone back to Sussex to stay with the Colmans, having installed Rose in a nearby mental hospital.

“November 1959. We found a place with a sea view. I hope that was the right thing to do, although in her current condition (much more powerful drugs) I doubt if it makes any difference to her where she is. Have had several consultations with the psychiatrist, told him all the background. He was most interested to hear that the symptoms of psychosis are so similar there and here. Seemed to confirm a personal bet. Though he favours the, presumably more precise, diagnosis of schizophrenia. He doesn’t hold out much hope. They will probably try some electric shock treatment.

“Colin and Penny being so very kind. Say I must stay as long as I like. Lovely ancient church with fine stained glass windows, small village, lying, no, nestling, at the foot of the Downs. I walk on the Downs most days, up through lanes sodden with dead leaves. Shall pay a visit to my parents sometime soon.

December. I think I must count it a blessing that my parents are too old to take in why I am home unexpectedly, or to want me to stay long. Routine replies to their questions (‘How’s Joseph? And Rose?’) satisfy them. I never thought I would envy those who have lost their mental powers. My suffering is constant. I fall on frozen furrows, the earth, hard-faced, has turned away. The skeleton trees point black fingers at the sky. The sun is pale and weak, it falters soon after it has risen. The nights are long and full of shadows.

On my return, Colin made me a prisoner in his study. A glass of whiskey, a log fire. Made me confess. Of course, it was more than he had expected. And far worse. I have never seen him so shaken.

He soon bowed his head, did not look at me as I spoke, but, good man that he is, held my hand throughout. 'Let yourself be Broken,' he said. 'It is time, more than time.' I have heard him use this word before, and others of a Revivalist leaning, but never truly understood. I was always on the other side, helping others find their faith, overcome their sorrows, leave their sins behind.

1960 January. A new decade. I have made outward efforts for the sake of my dear friends and the festive season. Attended services, though not Communion, and tried to delight in others' happiness at this joyful time. The boys have returned to school. Enjoyed helping them make some aeroplanes. Using a fretsaw requires great concentration. Took myself off when I felt the horrors welling up again. Visit Rose every week but there is no outward response. They say she sits all day looking out of the window. What she sees is any man's guess.

Colin has been very busy of course (did not ask me to help him, which is quite understandable) but manages a quick word most days: sets me texts to study as if I am on some course. Today it was Philippians 2:8. 'And being found in fashion as a man, he humbled himself, and became obedient unto death, even the death of the cross.' I have confessed, but only to a dear friend, who is now also burdened with my grief. Most people would surely turn away in horror.

I think I have sunk as low as I can go, and then am faced anew with the worst fact of all: I betrayed my God, I lost hope, did not keep faith. Despite my chosen occupation, despite having dedicated my life to proclaim His truths to others, whom I thought in more need of salvation than myself. Oh Joseph, Joseph, if only I believed you had not entirely passed from us, and I could find you in the spirit house.

Every morning I go alone into the church, after early Communion, before anyone comes to clean or renew the flowers. I sit, or kneel, and look up at the great Eastern window over the altar where Christ shows his disciples the lamb that was lost. They say that wherever you go His eyes follow you but I cannot see it. To me they seem cast down and I cast out, looking in like a beggar at the feast, as the snow falls steadily around and the cold stone strikes a chill to my heart through every bone.

February Luke 23:34 'And when they were come to the place, which is called Calvary, there they crucified him, and the malefactors, one on the right hand and one on the left. Then said Jesus, Father, forgive them; for they know not what they do.'

Penny saw that I was puzzled. 'Do you not feel at all betrayed by what happened?' she asked me. 'After all you had done for the people with only their betterment in mind?' I went for a long walk along the ridge of the Downs, towards the distant Solent glinting grey and sullen, and back into a storm of snow like grains of sand driven into my face by a bitter wind. 'No,' I told her on my return. 'They acted according to their beliefs. It was I who did what I knew to be wrong.' She laid her hand on my shoulder. 'But did you really know what you were doing?'

Then we all listened to Harold Macmillan's speech to the South African Parliament. He has been on a tour of countries in Africa that are newly independent or shortly due to be. Have been too sunk in my own troubles to take much notice but this made me sit up and pay attention. He said that the same processes that gave birth to the nation states of Europe have this century been repeated all over the world, in Asia about 15 years ago and now the same thing is happening in Africa.

'And the most striking of the impressions I have formed since I left London is of the strength of this African national consciousness. In different places it takes different forms but it is happening everywhere. The wind of change is blowing through this continent and, whether we like it or not, this growth of national consciousness is a political fact.' Strong words, especially in such a setting. This year will see the independence of eighteen new states! Colin and Penny exchanged looks. I know they wish they could return and be part of it all. And that they think I should also.

March. Penny came early to my room and asked me if I could possibly take her Sunday School class. She had been called to the school. Mark is ill again. Could not refuse. It is the first demand either has made of me. A dozen little ones, between seven and ten.

They are writing entries for a competition. 'What makes a missionary?' We discuss but I don't tell them that I was one. There is no need. They have their own ideas. I have brought their lists home, ostensibly to correct them. Several make me smile: 'a missionary should be a good swimmer.' I wonder where that came from! 'A missionary must like children and be able to amuse them easily' (not so hard to understand that one!); 'be brave, cheerful and healthy'; 'be good at mending things'. Well, I certainly qualify on the last count. This was my favourite, written by a seven year old. 'A missionary must:

1. *Believe in Jesus our Saviour.*
2. *Understand the Bible.*
3. *Like all kinds of people.*
4. *Have another kind of knowledge, like medicine or farming or teaching.*
5. *Have patience.*
6. *Learn not to be lonely.*
7. *Understand other languages.*
8. *Ability to 'make do'.*
9. *Prepared for people not liking you.*
10. *Be able to draw.*

Out of the mouths of babes, indeed. The last item the only give away and not something I have ever considered! I am going for a walk. The first daffodils are out in the garden and there are new lambs in the field down the lane. Showers alternate with bright sun, the clouds race across the sky – it is officially the first day of spring tomorrow. I had forgotten how it feels to live where there are seasons.

21st March. Early this morning I slipped in at the back of the church, as Colin was about to celebrate Holy Communion. How I have missed the wonderful words of the Book of Common Prayer. Colin was facing the altar as I took my place in the line of those kneeling to take the sacrament, but when he paused at my outstretched hands I looked up. For one terrible moment I thought he might refuse me, or at least wish that he could. Of course he did not. Tenderly he placed the wafer on my palms, I raised it to my mouth and then I looked up again as he made the sign of the cross over my head. His eyes were closed but there was the joy on his face that I have seen so many times before when he has recognised true repentance and belief in a hitherto recalcitrant soul.

I felt truly saved; there is no other way to describe it. All my sins and heartache washed away in a flood of the Water of Life. I gave up my broken empty self and now I am filled to overflowing as it is promised. 'My cup runneth over,' said David. How could I not have understood before? As Colin passed on to the next person, the sun streamed through the marvellous window behind him, like a voice from the eternal into time and I felt Christ's eyes upon me. I know now what I must do."

Go back to Africa, that was what he had done, to devote the rest of his life to his mission and to raising the money to install another lovely window as a memorial to his son. He may never have ceased to grieve, or to blame himself, but at least he had achieved so much that was good and for which he was still remembered. While poor deluded Rose had spent her whole life in vain hope. Lilia closed the journal and looked up and across the harbour which was now in shade, the sun having slipped below the rooftops of the buildings behind her. A few lights had already appeared on the far side. She hastened to find a taxi back to the hotel. It was time she left Africa, time she went home.

The guest telephone was at the end of the bar in a partly covered space by the open air dance floor where two young men were setting up sound equipment and instruments for the after-dinner disco. On one wall of the bar room a large television screen was tuned to Sky News. Near it a group of Sikh boys were playing snooker and beyond them an African family was celebrating the youngest member's birthday. The barman had just brought out a cake bearing five lit candles when the telephone had rung and he had summoned Lilia. It was very hard even to hear oneself speak.

'Lilia?'

'Sarita?'

'I thought I should call you.'

Lilia clutched her throat. 'What's happened? Has Rajah –'

The family had begun to sing '*Happy Birthday*'. Lilia hoped she had misheard Sarita's reply. The Sikh boys joined in the singing.

Lilia carried the telephone as far away from the merry-making as she could and sat down heavily on the steps that led to the dance floor.

'What did you say?'

'I said he's *fine,*' Sarita emphasised the last word. 'At least, not fine, he's not well but – the vet wants to do some more tests. A lot of tests. Which will cost a lot of money. Should we wait til you get home do you think? Or –'

'Please ask him to carry on as he thinks necessary,' Lilia interrupted. 'And to look after Rajah til I get home. Then you needn't worry any more. I'll see you in a couple of days. I'm going to ask the hotel to make the arrangements now. Thank you.'

But she did not get up immediately. Heavy-hearted, she sat on, watching a perfect full moon rise and illuminate the distant ever-pounding line of surf. A middle-aged German couple walked past her pointing and exclaiming at its beauty, but to her it appeared coldly impassive. There was no comfort either in the thought of her home-coming, her mission having ended with such a tragic discovery that it had better never been begun, especially since it had contributed to the neglect of her beloved cat. Slowly she stood and was about to return the telephone when she realised something else. Nothing Ravi Makrani could tell her could be of any comfort to Rose either, in fact it was hard to see how it could have any relevance whatsoever. His visit would be a waste of time and money and she must tell him so immediately.

50

Ravi heard the telephone ring in his own distant half of the vast flat. It could wait, he decided, and let himself sink deeper into the ancient chintz covered armchair in his father's very large living room. If he didn't speak to his father over dinner it might be another whole day before he could book the tickets. Jay was almost through his evening prayers in the next room, the one that he kept as his *mandir,* where the various pictures and statuettes of the gods were dwarfed by the tinted photograph of his guru that occupied centre stage. It was one of the few times of day when one could be sure where to find him. Otherwise, from early in the morning he could be anywhere on the streets of Mumbai targetting 'Non Resident Indians', handing out his books and pamphlets by the big hotels, waiting for them to disembark from the cruise ships by the Gateway of India, and, if he had made a contact, he might rush off to a meeting without stopping to eat. If he was in town at all.

Ravi picked up a copy of *'The Science of the Soul: How to Discover Bliss'* from the low table in front of him and leafed through it. *'Short Cuts to Self Realisation'. 'Follow in Arjuna's Path'. 'Understand the Workings of God in an Hour.'* Ravi paused at a photo of the elderly, bespectacled one-time cloth merchant who had himself experienced such sudden illumination several decades ago. Jay was apparently spending more and more time at the ashram. And more and more money.

'I've told him it won't last for ever,' Ashwinbhai had said only yesterday. 'And that he ought to consider you. And don't say you don't care about the money. I'm your lawyer too.'

The telephone had stopped ringing and Jay was on his final *arthi.* Ravi heard the slight catch in his breath and knew it was the moment when he drew a curtain in front of the holy man's picture and bade him goodnight. Ramjidas Thakker, reflected Ravi, looked more like a lawyer than did musician manqué Ashwin Kotecha, who had been obliged to support his many younger siblings and carry on the family business when their father died. Or an accountant. Ravi sighed. He could not tackle his father on two fronts at once. Perhaps once he got him away from India he would listen. *If* he got him away from India.

He heard the final tinkle of the small brass bell and the beginning of the sacred *Ommm* with which his father always ended his rituals. Ravi glanced at his watch. Eighty seconds still to wait. He had timed this bit before. But then he heard a soft cough and a whisper.

'Telephone, *Masterraviji.*'

It was Bhimjibhai, still looking after them, long after someone should have been looking after him. Bent, frail and already clad in his night-time *dhoti,* he stood in the doorway, beckoning. Ravi frowned. Bhimjibhai was usually a reliable taker of messages and he knew Ravi wanted to speak to his father.

'It's an English lady,' the old man persisted. 'She says it cannot wait.'

'I'm coming.' Ravi stood immediately and followed the old man along the long dark passage and across the dim hallway that linked the two apartments. The desk light was on in his study.

'Lilia Zynofsky?' he sat down and picked up the telephone receiver in a single movement. 'Are you back in the UK already?'

'No I'm still in Africa, in Mombasa.' She had a low pleasant voice.

'I'm hoping to book tickets in the morning,' he told her.

'That's why I'm calling,' she hesitated. 'I'm afraid it won't be necessary.'

'Sorry? Has something happened? Rose…?'

'Rose is fine, the last I heard. No it's…' she stopped again. He heard the deep sigh. 'I'd better start at the beginning.' There was an intake of breath but still a pause before she began to speak, rapidly. 'I went to Africa to look for any traces of Rose's lost son, not just for any family background as I wrote in my articles,' she said. 'He disappeared fifty years ago. *That* was the 'family tragedy'.'

'As I thought.' Ravi shifted the phone closer to his mouth ready to give her the good news but she wasn't listening.

'But I've just found out what really happened to him. From his father's diary. Someone sent it to me. I can tell you all about that later if you like but the point is – oh, it's so terrible, I can hardly bear to tell you and I certainly won't be able to tell Rose.' Again the sharp intake of breath before she spoke, so quickly that he could not make out every word. 'Joseph was sacrificed, by the builders of a church, it was the local custom, his father found out a few years after he disappeared when Rose was still in Africa, in Mombasa in fact…'

'Joseph,' Ravi interrupted. 'As I thought. Joseph is my father. Joseph McCormack.'

'What? '

'My father. Of course he's nearly sixty now. And he is called Jayesh Makrani.'

'But what…' Her voice was faint. He imagined her holding the receiver away from her mouth, staring at it in disbelief. 'I mean, how…' She was close again.

'It is a strange story and I know you'll find it hard to believe, but…' Ravi took a breath and began to speak, almost as quickly as had Lilia.

'My father, Joseph, told me that he left his home town in Uganda and went to a wedding party in another town, where he then attached himself to some guests, who were leaving to go home to India, and travelled by train with them to the coast. At the port, they boarded a boat for India, believing Joseph to be staying with friends in Mombasa.'

'He didn't travel with a friend? Nilu?'

'He never mentioned any friend by name.'

'Didn't they think it was odd that no one was seeing him off?' Her tone made it clear that she didn't believe him.

'Oh I was sceptical too at first' Ravi said quickly. 'I think he must have told them some story. And maybe they put it down to the strange ways of the Europeans.' Ravi gave a short laugh. 'They certainly wouldn't have felt able to interfere, I think, not in those days, nor have wanted to tangle with the British authorities. Whatever.' He took a breath. 'Look, I have more or less persuaded my father to come with me to meet Rose, though he's pretty freaked by the whole thing, as you can imagine. '

'He's not the only one,' said Lilia, her voice taking on a very sharp edge.

'No of course not, I'm sorry, and you've been through so much. You will have a lot of questions, only…' He heard a sudden blast of western dance music, very close to Lilia, American soul it sounded like. He raised his voice. 'I don't know if my father will answer them. If he will even be able to.'

'What? Pardon?' He was not surprised to discover she had not heard. 'There's a disco just starting here,' she was saying. 'And I seem to be sitting right by a speaker. Wait, that's a bit better.'

She had shifted a little further from the noise but it was still not the time or place for a long discussion. He spoke slowly. 'We must meet and talk before we see Rose.'

'Definitely,' she shouted back. 'I'll email all the directions. I look forward to meeting you.' She paused, sounding suddenly less certain as she added: 'Both of you.'

Ravi sat cradling the receiver for some minutes after she had gone, wondering how the reconciliation between his father and his grandmother would proceed, how much to tell his father before this event, whether his father would have any idea of the shock that it might be to Rose. I must call Maya, he thought, she will know what to do – and then he remembered what he had been doing before Lilia called and, with bitter foresight, he leapt from his seat and raced back to the other end of the flat.

'Jayeshjimaster gone out.' Bhimjibhai was standing by the dining table his hands spread wide in a gesture of his helplessness to prevent the occurrence.

'Never mind,' Ravi touched the old man lightly on one shoulder. 'I'll see him first thing in the morning.'

The alarm clock rang as the very first gray of dawn lightened the night sky and stars were still clearly visible overhead. Ravi swung his legs from the warm bed with reluctance, found his *chappals* and a shawl to throw around his shoulders and was ready to head for his father's apartment when he saw the white rectangle of paper under his bedroom door. He picked it up, knowing more or less what he would find. His father had already left the house, long before the usual hour of his morning prayers.

'Sorry, dear boy,' the note explained. 'Motherji called. She is not well. She needs me. See you in a few days.'

With great anger, Ravi crumpled the paper and threw it into a corner. 'Motherji' was Thakkerji's heir. She had ministered to his following since his death a number of years before. Now she was grooming Jay to take over from her and Jay was very happy about it. Ravi had been very happy for his father to have new purpose so late in life, until his own constant search for anything related to the name 'McCormack' had begun to throw up significant results. Now his father's mission seemed more like a convenient excuse, a way to escape his real responsibilities, not to mention his mounting debts. Dear God, did he appreciate the irony in running off to an adopted 'mother' when his long lost real mother had just been discovered?

Ravi sank back on the bed, his head in his hands, wondering if he would be able to get back to sleep. Even Bhimjibhai would not yet be up. He wished he had called home the night before and then he did a swift calculation. It was so early here that it would only be late afternoon in Seattle. He went to his study and called, praying Maya would pick up, imagining her sitting out on the deck gazing at the ocean or maybe inside listening to music. With Ben sprawled at her feet, one ear cocked in case she suggested another walk. God, how he missed them and wished he were home. Be there, please?

'Hello?' her voice was a little abrupt, she didn't want to be disturbed. 'Oh hi! My, you must be up early. What's up?'

She listened, she understood immediately, she had met Jay more than once, as a matter of fact she was good with him, he was always more relaxed, more *normal,* in her company, even quite cheerful.

'You have two choices,' she said. 'Either go after your father and talk to him one last time. Or go to England by yourself. And then come home to us.'

'How about just coming home?'

'Someone has to go, don't they. That poor old lady.'

'I know. My grandmother. And Lilia, the one who's been searching. I've promised, of course I'll go.'

'Go for a run,' said Maya. 'By the sea. It always helps. But come back soon. We miss you, don't we boy?'

51

'One last chance,' Ravi thought grimly as the plane landed at the small airport by the dusty desert town. 'And then I'm through.'

He shared a cab with a retired couple from Kansas. He sat next to the driver. It was Keval and Veena Shah's fourth visit to the ashram, they were eager to arrive, enthusiastic about the great spiritual benefits of staying there.

'So quickly we learned how to stop binding our karma,' confided Veena, her plump face glowing. 'So now if only we are living without attachment and understanding how it is not I that am the Doer…'

'It is like applied spirituality,' Keval interrupted helpfully. 'Keep it simple, Vee. He'll find out for himself when he's ready.'

'Oh gee, pardon me,' Veena said. 'I just want everyone I meet to know how wonderful it is. Anyway, so we came a couple more times, just to be sure, and then last year we took the plunge and bought an apartment. It's real comfortable, American style, you know, proper bathroom? Not Indian.' She shuddered and turned to address her husband. 'Remember the bathroom, Kev, in that hotel in Ahmedabad on our first trip? I was set to go right back home?' Keval nodded, lips pursed. He obviously did remember. 'So how long are you going to stay?' Veena turned back to Ravi

Ravi was vague, he didn't admit to a previous visit and certainly not to his personal connection with the place. He looked out of the window at the lengthening shadows of the mango trees lining the road, at the passing bullock carts full of newly picked vegetables and people going home after a long day's work in the fields. There were women in bright saris with babies on their backs or bundles or water pots on their heads driving herds of water buffalo, children running alongside flocks of goats and packs of yellow dogs peacefully accompanying the cavalcade. Eternal India. A scene that would not have changed much in hundreds of years. Ravi sighed. How he loved the countryside here, especially at this golden time of day, whilst knowing he could not live in it.

'It feels like coming home,' Veena observed, not quite echoing his thoughts. They passed small villages, with houses of mud and thatch, outside which sat old men chatting and smoking *bidis*. Women squatted, cooking over open fires and cattle, tethered close by, munched at bundles of fresh fodder. A few miles further the scenery changed as they drove through open shrubby grassland, desert almost, in the midst of which they could see, in the fast fading light, the gleaming outlines of the ashram rising like a small walled city or palace.

'It looks more beautiful even than I remember,' said Veena, with a very happy smile on her face as they approached the electronically operated gates.

Ravi bade a rapid farewell to his surprised companions, who had imagined that he would need to be introduced at reception and made straight for his father's apartment. He threaded his way through a maze of wide, clean-swept, marble-paved paths, lined with bright flower beds, between more or less identical but attractive and substantial two storey buildings, more of which were under construction, each housing, he knew, four large apartments. As always, he was struck by the incongruity with what he had just seen of life outside the walls. None of this here would have been at all remarkable in America, or in some modern developments in India for that matter, but in contrast to the surrounding countryside it was like landing on another planet.

Obscene opulence. Ravi felt the familiar stirrings of anger and resentment. This was where his father's money was going. Not on these buildings, most of which were owned by their occupiers, a few being available to rent, but on the infrastructure, wages, even, no doubt, very low Indian wages. And all those publications he distributed so freely. Providing local employment was good but the rest? How much more happiness could the good couple from Kansas have created for others with even a fraction of what they must have spent on their hideaway. For that was all it was and why it suited his father so perfectly. An escape from reality, an escape that was unavailable to the vast majority of India's more than a billion people. What was the point of, what right did rich people have to inner calm when not far away, in fact very close indeed, their fellow human beings lacked the most basic necessities? Ravi was slipping fast into his usual bitter cynicism that even Maya, when she had accompanied him last year, had been unable to shift.

His father was not in his apartment and a programme of the week's activities attached to the notice board above the desk told him why. There was a bi-weekly broadcast, a phone-in advice service and his father was hosting it, presumably due to Motherji's incapacitation. *'7.30 pm Central Hall Pujya Shri Jayeshji Makrani, self-realised Follower of our Beloved Motherji, will channel the Divine Truth as revealed to our Supreme Masterji, and by the grace of his wisdom help Questioners discover solutions to the Problems of Life.'* At the bottom of the notice there was an important reminder to visitors and residents to don the garments provided for all public occasions, sets of which would be hanging in each wardrobe. Uniform he thought sourly. Always a part of indoctrination, brain washing. He showered quickly, put on a set of his own clean clothes and went out into the balmy night.

Ravi followed the starlit white paths deeper into the maze and slipped into the back of the dimly lit central hall. It was filled with white-pyjama-clad devotees sitting on rows of chairs. Most were Indians, past middle age, NRIs probably like his travelling companions, but as usual there were also a few younger westerners. He slid into an empty seat at the end of a row near the back, causing a few raised eyebrows, perhaps at his lateness, certainly at his attire. The broadcast was in full swing. On the stage at the front of the hall sitting upon an ornate wooden chair that was further raised on a dais, sat his father, spotlit, also in white with a white shawl draped around his shoulders. He wore his long curly greying hair knotted high on his head Shiva style, which suited him better, reflected Ravi, than his usual ageing hippy straggly pony tail. Shiva with headphones.

Behind him there was a row of helpers also wearing headphones, presumably fielding calls, probably filtering them too before allowing them on air. Ravi sat listening to the unfolding litany of troubles from around the world. *Should I give up my career to look after his parents? My daughter wants to marry an American boy what should we do? My son spends all his time on the internet and won't study. What can I do? My son/daughter wants to go out with her friends all the time/spends longer on the phone/on doing her makeup than on her school work, they won't listen to us/say we don't understand...* Many of the voices had American or Canadian accents, a lot of British too and others from the more obscure reaches of the Indian diaspora. There were some home-grown Questioners also with similar problems concerning marriages, in-laws and homework.

It was mostly the stuff of magazine problem pages, not spiritual crises or the meaning of life, about which one might expect a guru to have something to say, Ravi thought, unless the apparent prevailing sense of powerlessness in the face of a changing world counted as such. In which case what did Jay know of normal life anywhere in the world? Of everyday family matters? He offered platitudes. Things he'd heard from other people or read in all those books he gave away. Ramjidas Thakker's words of wisdom, allegedly acquired in blinding flashes of divine inspiration. Delivered in a soothing tone, Jay's manner could not be faulted and perhaps his elevated position lent his vague generalities a higher wisdom. For his interlocutors and the audience here seemed satisfied, while Ravi became more and more angry.

At the end of the broadcast the helpers all removed their earphones, one came to assist Jay with his, and another assumed the role of a sort of master of ceremonies and addressed the audience (or was it a congregation?) inviting a few questions, though *'you will understand that Shri Jayeshji is very tired after offering so much of his wisdom to the world.'* Almost without premeditation Ravi put up his hand. An assistant hurried to give him a microphone.

'Masterji,' he said in his broadest American accent. 'My question is also a family matter, but a very unusual and sad family matter, concerning the disappearance of a small boy, a much-loved only son.' Ravi was dimly aware of the sea of faces turned to look at this Questioner, the shock and then the avid attention that followed the recognition that this was more serious than the usual fare. He could see that Jay was straining to see beyond the spotlight and identify his interlocutor.

'For many years this boy was lost to his real family,' he continued. 'To his mother who grieved constantly, whose whole life in fact became devoted to waiting for him to return. For she never gave up hope when everyone else did, when they said he must be dead, had died a thousand deaths. For many years she was, one might say, insane with grief. She was in an institution, on medication, drugged senseless some of the time by all accounts.' Ravi was elaborating from Lilia's emailed account.

Jay cleared his throat and many of the onlookers turned back to the front, waiting for his advice for this poor bereaved woman. But Ravi hadn't finished.

'Then one day the boy, who is now a man, who was very lucky to be adopted by a very rich woman and who has had a comfortable life…'

Jay was now shifting very uncomfortably on his seat. He muttered an aside to an aide, who appealed to the questioner to be brief.

'I have almost done,' Ravi continued. 'My question is: one day this man chances on something which reveals his true name and identity, an identity he has long forgotten, or of which he has buried the knowledge so deep it has ceased to have any reality in his new life. What should he do? Given that these days it is so much easier to make enquiries, to put out information on the internet - or on the radio? Should he try to contact his lost family? And, if someone else thinks he has managed to contact them for him, should he go and see them? Can the answer be anything but yes?' Ravi could barely keep the scorn from his voice.

Jay had buried his head in his hands. There were murmurings in the audience, some hostile glances at the aggressive young man. Ravi was suddenly afraid that his father might suffer some sort of public crisis. He actually felt sorry for him.

The MC hurried back to the front of the stage and appealed to the audience. 'Shri Jayeshji is seeking the truth deep within him. Let us sing a *bhajan* to aid him in his quest.'

But Jay had sat up straight and held up one hand to command attention. The audience grew silent, expectant, as he opened his mouth. Still he did not immediately speak.

'The truth is many-sided,' he said at last. 'One can approach it but never know it in its entirety. Even those who follow the Path of Knowledge will discover this. But few people wish to know too much of the truth, whilst accepting it as their final goal. These are the ones who follow the Path of Action. Some are happier knowing only a little, but seeking union with the ultimate reality through worship, the regular performance of rituals. These are the ones who follow the Path of Devotion.'

The audience had visibly relaxed. The wisdom of Guruji was rising to the challenge.

'Some people believe that the best of their life is over and they prefer to spend most of their time recalling happy memories,' Jay continued. 'We can sometimes help them turn their thoughts to the future, to find a little optimism, perhaps in comparison with others less fortunate than themselves.' There were satisfied nods from many of Ravi's neighbours. This had become familiar territory after all.

'And then there are those,' Jay raised his voice. 'Who have lived with great personal uncertainty all their lives, or who have suffered deeply, perhaps in such a way as you described, so that their minds, their souls, are so attuned, so accustomed to this state of being that any change to this could be dangerous to them, could be fatal. And those close to them must simply care for and accept them as they are.'

Jay held up one hand as in blessing, then stood and, with a final *Namaste,* was gone. Was he talking about Rose? Or himself? Either way he wasn't going to come. Ravi stood up too. He would have to go to England alone.

52

Lilia closed her laptop and slid it onto the shelf under her desk, opened a top drawer and swept into it the small collection of pens and pencils that seemed to appear and disappear according to principles of their own.

'Just tidying up a bit. We might have visitors today, darling.' She addressed Rajah where he lay on the cold tiles of the kitchen floor. He seemed to prefer it there and, these past few days since Lilia's return, had rarely occupied his red velvet cushion on the carved Indian chair. She walked into the kitchen and crouched beside him. 'Rose is coming home for a visit,' she stroked him gently under one ear. 'You remember Rose? She has fed you more than once in the past.'

Rajah stretched to his full length displaying his grey shaved stomach. Lilia surveyed it sadly. 'I know, darling. Such beautiful fur you had.' She sighed. 'And someone very special is coming too, to see Rose. Someone I went looking for, in a manner of speaking, although, as it turned out, I could have stayed at home all the time with you.' Lilia sighed again and stood up, at which Rajah got up too and began to wind himself around her legs. 'But I wasn't to know that, was I?' She bent down again to stroke his back which he arched a little to meet her hand. 'I think I know what you want.'

She reached for his food bowl and took it to the sink to rinse, Rajah following her, his tail raised expectantly erect. Then she took a dish of chopped chicken breast from the fridge and forked a little into Rajah's bowl, while he pushed his head under her hands and started eating before she had finished.

'That won't last you long, will it?' Then, brightening, she added: 'Oh and Mike, you've met Mike. He's coming to take me to the station to meet Rose's special visitor. He's rather special too, I've decided. And he likes cats. He's the one who publishes all my stories about you. I've just sent him another one.' She swallowed the lump that rose unbidden in her throat as the doorbell rang. 'I expect that's him now. I'll see you later darling.' She crouched low and whispered in his ear. 'And you are very special indeed. You are the best cat that ever there was.'

'I got your story,' Mike said as Lilia got into the car beside him. 'I'm sorry it will be the last. For more than one reason.' He leant across and kissed her lightly on the lips. 'Feeling OK? I've written something too.' He reached to the back seat and handed her a piece of paper. It will be tomorrow's editorial, if all goes well today.' He started the car.

'ROSE REUNITED,' Lilia read aloud. '*The Observer is delighted to announce that Rose McCormack, the elderly lady who was found on the beach having suffered a stroke six weeks ago has been reunited with long-lost members of her family. This is entirely thanks to reports published in our pages by special reporter Lilia Zynofsky, who has just returned from Africa, where she was able to follow in Rose's own footsteps when a missionary there in the 1950s. Miss Zynofsky, as regular readers will know, herself faced dangers in her travels and was very ill, but I know she believes that it was more than worthwhile to achieve this outcome. I was privileged to see for myself how happy Rose is.*

If there are any other readers who have lost touch with loved ones, the Observer would be honoured to help them get in contact again. Details of a new online facility will be announced in these pages in a few days.'

'It's a lovely idea,' said Lilia and kissed him on the cheek. 'And I like the "special reporter" bit.' Her smile faded. 'Let's hope Rose *is* happy. Do you think,' she turned to him quickly. They had reached the junction with the road that on the right led to the seafront, on the left to the town. 'Do you think you could meet Ravi Makrani for me? And bring him down to the beach? He said he wanted to see the beach and Rose's hut? Only I'm suddenly really nervous.'

It was a brilliant sunny day as Lilia headed down the beach to the shoreline, but grey-tinged clouds already loomed over the distant tops of the South Downs. It had been a red dawn, rain was forecast, and an autumn chill was in the brisk off shore breeze. The tide was very low and the sea had left wave prints on the flat sand, each emphasised in an outline of small stones. Up and down the beach on either side wave- shaped hollows filled with blue water reflected the sky, like windows to a parallel world beneath. A line of gulls sat along the posts of the nearest breakwater, on the other side of which a steep shingle bank thwarted the restless waves. There were no boats or fishermen today, presumably they were out fishing. She inhaled deeply, tasting the salt. It was good to be back. She glanced at her watch, knowing he would not be long, then turned and saw a figure, standing in front of the fourth beach hut from the end. It had to be Ravi Makrani. She waved and he began to walk towards her.

He wore jeans and an open necked blue shirt under a thin grey cotton jacket and carried a cloth bag slung over one shoulder. He was quite tall and slim with dark unruly curls and a pale olive skin. She watched him approach, her heart beating faster and, when he was close enough for her to see his features, her hand flew to her throat as her breath caught in shock. An older image of Joseph as he appeared in the newspaper cutting stood in front of her, at the very least he could have been his older brother. The resemblance was so uncanny that she was slow to take his proffered hand and shook her head to clear her confusion.

'I hope you didn't think me rude not coming to the station,' she said at last. 'It seemed better somehow to meet here. On Rose's territory as it were.'

He looked around him appreciatively, clearly unaware of the effect he had produced. 'I can see why she liked to spend so much time here. It reminds me of home.'

'She was waiting for Joseph,' said Lilia. 'But I suppose she was happier here too. You live in Seattle.'

He blinked, surprised. 'Yes.'

'Thin Air FM.'

'You've been looking me up! "*Thin Air Community Radio provides a forum for non-corporate, neglected perspectives, reflecting values of peace, economic and environmental justice*".'

'Right,' said Lilia and Ravi laughed, as if reading her thoughts.

'I was quite a bit younger and more ambitious when I started it. Basically, it's about giving a voice to the underdogs of society, the homeless, the disaffected, of whom quite a lot wash up on the west coast.'

'Like Mombasa after the Mau Mau.'

'Sorry?'

'When Rose looked after all her lost young men. On the beach. One of the many things I must tell you about. But first I need to ask you a few things.' She folded her arms across her chest. 'Such as: what happened to Joseph once he got to Mombasa and what has he been doing all this time since? When all he would have had to do to get in touch with his grieving parents was talk to some British official.'

Ravi nodded as if he had been expecting some such question. 'Well, I think he must have run out of steam once he was on his own, once he had said goodbye to his travelling companions on the train. He wouldn't have known where to go, he must have looked lost and so was very vulnerable. He says he was kidnapped by some men and taken by boat to a number of places and that it seemed a very long time to him though it can't actually have been much more than a year. I say,' he shivered suddenly. 'Would you mind if we walk a bit, it's colder than I expected.' He stuffed his hands into his jacket pockets and hunched his shoulders against the wind's chill as they strolled to the water's edge. 'Because then, somehow, he ended up in Bombay and was adopted by a woman who was known as Mataji, a rich single lady, who filled her big house with poor boys, and, as in my father's case, lost boys.' Ravi looked away across the dazzling sea and narrowed his eyes against the glare. 'Maybe the kidnappers, whoever they were, approached her, got money for him. I really don't know and I don't think he does either.'

There was a short silence while Lilia considered. She was prepared to believe that Ravi was telling the truth and that he had probably already asked his father all the questions that might occur to her now. But she was not yet ready to give up. She needed to be convinced.

'Didn't he remember his parents? His home?'

Ravi nodded. It was an obvious question. 'He says he thought he was an orphan. That his parents had been killed in an accident. I don't know who or what gave him that idea. And this Mataji seems to have been a little crazy,' he added quickly. 'Though I have no clear memory of her as I was little when she died. *I* think she may have encouraged him to believe he had nowhere else to go so that he would stay with her. He was her favourite, apparently, perhaps because of his light skin, and she certainly gave him a life of luxury, hired tutors for him, he learned Sanskrit, to play the sitar. They lived in a big old house by the sea. It's all high-rise apartment blocks there now. He only left for a few years in his late teens when he lived up in the Himalayas, with some western hippy types. He says he knew the Beatles and that was when he learnt to play the tabla, you know, an Indian kind of drum? He still can, in fact he's rather good at it. And, when he was older, Mataji found him a girl to marry and they had me.'

'It's so cruel.' Lilia shook her head, still only half-believing.

'He's more than a little crazy himself.' Ravi smiled sadly. 'I used to think it was all the drugs he doubtless took in his hippy days. You know,' he turned to her, confiding. 'If you met him, you would probably understand better. Be more inclined to believe his story. My girlfriend thinks it all makes sense, sort of.'

Lilia frowned. 'I am wondering if I would like him now that I've found him. I suppose it's better than what Edward thought had happened. What does your mother think?'

'I'm afraid she died a long time ago, when I was still at school, before any of this came up.' Ravi sighed and again looked away. 'You would have liked her,' he added.

'And you will love Rose,' said Lilia, suddenly angry, drawing back. 'Poor Rose, who has spent more than half her life grieving. My God, if I could get my hands on that man!'

'Child, he was a child.' Ravi demurred softly, bent to pick up a flat stone and sent it skimming far out over the shallow ripples of the ebb-tide.

'Rose is better off not knowing that he simply ran away from her.' Lilia was not diverted.

'He didn't mean to run away for ever. I'm sure he was very soon desperate to go home.'

'And has spent his time living the life of Riley. Or whatever might be the Indian equivalent.'

'It's not what he chose, Lilia.' It was Ravi's turn to insist. 'And we don't know what he was told. Or what was done to him.'

'Huh! I know what I'd like to do to him. Wring his damn neck for all the pain he's caused Rose. Not to mention the trouble to the rest of us.'

'You haven't wasted your time, Lilia.' Ravi reached out and laid a hand gently on her still folded arms. He looked her directly in the eyes. 'You've found me. Rose has a grandson she didn't know about.'

'Huh!' she almost shook him off. 'Fat lot of comfort that's going to be with you living in Bombay and Seattle. Both a very long way from Bognor Regis. You're going to be no help at all looking after her. No help at -' Her sudden fury crumbled into sobs, interrupted by fierce sniffs and irate throat clearing.

Ravi held up his hands. 'Lilia, I can really understand why you are upset. You've done so much and been through so much …'

'No no, I'm sorry,' Lilia's voice was a wail as she waved away his attempts to calm her. 'It's not that.' She sniffed again, swallowed and spoke more calmly. 'It's my cat, Rajah, he's got cancer, he's dying. And I went away to Africa and left him when he was already sick and maybe if I hadn't…. I'm going to miss him so much. I know, it's just a cat, you'll think me silly but…'

'Perhaps we should sit down,' Ravi suggested and helped her climb up and over the breakwater to the dry stony beach beyond, temporarily dislodging a few seagulls, who resumed their perches amidst much ruffling of feathers as Ravi and Lilia themselves settled in the shelter of a slight hollow.

Lilia cleared her throat again and spoke in her normal voice. 'I'm sorry. He has still a way to go, at least a month the vet said. Look,' she reached into her bag and drew out the photograph of Joseph. 'You look so much like Joseph. And Rose too, for that matter. I can show you an album when we go back to her flat, with more photos. '

Ravi was silent. Slowly he traced the shape of his father's face with one finger and drew it across that enigmatic curled lip. Then suddenly he held it closer and stared at a point under the boy's chin.

'The *ddagala*,' he whispered.

'Sorry? Oh the – charm. Yes, Rose talked about it. How she threw hers away, when she lost hope of finding Joseph. She became very upset about it.'

'You're supposed to pass it on,' Ravi nodded, undid another button of his shirt and leaned towards Lilia so that she could see the polished oval shell hanging on a leather thong around his neck. It was almost like an eye or a miniature television with a square shaped tawny brown centre and a surround of lighter greyish white streaked with brown. 'It's a cowrie shell,' he said. 'My father gave it to me when I was twenty-one. That was when he told me what he remembered of his history.'

Lilia looked from the *ddgala* to the photo and back again and then, frowning, she turned away and gazed out to sea. Something still bothered her, something that didn't quite make sense.

'If only Rose had followed her heart and gone to India,' she said at last. 'Though she still might not have found Joseph.'

'And if she had I wouldn't be here,' Ravi added.

Suddenly Lilia saw clearly the puzzle that had been eluding her. 'Joseph remembered his name!' she said. 'Or else you wouldn't have made the link with Rose. And if he knew his real name how come no one ever made any enquiries about him, or tried to trace any other relatives? Surely there must still have been quite a few British people around who would have thought the way he was living very odd?'

'Except he doesn't look typically British, English, Scottish, whatever, more like a very light-skinned Indian, or Anglo-Indian,' said Ravi. 'And anyway he didn't always remember his name. Or so he says. He certainly didn't use it. He says he discovered his 'earlier name' when he found something in a drawer, long after Mataji died, after my mother died. Look.' Ravi reached into his bag and pulled out a blue woollen object. He held it up. It was a small hand-knitted V-necked blue sweater.

'As in the photo,' said Ravi.

'And as I found in Rose's flat by the bagful,' Lilia said softly as she took it from him. 'And as she was knitting on the beach when she had the stroke. I think it was his school uniform. In England.'

'There is a name tag.'

'Joseph McCormack.' Lilia read the printed cloth tape sewn neatly into the neck of the sweater, surely by Rose and no doubt as required by the rules of Joseph's school. 'He must have taken it when he ran away. It would have reminded him of his mother.' She could not control the waver in her voice.

The sky abruptly darkened and they both looked up and behind them. The looming clouds had slipped slowly over the Downs towards them as they talked, engulfed in shadow the coastal plain to the west and finally swallowed the sun.

'We should go and see Rose,' said Lilia. 'She knows someone is coming who might be related to her. But not exactly who. What are we going to tell her?'

'Not the whole truth.'

'OK. But where to start? Where to stop?'

'I've thought a lot about it.' Ravi stood and reached out a hand to help Lilia to her feet. 'And I think we just have to see how it goes and play it by ear.'

'Oh look,' Lilia pointed. 'Rose has come to find us. That's her nurse with her, I think.'

Someone, it looked like Maureen, was pushing a wheelchair along in front of the line of beach huts. She stopped outside the fourth one from the end and appeared to be looking in their direction. Lilia waved, the other person waved back and then returned the way she had come, leaving Rose sitting alone.

'You go on ahead,' Lilia told Ravi with sudden decision. 'I'll catch up with you.'

The tide is on the turn, Rose can tell as soon as they reach the beach from the slight breeze in the air, the stirring in the pools and the excitement amongst the birds. Soon the waves will be running towards her across the sand and the gulls will take off in a flurry from the breakwater and circle the incoming sea. It is the moment she loves, when her spirit rises and her heart fills with new hope. How glad she is to have come in time today. How long is it since she has been here? She turns to ask the woman who was pushing her until they reached her hut, where she had asked her to stop. But she has disappeared. No matter.

Rose breathes in deeply as she gazes out across the water, still dazzling bright despite the gathering clouds. A sudden flurry of black and white draws her attention. A small bird has landed quite close in front of her, almost at her feet. A – what *is* it called? Some strange word. It will come to her. Then her eye is taken by some movement further down the beach. Someone is approaching her, a man, a young man surely, with a lift in his step and a blue shirt open in a V at the neck. The bird has seen him too, it is running to and fro between them as he comes closer.

'*Namunye!*' She remembers the bird's name and, in the very same instant, she recognises the young man with the black hair falling in curls onto his forehead, his mouth slightly open and the unforgettable curl to his upper lip that breaks into a smile as she calls his name.

About the Author

After ten years working as a medical sociologist in universities in Scotland, England, and Canada, Maggie started writing fiction while bringing up her three sons.

Five of her children's books were published and several plays read or staged in various fringe venues in London and Brighton.

She later worked for many years as a parliamentary assistant.

Most of her writing has something to do with the meeting of cultures.

Sacrifices is her first novel for adults.

SUGGESTIONS FOR FURTHER READING

Dinwoodie, J. *Mackay of Uganda (*Marshall Bros., 1921? No publication date)

Dougall, J.W.C. *Missionary Education in Kenya and Uganda* (London, International Missionary Council 1936)

Lawrence,V. & Warr, W. *Coming and Going in Africa* (Edinburgh House, 1963)

O'Neil, R. *Mission to the Upper Nile* (Mission Book Service, 1999)

Pulford, C. *Eating Uganda* (Ituri, 1999)

And A SHORT TREATISE ON THE PHILOSOPHY OF HEATHEN PRACTICE IN UGANDA, Kampala, 1957, unpublished and 'contributed anonymously'. Archives of the St Joseph's Missionary Society of Mill Hill